"C
ar
th
an
th
be

# Call of the Bone Ships

## Ships

### RJ Barker

orbit

ORBIT

First published in Great Britain in 2020 by Orbit

Copyright © 2020 by RJ Barker

Inside images © 2019 by Tom Parker

Excerpt from *The Rage of Dragons* by Evan Winter
Copyright © 2017 by Evan Winter

The moral right of the author has been asserted.

A CIP catalogue record for this book is available from the British Library.

ISBN 978-0-356-51184-9

Typeset in Apollo MT by Palimpsest Book Production Limited,
Falkirk, Stirlingshire
Printed and bound by Clays Ltd, Elcograf S.p.A.

Papers used by Orbit are from well-managed
forests and other responsible sources.

Orbit
An imprint of
Little, Brown Book Group
Carmelite House
50 Victoria Embankment
London EC4Y 0DZ

An Hachette UK Company
www.hachette.co.uk

www.orbitbooks.net

# Contents

Berringhulme Sound

Namwen's Pass

Keyshanhulme Sound

GAUNT ISLANDS

Sparehaven

She left her Kept to shipwife be
To fly across the shining sea
To walk the slate, the shining bone
With promises she'd soon come home

She flew up high, she flew down low
*Heave on, crew, heave on.*
From north to south she flew the storms
*Heave on, crew, heave on.*
She flew to east, she flew to west
*Heave on, crew, heave on.*
And always thought of home, hey!
She always thought of home.

> From "The Black Pirate" — traditional ballad

# 1

# Brought Up on a Hard Wind

Waves as monuments: huge and uncaring, crowned in furious white. Freezing salt water ripped across the decks of *Tide Child*, grasping careless feet, numbing hands. Wind; all noise and anger, rigging singing the high-pitched song of rope on the edge of panic; the lone topwings bellied out, on the edge of cracking. Ice on the ropes and the decks and the faces of the crew, making every movement treacherous. The bone hull of the ship groaned in complaint at the treatment of the waves. Women and men, wrapped in stinker coats, pulling and pushing ropes and windlasses, tying knots with cold and nerveless fingers. Tired after days of this, weeks of this, a lifetime of this. But no rest, because one moment of inattention was all that was needed and then the ship would be gone. Turned over, bone keel sticking up into the air while the crew tumbled down through the grasping water into the waiting hands of the Hag.

This was the Hagsbreath, the Northstorm's fury.

In the midst, one figure stood unmoving and uncomplaining – but watching, always watching. She stood at the rump of her ship and it was as if the storm could not touch her. The ship bucked and rocked as towering waves pulled him seaward to landward, landward to seaward, but she did not move.

Lucky Meas, the witch of Keelhulme Sounding, the greatest shipwife who ever lived.

"Ship rising!"

The call from the topboys — amazing that a human voice could cut through the noise and fury of the storm — and in that moment Meas went from stone-still to action. Passing her deckkeeper, Joron Twiner, shouting: "The rump is yours, Joron!" And she was gone, up the mainspine as if the wind did not threaten to rip her from it, as if the stressed rigging may not snap and cut her in two.

Far below, Joron dragged himself across the deck. A word here, a nod there, and in return a strong hand helped him across the constantly shifting slates. All the time his eyes scanning the horizon — grey water and black skies.

"Steer four points to the for'ard shadow, Deckkeeper." Her voice calling from above; his own voice hoarse as he relayed the order to Barlay at the steering oar behind him. The battering of the sea, constant, fighting *Tide Child* as he began to turn. Orders given, stolen from his mouth by freezing wind, ice in the corners of his eyes making the shape of the descending Meas waver in his vision.

"Deckkeeper!" That voice, able to cut through any storm. "There's a ship in trouble out there, trader of some sort, near to foundering on the rocks of a small island." One hand on her ornate two-tailed hat, holding it in position, just as Joron was doing with his one-tailed version. "We'll need the gullaime on deck. Bird needs to make us some slack water or we'll be on the rocks ourselves."

"Ey, Shipwife. We shall attempt a rescue then?"

"Or die trying, for that is our lot." She smiled the words at him as she shouted them through horizontal, icy rain: because *Tide Child* was a ship of the dead, and all those aboard were condemned to fly the seas of the Scattered Archipelago until they found themselves in the Hag's embrace. "Ready the flukeboats and crews." Water poured from the braided edges of her hat, from her nose, gathered on her lips, droplets chased across her weathered face by the wind. "We'll throw grapples on board and tow them away from the rocks." The ship lurched, hit by a rogue wave. A groan ran through *Tide Child*'s bones. Meas turned from Joron to Barlay on the oar. "Keep him steady, Barlay!" Then she screamed into the wind: "Solemn Muffaz!" The deckmother, a giant of man, appeared from the fug of driving rain. "Help Barlay on the oar, I'll not want us drifting onto the rocks." She turned back to Joron. "Take Dinyl, he can command the oared flukeboat. You take the wingfluke."

"Ey, Shipwife," he shouted, rainwater filling his mouth. The coldness of it nothing to the cold he felt at Dinyl's name. Once he and the deckholder had been friends — more than friends — but no longer, and what lay between them now was as cold as the Hagsbreath. He crossed the deck, guyrope to guyrope, and passed the gullaime; the bird-like windtalker was wrapped around the mainspine, its robes and feathers plastered to its spiky frame, and though the creature was anything but human, if anything on this ship embodied the misery they all felt in the constant wind and cold it was their gullaime, pressed against the spine.

"Do not like, Joron Twiner," it screeched. Then snapped its beak shut to stop more freezing water getting in its mouth. There was something of the land to the gullaime, something of southern islands, places of heat and sand that made its being here in the wet and ice and cold all the more alien.

"It will pass, Gullaime," he shouted. "Help Meas keep us off the rocks."

"Not like, Joron Twiner." A screech into the wind. "Not like!" Then Joron was past.

"Farys! Farys! Get me a crew for the wingfluke."

The girl — no, a woman now — appearing from the rain, her scarred face almost invisible under the stinker coat's hood. "Ey D'keeper," said Farys. "Won't be much fun on the sea in this."

"I cannot disagree, but go out we must. Have Dinyl ready the flukeboat."

"I'll tell the d'older, ey," and she vanished into the rain. Water swept the deck once more. The ship rose and fell and rose and fell. He was cold and damp but had been that so long that he could not imagine being any other way – though it was not really that long, six weeks only. Six weeks combing the most northerly parts of the Hundred Isles for a ship Meas was sure did not exist. A Gaunt Islands four-ribber that Kept Indyl Karrad, spymaster of Thirteenbern Gilbryn, swore was up here waiting to raid. But this had been their lives ever since *Tide Child* had been refitted, mission after mission supplied by Indyl Karrad, make-work rather than real work. It was becoming clearer to Joron and Meas that, whatever his reasons, Karrad did not want them in Bernshulme. Joron believed it was simply punishment for not killing the arakeesian sea dragon as they had been ordered, which Karrad had seen as the quickest way to the end of war. Meas, ever one to look on the gloomiest side, was sure she saw darker purposes in these missions. She had also dreamed of peace – an end to the war with the Gaunt Islands that had raged for as long as all could remember – but in the end had spared the keyshan, let it go to whatever waited it beyond the storms. Now she worried that their shared goal of peace was to be put aside, that Karrad had placed his ambition on another course.

Yet Meas had not abandoned her dream of a sea where warships no longer roamed. In the time since they had let the keyshan go she had introduced Joron to Safeharbour, and he had been stunned by what Meas and Karrad had wrought. For eight years they had been putting their energies into a freetown, built of the rejects, the lost, the unwanted and unwelcome. A place Meas barely ever set foot on herself, wary of the inevitable spies, but a place of succour and safety for those that desired to escape the grind of the Hundred, or Gaunt Islands, and a place that continued to grow. It was not a great or beautiful place – the roads were more mud than stone, its people rough, life hard and its Grand Bothy not that grand – but Joron had walked its streets, and marvelled that this place could exist. He knew Meas felt a quiet pride for it, and he shared it with her, as did all the shipwives of the black fleet that had come into being around Meas. It felt like something solid, something real that made their struggles worthwhile.

"Flukeboats are ready, D'keeper." This from loyal Anzir, shadow to Joron. "Dinyl is already in the water and rowing. Here is your sword."

"Well, the d'older is efficient, he knows his work." He buckled the sword to his belt, a straightsword of great workmanship, given to him by Meas and his most prized possession. Sooner see himself go to the depths than lose that sword. Sooner run into the Hag's arms than let his shipwife down.

*Tide Child* bucked and reared on giant waves, the space between the big boneship and the smaller flukeboat opened and closed like a hungry mouth. Anzir's strong arms helped him across and hands reached for him because, despite his rank and his familiarity with the sea, he had never quite got the hang of crossing from ship to boat – the spines and spikes of *Tide Child's* sides engendered a certain timidity in him. But despite this strange inability Joron had become well-liked by his women and men, and they helped, as to go into the water in weather like this was death. A kind death maybe, where the cold would take you before the creatures of the sea found you, but death nonetheless.

"Row, my girls and boys," he said, once safe and sat, "let's see if we can catch the d'older. No, better than that." He raised his voice into the storm as the boat was raised up on a wave, "Let us see if we can outpace him."

"That'll annoy Cwell at his helm," shouted Farys, "and who does not enjoy annoying Cwell, ey?" Laughter at this, smiles beneath hoods, grins as aching muscles pulled on heavy oars and the movement of those muscles chased away some of the ever-present cold. Joron stood in the beak of the ship, the sea so much fiercer and more dangerous in this small boat: picking them up, throwing them about. Two of the crew were forced from their oars to bail water from the hull as the waves threatened to swamp them. The flukeboat, usually so responsive, was unwieldy, weighed down by the coiled rope they carried in the rump. There were, he knew, deckkeepers who would have managed every oar sweep and movement of the tiller in weather like this, but not Joron; he knew those with him and he trusted them to keep the little boat afloat and headed in the right direction. He stood, staring into the ever-changing landscape of whirling water, looking for the stricken ship. In his mind was the deckkeeper's voice, his father's voice in many ways: *If it is this hard to row now, how will it be when we are paying out rope behind us, trying to tow some unwieldy brownbone merchant? How much more likely we will be cast over, our sentence of death finally carried out?*

And behind that voice was another, the one he had heard more often and more clearly with every day. The one he never spoke of. The song of the windspires, the song he somehow shared with the gullaime. Once he had loved to sing, and then for so long hated it, the memory of singing for his lost father too raw. But his voice had returned, and there were those among the crew who believed he had sung a keyshan into saving them from certain doom. Then, for a short while, he had loved to sing again. Though he felt his melodies subtly distorted and changed by the alien melodies of the windspires which recharged their gullaime's ability to control the wind, and which he now had some link to. A constant awareness, as if something vast and, for now, placid moved through the matter of his mind, and though he felt great joy when he sang, it scared him also.

There!

Glimpsed through the weather, a shape he knew well, the torn wings of a ship rising from a deck, wingcloth flapping and cracking in the high winds.

"Two points on the for'ard shadow to landward!" The boat moving to his call as Farys leaned into the tiller. The shape in the mist becoming clearer, no sign of the other flukeboat, no doubt lost in the troughs of the waves. Then he saw it, rising above him on a wave, women and men pulling hard as they drove the rowfluke up the sheer water. Hag's tits, it was dangerous, the merchanter was big and if they judged this badly it would smash the delicate flukeboats to flinders.

"Gavith!"

The boy came forward, keeping low so as not to tip the boat.

"Ey, D'keeper,"

"How far can you throw a grapple and keep it on the target, Gavith?" The rowfluke vanished over the crest, no doubt racing down the other side of the wave while his boat now fought its way up the side of a wave which was steeper than any hill. Vertigo span in his chest, stealing breath already thin with cold.

"I can throw it twenty-five spans, I reckon, D'keeper." The boy screamed the words through vertical rain, sheets of water running off him, glazing his skin. Joron nodded, water falling from the hood of his coat. Reckoned in the usual overstatement any deckchild gave their skills when they were young. They would have to be far nearer than he liked; the flukeboat was what, ten spans long? Even side-on they would be nearer than anyone with a mind would choose in a sea such as this. Two good waves and they would be smashed into the side of the merchanter.

"Be ready then." He took the grapple, a thin rope tied to the end of a thicker towing rope, and pushed it into the boy's hands. "The sooner we are rowing away from that great lug the better."

They crested the great wave and Joron was looking down on the merchanter. Its women and men – not many, maybe twenty – ran hither and thither over the slate of a deck crusted with ice. It had two large spines but both were broken and dragging in the water, the crew trying desperately to cut them free with axes. Behind it was a small, shallow island, one of a thousand that showed up as little more than smudge on the charts, but it had rocks enough to break a ship and with sight of the island the song within Joron became a little louder. Then the flukeboat tipped and he was screaming at the crew to row against their speed as the boat careened down the wave toward the blocky merchanter, but no matter how hard they rowed the boat continued to gather speed.

"Farys!" Water breaking over them. Wind grabbing at them as he scrambled for the rear of their boat over women and men grunting and fighting the oars. "Steer for the beak!" Screaming it through wet air. Picking up speed. The wind changing, coming from the front. The merchanter growing bigger, bigger. "Get ready, Gavith!" Skearith's Eye, if they smashed into it they were done.

The wind screamed.

The grapple whirled.

Speed picked up.

"Row hard my girls and boys! Slow us or we'll be food for longthresh!" He didn't need to shout, his little crew knew the danger, strained at the oars while the cold sea tried to smash them against the bigger ship. The grapple spun in Gavith's hands then flew through the air. "Turn, Farys! Turn!" he yelled, and the flukeboat was rushing on, the side of the merchanter growing in his vision as it raised up on a wave.

Not enough time.

Too fast.

Sure to die.

But the rising wave slowed their boat, just a little, and they flashed past the beak of the merchanter; a brutal, blunt and stubby prow. Gavith watched the rope fly. Joron saw the boy's face light up, knew it for a hit.

"I got him! I got him!" He held up the looped cord of the grapple in victory.

Joron dove forward, fist lashing out to knock the boy flat as they sped past the merchanter and the cord the boy had been holding was stretched taut as the thick rope tied to it was pulled from its coil. The boy's face a picture, looking hurt, insulted by his deckkeeper's attack until one of the deckchilder, pulling hard on an oar, shouted at him.

"D'keeper saved your arm, boy! You didn't let go, the rope would have had it off." Gavith's eyes widened, then he looked from the deckchild to Joron and nodded, started to get up but Joron knelt by him.

"Wait," he said, watching the rapidly shrinking coil of rope. "Wait." The deckchilder rowed hard. The wind howled and the waves swelled and the rain beat upon them. "Row my girls and boys. Row." The rope spooling out. "Row hard." More rope, hissing as it passed. The merchanter looming behind them as it rose up on a wave, and though it lacked the keyshan-skull front of their own warship, it was just as threatening, just as hard and unyielding. The spool of rope ran out. "Brace!" shouted Joron, and the crew threw themselves forward over their oars. The flukeboat jerked to a halt and the rope was ripped from the sea in a curtain of water as it came tight, throwing the braced crew of the boat hard against the woman or man or hull in front of them. A great groan coming up from the small vessel as its varisk skeleton was tested. Then Joron was up, despite his chest throbbing from where he had been cast against the side of the hull.

"Row! Row or that great brownbone will be on us. Row for your lives!"

Then the real work, and the real danger, began. It was as if they sought to drag a huge and angry keyshan from its slumber. When they wished to go to landward it pulled to seaward, when they wished to go to seaward it pulled to landward. Communication between the two flukeboats and the bigger ship was impossible with the whipping wind and driving rain. Occasionally he would see the merchanter's shipwife on the beak of the ship, plainly shouting something, but what they said was heard only by the Northstorm, which stole words and hoarded the secrets of storm-wracked deckchilder.

They fought on, pulling on the oars, muscle set against storm winds, against the sea, against the weight of the ship, and with nothing to fight the tired ache of their arms but their will. With the howling wind and scudding clouds no landmarks could be made out. All Joron had was that sixth sense that a life on the waves had given him – a mixture of a million intangibles: the cut of the waves, the direction of the wind and rain, even the smell and the taste of the water on his tongue. He felt it, felt the way to go, felt *Tide Child* out in the storm, not as a real thing, not something he could touch. But he knew where he had left the ship, knew the speed of the ship and the strength of the wind and the likelihood and length of drift in the howling gale. But he doubted, even as he screamed through the freezing rain for them to row, shouted directions at Farys on the tiller. Worried the rope would rip their boat in two if he misjudged the pull of the huge ship. Worried he misread *Tide Child*, that he sent them heading heedlessly out into the ocean.

And then there was relief as he felt a dot of warmth in the storm, a pulsing tiny dot of heat he had come to associate with the gullaime. Sometimes he felt it out there, sometimes not. But it provided him a point of reference. He knew if not for that he would have doubted more, worried more about his mental calculations, his instinct; but with the dot out there he knew he was right.

Little solace.

Rather not have it, rather get it right himself and know he had done it. Rather do that again and again and again until the doubt was worn away like rock by the tides.

But if wishes were wings gullaime would fly. This was his world and he must live in it, could not change it any more than he could rid himself of the slowly growing sores on his shoulders and legs.

Then, as if she could tell the deckchilder were finding the end of their strength, that the ropes were chewing through the soaked varisk of the flukeboats, that tiredness was beginning to mask his ability to react to the movement of the waves, Meas came.

"Ship rising!"

The black ship, *Tide Child*, Meas Gilbryn on the prow and her grey hair, black with rain, streaming in the wind.

"Throw me the ropes!"

No storm could hold her words, no wind could steal them nor woman or man deny them.

For she was Lucky Meas.

She was the greatest shipwife who ever lived, and she would be a legend.

# 2

# Ill Found the Flotsam

They flew the ship for three days. The gullaime never moved from its favoured place to bring the wind, crouched before the mainspine, and it never looked up or spoke as it concentrated on finding the most favourable currents of the air and bringing them to *Tide Child*. When Joron passed close to it he thought he could hear its song in his bones.

They towed the merchanter, named *Maiden's Bounty*, a full five ship-lengths behind them – for Meas would not trust an unknown shipwife any closer to her precious boneship.

"Too easy for the brownbone to wreck us, Joron."

Five ship-lengths gave them room enough to cut the bigger ship free if it did anything foolish, or if the gullaime could not calm the storm around them. But the ship did not do anything foolish and the gullaime did calm the storm. They moved in a bubble of relative quiet – not comfort or safety, never that, but the gullaime took the worst of the bite from the waves and the wind. Occasionally, Joron would imagine he felt heat cross the deck of the ship, a great wave of it – but, like all aboard, he was tired from long watches and short sleeps. They were leaden, the women and men aboard *Tide Child*; muscle memory powered the ship through those grey days and howling nights.

On the night of the fourth day, Menday — though none had time to mend — the winds subsided and the Northstorm's anger ebbed a little. When Skearith's Eye rose that morran it rose bright and cold, the light crystal sharp and clear, the sea no longer staccato-rhythmed into jumbled ranges of knife-edged mountains, became rolling hills of oily looking water. The gullaime vanished from the centre of the ship and Meas stood on the rump, her hair once more dyed through with her rank's reds and blues underneath the two-tailed hat of the shipwife.

"We'll go over there today, Deckkeeper," she said, pointing at the rising and falling beak of *Maiden's Bounty*. In the light the merchanter looked more damaged, more bedraggled than it had in the teeth of the storm. The hardened varisk that made up the hull had rips in it and he could see keyshan bone, the skeleton — literal and figurative — of the ship below. The spines were gone, just two broken stumps to mark where they had been. On the deck, crazily cracked with the flexing of the ship, the crew milled about. Joron picked out the shipwife, stood on a barely raised rump next to her oarturner. She was a stout woman, with hair cropped short, and she leaned on a crutch, the badge of some old injury. It must be injury, not birth, for few, if any, Berncast made shipwife of even a brown-bone merchanter. Only the families of the Bern, the women who birthed healthy children and rose through the Hundred Isles aristocracy, or the Kept, their chosen concubines and warriors, became officers. Joron watched the shipwife of *Maiden's Bounty*, thought it curious that she displayed little interest in the ship towing her.

Meas went to the rear rail. "Shipwife of the *Maiden's Bounty*!" she shouted. "Ready yourself to receive my wingfluke. We will assess your damage and do what we can to help."

The sea rose and fell and fell and rose while the other ship-wife walked down her web-cracked deck and Joron went to join Meas at the rear of *Tide Child*.

"I thank you for dragging us away from the island, Shipwife," was shouted back from *Maiden's Bounty*. "But we are well supplied. If you will allow us, we will loose your ropes now and be on our way."

Meas leaned in close to Joron and whispered to him.

"Be ready to untruss our rearmost gallowbows," she said. And he in turn passed the order on to the deckmother, Solemn Muffaz, who brought up the two bowcrews and had them stand near enough the great weapons of the warship to ready them should they so need it.

"Shipwife," Meas shouted once that was done, "I am afraid I must insist. Should you be found wrecked for want of a spar I could never forgive myself."

They watched the crew of the other ship: a smaller woman joined the shipwife and the two spoke, heads almost touching. Black Orris fluttered down from the rigging to land on Meas' shoulder. "Hag's arse!" it croaked and Meas reached up and fondled the black feathers of his throat.

"Shipwife," came the cry from *Maiden's Bounty*. "Of course you may come across. I did not mean to give the impression that we were ungrateful. I will prepare my crew to receive you." Meas gave the other shipwife a wave and turned to Joron.

"Something is off here, Twiner."

"What?"

"I do not know, but smell the air." He did, took a great sniff of the sea air and behind the freshness brought by the north wind there was another smell, a stink like a ship left too long in harbour, when the rubbish gathered around it and the bilges swelled with sewage.

"Are its bones rotting, do you think?" he said.

"Something is definitely rotten, Deckkeeper. We'll take Coughlin and our seaguard across with us, I think. And you shall bring that fancy sword I gave you."

"Will they not suspect we are up to something?"

"Possibly," she said, "but I do not care. A fleet shipwife should have a guard with her, so it will not be too strange. It is not only the smell of the ship that bothers me, Twiner, it is the placing of it. Such ships are meant for traversing between islands, they are not strong enough to fly the true ocean alone, so for it to be so far out is odd in itself."

"Smugglers?"

"It would be my first thought."

"There is a decent prize to be had for taking a smuggler's ship."

"Well, I doubt that ship is worth much, but it may have a valuable cargo. Keyshanbone is likely."

"It will give our crew a good amount of money to send home if it is."

"Ey, even Cwell may smile, eh?"

"I doubt it."

"Well, she would be right not to smile. If it's keyshanbone we will have to take this ship somewhere safe and contact Kept Indyl Karrad back in Bernshulme. He can have it shipped to Safeharbour for our own fleet. We will not see any money from it; the crew will have to be content with serving a higher purpose."

"Arse!" The call came from Black Orris as the night-black corpsebird flapped its wings for balance on Meas's shoulder.

"I suspect many will agree, Black Orris," said Meas. "But this is my ship and those who crew it follow my rule, happy or sad, rain or shine." She turned away. "Well, Deckkeeper, is my boat ready or not?"

"I will see to it, Shipwife," he said.

Within a turn of the sand they were making their way to the merchanter, across freezing choppy water in the windfluke, the great slab sides of the *Maiden's Bounty* growing with every stroke of the oars. At the rails of the bigger ship stood crew – not many, mostly women with a few men scattered among them. They leaned over the railing watching Meas, who watched them back from the beak of her small boat. Ten of the *Tide Child*'s deckchilder rowed them, and squeezed in among them were Coughlin, his second Berhof – an enormous though affable man who Coughlin had raised from in among his seaguard. Coughlin had chosen well there, thought Joron, Berhof was well-liked by all aboard *Tide Child*, even though he had never really found his sea legs, a thing that would have brought ridicule had Berhof not been so popular. With them were eight of the seaguard, hunched around their small circular shields. It always seemed such a strange thing to Joron, a man raised on the sea by his father, that there could be those in the Hundred Isles who had never stood on the deck of the ship. There were few women and men more miserable on the waves than Coughlin's seaguard – though Coughlin himself had almost managed to come to terms with the ocean, even enjoyed it on occasion.

The crew of *Maiden's Bounty* threw down a rope ladder and as Farys tied the flukeboat to the bigger ship Meas ascended, followed by her crew and then Coughlin, Berhof and the seaguard. Joron came last, fighting the ladder as it twisted and bucked beneath his booted feet.

On the deck of the merchanter crew stood about, appearing aimless and innocent though Joron noticed that each and every one of them held, if not a weapon, at least something that could be used as such.

"Welcome," said the merchanter's shipwife. Up close he could see she had been imposing once, but had gone to seed now. "Shipwife Meas, the greatest of us, eh?" She spat on the deck. "Well, we owe you our thanks, it is true. I will feed you for it if you come to my cabin."

The wind, which had until that moment been blowing on Joron's back and over the ship, dropped for a moment and the smell – that almost unbearable, clinging stench he had caught a hint of on *Tide Child* – came close to overwhelming him. He felt the world spin, the deck move beneath his feet in an unfamiliar way, just like stepping onto land for the first time after weeks afloat. Meas's hand closed round his arm.

"Breathe deep, it will pass."

"Heh," the *Maiden*'s shipwife coughed, "boy can't take a little stink, eh? And he's your deckkeeper? Always say it's a mistake to put a man in charge, ey, Caffis?" She glanced over her shoulder at a slender woman behind her.

"Ey, Shipwife Golzin. Men don't have the tits for command."

Meas's hand tightened further around his arm. "Breathe deep, Deckkeeper," she said again, then turned. "It is an uncommon stink aboard this ship, right enough, Shipwife."

"You get used to it," said Shipwife Golzin. "But if you cannot eat, I will understand. And if you are here to help then maybe we need enough material to get a mainspine up and to patch the hull. We can manage ourselves after that."

"You said you were well supplied," said Meas.

Golzin shrugged in return. "Well, it seems I were misled by my purseholder, corrupt lot that they are."

Meas nodded, as if in agreement. "What is it, Shipwife Golzin? The stink?"

Golzin shrugged again. "It is simply an old ship, Shipwife Meas."

"Brave to bring an old ship this far out into the ocean," said Meas.

"I do this route a lot," said the shipwife, and she turned away from Meas. "I know these seas."

"Apart from that island, ey?"

Golzin turned. "Ey," she said. Something crossed her face – confusion? Anger? "That island wasn't on the charts, wasn't there last time we passed. I am sure of it."

"Moving islands?" said Meas. "I will have to warn my courser of this development."

Golzin shook her head. "Mock if you wish, I tell the truth. Now, do you want to eat or not?"

"No," said Meas, "what I really wish is to see your cargo."

Golzin leaned on her crutch.

"You cannot do that, I am afraid."

"I am a shipwife of the fleet. I can——"

"You are a disgraced woman, on a ship of the dead." Golzin laughed, quiet but real, and her amusement sparkled in her eyes like light from Skearith's Eye on the water. "I fought a fleet ship of fifteen years as deckholder, until I had a leg broken by a spar." She tapped her left leg. "This ship is my reward and my word is law upon it, Meas Gilbryn. I need not listen or bow to what a woman like you says."

Meas did not flinch at words loosed to wound. "You are a merchant shipwife, and I am a fleet shipwife. Ship of the dead or no you must still bow to my commands." This said with the pleasant air of two Kept discussing the latest fashion in shoes, though her next words bit. "And you *will* listen and bow if I command it. Do you understand?"

Golzin reached inside her stinker coat – never a piece of clothing more aptly named to be worn on this ship – and took out a small scroll of birdleather.

"I will not, nor will I let you below, Unlucky Meas, and I do it on the word of your own mother. Here, read."

Meas took the scroll and unrolled it. On the back was an imprint of children bowed under the weight of the Hundred Isles throne. Meas scanned the words and passed the scroll to Joron.

*On pain of death, and by Command of Thirteenbern Gilbryn, this ship is to be given safe passage and left to itself. None are to interfere or interrupt. All assistance needed must be given to this crew.*

Below, the watery swirl of a signature.

"Such things can be forged," said Meas.

"These were not. You would think your own mother's writing would be easy for you to recognise."

Meas rolled the note, tapped it against her chin.

"Where do you fly for?" she said.

"Well, I am sure you would like to know, but I am afraid knowing that, I would say, comes under the remit of you interfering." It did not escape Joron's notice that the members of Golzin's crew were encroaching on them, and more were coming up from below. At the rump of the ship two small gallowbows were being untrussed. Meas glanced at Coughlin, who gave her a small nod, turned his head to Berhof and exchanged a look.

"Out here, in the ocean, Shipwife," said Meas, "there's no way to check if you've forged that or not. So I think I should check your cargo anyway. I am sure my mother will understand, she has always respected thoroughness."

Golzin stared at her.

"Out here in the ocean, Shipwife Meas," she said, "anything can happen, and I am also sure your mother would understand if it did."

And on one side or another a signal was given, Joron did not see it made. He only heard the result, the drawing of blades, the command to spin the bows and, like a bolt fleeing a gallowbow, he felt the release of tension among the merchanter's crew.

Saw the dangerous smile on Meas's face.

Reached for his precious gifted sword.

Shipwife Golzin stepped back and her crew came rushing in. At the same time Meas drew her sword, shouting, "Coughlin!" She dodged the slash of a curnow blade from one of Golzin's crew and ran the women through with a leisurely thrust. Then she pulled one of the small crossbows from the tethers on her jacket and loosed it at Golzin before retreating to where Berhof and a small group of Coughlin's men had locked their round shields. The leader of the seaguard had taken three of his men and was running up the deck of the ship in a desperate race to reach the small gallowbows before the crews could lose the cannisters of rocks they were loading. Had they been a fleet crew Joron had no doubt Coughlin and his men would have been cut to ribbons by a hail of sharp stone, but they were not, and the seaguard fell upon the deckchilder like sankrey on their prey.

The violence aboard *Maiden's Bounty* was sudden and total. One moment Joron stood and waited, the next he was thrusting and slashing with his shining steel blade. There was little skill to it; Meas had, for months now, been teaching him to use a straightsword like hers, and he had proven more apt then he had dreamed of, but here on deck there was no time for such dainty fighting. It was about brute force and quick reactions, both of which the seaguard had in abundance. A blade from the front, one of the seaguard caught it on his shield and Joron thrust the tip of his sword into an unprotected neck. A woman lifted her curnow to slash at Joron's flank and Anzir struck out with a club, smashing a leather hat into the skull beneath. The deckchild to landward of him fell, a curnow cutting through her ribcage and Farys, screaming, struck back at the man who had killed her friend. Further down the line Meas stood, and only she seemed not to be taken up by fury, her thrusts and ripostes almost leisurely. A man jabbed at her with a wyrmpike, its great reach making him a real danger, but where Meas went so did Narza. The small woman ducked beneath the wyrmpike and slid her body down the shaft, impaling the wielder on a bone dagger and putting herself amid a knot of the *Maiden's Bounty*'s crew where she was a whirlwind of black hair and razored edges.

Oh, the crew of *Maiden's Bounty* were a world-worn and hard-looking lot, and Joron had no doubt they would happily have stabbed him in the back as soon as blink, but this sort of fight was not for them. The deckchilder of Golzin's ship had little stomach for the fight and they broke upon the discipline of Meas's women and men, backing away, dropping their weapons, muttering, leaving the dead and the maimed to bleed upon the slate. Meas strode forward.

"Your shipwife, where is she?" No answer. Narza darted forward, grabbed the smallest of the deckchilder and dragged her over to Meas with a knife at her throat. "Where is she?" said Meas again. The woman stared. She was missing an eye – not a wound, just another defect of one born in the Hundred Isles. Her good eye was wide, terrified.

"Tell me where she is or I will have Narza take your other eye," said Meas, and Joron suspected it was not the threat in her voice that frightened the woman — it was the offhand, matter-of-fact way Meas put it, as if blinding her enemies was something she did each and every day.

"Her cabin," stuttered the woman, glancing toward the rump of the boat where a ramshackle building of varisk and gion stalks was lashed in place. A small chimney on top was bleeding smoke to be quickly whipped away by the wind.

"Hag's breath," spat Meas, "she burns her charts."

Then they were running for the cabin. Finding the door locked against them Meas kicked it until it burst open, and there they found Golzin, leaning against one of the varisk uprights, a small brazier smouldering before her. All it contained was ash.

"You may have burned your charts, Shipwife, but I will find out what you were doing here and I will take the knowledge from your body if I must."

Golzin shook her head, a slow and painful motion.

"I think not," she said, coughed, spat on the deck. An attempt had been made to whitewash the floor of the room, to make it look like a real shipwife's cabin, but the white was scuffed and scratched, though enough remained to show Golzin spat blood. "You're a good shot with that crossbow," she said. Coughed again, more blood. "But, unlike you, I am loyal to the Hundred Isles." She was struggling to get the words out, each one coming slower than the last. Golzin fell to her knees, looked up at Meas. "Loyal," she said, and fell forward to show the crossbow bolt in her back that had taken her life.

Meas shook her head. "I cannot fault loyalty, however mistaken," she said. "Hag embrace you, Shipwife Golzin."

She turned from the corpse. "Now, Joron, let us see what Golzin has in her hold. Let us see what was worth dying for."

*Tide Child*'s crew were outside the cabin, menacing those left of the *Maiden's Bounty*'s. Joron did a quick count of his crew to find how many had been lost, found three deckchilder from Meas's ship of the dead who had now had their sentence completed. Their corpses lay cooling on the deck.

"Coughlin," Meas said, "find some black material and make armbands. These women and men do not know it yet but they have volunteered to join us. Their shipwife is dead, and as of now so are they." As she walked past the crew of the *Maiden's Bounty*, she stared at them. "And the dead belong to me," she said.

Joron followed his shipwife across the deck and to the main hatch of the merchanter. A hefty lock was in place on the hatch and the smell, ever-present on deck, was noticeably stronger here.

"Mother's mercy," said Joron. "Do you think she died to protect a shipment of rotten food?"

"No," said Meas quietly. "I think I know what she ships, and why she did not want me to have her charts." She turned to Narza. "Find me something for the lock. I have no wish to break my good sword." The smaller woman nodded and walked away.

"What do you imagine it is?" said Joron.

"I'll not sully Golzin's name without knowing," said Meas, "but if I am right I will take back my wish for her to rest with the Hag."

Narza returned with a gallowbow bolt and placed it within the hasp of the lock, pushing her weight onto it and using it as a lever to break the metal with an audible crack. "Lift the hatch, Joron," said Meas, "but before you do, we should get torches, and something to cover our faces with."

"Why cover our faces?"

"You will find out."

# 3

# What Lies Beneath

It was dark in the underdeck of the merchanter, not even lit by the weak glow of wanelights. He found that lack of the small glowing bird skulls disquieting. But he did not think about it for long, because the smell hit him with its full force. It was a thing with a presence, a hard wall of stink that he had to fight not to reel away from. Instead he pushed the borrowed cloth harder against his mouth and nose, fought the vomit rising from his gut, pinched his nose shut and tried to breathe through his mouth – though that was almost worse. This was a stench so pervasive he was sure he could taste it, and it felt like he imagined it would to drink bilge water, that concoction of rotten bone water, sewage and refuse that collected at the bottom of every ship. He coughed, held up his guttering torch, illuminating the overbones of the deck above and the walls close around them. They were stood in a small room with three doors leading from it.

"They have shut off the hold," said Joron. "Would that not make it hard to load cargo?"

"It depends on what the cargo is," said Meas. She reached for the door to landward of them – like the whole boat it was ill-kept and stiff and took all she had to open it.

Behind the door a scene that Joron felt sure not even the Hag would visit on those she punished. The stink thickened the air around them. It took a moment for Joron to make sense of what he was seeing in the flickering light of his torch, and when he did his stomach threatened to rebel again.

"Mother's mercy," he whispered.

The cargo deck ran the length of the *Maiden's Bounty* and was separated into three levels of shelves, each about the length of Joron's forearm and hand above the one below. This strange deck was filled with a low moaning, and now he heard it Joron knew it had been present on this ship since the moment he had stepped aboard. He had presumed it to be the ship, the old bones, the tortured varisk, but it was not. It was the cargo.

People. Women and men stacked on the shelves with barely any room to move or breathe. The head of one by the feet of those next to them and on throughout the hold, nose to tail the length of the ship. Joron brought his torch nearer to the body closest to him – a corpse, one that had clearly been dead for a long time, weeks maybe. The feet next to its head moved weakly and that horrified him more. Imagine, being here in that confined space in the pitch black for weeks on end next to a corpse. Did they know that body rotting beside them? Was it once a friend, a lover even?

"Hold fast!" shouted Meas into the moaning deck. "Those who put you aboard are no longer in charge, I am. We will have you freed as soon as we can, so hold fast." Did her voice shake? There was little response from the people on the shelves and Meas pushed Joron back, opened the seaward door and said the same to those there.

"What is this, Meas, slavers?"

"I do not know, Joron. I suspected it at first because of the smell. That was why I doubted the papers, my mother would never allow it." She stared in once more before closing the door. "But even slavers treat their foul cargo better than this." She turned and opened the last door, the central one, into the smallest of the three holds and in there found something different. No shelves, just a wide space and in the centre, cowering back from the torchlight, were gullaime. All masked, as was right and proper, but smaller than the gullaime aboard *Tide Child*, Joron was sure of it. When they moved he heard the clink of chains and saw metal gleam in the weak light. Meas repeated her words to the crowd of windtalkers, told them they were safe and then shut the door of this hold as well. The sight of them seemed to bother her even more than the humans. "Go over to *Tide Child*, Joron, bring our gullaime to speak to its people. I doubt they will trust me nor any other human after being kept aboard this ship." She took off her hat, ran her hand through her hair before putting the hat firmly back on her head. "No wonder Golzin burned their charts, something truly wicked is happening on this boat."

"I shall arrange to have the deckchilder questioned," said Joron. Meas nodded.

"Have Solemn Muffaz do it, though I doubt he shall learn much. Did any of the ship's officers survive the fight?"

"I do not know."

"Well," said Meas, and she started up the ladder, "it would be best for them if they have not. I will not look kindly upon them."

When they were back on deck and Joron could take in great lungfuls of the cleaner air, Meas gave out orders. "Coughlin, belay those armbands. Instead, bind this ship's crew and put them in the flukeboat. Joron and Berhof will take them over to *Tide Child* and they will not join my crew just yet. Then find axes, food and water. There are women, men and gullaime cruelly chained in the holds below. Start with freeing the women and men, and treat them kindly. You will see why when you get there. Pick those of your seaguard with the strongest stomachs." A pause. "You will find many dead in the hold. You are to lay them out before you throw them overboard. They may have loved ones among those on the ship who wish to say goodbye. Joron will bring back our gullaime." She turned to him. "And bring the hagshand, Garriya, to see to those this ship carries." Meas took a step toward Joron, standing close to him so she could whisper. "Make sure Garriya brings all her medicines, Joron, especially those that will kindly let a woman or man leave this world."

"But—"

"You saw it down there, Joron, smelled it. The stink of death and rot. The slightest wound in those conditions will fester, the slightest crack in a mind will be broken wide open. I would wish such imprisonment on no one and will prolong the suffering of none."

"What will we do with them, Meas?" he said. "There must be hundreds of them and we are in these waters to find a raider."

"We shall stay here long enough to see how many of those in the hold can be saved, then put a crew on this ship and send it to Safeharbour. The rest of us will continue in our hunt for the raider, though I doubt we will find anything. 'Tis all smoke and mirrors to keep me away from Bernshulme and embarrassing my mother."

# 4

# The Unwanted

On *Tide Child* Dinyl waited with Cwell, who now shadowed his every move, two pairs of resentful eyes meeting his. Behind them stood Sprackin, who had once been purseholder until Meas removed him. Now he made himself a thorn in Joron's side. The man had been deckchilder long enough to know just how close he could walk to the line of insubordination before attracting the wrath of Solemn Muffaz.

"The shipwife would have you take those aboard my wingfluke and put the black armband on them," said Joron, "but hold them apart from our crew and keep them bound, for now. I am to return to the merchanter with the gullaime and Garriya; there are many sick aboard the ship."

"And why do you need the gullaime also?" said Dinyl. They had been shipfriends, lovers, once, but that close friendship had been cut away by Joron, along with Dinyl's hand – and now, just like the hand, nothing of it remained. Dinyl, Cwell and Sprackin had formed a friendship through their dislike of him that cut Joron every time he saw them together, which on a ship the size of *Tide Child* was often.

"Because the shipwife asks for it, Deckholder," said Joron, and he was aware he held his body as stiffly as his language.

A cold formality had replaced the heat of the emotions they had once shared. Behind Dinyl, Cwell smirked, she had never liked Joron, and liked him less the more he grew into his rank. She in turn, with her vicious nature, frightened him. Though he could never admit that. He felt sure that both Cwell and Dinyl judged his every move. Sprackin simply sneered and watched for any opportunity to trouble him.

"It is our duty to give the shipwife what she wants, ey?" smiled Sprackin, but there was nothing pleasant there. Dinyl ignored him and stepped forward.

"Cwell, do your duty, bring up the hagshand and the wind-talker," he said, cold and formal. "Then take these women and men and stow them in the brig until they are ready for duty."

Joron turned away. He did not fail to notice how often the word "duty" fell from Dinyl's mouth, and from those around him. It was his sense of duty that had cost him his hand, and Joron's sense of duty that had caused him to take it. In their own way both men had been right to act as they had, and as such Meas had kept Dinyl in his place on the rump of the ship even though he had threatened her life. But each day they stood together Joron felt this was a mistake, and he suspected Meas did too – though she would never admit it. "A shipwife only ever moves forward," she had said. "I'll not look to the errors in my wake, Twiner, not once I have set my horizons straight by 'em."

Joron did not stay long on board, the atmosphere was too chilly on deck. He left Dinyl to sort out the new crew and rowed back to *Maiden's Bounty* with the gullaime and Garriya. The old woman sat huddled up in the bottom of the boat between the rowers. She was brought on as one of the stone-bound, the lowest rank on a boneship, as she knew nothing of the sea, however she had shown herself to be a skilled healer. This was a rare thing for a ship to have, and almost unheard of on a ship of the dead such as *Tide Child*. Now she held the rank of hagshand. Like Dinyl she also made Joron uncomfortable, though in very different ways. When they first met, the woman had named him "Caller." And then, months later when all seemed lost and death had become inevitable, he had sung and an arakeesian had come as if called to that song. The last, vast and mysterious sea dragon had saved them from complete destruction, and although Joron was sure it was not his doing, he could not help wondering if he lied to himself. Because he had heard its songs and felt its presence in ways no one else seemed to.

Except the gullaime.

The windtalker had got over its terror of the Northstorm and reverted to its usual mood of being interferingly curious. At the moment it was fascinated by the rowers. The deckchilder, as they rowed, took in the gullaime's curiosity with good grace. Where most crews were frightened of the windtalkers, the crew of *Tide Child* had accepted theirs and looked upon it with the same fondness they reserved for Black Orris, the foul-mouthed corpsebird that nested in *Tide Child*'s rigging.

"What for these?" It pointed at the oarlocks.

"To rest the oar in," said Farys from her place at the rump of the boat. "So it is easier for the deckchilder to row."

"Why row?" said the gullaime, its sharp beak opening and the words tumbling out from within its throat, rather than being formed by lip and tongue as was proper and right. "I make air." It pointed at the furled wing of the ship with the claw that tipped the elbow of its own wing, hidden within colourfully painted robes.

"Save your strength, Gullaime," said Joron. "The deckchilder row because speed is not important right now. Your magic may be important later and it would be foolish to use it up."

"Joron Twiner is foolish," squawked the gullaime and it hopped down the centre of the craft, scrambling up so it stood before Joron on the pointed beak of the small boat. It orientated its whole body toward the merchanter rising from the sea before them. "Bad things," it said. "Bad things start here."

"What bad things?" said Joron.

"Raise your voice, Caller," said Garriya from the bottom of

the boat where she squatted with her bag of herbs. "What was long buried is being unearthed."

"What do you mean?" Her words were curious things and they swam around him. He felt that he existed separately in the boat to the deckchilder heaving on the oars. The sounds of the shifting sea receded, the brightly coloured clothing faded and there was only the voice of Garriya in his ears.

*"Keyshan rising, Joron Twiner, keyshan rising."*

The rushing back in of sound and sense and the old woman was in the bottom of the boat, burrowing through her bag as if she had never spoken.

Had she spoken?

Once he would not have doubted it, but recently he had become unsure of his own senses. Whether it was the long hours and constant wakefulness or something else that had changed him, he did not like to think about it. He scratched at the top of his arms where the skin was sore. Keyshan's rot, he was sure, but at the same time he hoped it was not and he dare not share his worries, for first it brought sores and in the end it brought madness. Increasingly he was given reason to doubt his world, doubt his eyes and ears and sense.

Could it come upon a man so quick? The bonemaster Coxward had it, and he had for years. But was it different in each case?

"'Ware below!" was shouted from before them and Joron shook himself as a rope came down from the merchanter. He tied on their flukeboat and climbed the side of the bigger ship. As he did the gullaime effortlessly scaled the side of *Maiden's Bounty* without need for rope or ladder, its clawed feet and wings made for climbing. They were not creatures of the open sea, the gullaime, and Joron felt sure they never had been. If they had not possessed the power to control the winds no one would ever have brought them out here, where most gullaime suffered sickness, neglect and ill-use. And the work they did, controlling the winds, only brought them more pain, through draining whatever strange force was within that let them do their magic. This gullaime, the one they thought of as theirs, still needed to visit land and charge at a windspire, but it held more magic than any of its kind and, unlike any other gullaime, it still had its eyes under its painted mask. A secret shared only with Joron, for gullaime were blinded when they were young to stop them straying.

Joron had always believed what he had been told, that this was done to keep them safe.

But so much of what he had been told was lies. Was there any reason to believe this was different?

On the deck of *Maiden's Bounty* Meas had already started bringing women and men up from below. These people were broken, little more than skeletons, their bodies covered in sores that Joron recognised – the tops of his arms itched abominably – and they had wild, frightened eyes. He watched the huge deckmother, Solemn Muffaz, discretely sorting those brought up from below. Some went to landward but the vast majority went to the seaward side of the ship. They were people of every creed and colour the Hundred Isles possessed, and he could make no sense of it: this was not the fruit of some raid where all were of one type, more like a deliberate gathering of all the island's peoples.

Meas intercepted Joron on his way with Garriya to the sick and infirm, gently leading them both aside. "Garriya," she said, "I trust Joron told you to bring what drugs you had that would let a poor wretch slip away?"

"Aye, Shipwife. Though I will save those I can."

"Well, there may not be many. Solemn Muffaz has sent to landward those he thinks may survive, the rest, well" – she bit on her lip – "it is kinder to let them go than make them suffer."

"Why kill—" began the gullaime but Meas's hand shot out, closing round its beak.

"Squawk quiet, Gullaime," she said. "I'll not risk those that may live hearing what I say. They may not see it as the kindness it is if they have loved ones among those I send to die."

She let go of the gullaime's beak and it twitched its head so it sat at an angle. Then, just above the rise and fall of the sea, Joron could hear what he thought were tiny squawks leaking from its beak.

"I don't mean you have to be silent, Gullaime," said Meas and the creature let out a cry of frustration, drawing all eyes to them.

"Strange creatures! Strange creatures. First be silent. Now be loud. Make no sense."

"She does not wish the ill people to hear you, Gullaime," said Joron, and the predatory curved beak whipped round so the painted eyes on the creature's mask were fixed on Joron.

"Why bring Gullaime?"

"Because I need your help," said Meas. "Now come, we will talk more below."

As they entered the underdeck Joron and Meas once more tied cloths around their faces.

"Why do that?" asked the gullaime.

"The smell," said Joron.

"Humans smell bad," it said. Then they were down the stairs in the darkness and the almost unbearable stink. Meas swore, left them and returned quickly with a torch, and Joron wondered what had happened that she should forget something she needed. It was not like Meas.

"In here," said Meas, pointing at the door before them, "are some of your people, Gullaime. They look as healthy as can be expected in this place, but I do not know why they are here."

"To fly ship," it said without looking at her.

"There's a lot of them, for a ship like this," said Meas. "And if that is the case, why were they not on deck when the ship was in trouble? No, there is a mystery here, Gullaime." She held out the torch.

"For me?" it said.

"Yes. Judging by the way the humans have been treated on this ship I cannot imagine the gullaime have been treated any better, or will be too trusting of us. But seeing one of their own may help." The windtalker curled its wingclaw and took the torch from her. Then it extended its neck so its head was directly in front of Meas's face.

"Kill gullaime too?"

"They are your people; you will know when suffering is intolerable for them. So their fate is your decision."

The gullaime kept its head utterly still and the flames licked around its neck, the air tainted with the smell of singeing feathers. If anything, an improvement.

"My people," it said, and retracted its head to roost between its shoulders.

"Joron and I will be in the ship's cabin on the deck, come to us when you are ready."

The gullaime let out a squawk, almost deafening in the small room. "Go!" it said. "Not scare my people. Go!"

They turned and climbed the steep ladder back up the deck, Joron following Meas towards the cabin. The sides of the ship were now filling with bodies, many simply lying inert, eyes closed. Those with their eyes open stared blankly, as if blinded. It was small solace to Joron that the wind stole the smell of them away, and he pulled off the mask from his face. He had seen the poor and sick on the streets of Bernshulme, but they were not like this. They fought for life, just like all had to in the Hundred Isles. But these? Their fight was gone. The under-deck of this ship would forever be his image of what awaited those denied the warmth of the Hag's bonefire, and he knew he would do anything to avoid such a fate.

Anything.

"In here," said Meas, pushing open the ill-kept door of the shipwife's cabin. Within, a woman was tied to a single chair, the shipwife's desk had been pushed to the side and the white painted floor was spotted with blood.

"This is, or was, Caffis," said Meas, "deckkeeper of the *Maiden's Bounty*." The woman was slumped forward, the front of her clothes black with blood.

"She was wounded in the fight?"

"Ey." Meas did not look at him as he lifted Caffis's head — a broken nose, smashed lips, bloodied and cut around the eyes. "But it was the beating that killed her." She let time pass, its gentle waves lapping between them. "The beating I gave her, before you ask the obvious question."

"Why?"

"Information," Meas said. Left a gap in her speech for him to jump into, but he did not. "And anger," she added, and he could hear it in the word. "Fury at what this ship had in its hold, at what she was part of."

"I understand that, but you always say all lives are precious, crew is necessary."

"I do." She put a hand on his shoulder and pulled him backwards, gently. She let go of Caffis, her head falling forward, hiding her broken face.

"I would have thought you had seen slavers before. I know it is not allowed but . . ."

"This is not a slaver, Joron," she said. "A slave, or a sacrifice, is valuable in the places that will buy them. Too valuable to transport like this."

"Then what is this ship transporting?"

"I do not know. I had hoped she did," Meas said, pointing at the corpse.

"But she didn't?"

"No. She knew nothing. Her shipwife had all the details. They have made this journey twice before. They take these unfortunates from one ship, meet another at a different island each time. Any that still live are taken away onto that ship, the dead go overboard."

"It sounds like slavery is the intention."

"You have seen those on the deck. How much use would they be for work?" She did not wait for him to reply. "No, what they are being transported for, and why, remains a mystery."

"What do we do now then?"

"We do one more sweep for this raider and then head back to Bernshulme. Answers will be there; the answers are always there. Indyl Karrad will know something; his spy network is far reaching."

"If we are not sent away again."

"I have let my mother push us around too many times. I will do it no longer. I will find some reason for us to stay in Bernshulme and we will search. I did not want it to be true, Joron, but the papers the shipwife showed me, it did indeed look like my mother's hand." Her voice drifted away then she shook her head. "And to have so many gullaime, there has always been illegal trade in them, but only in ones and twos, never so many at once. I do not understand. Something is off, Joron, something—"

Her words were cut off by the gullaime storming in. "Windshorn!" it squawked,

"What?" said Meas.

"Windshorn!" it squawked again.

"I do not know what that means, gullaime," she said.

The creature hopped from one foot to the other, slowly, and it almost seemed as if it hovered in the air for a moment between each step. Then its head orientated towards the corpse in the chair.

"That one not smell sick," it said.

"What is windshorn, gullaime?" said Joron.

The windtalker clacked its beak at the corpse in the chair before turning back to them. "Some gullaime windtalk. Some gullaime windshorn."

"Do you mean that they cannot control the weather?" said Meas.

"Wind. Shorn," it said, as if it was the most obvious thing in the world.

"I did not know there was such a thing," said Joron.

"Humans do not know gullaime," it said. "Windshorn no use."

"So," said Meas, "we have a ship full of the sick and the

useless, on their way to somewhere unknown." If the woman in the chair had not already been dead Joron felt sure Meas would have hit her again – there was exasperation in her every movement. "It sounds like slavery, Joron, you are right. But if this ship really does come from my mother I cannot imagine it. She has many bad qualities but she abhors slavery. The idea someone else may profit from her people infuriates her." She paced up and down the bloodied cabin floor. "We will return to *Tide Child*. Decide what to do there and sort out a crew for this ship."

"Gullaime," said Joron, "what should we do with your windshorn?"

Painted eyes stared at them.

"Kill all," it said.

# 5

# In the Depths, Only Darkness

**B**ack on *Tide Child* they sat in the great cabin and Meas poured them both anhir, while Mevans bustled about bringing food they had no stomach for.

"I said we were not hungry, Mevans," said Meas.

"Ey, but the body must be fuelled even if you do not like it," he placed steaming bowls of fish stew before them both. Meas shook her head slightly and cast Mevans a dark glance before picking up her spoon and placing a measure of stew in her mouth. Mevans rewarded her with a smile and left the great cabin.

"Acts like a Hag-forsaken mother bird."

"Talking of birds," said Joron, "will you do as the gullaime asks and kill these 'windshorn'?"

Meas shook her head. "No. Not unless it chooses to share more of why it feels so strongly about them, and even then I may not."

"So what shall we do with them?"

"Send them to Safeharbour with the *Maiden's Bounty*." She stared into the distance as she spoke.

"You worry about something, Shipwife Meas?" She took another spoonful of stew and Joron, despite the horrors of earlier, realised he was also hungry.

"Ey, many things," she said quietly. "Mostly I worry about sending my crew away on the *Maiden's Bounty*."

"That they will run?"

She shook her head. Gave him a black look.

"The ones I send will not run. I worry that the ship will not make it back. It is in poor repair and I cannot afford to lose loyal crew." He knew what was unsaid there. More and more it had become clear there was a faction on *Tide Child* who believed things could be run better by them. Better, and not run as fleet, but as pirates. Those who were cruel or thought themselves wronged had found one another, bonded, come together. At their head stood Cwell, and though she was a fierce and violent woman she was also intelligent enough to know she did not have the skill to be shipwife. There were reasons the poor were not taught navigation or reading in the Hundred Isles. But now Cwell had a friend in Dinyl, and there was a man with reason to be resentful, and skill to pilot a ship, and with Sprackin they had a man who, though corrupt, understood the financial workings and how to properly stock a boneship.

They ate in silence, mechanically fuelling their bodies while not looking at one another. Once done Meas went to one of the shelves in the cabin, boots knock-knocking on the bones of the deck, and took down her ledger. She opened it, Joron had time to see lists of names before she angled the book so he could not read what was there.

"Bring me the gullaime, Joron," she said.

"I could have Solemn—"

"Do it yourself please."

He nodded. Stood and gave her a small bow of respect before making his way through the ship. Along the black decks, down the black stair to the underdeck. Aware of each body around him, the ones who greeted him with a friendly nod and shout of "D'keeper," and the ones who turned away, and those rarer few who stared at him without subservience. The few who he knew would push him on every order, react just too slowly, give not enough respect to their officer. It was never quite enough disobedience for Solemn Muffaz to bring out the cord and have them disciplined; these deckchilder were old hands like Sprackin and knew the exact width of the tightrope they walked, how much disrespect could be shown without it actually becoming enough to warrant discipline in return. And though Joron hated himself for it, he knew he avoided giving them orders if he could. He passed the job to Dinyl, though he was sure it only strengthened the deckholder's hand.

He knocked on the gullaime's cabin door. Once he had walked in and caught the creature without its robe, preening the long feathers of its body with its beak – feathers that had once been white but now other colours were growing through. The moment he walked in that day, he had known he intruded upon something intensely personal. It may have been the link between them that Joron felt growing day by day that let him know, or it may have been the fury the gullaime blew into when it noticed him – throwing rocks and rags and dust and all the strange bits and pieces it had gathered to itself. But he had been careful to knock ever since.

"Come, Joron Twiner," it said.

The gullaime's cabin was like no other on the ship. The bowpeek was always open, the cabin always cooler than anywhere else. The wind blowing through it set the trinkets strung across the ceiling on lengths of rope – feathers, glass, rocks with holes in that it had a particular fascination for – to jingling. In the centre of the room was its nest – a circular construction of cloth, feathers and varisk stalks stolen from the hold – the place where the gullaime slept. If slept was the word; it never seemed to truly be asleep, just squatted there in what approximated a meditative state. No matter what time he came for it, the gullaime always seemed to snap straight into full wakefulness. When Joron slept, sometimes he saw this room as if through the secret eyes of the windtalker.

"Meas would speak with you, Gullaime."

It squawked, a loud "Awk!" that was almost deafening in the

small room. "Shipwife, shipwife," it sang, then stood. "I come."

They made their way back to Meas's cabin, slower this time. The crew of Tide Child were checking over the gallowbows – the six great bows on the slate and the twenty lesser bows on the underdecks – and the gullaime, with its incessant curiosity, felt the need to stop and watch each crew. To inspect what they were doing, sharp curving beak darting in and out of the mechanisms as they were checked; and, when its curiosity was finally sated, it would say "good job" or "well done" in what, if not an exact copy of Joron's voice, was at least close enough to make him uncomfortable. And in this stop-and-start fashion they moved through the ship, and if the deckchilder were at all bothered by the attention of the gullaime then none showed it. Indeed, it was met with a good humour and stifled laughter at its fleet and officer-like ways.

In Meas's cabin they stood while she stared at the ledger. On her desk was a loose assortment of scraps of parchment, each scribbled over in her beautiful hand, and as they entered she gathered them together, twisted them into a taper which she lit from one of the wanelights on the back wall. When the parchment was burning good and well she opened one of the rear windows and let it fall, lost forever in the great waters of the Scattered Archipelago, and that probably for the best if those scraps were what Joron thought they must be: lists of who she considered loyal and who she considered not – and maybe her plans on how to deal with them.

"Gullaime," said Meas.

"Shipwife," said the gullaime, and it moved its head down, so it appraised her from just above the height of her desk, its head low and tilted to one side.

"You said we should kill the other gullaime?"

"Windshorn." It snapped the word out, its predatory beak clacking open and shut three times after it said the word.

"You said we should kill these" – Meas paused – "windshorn. Why?"

The gullaime made an odd sound, part snort, part outrush

of breath through its nostrils and it spun around on the spot twice in a whirl of shining feathers and brightly coloured robes.

"Traitors! Egg snatchers! Tale tellers!" It stopped, stood utterly still. "Hated by great bird." It angled its head at Meas. "Kill all."

Meas stared at it, taking the time to consider the windtalker's words.

"I will take this under advisement. You may return to your cabin if you wish."

The gullaime let out a squawk and bustled out of the great cabin holding its head beak-up, like it was a creature of great distinction, too important for the shipwife and her foolish ways. Meas waited for it to leave then sat back in her chair.

"And what of you, Joron Twiner? Would you condemn these creatures on the word of your friend?"

He waited, thinking. "Once, maybe," he said, and sat in the chair opposite Meas. "But once I would have cast the gullaime adrift upon a bell buoy to escape my fear of it."

"You think it is afraid of them?" A flash in her eye. She had her own ideas already; of course she did, she always did. He was her sounding board, something to catch her ideas and throw them back so she could consider them from different angles, see them anew as if they were some strange and new creature brought up from the depths.

"Maybe it is not afraid, but it is uncomfortable, definitely," he said. "It is twitchy when it talks of them."

"It is twitchy all the time."

"There is a difference."

A silence while she thought, while she moved ideas around in her mind. She stood.

"Come with me to the *Maiden's Bounty*. We will talk with these windshorn, you can tell me what you think of them. See if you think they are also" — a smile breezed across her face — "twitchy."

They were rowed across, the journey too short to bother with the boat's wing – Mevans in the rump, calling the rowers' beat, Narza at the rump with Anzir by her. Joron stood next to Meas in the beak of the wingfluke and they watched the brown sides of the merchanter grow.

"Have you decided what to do with it, yet?" he asked. She shook her head.

"I have sent Coxward aboard to look it over properly. It is a big ship, useful if it can be kept afloat, but if it cannot then it is weight only."

"The bonemaster is the best judge of ships we have."

"Ey, part of me hopes it is sinking and we can leave the thing here. Then there will be no need for me to split our crew."

"Why not just say it is?"

She stared at the ship as it moved gently on the waves, thinking on that.

"Because we need it. The Hundred Isles, the Gaunt Islands, they have hundreds of ships to fight their war and our little movement for peace floats between them, ill equipped and ill prepared for when they chance upon us." She grinned at him, then grabbed the ladder thrown over the side of the *Maiden's Bounty* and nimbly made her way up it. He followed, more slowly and carefully.

At the top of the ladder the bonemaster, Coxward, waited for them. He too was wrapped in a thick stinker coat against the cold, and Joron knew that below it his body was wrapped in bandages to cover the lesions and sores of the keyshan's rot that slowly consumed him, the fate of all bonewrights and those that had once worked the vast bodies of the sea dragons.

"It'll fly the sea, Shipwife," said Coxward; he did not look happy about it. "But this ship" – he stamped his foot hard twice on the cracked slate of the deck – "it is not a happy ship. Would be better sent to the Hag, as it will ever harbour the stink of misery."

"You'll find no argument from me there, Coxward, but the ship is needed. Can you make it bearable?"

"Well," he took a deep breath, "we have removed the shelves from the seaward side. It still stinks like a keyshan's guts and it always will. My crew have made a start on the landward shelves." His face was downcast.

"They'll be rewarded for this," said Meas. "I know it must be hard work."

"There's more corpse than ship down there, Shipwife," he said quietly. She nodded, reached out and touched Coxward's arm. "We are stowing the corpses in the lower hold," he said quietly. "We began to throw 'em over but so many dead are like as not to attract something big in these seas, something we'd rather not see, I reckon."

Meas nodded. "Where is Garriya?"

"She has made the shipwife's cabin into a hagbower. We are taking people to her for" — he looked away, uncomfortable — "for treatment."

"I will speak to her," said Meas. "Carry on with your work, Coxward, and know you have my thanks."

From there they went to the cabin. Meas knocked, heard Garriya croak: "Enter, Shipwife. Enter, Caller." Inside the small cabin had been transformed, most of the furniture removed, the brazier burned hot in the centre. Garriya, small and gnarled, squatted by the brazier and before her a young man, a boy, slumped in the shipwife's chair, his eyes barely focused.

"Garriya," began Meas, and the old woman held up a hand to quiet her. Had any other done this then Meas would have been furious, raised her voice for Solemn Muffaz to take out his cord, but here she acquiesced. Garriya had the boy leaning against her, the rags that clothed his bones did not hide the sores that marred his flesh. Joron noticed the old woman was chewing. She took what she chewed, a pellet of leaves, from her mouth and placed it in the boy's. Then she dipped a cup in the bowl of water by her and helped the boy drink, rubbing his throat to get the pellet and the water down his gullet. Once she had worked the pellet down his throat she began to gently rock him backwards and forwards, singing a wordless tune with her eyes closed. Within that tune was something that Joron almost knew, and just as he was on the edge of recognising it the boy's eyes shot open. He coughed, started taking great wheezing breaths. His weak muscles worked, trying to fight or run, but Garriya held him tight, crooning into his ear.

"Fret not, child, fret not. The Mother is waiting. The Maiden will welcome you. The Hag ensures your passage will be swift, the pain short, fear not." She repeated the words, over and over again as the boy's breathing became less laboured, his coughing slowed and his weak muscles gave up the fight until, eventually, he was still. The old woman's mouth moved, somewhere between a smile and a grimace and she reached over and closed his eyes. "Sleep well, child," she said, and gently laid the body on the floor.

"He could not be saved?" said Meas. Garriya bent over and swilled her hands in a water bowl, then took a rag from her pocket to dry them.

"On land, with plenty of food? Aye, I could have saved him, given him years of life before the rot truly took him. On the sea, in the cold and on deckchilder rations? No, he could not be saved."

Meas nodded. "Can any be saved?"

"They had four hundred aboard, Shipwife, that were still alive anyway," said Garriya. Then she chuckled to herself. "Aye, old Garriya can count, Shipwife, do not look so surprised. Old Garriya can do many things. But save all these wretches?" She pointed at the corpse of the boy. "Not here. There are maybe forty, out of all of them, who will be strong enough to pull through. It is a strange thing, this, Shipwife."

"Why?"

"Many of those aboard were not far along in the rot. Had they been treated more kindly there was years of work in 'em."

"They all have the rot?" said Joron. Garriya nodded. "Is there any clue as to where they are from?" Garriya shook her head.

"Even the strongest are barely conscious," she said. "It will be days at best before we hear anything from most of them. The few that can speak, well . . ."

"What? Speak up, old woman."

"One fellow croaked out a story. I reckon it is not helpful. Said they are the least wanted, the Berncast, picked up off the streets with promise of work, moved from ship to ship over weeks. Many on his ship were from Bernshulme though, the fellow said."

"Where is he? I would speak with him." Garriya let out a chuckle.

"With the Hag, Shipwife, gone to the depths with the rest of the dead." Meas did not speak then, only stared at the hagshand, letting time pass while she thought through what had been said.

"Very well," said Meas. She glanced at the corpse of the boy. "Make them as comfortable as you can, Garriya." The old woman nodded.

They left the makeshift hagbower and made their way down into the stink belowdecks to see the windshorn.

Within the ship, the sound of hammering filled the air as Coxward's bonewrights worked, taking down the shelves of cured gion that had once harboured people. The doors to seaward and landward had been removed and light streamed in through the bowpeeks, though it did little to dissipate the stink. At the end of the hold Joron saw piles of what he thought at first was old varisk, but it was not. Bodies, wrapped in wingcloth, and many of them, so very many. Joron looked away, forged himself a little space to think by re-tying the cloth wrapped around his face. Meas opened the remaining door into the central hold.

No light in here, only the faint glow of the wanelights that had been filled with oil and set burning. The windshorn waiting within for them, huddled together in a corner of the central space under the decks. They reminded him of the gullaime the first time he had seen it, sticks and bones beneath filthy and threadbare robes. As they approached he saw the windshorn existed in two groups – one, the larger, at the rear and a smaller group to the fore. Was it Joron's imagination or were these gullaime smaller than he was used to? They were more timid definitely. He understood how much posture and attitude could affect appearance, but nonetheless he was sure they were smaller. As the first group of windshorn shuffled forward he noticed another difference: where his gullaime had a three-toed foot, each toe ending in a sharp claw, these gullaime's feet had two outside toes the same, but the central one was truncated and ended in a much bigger, sharper, curved claw.

"I am Shipwife Meas. It is I that has freed you from confinement."

The first of the small group came forward. It dragged one foot, approaching side on, keeping its head low and its masked face downcast. Only when it glanced up did Joron see that unlike most fleet gullaime it had its eyes – though they were not the burning orbs that hid behind the mask of the windtalker back on their ship. These were large black pupils in white eyes behind a mesh built into its mask; very human eyes.

"How serve, o'seer?" Its voice was a scratch on the air and it was careful to avoid meeting Meas's gaze. Joron noticed it was larger than most of the others

"I wish to know how you came to be here."

A shudder ran through the creature. Joron heard low noises, chirps and cracks from the gullaime behind them but their leader silenced them with a hiss. They were strangely unmusical, these gullaime.

"Lamyard o'seer say go ship. Gullaime go ship." Meas stared. This gullaime had a following, three or four that stayed with it, close behind, while the others cowered back. Joron noticed the leading gullaime, despite the terrible conditions, had better clothes, was slightly cleaner and had more feathers on its neck.

"Our windtalker," said Meas, "says you are traitors and that you can't be trusted. It says you should be put to death."

"No, no." The windshorn came forward a step, cooing out the word. "Windshorn help. Windshorn help o'seers. Windshorn do good work." Its voice dropped an octave, became full of threat. "Windtalker need cord. Need punishment."

"Only I can order the cord used on my ship."

"Yes, yes. Gullaime lie," said the windshorn. "Not like us. Us better. Better than it. We know place. Windtalkers not know place without cord. Shipwife show place."

Joron wondered if the windshorn knew enough about human expression to decipher the look of contempt on Meas's face.

"Can you work?" she said.

"Yes yes, Work hard. Keep windtalkers in place."

"Can you do other work?"

It stared at her and he saw the eyelids come down, a slow blink behind the mesh in the mask.

"Windshorn will do as told," it said.

"And do they agree?" said Meas, tilting her head at the other group, the larger collection of bedraggled and beaten-looking windshorn.

"Will do as told," said the leader.

"Are traitors!" This call came from one of the windshorn at the back and immediately, as if the creature was fire and those around it made of straw, a gap grew about it as the other windshorn moved away, quick to disassociate themselves from this lone voice.

"Quiet you!" came from the larger windshorn before them. It hopped over to the windshorn who had cried out, wings outstretched beneath its robe, and to all who grew up in the Hundred Isles and had a familiarity with birds, it was obvious it intended violence.

"Stop this!" roared Meas and the larger windshorn did. On the spot, as if rooted there. Then it turned, shrinking back down.

"Windshorn stop, windshorn do as Shipwife tells. Windshorn good worker."

"I want to speak to that one," said Meas, pointing at the windshorn who had spoken, so evidently out of turn.

The larger windshorn opened and closed its beak slowly, something Joron thought of as meaning a gullaime was either shrugging or thinking.

"That one wrong," it said. "Broken."

"You said you would do as you were told."

The windshorn lowered its head, then hopped to the side and Meas approached the other of the windshorn who stood, its body slack, beak pointed at the floor. Even though the gullaime were an alien, unfamiliar species it was difficult to read this creature's body language as anything other than dejected.

"Stealers," it said quietly. "Takers. Chainers. Biters. Corders. Jailers. Killers," it said softly. Some feeling ran through the gathered windshorn, like a cold breeze. They huddled together as if for protection from the words of their colleague.

"So the windtalker is right. You are traitors to your kind."

"What choice?" it said. "What choice without wind?"

Before Meas could answer there was a screech of fury and the larger windshorn flew at the smaller one, wings outstretched, running across the deck.

"Trouble causer! Liar!" screeched the larger and Meas's hand went to her crossbow but the attacking windshorn was too quick. It launched itself up, one clawed foot outstretched for the smaller windshorn, and as it came in the smaller gullaime dipped to the side, the claw passing over its head, scoring through the back of its robe, cutting into the body beneath. But the victim was not defenceless – it span before the hook of the claw got purchase in its flesh and it brought up its own clawed foot. As the larger windshorn landed, turning to face its opponent, the smaller windshorn's leg was already coming around and the claw, curved sharp and cruel, cut straight through its attacker's throat. The larger bird staggered back. Opened its beak to speak but no sound came out, only blood. It collapsed to the deck, quite dead. And the smaller windshorn walked over to it, a bright streak of blood on its dirty robe.

"Traitors," it said to the corpse. "Not lie."

There was a furore among the rest. Wings were spread, beaks opened to cry, battle lines swiftly drawn. Meas opened her mouth then. "You will be quiet!" she shouted.

An instant cessation, as if obeying a human voice was a compulsion, a part of them.

"I am Shipwife Meas and my word here is law. My rule is absolute. Should any of you wish to be kept separate from others in your group, then simply stand to landward of me." She glanced around the hold. "Do you understand? Landward is this side," she said, pointing. Nothing, no movement. "My ship and my rule are new starts for all," she said. "That is what we are. That is what you may have with me." She stood, imperious and sure. Then, with a small amount of hissing and posturing, the gullaime split into two groups, one to Meas's landward and one to seaward.

She pointed at the last windshorn before her, blood still on its robe.

"You can fight," she said.

"They make us. Keep order. Sometimes amuse them. Can fight."

"Well, I will have Garriya look to your wound. I think I may have a job for you."

# 6

# What Ill Cargo Is Found Upon
# the Sea

"Not want!" The screech was followed by a rock that
rebounded off the bone wall behind Meas's head as the
gullaime backed into a corner of its nest room, wings spread
beneath the robe as if to wall off that area and keep its precious
possessions safe. "Not want!" it screeched again.

"Joron has a shadow and I have a shadow because we are
important to the running of the ship. You are important to the
running of *Tide Child*, so you too will have a shadow to protect
you."

"Not want!" it screeched again and this time a small metal
mug was thrown, aimed well enough that Meas had to dodge it.

"Joron, see if you can talk some sense into it," she pointed
at the gullaime. "I will be in my cabin discussing our next
move with Dinyl and the courser." She turned and left. Did
Joron feel an odd stab of jealousy that she still respected the
deckholder, even though the man so obviously hated him?
Possibly, but he put that aside for the good of the ship, as he
had learned to put aside the constant damp and discomfort
and the cold and the tiredness and a thousand other things.

"Not want, Joron Twiner," said the gullaime, but its fury was gone now. Its voice gentle, sad even.

"Meas has said it will be."

"Bad shipwife."

"You know she is not." The gullaime hissed. "I will tell the windshorn that it is only to be near you if you are in danger."

"Not nest." It stepped over to its nest and settled. "No thief in nest."

"I will make sure it knows."

"Not want."

"We will make a show of you accepting it, and then maybe Meas will forget and we can quietly sideline it?" He knew she would not, and his thinking was that the gullaime would eventually forget its dislike of the windshorn.

"Bad shipwife," it hissed. Joron ignored that and left.

Outside he found the windshorn, the same that had killed their old leader.

"Not wanted," it said.

"Well no," said Joron. "It would maybe be best if you kept your distance while the gullaime gets used to the idea of you.

"Distance," it said.

"Yes." The windshorn nodded, then huddled down outside the door.

"I'm not sure that is what distance means," said Joron. But the windshorn did not reply or look at him, and if he knew one thing it was that the gullaime, as a species, had an uncanny ability to hear what they wished to hear and act upon that. In the end, it was often easier to let them work it out for themselves. So he left the windtalker and the windshorn separated by a screen of bone and a thin door and hoped he would not be called back later to break up a fight. Though if what he had seen in the hold of the *Maiden's Bounty* was anything to go by then gullaime fights were short, brutal and deadly. He thought about the vicious claw on the windshorn, and hoped he was never pitted against one.

Joron passed up through the ship, noting that despite the

new and strange crew that Meas had brought aboard, the life of the ship went on as it always did. Women and men of the day shifts moved about purposefully while those of later shifts slept. Some were in the hold restowing cargo to help the ship fly better, others up the spines to bring in the wings. Some checked the great gallowbows on the maindeck, some cleaned, some painted. As he passed, he tried to have a word on his lips for as many as he could, though some met him with little but polite surliness. He passed Sprackin, who was doing nothing in particular. Joron knew he should have picked the man up on it, but then he noticed Cwell, and Joron chose to pass by as if he had not noticed them. In the great cabin he found Meas and Dinyl bent over a chart – was that jealousy he felt? – and the courser, Aelerin, stood behind them, their features hidden beneath their robe.

"Joron," said Meas. "Aelerin tells me they have dreamed good winds and calm seas for the next few weeks we will fly toward Safeharbour, so I have decided we will accompany the *Maiden's Bounty* back there. Karrad is always telling me they need more ships. We may also leave the windshorn there."

"That will please our gullaime."

"Ey," she said. And all the while they spoke Dinyl stared at him and Joron had to fight the urge to fidget under his judgement. In all things of the fleet he knew Dinyl was his better – the man had been favoured by Indyl Karrad and gone to the grand bothies of the fleet to study, while Joron was simply a fisher's son. And yet Meas had, for her own reasons, chosen him over Dinyl and two years had passed since that day. One year since he had cut Dinyl's hand from his body to save Meas, and destroyed the budding relationship he had with the man. And every day Joron had to work hard to ensure none saw that Dinyl was a better officer, one more suited to command than he was. Every day he had to work and live under the cold, judgemental gaze of a man who had once been his shipfriend, his comfort and his warmth.

"They will be glad to see us at Safeharbour," said Joron,

"and glad of more hands to put to building. How large is the colony now?"

"A thousand, last I heard," said Meas. "And it grows. Those with a desire for peace hear of it, and they find us, or we find them."

"Your mother will find us one day, Meas, you know that," said Dinyl, his words blowing a cold wind into the cabin. Meas stared at the chart, nodded.

"I do not doubt she knows already."

"And yet she has not moved against us?" said Joron.

"Karrad is her spymaster, he controls what information comes to her. She may know of our movement but not the size of it. She probably does not think us worth moving against."

Dinyl nodded. "Let us hope so," he said.

They flew across the sea for a week and a day, the wind kind and the services of the gullaime unneeded. Every time Joron passed the gullaime's nest room the windshorn was still there. He never saw it eat, never saw it drink, never heard it talk nor saw it move, and though it was Joron's nature to want to help all those he saw suffer, he dared not for fear of upsetting the friendship he had with the windtalker.

Still, it seemed that their passage would be an easy one, and no deckchilder ever complained when their way was eased, and the weather, if not becoming warm, at least lost some of its bite.

"Ship rising!"

The shout came on Joron's watch, in that morran moment where Skearith's Eye was not yet fully open and gilded the early clouds with silver and the lapping sea with gold. At the call he was up the mainspine. Not with the ease of Meas or the deckchilder, and Joron would never have that — he still had dark moments haunted by the frailty of his body and memories of his father's death — but with more ease than he had once been capable of. The topboy pointed out the sighting, four points of the landward shadow, and Joron took Meas's nearglass from within his stinker coat and found the ship. Two spines, black sails.

"A ship of the dead," he said. "I think it is our allies in the *Snarltooth*, but being overly prepared never hurt a ship." He leaned over the side of the topboy's perch and shouted down. "Farys! Call the shipwife, clear the decks for action!" And then he heard Farys call out and a moment later the bell rang out and the drums beat and he knew the deck below would be like the ground around an insect nest disturbed by a foraging kivelly, the crew boiling out of the hatches to strip *Tide Child* down and prepare for combat.

By the time he was back on the slate *Tide Child* was arrayed for war: bowcrews stood by their bows, ropes were arrayed across the deck and he knew that below the smaller cabins of the D'older and the deckmother and hatkeep, walls would be down, hammocks stowed against the sides of the hull, bows ready to be untrussed. Meas stood on the rump of the ship.

"Ship rising, Shipwife." He was always surprised by how calm he could make those words, as if they were not harbingers of death, pain and havoc. "Four points off the landward shadow." He held out the nearglass and she took it from him, climbing a few steps up the rumpspine and hanging, one arm wrapped around a rope, her feet against the bottom of the bone as she stared out across the dancing, gilded water.

"It is the *Snarltooth*. He flies message flags and makes for us." She put the nearglass away and turned to Barlay on the steering oar. "Three points to landward of the shadow," she said. "Ready to meet with *Snarltooth* and receive Shipwife Brekir." She turned, looking for her steward, Mevans, who was, as usual, already there before he was requested.

"I will arrange food and drink, Shipwife," he said with a grin, bobbing his head. Then she turned to find the deckmother, Solemn Muffaz.

"Coughlin and his seaguard will be ready to receive Shipwife Brekir, Shipwife Meas," said Solemn Muffaz. He received a nod of acceptance from Meas, not thanks, as this was what the shipwife expected. *Tide Child* ran as a fleet ship now, her ship. No slackers, no slatelayers, none who did not know their place; and if she could not trust them all? Well, that may be true, but she trusted enough to know the ship was hers. It ran her way, and her way was to run it well.

So, when Shipwife Brekir left her ship to climb *Tide Child* she was met with a ladder and was whistled aboard. The seaguard, in blue uniforms Meas had supplied herself, stood with curnows raised to greet her and she could have been any great shipwife from any great fleet boneship, not what she was: the disgraced shipwife of a supposed enemy vessel.

Brekir stood tall on the slate of *Tide Child*. She was from the south, like Joron's family had been and her skin was even darker than his. Unlike Joron, she rarely smiled and carried the feel of a sea drizzle along with her, though Joron knew that beneath the dour exterior a wicked wit lurked. With her she brought two of her deckchilder and her deckkeeper, who was as big as almost any three others with a beard covering almost half his face, dangling down to his belly. He looked around suspiciously, for he, like Brekir, was a Gaunt Islander and the *Tide Child* was a Hundred Isles ship – nominally his enemy, if not for the dream of peace which united them.

"So it is true then," the deckkeeper said quietly to Brekir, "we are traitors."

"You have a problem with that, Vulse?"

"Oh no, Shipwife." Something sparkled in his eye. "In fact it brings me great pleasure."

Behind them stood a woman, small and bent and shivering, who glanced about herself as though frightened Skearith the Stormbird herself was about to descend and pluck her from the deck of the ship. Joron wished to reach out to her as he recognised the woman as a fisher from her clothes, a position in life fate had decreed for him. Though his body was sound and whole his mother had died in childbirth and he would never be chosen as Kept, his bloodline judged as weak in a land that only valued the strong. One of the fisher's arms was bent out of true and she stared miserably at the deck, uncomfortable around the officers, but Joron knew he could offer her no comfort.

"How goes it, Shipwife Brekir?" said Meas. "Well, I hope?"

Brekir shook her head. "I see you have been busy," she said, nodding toward the hulk they towed.

"Ey, I thought that Safeharbour could use another ship."

"Well, I bring ill and iller news for you, Meas," said Brekir.

"We shall go to my great cabin," said Meas. "If I must sup bitter news let us at least do it over sweet drinks, ey?" Brekir nodded and Meas led them down through the ship to her great cabin where a table waited, laid with the best plates, and what food they had left that passed as half decent.

"Sit," said Meas. They did, all but the bedraggled woman, who hovered at the back of the cabin. "You may sit too, fisher," said Meas. Joron wondered if his father would have been cowed just like this woman. Thoughts of his fishers and the closeness of this woman, who had hands covered in cuts from gutting fish and fixing nets, and carried some indefinable scent that he associated with the boats of his childhood, caused memories to surface of the terrible day he had lost his father – *his strong body crushed between the hulls of two ships*. Joron blinked, Swallowed. Pushed the image out of his mind.

"Thank 'ee, Shipwife," said the fisher and took a chair at the end of the table, perching uncomfortably. Mevans brought them drinks, thick anhir heated in a pan to chase away the cold touch of the sea winds. The fisher stared into the drink, looking utterly miserable, and Joron leaned forward.

"Good fisher," he said, "Shipwife Meas has you here as she considers you as much a shipwife as herself, but if you would be more comfortable outside this cabin I am sure Mevans can find you a place to eat and drink elsewhere on the ship."

"I would like that," said the fisher quietly.

"Stay close enough that I may call upon you, Fasni," said Brekir softly, and the fisher nodded as Mevans led her gently from the great cabin. Meas watched her go and gave Joron a nod as if to say "that was well done," for if she had offered the fisher the chance to leave it would have been seen as an order and may have made the nervous woman worse.

"So, Brekir, how ill is your news?" Meas smiled, for Brekir's news was always ill, even when some others may have thought it anything but, Brekir would find a dark edge to worry at.

"The illest, Shipwife Meas," she said, staring into the steaming drink, "and from there it only gets iller."

"Well, let us eat first then," said Meas. "Bad news is better digested by a full belly. I will bring you food in the name of the Maiden, the Mother and the Sea Hag. Enjoy and be thankful."

They ate, and while they ate Joron wondered if the news could possibly be as bad as the food, a roasted whole fish caught two days ago and with a gelatinous texture that gave way under his teeth only to reform on his tongue, as if the fish struggled still to live. After the seemingly unwilling main course was eaten, if not enjoyed, by all, silsh was served, the hot invigorating drink beloved of all who worked late watches on cold nights.

"So, Brekir," said Meas, "tell me this this ill news of yours."

Brekir sipped at her silsh, swilled the burning liquid around her mouth.

"All we did, Meas, in protecting the wakewyrm, it was for naught," she said. Looked around the table, shook her head. "The death, the sacrifice. For naught. Keyshans have been seen again."

Meas put down her cup, her pale face paler. "The wakewyrm has returned?"

"No," said Brekir, "others have come. Three have been reported so far, and though none have managed to kill one I have no doubt towers are being built right now. The boneships will rise again, Meas, and our war will last forever."

Meas turned her glass, her face unreadable, but when she spoke, her voice was as dead and black as her ship.

"You said you had iller news, Brekir. What could be iller than this?"

Brekir waited, as if the words she needed eluded her, her face contorted by misery.

"It seems your mother has finally tired of us, Meas. She sent her ships for Safeharbour and what your mother wants she gets." She looked up, straightened as if to find some inner strength. "Safeharbour is gone, Meas. We have no place to run to. The dream is dead now."

None spoke then. None had a word. Their hope, slowly growing over time, along with their hidden harbour, dashed on the rocks of Brekir's words.

"Gone? How?" said Meas, the words barely a breeze in the still cabin.

"I was not there, that is why I brought the fisher. She saw it and it is her tale to tell." She walked to the door, "Fasni," she shouted, "it is time."

# 7

# The Fisher's Tale

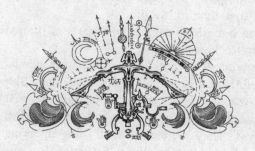

I sit before you, shipwife Meas, and I must tell my tale all at a rush and in one, for I do not lie to say you are a hero of mine from when I were young and running round the alleys of Bernshulme. To sit here, afront of you, well, to say it is hard to find words is the least of it so I shall speak and if you would be good enough to listen then I will think you kindly indeed.

This is my start. I found myself to Safeharbour after the sea took me and my flukeboat, *Corpsebird*. Some fell wind came up and pulled me far from home and would not let me go. Which is when I found myself falling under the hull of a black ship, and a shipwife name of Arrin.

Ey, you know him? He is a good man despite him missing a leg and so being, most would say, fit just for cobblering.

Anyways, I knew him for a Gaunt Islander as his ship flew the black circles and I were ready to be begging for me life, see. Told him I had no love for the Hundred Isles as my boy was sacrificed as shipblood, even though he had two fingers missing from his right hand and were not proper; the hagpriests did not care. So Shipwife Arrin brought me to Safeharbour, said I could ply my trade there. Fishers were always welcome and the water round it were warm and easy to cast my nets in. I thought the Mother herself watched over me, shipwife, for it seemed she chased my nets full every time they were cast. I even met a fellow there and thought to have me another child for my time of grief was starting to pass. Life became good and though it were hard work to live it were still gentler than any other time in my life.

Then the boneships came. This was less than two months past, by my reckoning.

No Shipwife, I do not know the names of all those who commanded them. I heard talk on the docks of a Shipwife Barnt being him who led them on us, and he had a two-ribber named *Keyshantooth*, but those such as myself are not privy to the talk of shipwives. They were four that came upon us, a pair of two-ribbers such as good Shipwife Brekir has and a pair of four-ribbers which I swear were the biggest ships I ever did see, and me growing up in Bernshulme and all — but these ships seem so much the larger when arrayed for war and coming for you, maybe that is it. The ships stationed themselves in the outer bay of Safeharbour and none could get in or leave, and they did not come near enough for the tower gallowbows to act on them, but sent in an envoy to speak to our Bern Council. An offer was made, said all that came from the Hundred Isles could return home and those that came from the Gaunt Islands must be given up as shipblood or to mine slate for they were the enemy.

I do not think they expected us to say no but we was not Bernshulme where one decides, and the Bern Council put it to the town. You would have been most proud, Shipwife Meas, for not one woman or man there wavered in the least, all were resolute that we would fight. So the whole of Safeharbour were done out as for war, or as near as we could get to it for we were not warriors, just those people as what were tired with the way of things. Still, we had our own boneship in harbour and we had the spares and parts for it, and with Shipwife Arrin and the *Sea Louse* with us we felt good, for by then we all knew him for a fighter. We did the best we could to fortify the town and while we was doing that them outside the harbour brought up a big brownbone, like the one you is towing, Shipwife, and put catapults on it and started loosing fireballs into the town.

Were a terrible few days and, well, you know Safeharbour, Shipwife. Built onto the stone of the island, ain't nowhere to hide so we weathered it best we could and the Bern Council had us gather up every bit of written word that we had about all the comings and goings and burn them – so none would know who had visited us and who stood with us. So don't you fret none, shipwives, for you are as safe as we could make you.

On the second day they made a run at the harbour chain but with the towers and *Sea Louse*'s gallowbows and the militia we kept 'em off, though it were hard fighting and I lost my new man in it. Arrin were not that happy with the way it went but he did not say why, not to such as me at any wave, for I am just a fisher and that is all, so why should he tell me? And 'sides, grief were my companion that day and I wished for no other. But after the first run at the harbour chain the Bern Council stepped back and let Arrin run the town for it were a military operation now. He gave us some speeches, good they were, rousing. Though weren't no one in the crowd fooled, seemed nothing short of Skearith the Stormbird dropping from the sky were likely to save Safeharbour and by the end of the second day all that was not stone were burning, and we all had moved up to the great Bothy, which them catapults could not reach. That were where Shipwife Arrin told us the plan what he had and I do not lie to say it caused a true ruckus among those of us that heard it. He did not mind, said he understood an' all, but that he saw no other way.

You ask what were his plan?

Oh, Hag curse me, Shipwife, I forget you do not know all. Arrin said that Safeharbour could not survive alone. Said the fight we had at the chain were nothing great, called it *ex-ploraytory*. Said they would come back harder and faster and with more seaguard, and Mother help me I have never seen fighters as big as them, or as ready to die, and with the death of my man so raw in me head I had no wish to fight them again. Arrin said we must get out and he gave us each a message to take. He gathered all us fishers – thirteen there were, which as you all know is a Hag-blessed number – and said we must escape the harbour, even with them big ships out there waiting, cos it weren't just the boneships and the brownbones by then, there were others too, big wingflukes, almost as a big as *Sea Louse*. Shipwife Arrin said we must run; he would take out *Sea Louse*, fight the ships waiting outside the harbour and behind him the fishers would come, making all the speed they could out to the open sea. He did not lie to us, said many would die. But we all knew he were one of them for a ship like *Sea Louse* could not take on four boneships alone, he did not ask anything of us he was not prepared to give up himself. I do not think, in my life, I have ever been more scared, even when a jellybeak rose out the water once and grabbed the spine o' my ship, and I tell you that were a close-run thing if ever there were one.

But that were how it were to be. He said we would break under cover of night and those that got away were to seek out the black ships for that was where friends would be found, and the worst that could happen to us was we would be pressed into the crew.

We went that night and I have never known such fear. *Sea Louse* led, and how grand he were, all his wings raised, black as night. Had fire burning at every gallowbow and, well, you know the wind in Safeharbour, comes right over the island and can drive a ship out past the towers at a hearty speed. Well, that is what Arrin did. The Hag sent that wind for him, and he went out determined to take as many to her as he could. Truly, when I saw *Sea Louse* under war, when I heard the warmoan of his bows, I thought us invincible. He led us out, the big ship and thirteen little fishers. I saw his first salvos and the way he steered his ship between our attackers. I do not think they expected him. Far as I can tell he took them by surprise and they paid the Hag's price for it. One of their two-ribbers was spinebroke almost straight away and it got in the way of the other ships. I truly thought for a moment we may make it.

But someone in that fleet, they were canny, clever. Knew what we were about, see. For they did not turn their bows on *Sea Louse*, not straight away. They turned them on us, on the fishers. I have never seen the damage a . . .

No, please Shipwife, let me finish. I will be alright. The Hag knows tears for the dead are prayers, so you let me pray for if I do not finish this tale now I never will.

See, I had never seen the damage a gallowbow bolt could do to a flukeboat, never thought one shot could wreak so much havoc. We did not stand a chance. Shipwife Arrin told us to split the moment we left the harbour and those that did not follow that order quick enough went first — one broadside from a four-ribber, name of *Wyrm Sither*, took them all out. Them who didn't die straight away was ripped apart by long-thresh. They took their time with t'other boats. Taking them down one by one, the boats too. Not the crews. They let them go into the water. More cruel than needed, that were.

Only I as far as I know, Shipwife, ey — only I escaped.

No, Shipwife. Do not call me brave, for it is not true.

I live because I were a coward and did not follow the orders from brave Arrin. Rather than make for the sea I hugged the outer harbour wall, stayed in its shadow, made my way back to the island and round the coast a little. I hid my boat in a cove while *Sea Louse* burned behind me, and if I had not then I doubt I would be here.

Well, it is kind that you say it was clever. But it was all done from fear and I will not lie to myself about that, Shipwife.

I stayed on the island for two days, watching. They moved their fleet into the harbour, put down the staystones and then, oddest of all, started loading people onto the brownbone. There was maybe five hundred people left in Safeharbour when I made my run.

Help, Shipwife? No, Arrin did not sent us out to bring help, not in the end. He sent us out to tell you Safeharbour is lost, he sent us out to warn you.

He sent us to tell you to run.

Five years upon the sea was she
Brought havoc to her enemy
Left wrecks behind in fire and blood
Thought always of her perfect love

She flew up high, she flew down low
*Heave on, crew, heave on.*
From north to south she flew the storms
*Heave on, crew, heave on.*
She flew to east, she flew to west
*Heave on, crew, heave on.*
And always thought of home, hey!
She always thought of home.

                    From "The Black Pirate" – traditional ballad

# 8

## To Follow a Foul Course

When the fisher finished her tale the officers sat, stiff and unable to speak. Watching as tears coursed silently down her weathered face. Meas opened her mouth, coughed to clear her throat and went down on one knee by the fisher.

"The Mother and Maiden see your service, Fasni, and know it a great one. Do not berate yourself for fear. Sometimes fear is what makes us canny, eh?" She put a hand on the fisher's shoulder. "Now, I have one last task to ask of you, but you need not take it up and if you do not wish to I will think no less of you."

"I will do whatever is needed, Shipwife," she said quietly. "I am yours to command."

Meas nodded once then kept her head bowed, staring at the white floor of the great cabin. When she eventually looked up it felt to Joron as though Meas was struggling to lift her head against a great weight.

"Do you know the island of Falsehulme?" The fisher nodded. "There is a message flag there. I will write you a message, I would have you take it to Falsehulme and put the flag to half mast. Two hundred paces toward the Northstorm of the flag is a ring of large rocks that were put on their ends in the time of the Stormbird. Stand so you look at the biggest. To your landward will be a rock and at its base is a smaller stone that is almost a perfect circle. Place my message under that, if you will."

"I will," she said.

"Mevans!" shouted the shipwife and her steward appeared. "Take this fisher, give her whatever she needs. She has done us a great service. Then send Aelerin to us." Meas clapped Fasni on the shoulder and moved out of the way so she could leave. Once she was gone those gathered stood around: Joron shocked by what he had heard, Brekir and her deckkeeper deep in thought and all waiting for Meas to speak — but she did not, not until the courser appeared. "Aelerin, prepare a chart for Shipwife Brekir," she said, "showing the route to Leasthaven." The courser nodded and backed out of the cabin.

"What is it you intend to do?" said Brekir.

"The fisher's message will warn our ships we are discovered, give them a new place to meet with us or leave messages. At Leasthaven, Brekir, you will find what we have of our small fleet that is currently laid up."

Brekir's eyes widened. "Leasthaven? We have another port?" she said. "Is this a secret you did not think me worthy of, Meas?"

"A secret Arrin and I told no one. The fewer know a secret, the less likely it is to spread. But you have had my implicit trust since we flew together in chase of the wakewyrm, Brekir, you know that." Brekir shrugged then sat down. "We have nothing big there, nothing truly impressive. Most of our fleet are out, pretending loyalty to the Hundred or Gaunt Islands. At Leasthaven it is mostly repurposed brownbones, a couple of two-ribbers that need work. I would have you bring what you find of our fleet toward Safeharbour. Aelerin will find a place near enough we can meet without fear of being seen. Brave Arrin's death will not go unavenged."

There was a space then, a moment for the ghost of Arrin to pass and the grief of losing a friend to settle in the room.

"Can we fight four boneships, Meas," said Brekir, "with a couple of brownbones and some broken two-ribbers?"

"No." Meas shook her head. "No we cannot. But the island is taken now and I imagine there will no longer be four bone-ships there. Two at most to hold it and catch any stragglers who appear, or that is what I would leave. If we turn up with what looks like a fleet they may even surrender straight away."

There was no doubt that Brekir, Vulse and Joron knew what Meas said to be unlikely, but they did not pursue it further because Meas had spoken and she commanded.

Brekir stood. "I will bring your fleet, Shipmother," she said. It was respect that had Brekir raise Meas's rank, though Joron knew it must be as if another weight was pressed upon her shoulders.

"Shipwife only, Brekir."

Brekir nodded. "I have been wondering ever since Fasni gave me her story, why attack Safeharbour now, Meas?" she said. "You have said before, you were sure your mother must know about Safeharbour, so why make her move now?"

"Because the keyshans have returned," Meas said. Brekir's eyebrow raised in question. "My mother is far from stupid, she knew that without the arakeesians to supply bones the age of boneships was passing. War would grind to halt and new ways would have to be found. I expect she saw the community at Safeharbour as an experiment, and when the time came she may have legitimised it, brought it into her government even. Oh, she would have had conditions, my head among them once everything was made clear to her." She picked up her cup from the table, put it back down. "But with the return of the arakeesians comes war, and war is what she knows well. It will mean she can fasten her grip so tightly on the Hundred Isles it will never be loosened. First Bern of the new keyshan age, how she will love that."

"Meas," said Brekir, "forgive me this but I must ask." Meas looked up, met her doleful gaze. "Do you send us to Safeharbour for the sake of our people, or to spite your mother?"

Another silence then, a long one, a stilling of the air within the cabin, a moment where the ever-present noise of deckchilder about their duty seemed to cease and *Tide Child* seemed to stop rocking on the restless sea. A single shaft of light from Skearith's Eye lit a column of dancing dust.

"In truth, Brekir," said Meas, "I am not sure."

Brekir nodded. "Well," she said, "that is an honest answer and I can ask for no more. Come, Vulse, we have a trip to make and we must make it with all the haste we can muster."

When they were gone, and Joron had heard the whistles and shouts of them being saluted off *Tide Child*, Meas stood.

"Say what is on your mind, Deckkeeper," she said.

He waited a second before speaking, deciding how to phrase the words in his mind, realising that however they were phrased there was no escaping the brutality of them. The finality.

"Arrin gave his life to warn us away from Safeharbour," he said. "And now we rush toward it." Meas nodded at that. "I think only that *Tide Child* is our most powerful ship. We may risk losing him and that will turn a disaster into a calamity."

Meas tapped her finger on the desk and then went around and sat behind it.

"Eight years, Joron. That is how long Indyl Karrad and I have been building Safeharbour up. Bringing women and men who wish to escape the Bern, on both sides of our ancestral war. Eight years, Joron. And we worked together for peace for many years prior."

"But we still exist, even without Safeharbour," said Joron. "Is it worth risking losing our biggest ship taking back a town we cannot keep? And you know we cannot — as soon as your mother knows we have taken it back she will return with more ships. She will not let you win. Going to Safeharbour may mean we lose what small chance we have to rebuild somewhere else."

Meas sat back in her chair, stared at him and then stretched. "Anyone listening would think you the shipwife, not I, Deckkeeper." And at that he seemed to shrink, the veneer of command he wore cracking and slipping away to expose the fisher's boy beneath, so unsure of himself.

"I . . . did not . . ."

But Meas showed no sign of seeing these cracks, only broke out into a wide smile, though it was a cold smile too, one of amusement that told him she saw things he did not.

"You are well worthy of that sword I gifted you, Joron" — he felt a warm glow within him at her words, and he touched the hilt of the blade at his hip — "and you are right to question me, in here at least." Her face hardened. "But never out there, in front of the crew. In here it is your place on this ship to make me think. Now, tell me, did anything strike you as odd in the fisher's account?"

"You think she lied?"

Meas shook her head. "No. Definitely not."

"Then no, not odd, Shipwife, only terrible. And sad, ey — terrible and sad."

"It is both those things, ey," she said. "But is it not strange that this Shipwife, Barnt, did not ask for me?"

"You never go ashore; why would it be odd you are not expected to be there?"

"But I am recognisable, Joron, as is this ship," she waved a hand at the bone walls around her. "And even in Safeharbour there were spies, that is why Arrin and the Gaunt Island ship-wives ran it. But the attackers not asking for me makes me suspect my mother is not sure of my involvement, she would surely have wanted me taken." Meas tapped the desk with her finger, thinking. "As it stands, to destroy Safeharbour may have been enough to sate her for now." She smiled and leaned forward, "We do not go back for vengeance, despite what I let Brekir think, and I will make no attempt to repopulate Safeharbour."

"Then why do we go there?"

"Our people, Joron, they need us." She looked up, face dark with worry. Shoulders heavy with responsibility. "They had brownbones, like that great lug we tow, Joron, and Fasni said many were loaded onto them. Think of what we found on it."

"But they were the sick and broken, useless people. The people of Safeharbour are healthy, they are—"

"Traitors, Joron. That is what they are to my mother. They are traitors and I do not believe that they will go to other lives, nor even a get a quick death. I go to Safeharbour to get what remains of my people there away. I will not let them suffer like those we found on the *Maiden's Bounty*."

"And if they are already gone?" She looked away. Continued to speak as if he had not.

"I intend to find the brownbones that left with my people. After we have saved those who remain at Safeharbour we shall go to Bernshulme and find out where they are being taken and why."

"Surely you cannot risk Bernshulme, Shipwife. Your mother . . ."

"As I said, I don't think she knows about me, Joron. Now, set us a course for Safeharbour and hope Aelerin dreams us good winds and swift passage."

On *Tide Child*'s deck was a ruckus. The gullaime had emerged from its nest and was doing its usual curious round of the deckchilder and their jobs – sticking its beak in with those it knew would tolerate it, hissing and cursing at those who it did not trust or had taken a dislike to. But it was not this that was causing the upset; the ship was used to and knew this. It was the attention the gullaime was showing the windshorn.

Meas, true to her word as ever, had brought some aboard then put them to work. Knowing gullaime were dextrous she had the windshorn mending ropes and nets and wings for the ship, and now *Tide Child*'s own gullaime was showing its displeasure, hissing at the gaggle of windshorn as it passed, making them cower. If one had its back to the gullaime it would nip with its beak, making the windshorn squawk. In response their gullaime would open its beak and make an almost human laughing sound, something false and sinister.

Behind their gullaime followed the windshorn that had

sworn to protect it, staying low as if that may make it invisible. It would sneak forward and then, as if possessing some sixth sense for such things, the gullaime would swing round. Begin spitting and lashing out with its clawed feet. Shouting, "Not want! Not want!" The windshorn would react immediately, jumping backwards out of reach of the sharp beak, the wings under its robe outstretched as the gullaime continued to screech and squawk and swear in the many inventive ways it had picked up from the deckchilder. The windshorn would shrink under the onslaught until, finally, the gullaime became bored and returned to tormenting the other windshorn on the deck.

It was not something Joron found tolerable.

"Gullaime," he called out, "attend me on the rump of the ship." It turned to him, tilting its head, hissing, then hopping up to join him.

"What want?"

"You are not acting in an officerly fashion, Gullaime."

It stared at him, the painted eyes on the mask focused on his face.

"Officerly," it said.

"Ey. Shipwife Meas has expectations."

"Bad shipwife," it squawked.

"Would you wish to tell her that? Deckchilder are corded for such talk."

The gullaime cooed, then bent its head to preen at the long feathers that sprouted around the single claw on the elbow of its wing, the rest hidden beneath its robe.

"Shipwife needs Gullaime. Cannot hurt."

"But she can make your life more inconvenient," he whispered. "No more pretty rocks or soft rope for you. No more clean robes."

"Traitors," it hissed. "Traitors die."

Joron leaned in close, letting the sand and heat scent of the gullaime surround him, fighting the drift of his mind, the scintillating cascades of notes that such closeness to the wind-talker always brought on.

"All who are brought on this ship, Gullaime, are criminals, are lost and unwanted and hated by others. Meas says *Tide Child* is a new start."

"Hate them."

"As you hated me," said Joron.

The gullaime took a step back. Its beak opened and shut.

"You do not have to like them. But you must treat them in an officerly fashion for the ship to run." The beak, so wicked, opened and shut again. The windtalker hissed. Then cocked its head to one side, aggression replaced by curiosity.

"Officer Gullaime?"

"I suppose so," said Joron, unsure quite what he had promised.

"Get shiny badge? Get dye for feather?"

"I am sure it can be arranged."

The gullaime trilled, a high-pitched fanfare of delight. Then it span in a circle.

"Officer Gullaime!" He heard a chuckle from behind him and turned to find a familiar face. His shadow, Anzir, was at the steering oar, as she often was when he did not require her direct protection. She grinned at him.

"That'll cause trouble, D'keeper," she said. He nodded and turned to shout after the gullaime.

"Only an Officer over the others of your kind," added Joron, "not the ship."

But the windtalker's dance did not stop – the gullaime had found some joy and did not intend to lose it and so it danced, whirling and spinning and squawking up and down the deck of *Tide Child* while they set their course, toward Safeharbour. Toward war. Toward death.

# 9

# A Home to Only Heartbreak

They travelled for twenty days, the rhythm of the sea matching the rhythm of the ship, The constant shifting movement of water and crew made it easy to lose track of time as each day aboard ship was essentially the same: wake, eat, work, eat, work, eat, sleep and round and round it went. Sometimes the flying was easy, following winds pushing them across the waves, and sometimes it was hours and hours of painful tacking across the wind in huge zigzags, only to make small headway. All their work made harder by the great brown-bone they still towed, and when Joron asked why they had not sent it with Brekir, Meas simply shrugged.

The only exception to their routine being Menday, when Meas would read the Bernlaw and then all aboard would set to fixing and mending their clothes and equipment. Deckchilder would bring out games, cards would be played and the officers would turn a blind eye to the gambling as long as it caused no trouble. Good-natured games were played on boards chalked on the slate deck — and yet still, even on this relaxing day, the ship must be served. The wings must be furled and unfurled, the gallowbows greased and checked, the decks cleaned, the bone hull inspected for leaks; the work on a ship was never-ending. Sometimes he found himself watching the courser, Aelerin, as they measured the angle of Skearith's Eye, listened to the stormsong and communed with clouds. Found himself a little jealous of their easier life.

Meas kept to herself on that long passage. The entire journey was one of curt orders, of her standing on the rump, transfixed by something in the distance. Once he would have taken this as an insult, or worried that he had displeased her somehow but now he knew this was simply her way. The running of the ship, the day-to-day activity, that was for him and for Dinyl, and while the two men shared no love they marked the log accurately and exchanged all the information needed — though Joron could never quite meet Dinyl's accusing eye, nor ever quite forget that the reason the deck-holder's writing was almost unreadable was because Joron had taken his good hand.

Meas talked more to the courser than any other in those weeks, and plainly the courser had her trust, not that it made Joron any more comfortable around them; never showing their face, never staying long enough to enter a conversation, always slinking off to their cabin and hiding away. Of all the crew he felt like he knew Aelerin the least, though if he was to tell the truth to himself he might admit that maybe of all the crew, he had tried the least to get to know them.

On a couple of mornings Solemn Muffaz rigged the grates and there were cordings of particularly recalcitrant deck-childer, mostly among those new crew taken from *Maiden's Bounty*. Once of Sprackin, emboldened by Joron's laxness with him, who had ended up answering back and being rewarded with ten strokes of the cord. His punishment delivered by Anzir, while Solemn Muffaz looked on approvingly. Sprackin swore revenge with every stroke but Joron ignored him. The man was all talk and while Sprackin cursed Joron wondered whether he would lose his shadow one day. He felt sure that Solemn Muffaz was grooming her to take his place should the deckmother fall. Joron approved, as he thought Anzir may make a good deckmother one day, maybe when Joron had his own ship.

All these things were the normal workings of a fleet ship, and the passage of *Tide Child* was as uneventful as the arrival at its destination was likely to be eventful, and that in the extreme.

Joron did not know how Meas chose the place to drop the seastays and furl *Tide Child*'s wings. As deckkeeper he ran the ship — occasionally Meas would ask him for help in navigating as his numbers were good and his instincts sharp, or so she said, but there had been no need this time, and when the orders were given they were as much a surprise to him as to the deckchilder around him.

"Now it begins, ey, D'keeper," said Farys, the girl's burned face stretching with her smile as she stowed the great gallowbow she had been lovingly polishing. "Pay them Hag-cursed souls back for Arrin soon, ey?"

"Ey, Farys," he said, and he was proud that his voice did not tremble at the thought of the trial to come. "Now our work begins, but we must wait on the shipwife to tell us what that work is and how it will be done."

He closed his eyes and tried to push away thoughts of the violence to come. Saw in his mind's eye that moment when his father's strong body was crushed between the hulls of two ships — the constant reminder that strength counted for naught in the Hundred Isles, that the Hag would have her way. He tried not to shiver, tried to give himself up to the inevitability of death. Clamped his hand around the hilt of the sword Meas had given him, but he must not have hidden his shudder as well as he thought. "There's kivelly-fuzz jerkins in the hold, D'keeper," said Farys. "I hid some in a place where they are kept dry and will give you one if you are cold."

He shook his head, smiled at her.

"A passing glance of the Hag is all, Farys," he said. She gave a quick nod and made a sign of protection against her chest.

"Oh, D'keeper." He turned to find Gavith, the cabin boy,

evidently surprised to run into him. He was hardly a boy now though.

"Can I help, Gavith?"

"No I . . ." He looked stricken and Joron wanted to laugh – he knew all too well what it was to be nervous around an officer, though he had thought Gavith over it. Maybe he was still embarrassed over nearly losing his arm to the rope when they saved the *Maiden's Bounty*.

"I was just leaving, Gavith. I will let Farys find something for you to do."

"Deckkeeper," came the call from Meas, "my cabin. I would talk." He followed her voice, out of the cold light on deck and below to the underdecks where the smell of damp was ever present, through into her great cabin where the rear windows of *Tide Child* showed the endless shifting sea and once more filled the world with light.

As soon as he was through the door Meas started talking. "I need to meet with Brekir and whatever ships she has, and I need to know what awaits us at Safeharbour. I cannot do both myself." She sounded somehow as though she had let him down, by not being in two places at once.

"Of course not, Shipwife," he said. Meas ran her hand across the top of her desk.

"You will take the wingfluke, dirty yourself up so you look like a trader and go spy out the place for me."

"Go into the harbour?"

She shook her head. "No, I do not think that would be wise. Get near enough to look at what is there." She took the nearglass from her jacket and placed it on the desk before him. "See what awaits us and return. Take Aelerin with you."

"The courser?"

"Ey, I need to know how the wind will blow around Safeharbour and the nearer you take them the better their dreams will be." She tapped the top of the nearglass. "And take Cwell, also."

"Cwell?"

"I know she has no love for you, nor you her, but you are her officer and she will obey you. Staff the rest of the crew with your true people – Farys, Anzir and the like."

"But why Cwell, Shipwife?"

"To get near enough to spy out the harbour you will no doubt be seen yourself. If they intercept you then you must pass yourself off as traders. Cwell knows the trader's cant, she was raised on the trade docks of Bernshulme, and if any of us can pass as a trader who strayed too far she can."

"If she does not simply give us up."

"It is a risk, I grant you. You will have to ensure she does not." Meas took her hand off the nearglass and reached into her desk for one of her many books.

"Shipwife," said Joron, picking up the nearglass as she looked up and raised an eyebrow. "If we may be chased, then the gullaime would serve me better than Cwell, surely. Give me the winds and I'll outrun whatever they have."

"Tell me Joron," said Meas, "how many wingfluke traders do you know that have a gullaime on board?"

He waited, as if he was thinking about it even though he immediately knew the answer, "None, and if they spot the gullaime then they will know something is afoot."

"Ey, Joron, ey," she said, and opened her book. "You may leave now." He started to turn and she added, "But in future, try not to ask questions to which you already know the answer."

# 10

# What Is Given May Be Easily Lost

It was a surly boat that headed out for Safeharbour from *Tide Child*, rigged to look like a trader rather than the flukeboat of a ship of war. Though Joron had given up his clothes and hat of command, he kept the sword Meas had given him after they had freed the wakewyrm. It had become too much part of him, a piece of metal that proved his value to Lucky Meas, and though he felt he should not need such a simple thing, he did. Especially with Cwell in the boat.

At the tiller was his shadow, Anzir, and Farys was in the small cabin in the rump of the ship sorting rope while Cwell – unhappy, sour, violent Cwell – glowered at Joron from where she sat, carving slices from a gnarled fruit with one hand. The remainder of the crew was made up of Tarin and Vosar, two of the seaguard, and if they were not exactly shiply men they had at least been with *Tide Child* long enough to know how to handle a rope and wing and to take an order. For the purposes of their journey, and because she spoke the trader's cant, Cwell wore the brown birdleather coat of a trader's master, though she showed scant sign of mucking in with Joron and the crew as they worked the boat, as any true trader's master would.

The sea about them was grey and eternal, a continuous shifting of waves that gently jostled the little boat as it coasted across the sea, wings full of the storm's gift and the sky above as blue as promises.

Cwell only continued to glower.

As Joron took measurements of the sun's shadow so he could estimate their place, Cwell glowered. As Aelerin matched their charts to the sea, Cwell glowered, and as Anzir leaned into the steering oar and Farys pulled taught the spinestays, Cwell glowered.

*You hate me*, thought Joron. *You once thought me a joke and I have risen above it, risen above you and you hate me for it.* He wondered if Meas had sent her in the hope Joron may find some bond between them, as he had done with the gullaime, as he had done with many of the crew, but he knew that would not happen. Cwell's hatred was implacable – she hated officers, hated being consigned to the black ship and she hated Joron the most, and he knew why. What was he to officer over her? A fisher's boy, not even trained in the Grand Bothies at Bernshulme, where she was blood to Cahanny, Bernshulme's crime lord.

But he could do nothing about her thoughts, so for long hours he worked the ship and lost himself in rope and knot.

"D'keeper." He turned to find Aelerin next to him, the wind plucking at their white robe. "We should be in sight of Safeharbour within the hour." It amazed him how still the courser managed to be, hands clasped together within the sleeves of the robe despite the rocking of the boat.

"Thank you, Courser," he said, "and how long until they can see us?"

"Half that time, maybe, it depends whether they use the lookout tower on the top of the island or not."

Joron nodded, unsure why he had wanted to know that. His mouth had moved and he had said the words because he thought they were the sort of words an officer would say in this position.

"Smoke," said Farys, pointing southward of them. "It seems Safeharbour still burns, D'keeper."

"Ey," he said and lifted the nearglass to his eye. Nothing to be seen yet but the greasy tower of smoke turning in the wind. He placed the nearglass carefully back into his jacket, noticed his hand trembled. It was not the column of smoke that made him shudder. It was that he knew if Safeharbour dispatched a ship with a gullaime aboard he could not escape it. The wind was kind for him travelling toward Safeharbour but to return to *Tide Child* he must go against it, and that meant hours of painful tacking. Zigging and zagging back and forth to make their way forward. A ship with a windtalker aboard had no such problems, it would cut through the sea to intercept them, and then his life, all their lives, would be in the hands of Cwell. Joron would not even be able to show his face, he would have to hide in the small hold or behind the doors of the cabin in the rump. It was unlikely he would be recognised, very unlikely, but at the same time he had been ashore in Bernshulme many times, carried out business at the boneyards for *Tide Child* and unlikely was not impossible, so it was best he was not seen.

Which meant trusting Cwell not to give them up, and why would she not? The woman was a seething ball of hatred for all those around her — outside of her little clique, and Dinyl.

But Meas must know that.

She must.

The wind carried the windfluke on, and Joron let his mind drift a little. The small craft was so similar to the boat his father had owned, he should name it. But not after that boat, as that would only be ill-starred. Maybe he would ask Farys to name it; she had a knack for such things.

"Here, D'keeper, land should be in sight now," said Aelerin and Joron nodded.

"Hide yourself away, Courser," he said, "a courser aboard marks us a rich merchant if nothing else, and we should attract as little attention as we can." Then he climbed the short spine, and how alarmingly it swayed compared to the sturdy spines of *Tide Child*, how flimsy it felt. He lifted the nearglass to his eye, the horizon jumped and jittered until he found himself a more comfortable perch, felt the rhythm of the sea below the hull and managed to focus the glass on Safeharbour.

Poor Safeharbour. No longer any streets, no longer any houses or varisk and mud, no slowly rising, rounded bothies, for the governance of the island. All smashed now and destined to remain unfinished, bar the first one, the grandest bothy. Joron had travelled to many places, but Safeharbour had been the first to feel like he had found a home again after the death of his father. Meas had often sent him ashore to do the jobs an officer was needed for, and his visits and familiarity had bred a fondness within him for it. Awful that the town was still smouldering, even now, so long after it had been taken. He wondered if this was deliberate, if they smeared the ground with hagspit which would burn and smoulder for months as it scorched and sucked out all the life in the ground beneath it. He saw people moving — it was difficult to tell from such a distance, they were so small, but he did not think them deckchilder; a deckchild had a certain way of walking, their bodies used to the roll of a ship beneath them, and these figures did not. They carried barrels between them and he saw a couple of people struggling to tip over a barrel and pour the contents onto the ground, then a man — an officer, definitely — came and lit the ground and more greasy smoke added itself to the lofting pyre.

"Ah, Safeharbour, they make sure you can never be used again," he found himself saying under his breath. Then he stopped. This was not why he was here. Not here to watch the plight of those still there, not here to watch the town burn or wallow in his own sense of loss. He was here to see numbers and positions so his shipwife could form a plan. He moved the nearglass to focus on the harbour.

Boneships — a four-ribber at the staystone, and a pair of two ribbers. One was under way, women and men crawling through the rigging, wings falling and filling with wind, blowing outwards to show a huge and staring eye painted on it. Behind the boneship were wingflukes similar to his own, and two of these were making ready to follow the boneship. He counted all in the harbour quickly, including those leaving. Three boneships, eight Wingflukes. It was a formidable force, more than was really needed to hold Safeharbour. He did a final quick scan. Noticed the towers on the ends of the harbour piers had been burned, probably by the defenders when they realised all was lost. Noticed how well Safeharbour's walls continued to defend the ships within it, the curve of the island gathered around them like a protective skirt, the long stone piers ready to crack unwary hulls. Then he placed the nearglass back in his coat and descended the shifting spine.

"Farys," he shouted, "they have seen us. Get us under way, all speed we can make."

"Can we outrun them, D'keeper?" said Vosar.

"Not unless the wind changes . . ." He glanced at the cabin where Aelerin hid in the shadows and saw the gentle to and fro of the courser's hood as they shook their head. "And it seems that is unlikely. My hope is they do not drive their gullaime too hard or at all, and are not on us by nightfall. Then we can extinguish the wanelights and escape under cover of dark."

"And if that is not what happens, D'keeper?" said Farys.

"Then we must hope Cwell's tongue is quick." Cwell, from her place in beak of the boat, looked up, her ice-blue eyes squeezed into slits against the brightness of Skearith's Eye, reflected back from the water in a million winking glints.

She cut a slice from her wizened fruit and placed it in her mouth.

Then all was work. Wings were rigged and ropes pulled taut, the little wingfluke heeled over and sped across the choppy sea but its speed was illusory, as it moved forward in huge zigzags so its speed toward its intended destination was slow, achingly slow. Constantly re-rigging and jigging of the ship and the pulling on the steering oar. The shouting of orders.

"Heel!" As the boat began to turn and the deck leaned over at a precarious angle.

"'Ware yer heads, boom coming over," as the wind caught the wing on its moveable spar and the boom that held the bottom of the wing moved across the deck, always ready to clout an unwary deckchild insensible.

In the moments when he was not pulling on ropes or leaning against the side of the ship to stop it capsizing, Joron would pull the nearglass from his jacket and scan the horizon.

First, a clear sea, only the smudgy column of smoke showing where Safeharbour had once been.

Zigzagging onward, all hands to the ropes.

And they turned the boat. "Heel!" "Ware yer heads, boom coming over!"

Bringing out the nearglass once more. A dot on the horizon, a nothing to those not looking for it. Could merely have been a seabird. But Joron was looking for it and knew what he saw, the tip of the mainspine of a boneship. On it would be the topboy, scanning the horizon for the wingfluke and he had the advantage of height over Joron, who had no doubt they were already spotted.

All hands to the ropes.

And they turned the boat. "Heel!" "Ware yer heads, boom coming over!"

Now more than a dot, a vague shape, a blot, a sparkle of white against the grey sea, heeled over slightly to Joron's landward.

All hands to the ropes.

And they turned the boat. "Heel!" "Ware yer heads, boom coming over!"

Now bigger, no longer needing the nearglass to make it out. A tower of white wing coursing across the grey water toward them. All its varisk canvas out and even the flyer wings out to the side, a ship rigged for best speed. A beautiful thing, but less attractive to Joron's eye, knowing it came for him.

All hands to the ropes.

And they turned the boat. "Heel!" "Ware yer heads, boom coming over!"

In the nearglass he could see the crew scurrying up the rigging, checking the ropes, pulling them taut where needed, loosening them when not. The shipwife stood on the beak of his ship watching. Behind him two bowcrews stood by the for'ard gallowbows. Behind them on the deck stood a courser and in front of the mainspine a gullaime, head bowed as it brought the ship the wind.

All hands to the ropes.

And they turned the boat. "Heel!" "Ware yer heads, boom coming over!"

Was there a desperation to those words now? Was there a certain worry that fouled fingers when they pulled at the knots? Was there a desperate look in the eyes of Anzir as she leaned into the steering oar? No, not that he could tell at least. If the crew felt the same way he did, if their hearts fluttered in their chests then they did not show it.

So he did not.

Or hoped that was the case.

All hands to the ropes, it was.

And they turned the boat. "Heel!" "Ware yer heads, boom coming over!"

No escape, no chance of it or thought of it. The boneship was outpacing them without even really trying; its flyers had been taken in now and its shipwife had clearly decided a leisurely pursuit would still haul in their prey before darkness. And Joron knew them to be right – oh, what he would have done for the Hag to send a sea mist at that moment, but the Hag rarely listened to deckchilder in their desperation, for if she did she would be deafened as there was no more dangerous place than the sea.

Tired hands on the ropes.

And they turned the boat. "Heel!" "Ware yer heads, boom coming over!"

"Bring us to a halt," said Joron. "We'll not outrun him."

He stared at the ship approaching, getting bigger every moment, the beak of the arakeesian skull on the front staring sightlessly at them, the ram pointing at their target. That head, so much smaller than the keyshan that *Tide Child* had protected – the skull of the wakewyrm would have built an entire ship, and now more of the beasts had returned. All they had done, all the sacrifice and fear, for nothing. War would never stop.

It was with a solemn heart that he helped bring down the wingfluke's wings, that he helped push the seastay over the side, that he turned to Cwell and for the first time was forced to speak to her.

"I will be in the cabin while you speak to the shipwife. I will keep my crossbow on you, Cwell," he said, "and if I think you intend to betray us you will die first, understand?"

Cwell stared at him, narrowing her eyes as if he were too bright to look at.

"Ey, Shipwife," she said, and her mouth was twisted into a mocking smile.

"It is Deckkeeper."

"Oh," said Cwell, "So it be, I forget, I do. Always remember the happy days wi' you as our shipwife."

To Joron's credit he did not blush or splutter or lose his temper when she tried to focus on the wreck of man he had been, rather the fleet man he had become. "Remember what I said, Cwell." He held up the small crossbow. "Get us out of here, do whatever it takes."

"Whatever?" She smiled at him, not a pleasant sight.

"Ey."

"You have my word on that," she said. "And my word is always good." A promise that sounded like a threat and he turned away from her before she had time to say anything more, to attempt to put him down. But she said nothing, only chuckled as he walked away and settled himself in the small cabin, the scabbard of his sword rubbing against his leg as if to cut through it, the handle of his small crossbow warming in his hand. Behind him he felt the gaze of the courser alight upon him but he said nothing to them, did not know what he could say.

It did not take long for the boneship to draw up, its shadow falling over the wingfluke, blocking out the heat of Skearith's Eye and sending shivers through Joron.

"Master of the flukeboat," came the shout. "I am Barnt Amstil, Shipwife of the *Keyshantooth*."

"Is Cwell, Shipper," shouted Cwell in reply, winding a rope into a spool as she spoke, "is Master 'f this 'ere boat, much thanks and break your bows for luck, ey?" Joron glanced out through the gap between door and jamb, sighted along his crossbow, but if Cwell intended to betray them then there was no sign of it. She made no signal to the shipwife of the boneship, only carried on winding up the rope as if she had no care at all in the world.

"You approached the town back there but turned away. In the name of Thirteenbern Gilbryn, what business did you have?"

"I hear in the Maiden's soaks of Bernshulme that good coin were to be made for those who will travel a bit a farther under the godbird's eye, and I am ever a traveller." She laughed. "Ever a traveller."

"And yet you turned away from that coin," said the shipwife.

"Saw through 'em nearglass were only ashes to be handed out at that place over yonder, ain't no great call for ash in trade."

Silence then, and Joron wished he could see the shipwife but all he could see was the white spines and hooks of the boneship's side.

"Safeharbour was a town of traitors." The shipwife spoke slowly, seriously. "And as you intended to trade with them, I reckon you a traitor too. Which makes all you own forfeit to me. Your boat, your cargo. I will have them and you will return to Safeharbour as a traitor to be dealt with as such."

Joron shivered. He did not think Cwell had betrayed them, or if she had then he had not seen it. No, they had just come across all the things he had once believed fleet officers to be — women and men out to make what they could from those less fortunate, and uncaring of the rightness of it.

"Oh Shipper, Shipper," laughed Cwell. "I are a trader's master, I walk the Maiden's line with all my kind and all know this. Surely there is no need for you to—"

"Aim!" came the call and Joron imagined the ship's great gallowbows swinging round to aim at the wingfluke — as no doubt they did.

"One moment Shipper," said Cwell, and now her voice was deadly serious. "One moment afore you send me to the Hag, it will cost you nowt, right?"

"You have your moment," came the reply.

"Aelerin!" shouted Cwell.

Behind him Joron felt the courser freeze at the mention of their name. He turned, but they did not move, only sat there.

"Aelerin!" came Cwell's voice again. "Get out here!"

"Go," said Joron.

The courser remained frozen in place.

"I know you fear her," said Joron, as gently as he could, "most aboard do. But we all may be about to die, Cwell included, and the shipwife has said we must trust her. If she has some plan to save us and it requires you, we must chance it."

"I . . ."

"It is what Meas would want and it is my order." Was his voice unnecessarily harsh then?

The courser sat, stock-still, then gave a small bow of their hood and stood, going out to join Cwell on the deck.

"A courser," said Shipwife Amstil.

"Ey," said Cwell.

"Not many traders have coursers."

"As not many can as afford 'em, Shipper," said Cwell.

"Why should this interest me? Apart from to think your cargo may be a worthy prize, ey?"

"A pail o' reasons, Shipper," said Cwell. "First, 'tis almost as poor luck to kill a courser out of battle as it is a gullaime;

even in battle 'tis something to think twice about. Second, as I said, I 'as a courser cos I can afford it. And there are those in Bernshulme, both family and trade, who know the keyshan road I fly. And rest assured, if I do not come back, they 'as friends who will find out why and whatever great family you come from, well, is likely it will find itself at a disadvantage in trade it can sore afford."

"So you threaten me, trader?"

Cwell laughed again, shook her head. "'Tis only a fool threatens a fleet shipwife. I am a trader's master, so I offer a trade, Shipper."

"And what trade would that be?" The shipwife sounded cold, disinterested.

"One moment, Shipper," said Cwell. Then she turned, leaving Aelerin stood uncomfortably on the deck and entered the cabin where Joron sat.

"Give me that fancy sword, Twiner," said Cwell, her voice harsh as the weather in the far north. He felt his face freeze in place.

"Meas gave it to me," he said.

Cwell's eyes sparkled, a rising tide of malice. "Ey, so it will be good quality. A man like that shipwife will recognise that. He'll like the fancy drawings on it too."

"We have coin," said Joron, quietly, firmly. "Meas gave us plenty of it for just this eventuality."

Cwell leaned in close, Joron could smell her damp clothes, the sickly sweet juice of the fruit she liked to chew. "The Amstil are an old and rich family, they will care little for coin. Novelty, that is what will hook this fish."

"Try the coin first," said Joron.

"If you wish to argue," Cwell grinned as she spoke, "I will argue my point all day but that shipwife out there will get bored of us and loose his bows, or come aboard, one or the other."

Joron knew himself caught in her words. Trapped by her. He began to unbuckle the sword.

"I will not forget this, Cwell. You do this to humiliate me." He thrust the sword in its scabbard into her hand.

"I would never do such a thing, Shipwife," grinned Cwell, then she was gone, back out to the deck.

"I have this blade, Shipper," she said, "it is a fine one." Then she threw it across to the other ship. Joron heard the shipwife catch it, draw it. Draw his blade. No doubt inspecting it.

"It is a fine weapon indeed." A pause. "Very well, trader, I imagine having to give up something as valuable as this will have taught you your lesson. Never come back here, do you hear?"

"I have no great wish to return, Shipper," said Cwell. Then the shipwife was giving the orders to move on, to drop the boneship's wings and for the gullaime to bring them wind to go about.

Joron imagined what it would be like to place his hands around Cwell's thin neck and squeeze until she could no longer breathe.

# 11

# The Blackest Crew Afloat

*Tide Child* sat at his seastay amongst a small flotilla of ships, three of them boneships, and two of those in a poor state of repair indeed, the sort of sorry-looking tubs that had Bonemaster Coxward sucking in air through his teeth and twitching his hands for wont of "a go at 'em, Shipwife, just a few days is all." But Meas had no time for such things. She had the shipwives of her small fleet in her cabin sat around her desk with their deckkeepers.

Stood with her were Brekir and Vulse of the *Snarltooth*, Tussan and Binin of the *Skearith's Beak*, and Coult and Rulfar of the *Sharp Sither*, each shipwife in their colourful finery and still with the paint of welcome beneath their nails; their deck-keepers, those slightly drabber consorts, stood behind them while Meas commanded their attention. They had eaten at Meas's desk, cleared and with supplemental boards of gion added to provide room to sit, and now she had arranged plates and gravy boats and cups and knives into an approximation of Safeharbour.

"There is our target, my girls and boys," she said. "Joron saw a pair of two-ribbers and a four-ribber. With them about eight flukeboats. So, say a crew of at least a hundred and fifty for each two-ribber, and two hundred and half again for the four-ribber. Add another two hundred for the flukeboats." She looked around the table at the serious faces. Brekir looked miserable, her long, dark features drawn into a frown. Tussan was hard to read; the man was round-faced and jovial as always but talk was that his wits had deserted him after a particularly fierce battle and that his deckkeeper, Binin, was all that kept the battered *Skearith's Beak* afloat. Coult of the *Sharp Sither* was his opposite, with everything he thought flying across his weathered and craggy face, and none of it good. He was a fighter, maybe too fond of it, and his deckkeeper never spoke, only stood behind him looking fierce. There was something brittle in that relationship, something overly stressed.

"Eight hundred," said Tussan, with a giggle. "And we can add maybe a hundred seaguard to that, for you only talk crew. We have maybe four hundred if we commit all we have. And only *Tide Child* and *Snarltooth* are capable of any sort of fight."

"Speak for yourself," said Coult. He rolled his head around on his neck — a thin man, small, but made of almost pure muscle, he was as hard and as taut and as weathered as old rope. "*Sharp Sither* may be down and damaged but he ain't out. My crew will fight." He sucked on his teeth; one of his canines was missing and had been replaced with metal. Behind him his deckkeeper, Rulfar, looked at the floor.

"It all sounds perfectly splendid to me," said Shipwife Tussan with a huge grin, the many feathers sprouting from his two-tail bobbing as he spoke. "And what a wonderful dinner Shipwife Meas put on for us. I think we should all compliment her on that." Only silence met his remark as it had not been a wonderful dinner at all. The food had been old and the conversation stilted by news of Arrin's death — though those gathered may be disparate in personality they had all respected the man.

"I think," said Meas, "my mother has underestimated us. And I think, despite what many would believe, we can take Safeharbour for as long as our purposes require."

"Why do you think we are underestimated?" said Binin.

"My mother thought so little of Safeharbour that she only sent her men to take it."

"You think men cannot be good shipwives?" said Joron, perhaps too sharply as, though Meas had said nothing about it, he felt the loss of the sword keenly, felt he had let her down. Felt she must feel let down.

"No, I think men can be great shipwives, Joron. However, my mother is more old fashioned."

"All this talk of your mother," said Coult. "Do you wish to raid Safeharbour only to bloody her face, Meas?" His gaze passed slowly around the table, meeting each eye there. "I have no problem with that, you understand. Vengeance is as good as any reason to fight."

"But not a good reason to throw away all we have worked for," said Binin. "Coult's love of a war is famed, but it does not make our little collection of ships in any better condition to fight such a force as is gathered at Safeharbour, and for no gain I can see."

"It would be a glorious victory, Binin," said Tussan to his deckkeeper. "Skearith knows why you must try to spoil everything."

"I tend to agree with Binin," said Brekir.

"Well, you would," said Coult, and there was nothing friendly in his words.

"We should gather the rest of our fleet. We are not all in such a rush to throw our lives away, Coult," said Brekir, and if Meas had not interjected at that moment Joron felt it would have come to drawn swords.

"Brekir is right, we cannot win a straight fight," said Meas. "Though Coult, you are also right, in that it would be good to give my mother a bloody face over this. I plan to do that, without us facing the force camped in Safeharbour in a ship-to-ship battle, one which we would lose."

"It is still a huge risk," said Binin. "Why not just fly away? That is why Arrin sent warning."

"But Arrin did not know about the brownbone we tow, Binin, or what was on it." She met each face around the table with her gaze. "That ship, and its terrible cargo, was expected somewhere."

"You think they hit Safeharbour because it did not turn up?" said Tussan. All turned to him. His face, momentarily serious, returned to a vacuous grin. "Was a passing fancy to say so, is all. I act upon all my whims."

A smile touched Meas face then left, a zephyr breeze of emotion. "No," she said. "The timing is wrong, but if the people aboard were some sort of resource then that resource will still be needed. The fisher told us they had brownbones at the island so I imagine they will be expecting more to come back and pick up those who remain there. How many did you say, Joron?"

"I saw upwards of a hundred working," he said.

"So we can reckon there are more. They would not let all out at once, only those they thought they could control."

"So what?" said Coult. "You plan to fly our brownbone into the harbour and simply load up our people without so much as a sword drawn in anger?"

"Oh, do not look so disappointed, Coult, of course not. There will be code signals and flags expected from any ship coming in. No, my plan involves plenty of violence, don't you worry about that. And as for me? Well, it does not involve me at all."

"You are too precious to be put into danger," said Tussan, and he fanned his face. He had been an attractive man once, a favoured Kept, but excess had stolen his looks, his body, and many said his mind, from him.

"Nothing of the sort, Tussan. But I am recognisable, as is *Tide Child*. This is a hit and run and we cannot risk *Tide Child* being identified by those that will remain. We are the only ship I feel safe sending into Bernshulme."

"You presume she does not know about you already," said Brekir.

"I have to," said Meas. "Something is happening with those brownbones, something I cannot countenance. If we can find out what it is, show people this horror, then it may be enough to bring my mother down. Safeharbour will be avenged, we take a step toward change."

"And win you no fair amount of acclaim, no doubt," Coult sneered.

"Aye, it will, Coult. And with it maybe I can ascend to some sort of power in the Isles, and bring you lot with me. No more black ships for you. No more war."

"No more war," he said quietly. "And what am I for then, ey, Meas?"

"War will not go away too quickly, Coult, do not worry so. There will be plenty for you to do. But first, Safeharbour."

"And what is it you plan, Meas?" Coult's voice was a low growl.

"*Tide Child* and I will remain here with *Skearith's Beak* and *Sharp Sither*. Brekir, *Snarltooth* we will rig for speed – it can be done, and we will need as many flukeboats as we can get, the big ones."

"The *Sither* can fight, he need not be left here," snapped Coult.

"But the *Sither* must not fight, Coult. If we end up fighting ship-to-ship we have failed." She stared around the table. "Here is my plan. Brekir, you approach under cover of night on the far side of the island, then send a force to make its way across land until you are overlooking the town. It is foolish to let prisoners work at night, the darkness makes them bold and more likely to try an escape. I am hoping that if we go in at night then those of our people Joron saw working will be imprisoned once more."

"And if they are not?" said Brekir.

"It breaks my heart to say it," said Meas, "but we may not be able to rescue everyone. However, we shall do our best." She looked around the table at those gathered. Met bleak and serious faces. "When Skearith's Blind Eye is two thirds across its journey we will fly in the brownbone loaded with all the hagspit we have aboard."

"A fireship," said Brekir with a shudder. "It will be hard to find crew for such an endeavour."

"We will only fully crew it until it is near enough the harbour for the gullaime to fly it straight in."

"That beast is our greatest asset and you would risk it on this?" said Binin. Wanelight gleamed on her dark skin.

"If needed," said Meas. "If the winds are with us then the gullaime will leave with the majority of the crew. It will need five, maybe ten to steer the ship into the harbour and set the fires. Then they must find a way to escape in the confusion."

"Good luck to them," said Coult. "Every deckchild in Safeharbour will be after their blood." He looked around the table. "What makes you so sure the brownbone will make it into Safeharbour?"

"Greed," said Meas. "The shipwife that stole Joron's sword, Barnt, was greedy. I reckon they will let you in, thinking to take you as a prize. Then I am counting on every deckchild wanting to find who set their harbour alight." She grinned at them. "While the attention of Safeharbour is on the fireship, Brekir and her force will hit the Grand Bothy. There is nowhere else large enough to hold our people. Take them back to the ships on the other side of the island and make your escape."

"It would be folly to crew that fireship, almost certain death," said Coult. "Who would command it?"

Joron reached down to touch his sword for comfort, found it missing.

"I will do it," he said.

What was it that crossed Meas face then – relief? Fear? Sadness? He did not quite know. He only knew that once the words were spoken he wished he had not said them, but knew he could no more have escaped saying them than he could have stopped breathing. Although, the latter had suddenly become far more likely. Coult stared at him, an odd smile on the old man's face, while Joron felt the cold of death fall upon him.

"You cannot give an inexperienced boy a job like this, Meas," Coult said. "I will command the fireship."

It seemed like the life flooded back into Joron; he felt weak, giddy, alive. "But do not look so pleased, boy," Coult added, "for I will take you with me." And Joron's feet were once more heavy on the deck.

"One thing, Meas," said Coult. "The minute they see this ship only has a tiny crew they will smell it is bad, like rot on a week-old kively corpse, and they will throw everything they have at us. We may well not even make the harbour entrance."

Then Meas grinned again, a terrible thing to see.

"Oh, don't worry yourself about that, Coult, I have a crew in mind for you, and believe me when I say they will be thirsting for vengeance against my mother."

# 12

# A Fire in the Night

"Ship of the dead, ey?" Coult was laughing into the night
mist wreathing *Maiden's Bounty*. "Ship of the dead," he
said again and wandered away down the long deck to be lost
in the foggy darkness.

Joron was not in quite the same jovial mood; in fact, he had
never in his life been so nervous. It was not that he headed
toward a desperate attack on a wildly superior force, it was
not that he feared for his life and limb, neither was it that –
horribly – Meas's idea to make *Maiden's Bounty* appear to have
a full crew was to take the corpses of those who had been his
cargo and tie them on all over the ship – in the rigging, at the
rails, by the steering oar. A hundred of the dead feigning life
in a last act of vengeance. A funeral pyre.

No, it was none of this. It was the firepots, the barrels of
hagspit that were dotted about the old brownbone, waiting
for the touch to set them alight. Fire was every deckchilder's
nightmare and hagspit fire the worst of it – once it caught in
a ship's boneglue nothing could put it out. Even those old and
seasoned hands that had volunteered to come were jittery about
it. They swaggered up and down the deck with an exaggerated
nonchalance, but it was not right and real, that bravado, and

that communicated itself to Joron, who felt it as if through the slate of the deck and the old bones of the ship.

The corpses did not help, though.

As he walked up and down the deck in the mist that had gathered as Skearith's Blind Eye rose he would see figures before him and raise his voice to greet them, for there is little more comforting in the cold and the dark and mist than a human voice. But he would be met by a silent, leering corpse roped to the rail and animated only by the rocking of the waves. So he had stopped talking, and now the *Maiden's Bounty* made his way to Safeharbour in a pillowy bubble of silence.

"Not want!"

Or almost silence.

The gullaime did not observe silence, nor had its wrath at the windshorn following it around lessened any. Both continued their dance — the shrieking, the leaping away, the head bobbing, the subservient return, and this going round and round and round, as eternal as the seasons.

"Joron!" shouted Coult. "Will you stop your bird making its infernal noise. If it blares so when we approach Safeharbour our trip will be a short one."

So Joron tracked the noise of the windtalker, finding it gently pecking at a barrel of hagspit and he had to restrain himself, then, from shouting.

"Gullaime," he said, voice as stiff as his posture, "I must ask you not to touch that less you wish to send us all to the Hag in flames."

"Fire?" It bobbed its head twice at the barrel. "Smells bad."

"Yes it does, and yes, it is fire. We will send this ship into Safeharbour in flames, and hopefully set the attackers alight."

The gullaime nodded thoughtfully. "Set windshorn alight."

"No, Gullaime. And you must try not to squawk at the windshorn so while we are on this ship."

"No squawk. Hate."

"You must still try. All aboard this ship must appear normal, and the voice of a gullaime will alert the guards at Safeharbour that it is not so. Please do this thing for me."

"Not want," it said quietly.

"I know, but I ask you this thing."

"Sing later?"

"Ey, we will sing later." How could he not? He heard music everywhere. Even now a song, a strange and beautiful tune, was rising within him as they approached land and something in him longed to let it loose. The gullaime preened the feathers around its wingclaws.

"Will quiet." Then it span on the spot, hissed at the wind-shorn behind it and scuttled off. Joron headed down the ship, toward the rump and through the stink of death that twisted through the mist. The moist air took on ghostly forms, as if the spirits of the wronged flew with them.

At the steering oar he found Anzir and Farys. Of all those on the boat he considered Farys the bravest; she had been scarred by fire in the belly of a ship and the marks of it on her face were clear for all to see. Fire still terrified her, she would do almost anything to avoid the galleys of *Tide Child* where a fire always burned for the cook, and yet she had volunteered for this. Because he had, and she served him.

"Land rising!" came the call from above. He imagined being the topboy, sat above the mist – it must be like flying across the clouds, like being Skearith itself as it opened the Golden Door and flew into the archipelago from beyond the wall of storms.

"Not long now, D'keeper," said Farys quietly.

"You can leave on the flukeboat with the rest, Farys," he said. "There will be no shame in it, you do not need to stay as part of the skeleton crew. Join up with the flotilla on the far side of the island." The boat creaked and Joron found it hard not to imagine this sound, as with every other creak and crack, to be the sounds of the dead moving, testing the ropes that held them in place as if hoping to escape the fire that was sure to consume them.

"I go where you go, D'keeper," she said, and behind her Anzir nodded. "Even if it be into the fire." And something in Joron's heart cracked at that simple belief in him. How could she not see that he lived his life scared and unsure?

"Deckkeeper." Shipwife Coult appeared from the mist. "When we have turned for Safeharbour I would have you ensure all those who are meant to be leaving this tub do leave it. You girl," he said, turning to Farys, "the Deckkeeper clearly trusts you, so you can light the fires. Start below on my order." Farys, usually so quick to answer an order, only stared at Joron, as still as any of the dead in that moment.

"Shipwife Coult," Joron said, "I would sooner give that job to Anzir and have Farys on the steering oar."

"She seems slight for such a job, takes muscle." He glanced at Anzir, huge where she stood. "But you know your people so you assign them as is best. I am going up the spine to join the topboy. Be ready for my shout and hope our enemies are complacent. If they are not and send out a boneship to investigate us we are lost before we start." With that he walked down the deck into the mist to vanish up the mainspine.

They flew on, a gentle breeze filling wings hidden by mist, pushing the boat of corpses and jittery women and men forward. Joron felt the tension growing with each creak of the ship. In his mind he saw a boneship, pristine white, pulling up its staystone and unfurling wings to intercept them. A shipwife, Joron's sword at his side, giving the orders to untruss the gallowbows. The smile on that shipwife's face upon realising that this brownbone was an interloper. The merciless onslaught as the boneship stood off, launching volley after volley of bolts into the defenceless brownbone.

"Do you think they'll come see about us, D'keeper?" said Farys from the steering oar.

"No, Farys," he said, coughed, cleared his throat. "Meas says they are greedy and will simply wait for us to fly into their trap."

"If the shipwife says that," said Farys, "then that is what

it will be." Somehow, her utter acceptance of Meas's plan calmed him.

"When the fires start, Farys," he said, "you are to ensure our gullaime is first off this tub, you understand? Listen to none of its nonsense, get it in the boat and if nothing else get it back to Meas safe."

"As you say, D'keeper," she said, and he was gladdened slightly to know that, whatever happened, Farys at least would escape the fires they would bring into being.

"Steer us a little to landward," came the shout from above. Farys leaned on the steering oar and he added his own strength to hers. "Enough! Hold this course." Together they brought the steering oar to for'ard and then Farys made a quick job of lashing it straight. Coult came striding out of the mist.

"Meas was right, they've seen us but they either think we're their own boat returning or they're greedy enough to let us come in and presume to take us then."

"They have sent no one out? I would expect at least a curious flukeboat."

"Ey," said Coult, "I would do that, but they may worry that in this mist we will simply fly right over it, and we would, but not for the reasons they think." He wiped a gnarled hand down his face. "Get those off this boat that are not staying for the fire. My girls and boys staying are Tenf, Hallisy – he's a big one – Colfy, Duny and Garent. They'll all fight like the Hag is sat on their shoulders and the Maiden's promised them a ride. You know yours that are staying, so get the rest off. Then gather all your people here for a quick speech and we'll get your gullaime working, coast in on a gentle breeze. I'll stand by the steering oar for the rest of the way."

Joron nodded and did the job of gathering up the women and men who had crewed the ship this far and were now setting rigging, winding ropes and doing the myriad tasks they would do on any ship. Then he saw them quietly over the side with many whispered well-wishes of "Good luck, D'keeper," "Mother hold you, D'keeper," and "Hag take your enemies, D'keeper."

That done, he returned to the rump where Coult had gathered those who remained, ten in all, including Joron and Coult. The gullaime and its shadow hovered behind them, waiting to be given orders. Coult spoke.

"My deckchilder will know I'm not one for speeches, and most on this ship wouldn't appreciate it." He nodded at the watching corpses. "But I'll not lie about the danger we go into. Few, if any of us, will see the dawn, so hear me now. Get off this ship before it burns, I'll wait around for none. When you meet the enemy, and you will, sell your life dearly. Remember the fallen."

Those who had come with Coult echoed him: "Remember the fallen," they said.

"Good, now, Joron here will have his gullaime take us in. You go splash paint around or do whatever will make you feel good about yourselves, then we've some of the Hag-cursed to kill out there, so make sure your curnows are sharp."

That was it, the entire speech. Joron returned from there to the rump of the deck and cut away the rope, placing a callused hand on the steering oar, Farys by his side.

"Gullaime," said Joron, "give us enough of a breeze to keep this course and this speed."

"Wind," said the gullaime. It crouched on the deck and brought into being whatever power it was that caused the winds to flow at its command. Joron felt pain in his ears as the air pressure changed, that strange woolly feeling in his mind as he heard echoes of the ancient songs he experienced whenever they took the gullaime to charge at a spire. At the same time it was as if heat washed across him; he felt a momentary warmth before the cold air once more bit at the end of his nose. He felt the world pause, felt a million tonnes of water run across his skin, felt himself entombed within a darkness and then with a *pop* he was sure must be audible to all around him the feeling vanished.

"Deckkeeper," said Coult quietly, "go up the spine. The mist is holding and I would have someone in the topspines to guide me in and set me on a path to collide with that four-ribber they have. The other ships are tied alongside it right in the centre of the harbour. Careless that is, they think themselves safe here. The fires will require at least a tenth of a sandturn to truly bite, so when you judge we should light this Hag-cursed tub shout down 'ware your speed' and I will know to act."

"And what if I wish you to ware your speed?"

Coult grinned at him.

"I would not anyway. We want to smash into them with as much speed as possible." He grinned into the smothering mist. "We will bring them all down in flames."

"Very well," said Joron. Then he was gone from the deck, climbing the mainspine to the topboy's nest to become the herald of a chaos yet to come.

Somewhere before him the fog ended, to be replaced by the smoke from burning Safeharbour, but Joron could not pick out where one replaced the other in the swirling cloud. Smudgy lines of red, embers still glowing where a town had once stood, told him where the land was. Further out, a diffuse carpet of soft blue light, ship's corpselights lost in the fug. Above that he saw the topboys of the boneships in harbour, the four-ribber tallest, a glowing wanelight at the point of its central spine. Either side the two-ribbers, their lights slightly lower. Before them another light, closer now, glowing in the mist. Atop one of the pier towers — it must have been rebuilt to act as a watch-tower. Joron hoped it did not hold a great gallowbow, doubted there had been time to build something strong enough to hold one. The four lights made a triangle, the ship lights the base, the tower the point and it seemed to Joron they pointed at him, as if to remind him of his duty. The harbour beyond those lights he knew well, knew that once through the two piers their ship must swing to landward to bring it on its target. Knew he must concentrate on that.

"Ho! Brownbone," the call came from the tower as they approached.

A figure resolving in the mist, from dark blob to crouching shape. Was she dark-skinned like himself? *Always good for the night watch, us Long Islanders* — his father's voice, chuckling as he said it.

"You're back early. Seven flags a-flying, ey?" The woman's voice had no echo, the mist ate it, and for a moment it felt to Joron that they were the only two alive in the world. "I said, seven flags a-flying," she shouted again and Joron knew there must be some agreed reply. Of course there was. And, of course, he did not know it. He loosened the knots holding one of the small crossbows within his jacket and pressed a bolt into the weapon. Placed the point of his boot through the cocking stirrup and pulled back the cord. Then used his arm as a rest for the weapon, sighting along the fletching of the bolt at the figure in the tower. "Ho! Brownbone," came the shout again. Could he hear it in that voice? The oily taint of a growing suspicion?

The tower gliding nearer, how strange this was in the mist — it dampened the sound of water running along the hull and the sound of the deckchilder below. He and the tower guard moved through the air like Skearith's Bones in the sky, inexorably coming into each other's orbit. He could make out the woman's clothes now. She was wrapped in a stinker, sat in a little nest with a small brazier — it was that which provided light, a glow on her chest. A perfect target in the lonely night.

"Seven flags indeed," said Joron to himself as he watched the figure slide into his aim, applied pressure to the trigger and felt the kick of the weapon's release. Watched the guard jerk. Saw them open their mouth and in his head he was wishing fervently, *Be dead, be dead, be dead*. And then the lookout slumped, and luck was with Joron for they did not fall from the tower or slump forward into their fire, and the *Maiden's Bounty* moved on through the entrance of the harbour. Joron counted to five as he glided through the mist before passing his words down the spine.

"Bring us to landward," and the ship came about. No further instruction was needed: all that had visited Safeharbour knew the place. He felt the *Maiden's Bounty* straighten. The topboys of the three boneships were pointing at him. He raised his voice.

"Ware your speed!" And these words did echo, some quality of the air about them had changed. It was no longer the clean, damp scent of sea mist. Now it was the smell of sewage and rotting rubbish that was normal to a harbour – and the smell of charred earth and flesh, which was not. It was clear from the reaction of the topboys in those other ships Joron could see that they had realised something was wrong. Below him he saw the glow of torches as the deckchilder hurried to light the hagspit on the decks, and he knew Anzir did the same unseen in the places below, where rags soaked in hagspit had been gathered.

One of the topboys stood. "Treachery!" came a shout from the fug before them and a crossbow bolt split the air above Joron's head. Time to leave. Down and down he went, spiralling around the mainspine, not taking the direct route for fear of some clever thinker with a crossbow who aimed at where a deckchilder climbing down a spine should be. Relief when his boots hit the cracked slate deck and the smell of burning hagspit filled his nose. The *Maiden's Bounty* was moving at a rate of stones now. To seaward Farys was chaperoning the gullaime and the windshorn over the side and into the fluke-boat. He could hear Coult shouting somewhere, though not see him as billowing smoke was pouring from the underdecks.

"Get up there, you slatelayers! Onto the maindeck! I need your curnows on the land, not your bodies burned at sea."

Two deckchilder appeared from the smoke, coughing and spluttering, followed by Coult. From the rear of the ship Anzir and the rest of the crew came running toward the flukeboat while around them the corpse crew began to burn, slack mouths silently screaming.

With a cough so loud he thought a keyshan must have surfaced by him, something in the beak of the ship exploded, knocking Joron and everyone else flat, covering them with a blanket of heat. When he opened his eyes he saw a sheet of flame, the entire for'ard spine and its wings alight, burning bright as Skearith's Eye, making women and men into strange beasts, their movements jerking in the twisting, living firelight.

Making corpses dance and twitch. With the fire raging he could see more of Safeharbour, see the three ships, see that *Maiden's Bounty* would make contact right between the two-ribber nearest the dock wall and the four-ribber. There was panic on those ships, women and men with axes laying into mooring ropes. Then Coult shouted, "Brace, you fools!" and Joron saw no more.

The *Maiden's Bounty*'s journey ended with a crash that threw those only just recovering their footing from the explosion back to the deck. The air filled with the ripping and creaking and cracking of splintering bones. And in the crackle of fire he was sure he heard the gleeful cackle of the dead. The for'ard mast, all aflame, came down on the four ribber, spreading the fire across its deck and, by some fortune, the impact sent a flaming barrel of hagspit flying into the air to smash against the side of the two-ribber. Fire ran across the unfortunate vessel, eating into the spiked bone of its hull.

"Off!" shouted Coult. "Get off this ship, he's already goin' down!" And it was – another horrendous groan from the frame and the beak of the ship jerked, the deck slanted and one of their number, Tossick off *Tide Child,* slipping and rolling down the deck, shouting and screaming for help, only to be lost in the furnace that the water to seaward had become, hagspit flames an orange glow beneath the water. Joron stared after him. "Hag has him now," shouted Coult, as the sound of roaring, crackling flame tried to steal his voice, eager as any wind. "Get to the boat." He ran forward, pushing Joron on. The deck tipped further. The air full of screams.

Then Joron was over the side. Blessedly cool in the fluke-boat, as the *Maiden's Bounty*'s hull protected him from the worst of the heat. He tried not to think about the terror, the fear that must be running rampant on those burning ships. Then, in a panic himself he checked for Farys, found her at the front of the flukeboat already at her station, the gullaime and windshorn crouched below her. "Hag take you all," Coult was still shouting, "grab an oar, we'll go round the back of the *Bounty* and head for land."

"Shipwife," said a woman near the front of the boat, "they'll be less likely to search for us at the other side of the harbour."

"And we'll be more likely to run into the second two-ribber, you fool, I saw no sign of it burning. Now row! Row for your lives!" And Joron had an oar in his hands, was pulling for all he was worth, the sweat on his skin no longer the cloying sweat of heat and fear, now the cleaner sweat of physical work.

He felt the rocking of the flukeboat as someone moved up it and concentrated on his oar, not the screams, not the smell of hagspit or rich scent of burning flesh that both revolted him and made his mouth water at the thought of fresh meat. He was almost surprised when Coult spoke into his ear.

"Right, Meas's boy, you'll have to command from here."

"Me?" he said, almost losing the rhythm of the oar stroke, "why me?"

"Listen to my voice, boy," he said. And Joron waited for him to finish the sentence before realising what he meant. Of course, Coult was a Gaunt Islander, from the other side of Skearith's Spine. Joron had spent so long under Meas's service that what had once been unthinkable, to work with the Hundred Isles' ancestral enemies, he now gave no thought.

"Of course," he said, and started to stand.

"They'd be on us the minute I spoke."

"I thought you liked a fight," said Joron, and the smile fell from Coult's face.

"Ey," he said, then leaned in close, "but I like to get my girls and boys home more." A flash of teeth. "Tell no one, they'll think I've gone soft."

"Do you have a plan, Coult?"

The old Shipwife nodded. "We get to the Grand Bothy, we free any remaining townspeople, meet up with our people, then get out."

"You make it sound so simple."

"Ey boy, most things are, till others try and ruin it. That's when problems start. Now give me that oar and get to the front of the boat where the shipwife would stand."

He passed the oar across and made his wobbly way down the boat, stepping around the gullaime and windshorn who were hunkered down in the bottom of the hull, not moving, not even seeming to notice him. It was if they were in some sort of trance. He glanced to the side, and like a ghost he saw a white shape moving through the smoke and mist – the second two-ribber making its way out of the harbour. Fires burned on the rear of the ship but they were small. Coult was right, it had escaped the inferno engulfing the other two ships. He watched as it passed, imagined the frantic activity on board and the panic as fire took hold of the other ships. He commended the shipwife who, from the rate the small fires aboard were being extinguished, must have kept large quantities of sand on deck for just such an occurrence. Meas would approve of such an officer. Then the ship was gone, gliding into the mist and smoke and Joron turned to the front, seeing the wharves of the harbour – not stone, not yet, and now never to be, built from varisk and gion for the time being until there was opportunity to build them properly. Now the unfinished structures were full of women and men, some staring at the two burning ships, the hagspit melting the ships' bones, making a puddle of fire around them that consumed a flukeboat desperately trying to make its escape from the burning two-ribber.

As they approached the wharf he saw an officer, a deckkeeper with his curnow out and his one-tailed hat in his hand. He was approaching where they aimed the beak of their flukeboat, shouting, but Joron could hear nothing but the roar of fire. Ash rained down, black flakes that fluttered like corpsebirds, and he saw deckchilder frantically scratching them from their heads in case they contained hagspit and set them to burning.

"You . . . whe . . . ?" yelled the deckkeeper.

"I cannot hear!" shouted Joron.

The man leaned over as the boat came up against the harbour edge. "You, where are you from?"

Hag save him, he did not know the names of those ships in the harbour. Words failed him for a moment, then he stepped back and pulled up the windshorn — not the gullaime, as he was never entirely sure how the gullaime would react. But he knew the windshorn would simply do as he asked.

"We managed to get off with these two gullaime," he shouted. "Will someone catch a rope for us afore we burn too?" The edge of panic in his voice was real, but not through fear of fire. For fear of being discovered.

There was a moment when he thought the deckkeeper may question him further, and if he did then he knew they would never mount the wharf, they would die here under the crossbows he could see some of the deckchilder carrying. But the decision was taken out of the officer's hands by the deckchilder around them — no crew could bear to watch their own kind burn — and hands were held out, the boat's rope was thrown and their flukeboat was pulled up next to the wharf. More hands helped them out of the boat. His feet hit the land and the song of the windspire increased in volume within him as a space grew around the gullaime and windshorn. The officer stared at Joron, as if there was some recognition, but if there was the events of the night were moving too quickly for him. Something exploded on one of the boats — the hagspit stores — throwing a column of vivid purple fire into the air and making everyone duck.

"Well? What are you waiting for?" said the deckkeeper to Joron. "Take them up to the lamyard at the bothy, they're too precious to risk burning. And Shipwife Barnt will want to talk to you and know what has happened to his glorious little fleet."

"Ey, Deckkeeper," he said, the words coming breathily with the sense of release at being accepted. "Come on then," he said to the group around him, "and bring the windtalkers." The gullaime let out a furious squawk and they set off through the chaos for the Grand Bothy.

# 13

## The Darkest Port

It was difficult for Joron to recognise this blackened, smoke-rimed place for the same peaceful and cheery Safeharbour he had known. There was something within him, a mixture of anger and pain that burned, just as Safeharbour burned. If the song of the windspire that topped the island had not filled him to overflowing the moment his feet touched the land he would have believed he was in some nightmare place, some Hag-cursed land for those found unworthy of the comfort of her fire. But the song was there, vibrating through him, beautiful and alien and strange, something as unique to every island with a windspire as its coastline. So he walked, the little group of deckchilder surrounding the gullaime creating an area of calm while women and men ran hither and thither around them. All this given a terrifying otherworldly edge by the towering purple-and-green-tinged flames of the burning boneships.

Once, houses of mud or gion and varisk had lined the wharf and the streets leading up to the Grand Bothy. Now they were gone, only blackened ground and the occasional stubborn, carboniferous upright remaining to show where people had lived. The ground beneath Joron's feet, that glorious singing ground, was scarred and blackened by hagspit that had been kept burning for weeks on end, and he knew a scar would remain on this island for at least his lifetime. Pure hagspit oil, distilled from the fiery hearts of arakeesians, was a poison so pernicious it could not be diminished. One drop of hagspit could make a thousand barrels of poisonous fire.

*Would it were as easy to clean water as it is to dirty it, Joron.* His father's voice, speaking from a place a million miles away, where he flew across the calm oceans of the Hag's realm.

"Would that it were," he said to himself, watching as a bevy of deckchilder ran past him, their faces streaked with black from the smoke that filled Safeharbour, both from the burning ships and the burned town.

Despite the cold air everyone sweated.

"Hag's tits, Joron," said Coult, "I have spent more time here than anywhere else in the last few years of my life and I know not which way I should be going." An errant wind split the smoke and mist for a moment and Joron saw a flag waving from the top of the Grand Bothy.

"That way," he said, pointing toward where the flag had swiftly vanished into the whirling smoke. They moved onward, coals crunching underfoot like a layer of ice on new snow, passing through groups of women and men who stood around, as if unsure what to do. "It seems," he said quietly to Coult, "that most of the deckchilder were on land."

"Ey," said Coult, "unfortunate for us that, but it is the way it is. I see no workers though, Meas must have been right thinking they would be locked away. We can at least thank the Mother for that," he grinned at Joron. "Come, we should hurry."

They did, and at one point they paused to let a group of hard-faced and angry-looking officers past. Joron stared at them, hoping to see his sword at the waist of one but it was too hard to see in the smoke. The officers passed slowly, talking heatedly of who was to blame for this. He scanned their faces, seeing one he was sure he had run into in Bernshulme once. He looked away and stared at the ground, pushing at the coals under his foot until he found the hard, packed dirt of the road beneath.

"Listen, my girls and my boys." Joron glanced up. One of the officers, young and angry-looking but wearing the two-tailed hat and pink-and-blue dye streaks of a shipwife, was stood on a barrel of hagspit, stacked where the roadside must once have been. At his side he wore Joron's sword. "That fireship, it did not fly in alone."

"Were flew in by ghosts," came a voice from the deckchilder who had stopped at the sound of the officer's call. "I saw 'em. Dead deckchilder lined the deck."

"It was not," the officer shouted back. "It was flown in by women and men, and as the *Keyshantooth* sits in the harbour entrance we know they have not escaped." One of the other officers raised a hand, trying to pull the younger man down but he shook him off. "So those women and men who burned my ships—" He stopped, breathing heavily, then got control of himself and seemed to calm a little. "Who burned your friends," he said, then added, "my friends," before turning his head, looking at those gathered. "Where are they? Ask yourselves that, and look at the faces around you. Look for those who you do not know."

Coult pulled on Joron's arm. "Time for us to move, lad," he said.

Joron knew he was right. But that shipwife had his sword and he recognised his voice as Barnt, the man Cwell had given it to and it seemed the island was his now. Joron looked up, committing Barnt's face to memory. He wanted his sword.

Another tug on his arm from Coult. "Come, Joron."

"Look for those strangers and make sure they are brought to me," said Barnt. "I will pay well for them, and they will pay well for what they did!" A roar went up at that – it was a rare deckchild that didn't like a good execution; the bloodier and harder someone died, the better.

Joron and his small group started to move off when the shipwife raised his voice again. "You!" Joron had no doubt the man spoke to him, it was the way his luck ran. He turned, head down in a way he hoped came across as reverent, not as an attempt to avoid being seen. "Look at me when I speak to you, man." Joron did, raising his head and, as he had seen so many deckchilder do, managing to look at the officer without meeting his eye.

"Ey, Shipwife," he said.

"What are you doing with those gullaime?"

"Came off the ships, Shipwife," he said. "Taking 'em up road, Shipwife." Quiet was falling around them, and from the corner of his eye he saw Coult's hand come to rest on the hilt of his curnow.

"I do not recognise you," said the shipwife. At those words, it was as if some spirit were invoked, as if the malign, choking smoky air suddenly came to life and focused itself on Joron and the women and men with him, and with its unkind attention came that of all the gathered deckchilder. "No, I do not recognise you at all."

A scattering of sand in the sandglass. The moment when the last grains are falling and the glass must be turned, the moment a hard decision must be made.

A breath taken in panic.

A surety of violence.

"Peace, Barnt." The man who spoke reached up, touching the shipwife's arm. He wore the one-tail of a deckkeeper and he was the same man Joron was sure he had seen somewhere before. "I know that man's face – not sure from where, but it is familiar."

Barnt stared down at the deckkeeper. "Very well, Viss," he said. "And you, man," he said to Joron, "you should not be standing around with something as valuable as two gullaime. Get them up to the lamyard."

"Ey Shipwife," he said with a quick bow of his head.

As they walked away Coult came to stand by him. "A stroke of luck there," he said, "I thought we were Hag bound for sure."

"That shipwife's words will spread though, and . . ."

"It will work well for us," said Coult.

"It will? We are strangers here and—"

"Think how many others are strangers to each other, Joron. Think how many, outside your own crew, from my ship, say, you would recognise on an island? Few, right? No, all that shipwife has done is sow chaos and that may help us."

"I hope so."

They walked on, climbing the steep hill, women and men making way for them as they guarded the gullaime and as ever, few wanted to be near the windtalkers. Arguments were breaking out as they passed, small groups demanding each other justify their place on the island. But the gullaime were like a day pass, allowing their little group through with no questions and it made Joron think. He found Coult and pulled on his arm.

"Ey?"

"I have had a thought," said Joron, "that shipwife gifted it to me." Coult raised a brow at this. "Gullaime, come here." The windtalker hopped forward.

"What want?"

"Do you think the gullaime from the ships out there, the ones in the lamyard here, would follow you?"

"Follow follow?" It snapped its beak at the air. "Some yes. Some not. Gullaime fear."

"We are here for our people, Joron," said Coult, and he gave a sideways glance to the gullaime. It was easy for Joron to forget how uncomfortable the creatures made those around them.

"Ey," he replied, "but you heard that shipwife, Coult. The gullaime are valuable to them. They have dealt us a blow in taking Safeharbour from us, maybe we could repay that blow by stealing their gullaime." Coult did not reply, and Joron added, "Think how much more effective would we be if every ship of ours had windtalkers."

A second, then Coult smiled.

"You're a crafty one, Twiner. But where will the lamyard be? We only have 'up the hill' as instruction."

"Near windspire," said the gullaime, "always near windspire."

"It is not on our route out," said Coult. "The easiest route out is around the base of the isle, and if our people here have been badly used they will not have the energy to climb a steep hill."

"I will go, they need not," said Joron.

"I will accompany him," said Anzir.

"As will I," added Farys.

"You have loyal people," said Coult. "Very well, I and mine will come with you but we must get our people away first. When we meet Brekir at the bothy I will tell her what we plan, and we only go if she has enough room in the boats for the birds."

"Very well, let us hurry then."

And they did, up the Serpent Road, not as grand or wide as the Serpent Road at Bernshulme but built along the same idea. Where Bernshulme's was a glory, Safeharbour's was sided by the blackened remains of people's lives. Twice Joron was sure he saw the remains of bodies, probably caught in the first fires of the attack. He wanted to go back and find that young shipwife, hurt him. Fires still burned all over Safeharbour, unnatural purple or green fires all the way up the road where hagspit had been left to poison the land.

But he had a duty.

The Grand Bothy appeared from the stinking smoke, the curved roof still unfinished, more through lack of materials than lack of will. It had been roofed with flat plains of cured gion. Walls of sharpened varisk stalks surrounded the base of the bothy and two seaguard stood at the gate. Joron glanced around – there were people in the dark and he did not know if they were his or Barnt's, then he saw a familiar figure emerge from the mist and approach the seaguard.

"Sent to bring more hagspit, I am," said Brekir.

"Well it ain't here is it?" said the seaguard. "Don't keep it where people live, do we? It's over there in the—" but he never finished. Brekir's straightsword flashed out through the man's neck, and from behind the second guard a shadow left the wall and cut his throat.

"Come on." Brekir's voice, clipped and sharp, cut through the air, and from all around them her deckchilder appeared, cutting down those they did not know before running past Brekir and into the bothy. They piled shields against the inside of the fence while she watched, and when the last was past and into the bothy she rushed in. Joron turned to the gullaime.

"Find somewhere safe to hide in the shadow of the wall, we will be back to free your people next." Then he was shouting, "Bands on!" and black bands were produced from pockets, tied around arms that marked them as of the black ships. Joron ran to join the fray, curnow raised and fear singing its weakening song in his gut, but at the same time there was that terrible exhilaration he had started to feel somewhere deep inside with every fight, something he felt was becoming a part of him, something he needed.

Into the bothy. To his landward he saw a shipwife with no black band. The man looked confused at what was happening, was doing up the belt around his trews, and Joron lashed out with his curnow, cutting him down. From seaward a man came out of the darkness, screaming as he raised his sword and was felled by a blow from Anzir, who carried a beaked bonehammer, of the type the bonemasters used. Farys, smaller than Joron and Anzir, kept low, using knives to stab the unsuspecting, and nearly all were unsuspecting, surprised by the sudden onslaught just as Meas had planned back on *Tide Child*. There were few about in the Grand Bothy, the action in the harbour having pulled everyone down there. Brekir stood with a bloodied sword, waiting at the entrance to the lower levels.

"Coult! Twiner!" she shouted, and cut down a man who ran at her, barely a thought in her movement. "We must hold the gates to this building. My first crew are clearing the bothy, my second are in the lower levels finding the prisoners. I've also set crew to cut through the varisk wall at the rear of the bothy. If we make a show of defending the gates it may distract anyone from noticing."

"We will," said Joron, "but Shipwife . . ."

"Ey?"

"They have a lamyard here, we think it will be up near the windspire. If we can take their gullaime it will hurt them as much as getting our people back."

"More even," said Brekir, but her doleful voice was far away. "We would not be able to protect you, Deckkeeper. Getting our people to the boats must be our first priority."

"I will risk it, Shipwife Brekir," he said, as they jogged back toward the gate, weapons jingling in the smoky dark. "It is worth it."

"Are you sure? When this is done the island will be crawling with those out for our blood."

"I have walked through Safeharbour, Brekir," he said. "I am ready to spill blood to avenge this place."

Brekir nodded. "Very well," she said, as a roar of anger came from out in the mist. "Ready yourselves. Here they come."

# 14

## Meetings and Partings

They locked their shields, making a wall between the two stout varisk gate posts; behind them two barrels of hagspit had been brought in and Joron wondered what Brekir had planned for them. A rut of half-buried varisk ran between the posts to stop the gates and Joron was curious as to why they did not form on that, use it as leverage for feet caked with mud and carbon. He found himself in the second row, as women and men boiled out of the night full of fury, eager to avenge the insult done to their ships. The time for thinking was over. Some brave but foolish souls ran straight at the wall of shields only to be skewered on spears that Brekir had the foresight to bring with her and her crew. After the first few fell those attacking stayed back, dim shapes in the mist. He heard a shout.

"Crossbows, get crossbows up here."

The man heading Brekir's seaguard yelled out: "Close the shields. If any fall to a bolt they'll answer to me."

The shields were brought closer together, overlapping, making a tent of treated gion that closed out the sky, concentrated the smell of humanity: sweat and bad breath and fear. A rattling on the shield wall, as if the shields were being repeatedly punched. In his mind Joron was thinking not of what was happening, not of the coming violence or the sharp bolts. He was thinking of tactics, of what to do, taking his mind into the future where he could have some effect on events, not in the now where he must simply stand with these women and men and weather the storm of crossbow bolts.

They were undisciplined, these deckchilder that attacked, not shooting from lines as Meas had told him you must. No concentrating their shot on one target. Instead an ill-timed and -aimed hail of bolts. This was angry women and men loosing off at random, furious, unthinking. This was not how fleet deckchilder behaved. This was not how Meas's crew would behave.

And he knew these fighters could be beaten.

A thud against his shield, a shock against the aching forearm with which he held it up. A bolt sticking through. It had punctured his stinker coat, not his flesh. He was cold.

Behind him voices, the first of the prisoners coming out of the bothy, confused, not dressed for the night's chill, wide eyed and blinking as deckchilder harried them on, started to push them toward the rear of the building, making them keep their heads down so they were not spotted.

"Going to be fun getting out of here for us," said the woman beside him, and she spat into the mud.

"No one wants to live forever, Girtane," said the man by her. "Weren't you just complaining about how much that bad foot of yours aches this morran?"

"Ey, I suppose it'll not ache at the Hag's fire."

"At them!" A roar, from outside the shield wall.

"Brace!" Brekir's voice from behind them. Joron dropped his shield, holding it at a more comfortable height and crouching down a little. In front of him women and men were running from the mist, shields of their own held up, using them to push away the spears of Brekir's deckchilder.

"Knives!" shouted Brekir. Short blades were drawn by those on the second rank and a moment later there was impact.

Bodies hitting the shields. Screaming bodies, wishing the worst of the Hag on them. Swearing they would find no warm place to rest. Promising desecration of those they attacked.

"Hold them!" shouted Brekir, "we don't need to beat them right now, just hold them!"

"Easy for you to say, glum sither," hissed the man beside Joron, grunting as he pushed against his shield. Joron was frightened – madness not to be – but it was a strange fear, a blunted fear. Not like the first time he had fought, that fear had been sharp, cutting. But now he had experience. He knew he was unlikely to die in this first rush. Knew few of them were. Maybe one. Maybe two. But this was the first engagement, muscles were fresh, minds were working. The death came later, when you were tired, or worse, if the wall broke – but these were Brekir's hand-picked seaguard and deckchilder, her finest. And Brekir served Meas.

They would not break.

Until they had to, of course, until they must leave. And Joron hoped Brekir had something planned for that because then he would be scared. Then he would be running with all his strength, because the fury of their attackers, currently contained by the shield wall, would be loosed on him and those around him.

All was shouting, anger. Someone screamed in pain. He could not see whether it was on his or the other side. He hoped it was them, they had more people. Behind him the prisoners were still coming out of the bothy.

"Move, move! Run, quick as you can." Could he hear those whispers or were they in his imagination? They felt like they were carried to him on the song of the island.

Another scream, a space in the shields before him as someone fell and he moved into it, his bone knife gripped tightly in a sweaty hand, momentarily meeting the eyes of the woman – filled with triumph – who had felled one of the deckchilder.

One of his deckchilder.

And all was noise.

All was violence.

He punched the shield forward into the face of the woman, heard her screech. Drew back his shield as she brought her hands up to her injured face and the man beside him ran her through. A blade came at him and Joron pushed the shield forward again. Shouting as he did, unaware of the noise he made, unaware of anything but the need to protect and to fight and to live. His shield trapped the arm of the attacker and Davand by him hacked at it – blood and flesh and bone – and it was pulled back. He was in the heat and the passion and the pressure. Thrusting with his bone knife, not seeing a target, more often hitting a shield than anything. Pushing and pushing. And it seemed to happen forever and it seemed to take no time at all.

"—dy. . ."

"—eady . . ."

"—ready . . ."

"Be ready!"

Brekir's voice – ready for what? He heard an axe against a barrel. Then smelled acrid stinging, pungent hagspit. Looked down, saw dark liquid running between his feet, pooling where it hit the line of buried varisk. *Oh Brekir*, he thought, *I see why they made you shipwife*.

"Be ready!"

He glanced behind him: no more were leaving the Bothy, only Brekir stood there now, with two deckchilder and an overturned barrel. In her hand a torch burned.

"Now!" she shouted. And they stepped backwards, the wall dissolving as they turned to run and those attacking them let out a great scream of triumph as their opponents seemed to retreat. One step, two steps, and the air behind lit up with purple and green fire. Triumph turned to agony as the hagspit ignited around those rushing forward, a cruel flame that could only be extinguished by sand, and there was none of that here. Then Joron and Brekir's crew were running round the bothy. Brekir stopped at the broken fence – there stood Coult, and

Farys, her face pale and drawn, her scars dark shadows. Behind them stood the gullaime and, far enough back from it to avoid its vicious beak, the windshorn.

"You still intend to free the island's gullaime, Joron?"

"Ey," he said.

Brekir put out her hand, clasped his arm. "Stay with Coult, he'll not lead you far wrong and his deckchilder fight like the Hag watches them. I will wait as long as I can on the beach, but I'll not endanger my boats or my ship."

"I would not expect you to."

"Mother's Blessing, Joron Twiner," she said.

"Mother's Blessing, Shipwife Brekir," he replied but she was already gone, vanishing into the brown and drooping gion.

# 15

# Dead Run

It was the season of dying. Gone were the riotous colours of the growing times, to be replaced by uniform brown as varisk and gion withdrew life from the plants above and stored it in their roots for the next season. In times of high heat sometimes leaves blackened, became sharp-edged and flaking to the touch, but the dying season was a time of softness, of wetness, of slipping and sliding along paths as they were slowly revealed by the withering vegetation. There were no firm handholds, no places to put your foot that you could be sure would stay; more often than not the vines and leaves that covered the floor would split and spill overripe, decaying and stinking liquid from their skin like pus from an infected wound. The smell was no worse than the burning town below, and while it did not choke Joron, it filled the air, coating his mouth and nose, restricting his breathing.

And he needed his breath to run.

Coult's words filled his mind. "Keep going uphill. Don't stop 'cause they'll be after us. If you can't find your fellows, keep going. If you think you're lost, keep going. If the deckchild by you dies, keep going. Get to the lamyard and we'll deal with whatever we need to when we need to." Then they were running, each of them carrying a curnow and a small round shield. The jungle around them alive with noise, but not animal noise. In the dying season the birds vanished into burrows to hibernate, flew away to cliffs to sleep and it was hard not to think they left to avoid the stink and the rot. Behind them, the fire that Brekir had set burned, and further behind that ships burned and it was as if that fire filled those chasing them. The dying forest was full of their noise. Shouting, whooping. Feet drumming. Voices cursing as they slipped on rot.

All was chaos in the dark. Joron saw vague shapes. Was it gion, was it a woman? Was it varisk, was it a man? Was it a sword, was it a branch? Was it? Was it? Was it?

Keep. Going.

With him ran Farys and Anzir and the two gullaime, though *Tide Child*'s gullaime would not speak to him, not now, as he had forced it to roll in the stinking forest floor, the better to cover its colourful robe, the white parts of which had glowed like a beacon fire in the darkness. The windshorn, ever eager to please, had immediately done what Joron asked, gladly rolling around and becoming filthy – but this only served to increase their gullaime's stubbornness.

"Not want! Not like! Not servant!" Screeched at the top of its voice, and only when that attracted a crossbow bolt did the gullaime dive to the floor, more to avoid the shot than to obey. Then there was fighting, hard fighting, their ten against an unknown number and Coult shouting. "No time for this, get away. Break! Break!" And they did, into the night, going different ways and whether the gullaime would roll on the floor or not became a moot point. Now everyone was covered with the filth that splashed up and soaked into their clothes with every step.

They followed the gullaime. Joron could not help believing that it knew the way better than all of them, that somehow its people would call to it in the same way he sometimes felt the presence of the gullaime as a warmth within his chest, but even that belief did not stop their flight through the decaying jungle feeling aimless and panic-stricken.

Once they stopped in a clearing. In the centre of it a huge gion, towering above them – and at that moment, just as they entered, something in the gion gave and the trunk ruptured, the giant plant coming down before them in a cascade of brown fluid. They had to run around it as it crashed and splashed down into the forest, filling the air with choking brown droplets that coated your tongue with sickly sweet slime even if you covered your mouth. They ran, their feet no longer moving so quickly. Their chests filling up with the miasma. Before them the gullaime, shouting.

"Come! Come Joron Twiner! Not far now. Not far."

On they ran. Up. Always going up. Struggling through knee-high, sopping, melting vegetation.

Fighting. Sudden and without warning. A squawk from the gullaime and then they were amongst women and men they did not recognise. Striking out, never stopping running. Not engaging. The enemy as surprised by Joron and his crew as they were by the enemy. On and ever on. Joron always aware that not only the enemy and the forest, but time was also against them. Brekir would wait as long as she could, but she would not risk her boats for him. Maybe she would stay a little longer than she should for the gullaime, but she would still go at the merest hint of being overrun. She was a careful one and that was why Meas had sent her.

Fighting again. Someone screaming. Someone dying. One of his? No. Not one of his. He still had all of his. Hag's curse, his legs were tired. Slipping and sliding making his muscles ache.

You never ran this much on a slate deck.

Then they were there, breaking out of the mouldering forest into a quiet clearing full of cages, and in the cages were gullaime. Only two guards, all others pulled away to the remains of the town. There was something intrinsically ugly about this makeshift lamyard. The cages were great boxes of cured varisk, their bars made of woven rope that had been treated with oil to make it hard as rock and black as Skearith's Spine. The cages rose to three times the height of a woman, and at the top the uprights curved over into vicious-looking hooks. Further down, where the bars of varisk intersected the cross-beams, wickedly barbed spikes stuck out to stop the gullaime climbing, for as Joron well knew, they were skilled climbers.

Within the makeshift lamyard about fifty gullaime huddled together in a circle, around them patrolled maybe twenty windshorn. Joron saw now why their own gullaime hated them so. The windshorn acted as guards within the cages; as he watched one chased a gullaime, with much squawking and posturing, back into the huddled circle at the behest of the two humans guarding the lamyard.

"Into them!" The words out of Joron's mouth even before he had the breath to shout them. But it came, that officer's voice, that fleet voice so practised at cutting through wind and hail and rain. It came. And his people obeyed. Running forward, curnows lifted. The guards barely had time to react before they were butchered, Anzir and Farys going about the business in as an efficient manner as ever. As the guards died the lamyard exploded into noise. Every gullaime within it crying out, screeching, screaming.

"Quiet them," hissed Joron at his gullaime, but the wind-talker simply looked at him, the blank eyes of the mask regarding him as closely as any true eye could. And of course, Joron was the only one that knew of the bright and shining eyes below those painted leaves. "If you do not quiet them, they will bring the whole island down on us."

"Not tyrant, Joron Twiner," said the gullaime. "Not wind-shorn, not leader. Not human."

"Hag's tits, Gullaime, now is not the time for games. If you cannot order then ask."

"I order," said their windshorn, and it set up its own screeching. Before it could finish the gullaime lashed out with its foot, smashing the windshorn to the floor and leaving a bright red smear of blood across its damp brown robe.

"Not want!"

But it was enough – the lamyard was abruptly quiet. Joron turned back to the gullaime.

"Can you ask them if they will leave with us?"

The gullaime opened and closed its beak, slowly, oh so slowly. "Ask, yes. Ask."

It hopped forward, scaling the grid of varisk stalks that imprisoned the windtalkers within so it sat upon the curved lamyard cage-top like an insect on a web. Then it started to sing, to croon and cajole the gullaime within – and as they listened so did Joron. The song worked its way into his mind, down into the cracks of his consciousness and here, in the stinking and suppurating jungle, he had a clear-as-day image of standing in the beak of his father's flukeboat. His father's strong arms about him as they rode the waves at a speed that seemed impossible, on a day so clear the air felt like it cleaned his body with every breath, the salt water a shifting floor of diamonds, catching the light of Skearith's Eye and reflecting it back at him in a million glinting lights. Then it was gone, though he still reckoned he could smell the scent of the sea from that glorious day above that of the dying plants around him.

"Here they come, D'keeper," said Farys, and women and men broke from the forest. Furious, screaming, angry. Joron, Anzir and Farys made a wall – a pathetic, small wall of three – and the windshorn joined them, dancing and fluttering in a display of threat that might have worked on its people but, to the approaching deckchilder, must surely have seemed ridiculous.

"Eleven of us, three of you," said the woman leading the deckchilder before them, drawing her curnow and swiping at the air. "Reckon we can have some fun afore we take you down to the harbour and give you to the shipwives, ey?"

Joron glanced over his shoulder, saw the gullaime was now working at the lamyard lock. He hissed to it. "Can you help us?"

"Big wind?"

"Yes."

"Need spire," it said, and Joron cursed – they had used the last of its magic up in bringing the *Maiden's Bounty* into the harbour.

"Get the key, from the dead guards." It looked at him, then hopped over to the bodies, turning one with its foot. "See if any of your fellows can help us."

"Need spire," it said again but it sounded distracted. Its beak flashed down and it reappeared with a set of keys.

"What's that beast doing free?" shouted one of the deckchilder, which brought Joron's attention back to them.

"It came with us," said Joron, "and if you don't leave it will blow you all back down the hill into the fires burning below."

The woman shook her head, smiled at Joron. "I don't think so, do you?" She grinned, raised her sword. The order to charge forming on her lips.

"There are more of us, out in the jungle, on their way," said Joron.

"A likely story," she said. "I am not so foolish as to—"

But it was not as unlikely as she believed. Coult and his remaining deckchilder emerged at a run from the forest behind, cutting her down. Only four of them, but that was enough as they came, rushing from the melting gion, swinging their weapons at the backs of the deckchilder. Coult looking like some dark creature banished from the Hag's bonefire, his clothes and face spattered with the brown detritus of the forest and the blood of those he had killed within it. As the enemy deckchilder turned to meet the threat, Joron ran forward, his own weapon raised, his bloodlust suddenly up and he was hacking and slashing, left and right, unaware he was shouting and cursing until it was over and Coult stood before him.

"Didn't think you had it in you, lad," he said, a longthresh smile on his face, "but I can see I were wrong about that." He pointed forward. "Come on, let's see how our bird is doing with those imprisoned. We can't wait around here for long.

Plenty more of them" — he pointed his blade at the corpses — "searching for us."

The gullaime was in the lamyard now, surrounded by a circle of its fellows. They were bobbing and shaking their heads, singing and cooing in a back and forth call and response. Though Joron could not understand, he felt a wave of calmness coming upon him. One soon spoiled by Coult.

"We don't have time for a sing-song, birds," he said, swaggering across to the bars. "We need to get away now if we're going to do it." The sounds stopped, most of the gullaime backing away from Coult, pushing themselves against the bars and between the spikes on the other side of the lamyard. Joron's gullaime was the only one not to move away — instead it turned, spreading its clawed wings slightly as it met Coult's gaze.

"Need spire," it said.

"You or all of them?" said Joron.

"Yes," said the gullaime.

"Don't have time for that, bird," said Coult. "We get them to the ships, find a spire later."

"No run. Hurt. Weak. Need spire."

"Then they stay here," said Coult. "More will be coming up from the town and we can't fight them all off." He turned away from the windtalker. "We tried, Joron, but it is not to be. Now, I like a fight as much as the next woman, but Brekir won't wait forever. I'll not endanger her boats any longer than I have to."

"Need spire," hissed the gullaime. "Fifth of sandglass all."

"Can we hold it for a fifth of a turn, Coult?" said Joron. "Do you think?"

The older man glanced up the hill, towards where the windspire rose from behind the lamyard. "If they come in dribs and drabs, and they don't have crossbows, maybe," he said. "But the lives lost will be on you, Joron Twiner, you understand?"

Joron took a deep breath, nodded. Wondered how Coult had got his reputation as a man too eager for a fight when he seemed to be a man of sense. Maybe he had learnt his lesson, maybe he had been condemned for something beyond his control. Maybe none of that mattered.

"Will be safe," said the gullaime. "Joron call." Then it let out a crowing, a call that made the heads of every gullaime in the lamyard snap around, and they trooped out of the open gate. Only then did Joron notice that each one was shackled to the one behind it.

"Farys," he said, "take the keys from our gullaime, and as these ones recharge at the windspire unlock their feet." Only then did it sink in what the gullaime had said: *"Joron call."* What could it mean by that? The last time it had said that he had sung with all his heart, and every woman and man on *Tide Child* had joined him and, just when he thought they were done, that they would be wrecked beneath the bows of the *Hag's Hunter*, an arakeesian had come. The sea dragon they had called wakewyrm had smashed the enemy ship to pieces. But that was coincidence, is all. A man cannot call a monster to him, and even if he could, what use was that at the centre of an island? A spire of rock sticking out of the endless ocean?

None.

The gullaime made their way to the windspire, a curved, pale bone-like piece of rock that sang to Joron — the spires always sang, and it was a song Joron could always hear, a strange counterpoint to his own thoughts, a constant low hum on a scale alien to his own sense of harmony and of what was sharp and what was flat, but still full of beauty and yearning.

As they approached the windspire three women burst from the brush and engaged Anzir. She killed one, maimed another but the third escaped, despite Joron sending a bolt after her into the brush; he heard her feet thudding away as a counter-point to the ever-present dripping of the decaying forest.

"They'll be coming soon," said Coult, "and plenty of 'em." He looked around, saw a fallen, sodden gion trunk. "Drag that over, make us a barrier before the spire." This spire was bigger than the last Joron had seen. It rose from a bone-white rounded base, easily big enough for all of the gullaime to fit inside. "We can protect 'em while they're in there. Not sure how we will get 'em out of here."

"Maybe they can bring us a gale," said Farys as she unlocked the windtalker's shackles, "Like the gullaime did at Arkannis Isle."

"Tired," squawked the gullaime. "So tired."

"That's a no then," said Coult. "We form up. Get ready." They made a line, a thin line.

Out of the forest came deckchilder, but none familiar, no arms banded in black. They came in ones and twos, then threes and fours, their numbers swiftly swelling.

"Too many," whispered Anzir into Joron's ear. "If it comes to it, get away, D'keeper. I will hold them off."

Joron stared at those gathering at the edge of the clearing. At the curnows, the clubs, the spears, the wyrmpikes. Thought of all the ways they would pierce and cut and crush his body. Thought of his father, crushed between two hulls. Tightened his hand on the hilt of his curnow.

"It is not your place, to give me orders, Anzir," he said. "I think I shall stay as long as I am needed." The huge woman stared at him, then she grinned and shrugged.

"Apologies for my presumption, D'keeper," she said, as more gathered at the edges of the forest, gathered and arrayed themselves, like they had no real need to hurry.

"How long, Gullaime?" said Joron, and he was surrounded by the scent of the desert, the touch of heat.

"Too long," it said. It opened its beak, closed it, then let out a gentle cooing sound before it spoke again. "Call, Joron Twiner, call."

"What?" A cold sweat slicked his body.

"Sing, Joron Twiner."

He knew the song the gullaime meant, and it sprang into his mind. He had sung it before when everything had seemed hopeless. Had sung the day the arakeesian had come to save them from the *Hag's Hunter* and he knew that there were those among the crew who believed he had brought it. But he did not. Coincidence was the word he had kept in his mind ever since. Though here and now, next to the windspire, with that alien song weaving through his subconscious, he was not so sure. The song – the moment he thought of it he heard it so much more clearly, powering through him: a harmony, a resonance, a set of strange notes that wrapped themselves around the shanties and songs he had grown up with and sung for his father, and here, near the windspire, the song was irresistible. The thought of it was too strong and he opened his mouth, let loose his rich tenor. The gullaime joined him in an eerie counterpoint, but he knew he did not need it. Did not need those around him joining in, though they did.

*Saw a world of darkness, felt the pressure of stone, the pressure of eons, the pressure of time, of water, of death.*

At the edge of the forest more enemy gathered, pulling together for a charge that would sweep them away like beach flotsam before the tide.

"Ready!" shouted Coult. "Be ready!" Bodies around Joron, the women and men singing with him even as they readied their weapons. Just as caught up in the song as him, notes whirling around them and it seemed, though surely it could not be, they were unaware they sang this strange and alien tune. The huddled gullaime calling out in fear, that fretful sound joining the song of the windspire, filling his mind and flooding from his mouth.

The enemy charged.

They faltered.

They fell.

They all fell.

The ground shaking beneath them, throwing them from their feet. The top of the windspire tipping back and forth like the spine on a ship caught in harsh seas. Then, with a sound like the greatest gallowbow the world had ever known, the ground between Joron, his deckchilder, and their enemy cracked. A great jagged line zigzagging across the top of the island, letting out a hiss of heat and steam and . . .

*Light*
*Light*
*Light*

Something rising. The noise, the smell, the suddenness of it such a shock that the song fled, all sound fled. The silence that fell upon him seemed eternal, dangerous. Then the gullaime's beaked head was in his vision.

"Sing!" it squawked in his face. "For life, sing!" And he did, opening his mouth, continuing the song. "All sing!" The gullaime sounded desperate, furious and scared at the same time. "All sing!"

"Everyone," shouted Joron, "sing with me!"

They did – massive Anzir, wiry Farys, fierce Coult and all those of their crew that still lived joined him, and as they started to sing a nightmare appeared from the crack in the ground. A creature he had seen only once before. On a beach with Meas, and even fierce and fearless Meas had warned them off from going near it, even she had been afraid the thing would sense them.

Three long legs coming over the cracked rim of stone, bending strangely as if they had no bones within them.

Tunir.

The creature looked like it was covered in wet, lank fur. It was without face or eyes or . . . He could not look away from those strange legs, the way they joined the rounded body. Had it not moved Joron would not have believed it could be a living thing, there was so little sense of any life Joron recognised, any creature he knew in it. Its emergence had drawn every eye, and every woman and man ceased to move or think, as if they were frozen by some ancient, primal fear. It was all Joron could do to keep singing, but by dint of this effort he pulled those around him back into song too. For a moment he thought them double-crossed, thought the gullaime had done this to kill them, for the singing seemed to drag the creature toward them in disturbing, staccato steps. It was Joron, the loudest and strongest singer, that drew it. It stopped in front of him. The smell of it stronger than the rotting forest – this was heat and age and illness, the stink of something corrupt, though not naturally corrupt like the forest. Something wrong, something that should not exist.

As it stopped in front of Joron he fought down the fear, studied the Tunir. The beast was not covered in fur as he had thought, but spines. They rolled, line after glimmering line of them, first laying flat like fur then rising, pointing out as if to impale him upon them before laying flat once more, now pointing up. This movement, this process, constantly repeating, working its way up and down the beast in a hideous cadence. And as the spines rolled, regular as breathing, he saw the skin below, shining wetly. Red within the black.

He had been ready to die. But he did not want to die on the spines of this beast. He feared he would never see the Hag's fire if he did.

"Tunir!"

The beast's name called in terror from the other side of the clearing. As if its name were a magnet the creature swept away from him, moving fast, unbelievably fast. Then it was among the enemy deckchilder and they were dying. Spined arms shooting out as it ducked and twisted around the strikes of weapons. Those facing it were not prepared to fight such a creature. Half of them ran, half of them fought – those that fought died first.

"Gullaime ready," squawked the gullaime, "Run. We run now."

Accompanied by the sounds of screaming and dying, Joron, his deckchilder and the gathered gullaime ran down the hill and tried not to think of what was behind them, tried to keep their minds on what was in front. Hoped Brekir's ships waited on the beach. Hoped not too many of the enemy were in the forest below.

And the screams behind them said going back was not an option.

# 16

# The Deepest Cuts Are Hardly Felt

The forest on the far side of the island was scabrous, like the skin of those who contracted keyshan's rot. Joron's upper arms itched. They ran through a variegated landscape, splashing through places open to the sky where the first rays of Skearith's Eye were gently lightening the dark. The growing blue above looking unbelievably healthy compared to the brown and wilting forest.

The ground they ran over was strewn with soft and yielding vegetation making them slide and slip along, and then they were back into the darkness, into the constant brown rain from the dying leaves above. And yet, the forest never fell away enough to give them a glimpse of the sea, of where their boats should wait, and they did not know whether they ran toward their own people or toward a shoreline full of the enemy, furious that their quarry had escaped, ready to spend that fury on those left behind.

How long would they last in that case?

Not long.

The gullaime were far ahead of them. The time at the wind-spire, though brief, had energised them and their clawed feet were far more sure footed than the booted and bare human feet. Joron had given the windtalkers instruction to stop in the vegetation near the shore but had no idea whether they would do as he asked.

Joron and those with him ran into a group of women and men as they came out of forest and into light. Half dazzled by changing light they were on the enemy before either realised what was happening. The enemy were facing the opposite way, no doubt staring after the flock of gullaime that had come thundering past, and Joron, Coult and their fellows fell upon them. Not stopping, not fighting in any meaningful way, only cutting holes in the ragged line so they could push through, dragging the enemy deckchilder after them the way a needle drags thread through cloth. Then Joron and his comrades finally burst onto a beach, running hard between the huge rocks that dotted the shingle and sand as pink as the new skin over a wound.

The second time they found the enemy they were not as lucky. These women and men were facing them, had heard the screaming from their fellows and had set themselves up in a rough line. They had no shields and spears, or the fight would have been much harder, and if not for Coult – furious, reckless, angry Coult, who lay about himself with his curnow with such fury none could or would stand against him – then maybe they would not have got through at all. Joron only retained fractured glimpses of the fight. Gouting blood, flesh being opened. A hard impact against his back as someone fell. Mouths wide in screams. Blades coming toward him. Blocking. Slashing. Hurting. Being hurt. Then a gap in the line. Running.

They lost three – two killed outright, one who took a cut to the leg and could not run. When Joron glanced behind him he saw the woman being hacked apart, heard her screaming for help but could only hope the Hag ended her quickly. Anzir ran by him, her face grey, blood streaming down her arm from an ugly-looking cut to her bicep. His back ached.

Twice they passed single gullaime, seemingly lost and wandering. The first time Farys tried to pull him to a halt, pointing at the windtalker which was aimlessly pecking at the ground near the drooping plant line of the forest.

"No time, Farys," he shouted and pulled her away. Running from the screaming, baying, bloodthirsty mob behind them. With every step the enemy grew in sound and numbers, and he knew, as he ran and slipped and slid along the ground, he knew that if they were late, if Brekir did not wait for them, then his life ended here; on a rocky beach at the edge of a stinking, dripping forest.

He wanted to stop, to slow, to look for boats on the shore, disrupting the smooth lines of waves lapping on the sharp pink sand. He could not. The baying behind him never stopped. He imagined a hundred, a thousand behind him, and how many waited further down the beach beyond the rocks?

He did not know.

He could only run.

And run, and run.

There.

Ship rising!

Brekir's ship. *Snarltooth*. His back hurt. *Snarltooth* moving, out in the channel, wind filling its black wings, making them ripple and billow as the ship came about to catch the wind and turn away from the island. He felt his steps faltering.

Too late.

They were too late.

So much pain.

"Come on, Joron," shouted Coult, grabbing his arm, "nearly there!"

He would have said "No point," or "Too late," but he had not the breath, it had been stolen from him. All he could do was let Coult pull him on, running and running, his legs starting to become numb, his bones feeling as if they bent within his tired flesh, his back on fire, stumbling between giant rocks and there – the sea. Blue as fine glass, kissed with morran light. Where the surf washed the sand, where gullaime – gathered in gaggles, milling about – pecked at the sand or lifted clawed feet to experimentally place them in the water, avoiding the corpses of women and men gently rocking on the waves. In the distance *Snarltooth* making its way out to the deeper sea, surrounded by flukeboats full of those they had saved from the island. His back hurt. The scene before him framed by two massive grey rocks, one on either side. Forward, still stumbling, his arm held by Coult. The island rumbled, ground shaking as it settled, as the rocks and material of it recovered from whatever it was Joron had done at the wind-spire.

And from behind came deckchilder. Ten, twenty, thirty. Not a lot, but enough. They held curnows and boarding axes, looked angry, spattered with mud and plant matter. The largest of them, a man in the leather straps of the Kept, pointed his axe at Coult.

"We have you now," he shouted. "Give up and you'll at least die quickly. Fight us and I'll give you to those who lost their loved ones in the fires." By him was the shipwife. The one with his sword. Barnt.

"Get ready," said Coult; he was breathing hard also but managed a smile. "Stay behind me, Deckkeeper." He seemed to know no fear. Joron clasped the hilt of his curnow.

"Sell yourselves dearly," said Joron, panting between each word. His back, such pain. "Don't get taken alive." More quietly, "He has my sword."

"You heard him," shouted Coult to the woman and men around them. "What are you waiting for?"

The big man stood before the enemy line smiled. Shipwife Barnt raised his sword, Joron's sword, as if this was something he had been waiting for all his life. Then the smile vanished, the sword arm faltered and Joron heard another voice.

"Down!"

He span, saw Brekir running out from behind the massive rocks with ten women, another ten coming from behind the other rock. "Down!" she shouted again and her deckchilder formed into two lines. One on their knees, one standing. They brought up crossbows to their shoulders. Joron threw himself to the floor, feeling the sharp sand cut into wherever his skin was bare, knowing that when he hit the salt water his body would sting everywhere, but that was a joyous thought because it meant he would be alive, and just a moment before he had not believed he would ever touch salt water again.

"First line," shouted Brekir. "Loose!" And the bolts flew, cutting into the men and women on the beach. Three hit the big Kept who staggered back but, miraculously, managed to remain standing. Shipwife Barnt used him as cover. Brekir's first line went to their knees, reloading. Brekir gave them a moment, then shouted, "Second line! Loose!" And the bolts flew again. This time the Kept fell and the volley was more than those still standing could take. Their shipwife shouted "Retreat!" and they vanished, running back up the beach. Then there were hands, too many hands, too many arms helping him up. Pulling him toward the shoreline, voices saying: "Lemme help you, D'keeper," "You just stand, D'keeper," "You lean on me, D'keeper," and why were they acting like he was some stonebound new to the fight? Why were they so intent on keeping hold of him as they moved toward the flukeboats hidden behind the giant rocks? And there was he foolishly saying, "No, no, my sword, Meas gave me that sword." Women and men were shooing gullaime aboard. Now they were half carrying him.

He had not realised how tired he was.

His back hurt.

"I can walk," he said, but the words barely made it out of his mouth.

"Worry not, Deckkeeper." A strong voice, one he did not recognise. "We'll get you on the boats and aboard the *Snarltooth*, and we'll have your wound sewn up and healed before you're back on *Tide Child*, don't you worry."

Wound? He had a wound?

He wanted to ask where, but his mouth was no longer working. When? The pain, a long line of agony from his shoulder down to his waist. The more he thought about it the more it hurt until there was a line of fire across his back and deep within his flesh and if there had been any air left in his lungs he would have screamed. If there had been any energy left in his muscles he would have screamed.

But there was not.

He did not.

Instead he closed his eyes, and let the Mother's cold hand usher him away to unconsciousness. His last thought being, *I do not even remember being hit.*

# 17

## The Depth of Scars upon the Ocean

He stood on the rump staring forward. He had been standing there so long he had become unsure about whether the ship stayed still and the sea moved or the sea moved and the ship stayed still — or was it some mix of both?

It hurt to stand. He felt the pull of the skin on his back, the complaining of the muscles beneath the broken skin, and each time he felt that pull he remembered pain and what had come with that pain: the feeling of enclosure, of terror and the certain knowledge that the Hag stood close to him. Sometimes he had felt his father's presence, seen his face, but when he had reached out his father had taken his hand away. Not cruelly, not because he did not wish to be with Joron while he suffered; there was a tear in his father's eyes when he removed his touch and Joron had cried out in his mind and he was sure, to his shame, he had cried out in the real world as well.

Brekir's hagshand had treated him first, or so Farys had told him, with much wishing of the man to the bottom of the sea. Joron even remembered some parts of the treatment. Biting on a piece of bone while the hagshand washed the long wound out with seawater, cold as he could get it, and then stitched it up with crude wingmaker's stitches. The next day he could stand, even joke with Shipwife Brekir about never seeing the curnow blow that laid him low. But then had come the fever, so it had been cold water again. Stripping him naked and standing him on the deck, pumping gallons of freezing water over him until he could not see straight for the juddering and shivering of his body. So weakened by it he had to be carried back to his hammock, to lie sweating and moaning as the cold water had done little for him. By the time *Snarltooth* met with *Tide Child*, four days later, he was lost to the world, his wound had become an angry, raised red line on his back that leaked yellow fluid and stained the hammock he lay in and blankets they wrapped him in.

Farys told him how Garriya had raged when he was brought aboard, cursed Brekir's hagshand for a fool and woken Joron from his delirium with some evil smelling spirit. She had even come on deck to shout and scream at Brekir's ship as it took the rest of the gullaime away. He remembered that, but only as a fraction of some terrible dream where he floated through black water, the blue glow of the Hag's bonefire the only point of light, managing to be both warm where he was cold and cool where his skin was raging hot. Then all comfort was removed, some foul current in the water picked him up, rag-doll light, and tossed him around, forcing him to the surface where he took deep, hard breaths and found himself looking into the aged and worn face of Garriya, her eyes piercing his fever.

"Do you want to live, Caller, aye? Do you really want to?"

He must have said yes, must have, but he did not remember it. And the rest was vague – he knew she cut the stitches, opened what flesh had healed with a cruel knife, sopped out the corruption with cloths. Farys told him, and he wondered if she made it up, that Garriya filled the wounds with maggots she had found in a rotten piece of fish in the bilges of *Tide Child*. After a week she sewed him back up again, but not fully, and this was the worst part for him, the repeated agony as she opened and re-closed the stitches on his back time and again.

"I do this all for naught you know," that creased and filthy face looking into his. "When you will just repeat all you have done and return here, under my knives all over again." Had she really said that or had it been a dream? It was the sort of thing she would say, but the next part was strange, even for Garriya, and he remembered it as if seen from the bottom of the ocean: the cold line of a blade at his neck. Her words – "Maybe better to end it all, aye? Better wipe the slate clean than open the door to go through it all again and again and again."

But she had gone through it, and so had he. She had drained the wound time and time again until she felt happy enough to close it properly, and that – had that only been four days ago? Four days, ey, and he had believed he would never have the strength to hold a curnow again, never mind walk the slate of *Tide Child*.

But he had and he did. And if any noticed Meas gave him softer tasks than usual then they said nothing, only seemed glad to have their deckkeeper back, and for that he was thankful himself, thankful he had made it back from the dark seas where the Hag waited, thankful his father had not taken his hand and led him back to the bonefire. Even Dinyl had stepped in and helped, though still no cordial words were exchanged, nothing but the bare minimum needed – but more than once Joron had noted Dinyl, when he thought Joron was not looking, taking the harder, more physical jobs. And if Joron was true to himself he did not know if he hated the man for it or not. Was it done simply to undermine him – Joron is weak now, let me take on his tasks – or to reform some remnant of their fractured friendship? He did not know.

His every moment was to ache, to feel pain, or so it seemed. For the first weeks of consciousness he had, for the first time in his life, hated the sea, hated the way it never stopped moving, that it never gave him a moment of comfort. In the hammock he would swing, and when he found a comfortable place to lie he would, by tiny increments, be moved from it until his wounds once more rubbed against the material and pain chased away sleep. When he was well enough to walk the slate again the sea became his enemy; he had never realised how much he moved, even standing still he was forced to move to keep his balance, and all those muscles he had never once thought about in his life, now complained every time he did anything but remain totally still. There was one thing he welcomed – he had been without the song of the spires through his illness, and now though he was hurting, always hurting, the song had returned to him. He had not realised how constant it had been; he had begun to think of it as part of him.

There had been no song under the sea at the bonefire. The dead knew no tunes and he had felt bereft, as if some part of him had been amputated.

"Long enough now, Joron." Meas's voice from behind him, gentle. The merest touch on his shoulder. He turned to find her huddled into her stinker coat.

"I do not need to be coddled, Shipwife," Joron said, and pointed at the sandglass. "I have served barely half my watch."

"You should not be on watch at all, Deckkeeper," she replied. "But I wish to talk to you in my cabin. I have a task for you that your wounds have you well suited for."

"Oh," he said. Then he followed her through the ship. Across the ever-shifting deck, boots crunching on strewn sand. Down the stairs into the dark where the wanelights glowed and past the gullaime's cabin door, slightly ajar, the latest of the crew's offerings outside, a jumble of oddments piled on the deck.

In her white cabin under the rump of the ship Meas sat before her wide desk and gestured for him to sit opposite. He did, shifting in the seat, trying to find a comfortable place on it.

"We rescued one hundred and fifty-seven, as you know. The rest were taken by a brownbone named *Toothless Longthresh*. It made two trips, each one taking it away for two to four weeks. It also had gullaime aboard."

"It could have gone anywhere," said Joron dolefully.

"Ey, it could."

"We should have waited for it to return."

"I have given Coult that job, but he must also play kivelly and sankrey with the two-ribber which escaped Safeharbour. I have told him not to sacrifice his ship under any circumstances."

"I have never seen a man as fierce as Coult."

She grinned at him. "Ey, he is something to see, right enough. Condemned for striking a hagpriest, I believe. But that matters not. If what *Toothless Longthresh* does is secret, there's a good chance it does not know the cargo's final destination. It may simply meet another ship and offload to them." She tapped the desk. "It is what I would do."

"Then our people are lost?" he said quietly.

"Something terrible awaits our people, Joron, do not doubt it. Something terrible is happening." She placed a hand flat in her desk. "The answer must be in Bernshulme."

He was about to tell her she was wrong, that Bernshulme was too dangerous after Safeharbour had been raided, but Mevans interrupted. He carried three drinks on a tray – two of alcohol for Meas and him, the third was Garriya's foul concoction of old bread and water that she had demanded he continue to drink to keep his wound fresh. He knocked that back in one, let it slide down his throat and fought the urge to vomit as it was not considered polite or fleet to vomit all over your shipwife. Once the medicine was down he sipped at the alcohol to take away the taste, and he found the outrage that would have been in his voice at the thought of going to Bernshulme had fled somewhat and he could speak more calmly, think his words through a little more.

"We should not go to Bernshulme, Shipwife, not if your mother knows you have betrayed her."

Meas sat back, ran a hand through her iron-grey hair.

"I do not think my mother does," she said. "None of our people I spoke to mention being asked about me, or about *Tide Child*. It may be my mother does not know or, at least, is not sure."

"Or does not want to admit," said Joron.

"Well," Meas smiled across the desk at him, "I am glad to see the sword cut did not take your wits. No, it would be a blow to her authority to admit her daughter has turned full traitor, rather than just being a . . . well, a let-down." He nearly asked it, at that moment, nearly let the words out of his mouth – What did you do? Why were you condemned to the black ships? – but he did not. Only waited on what Meas would say next. "But whether she knows or not does not matter, my mother does not trust me. I will be watched when we dock at Bernshulme, every step I take will be monitored."

"But mine will not?" he said.

"Oh, you would be, but you will not be if you are ill and confined to the officer's hagbower, up by the Grand Bothy."

"But I am not so ill, and I am deckkeeper on a ship of the dead, I will hardly be welcome . . ."

"Of course you will not be welcome. But all officers have access to the hagbower, Joron, and as for not being so ill, well, you will just have to play-act a little. I will send Farys, Hastir and Anzir as your servants, and Mevans also."

"How will I get out of the hagbower without attracting attention?"

"Well," she said, "that is for you to work out once you get there. Mevans has plenty of contacts within the town. You will have to meet with Indyl Karrad. I know you would rather not, but it is necessary. If anyone can put us on the right track it is him."

"So, I must play the invalid, and at the same time be sprightly enough to escape the hagbower?"

She nodded, a playful smile on her face. "I never said your life would be easy, Joron. But I expect you can use your people to do the running around, then you can handle anything that is truly important. I want you to meet with the crime lord Mulvan Cahanny too – little that happens at the docks gets past him – and try and get into the basement of the Grand Bothy and meet Yirrid, the chartmaster. If people are being taken somewhere then charts will have been needed. See if you can find out if there are areas my mother has been especially interested in. That may give us some sort of clue."

"Are there are any other well-guarded places I should not be that you would like me to get into, Shipwife?" he asked.

"Not at the moment, Joron," she smiled, "but when I think of them you will be first to know."

# 18

# The Invalid

Joron watched Bernshulme coming into view from the rump of the ship where he sat, swaddled in warm clothes, as the pilot ship guided *Tide Child* to his berth. Their welcome had been as cold as ever, deckchilder and officers of other ships turning their backs on the condemned of the black ship. A note was delivered to Meas from the harbourmaster that made it plain none from the ship were to come ashore except the gullaime, which would be allowed to visit the windspire; lists of what they required would be taken and delivered (if possible) and, should Meas wish, her deckchilder could be put aboard the prison hulks. Meas showed it to Joron.

"So, it seems my mother suspects," she said, passing him the note. But lists of much-needed stores and supplies she always had on hand, and made sure she claimed a dire shortage of all things and requested far more than *Tide Child* required in the hope of getting half as much as was needed – such was the lot of a ship of the dead.

But among those requests and notes was the important one, the one that had been closed with Meas's seal and addressed to her mother. She doubted it would see her mother's eyes, not once some low-level spy in Indyl Karrad's service to the

Thirteenbern had opened it and found it to be of no importance – only a request that her wounded officer be allowed access to the officer's hagbower with his servants. And then, from there it would be passed on and stamped and an order returned – far more quickly than it would have been if Meas had put in the request normally, where low-level officers and administrators took great delight in making life difficult for those they saw as below them. Simply by skipping that one level with her seal Meas saved time, and that was time she so desperately wanted, needed.

Joron had never thought of her as sentimental – if anything he thought of her as the opposite, as hard and as cold as a glacier – but that brownbone full of the dying had appalled her, and the idea that people she thought of as hers could be in a similar position gnawed at her. She was desperate to act, and he knew her infuriated that her mother's power kept her on this ship and made her use proxies, though she fought not to show it. Meas stood beside him, almost vibrating with energy, with need, and unable to do anything but trust in Joron. In turn he knew that whatever came, whatever happened, he would die before he let her down.

When had he become this person?

It had been hours since the lists and requests had gone in, sent well ahead of *Tide Child* who had sat at his seastay outside the harbour while ships and boats, of much less importance than a fighting ship, were let in and out of Bernshulme. As Joron watched, a boat left the quay – four hagpriests in the front, being rowed by a set of strong women and men straight for *Tide Child*. He felt another presence at his side and turned. Garriya, the old woman stared hard at him.

"I don't trust them, Caller," she said. "You should not trust 'em either." She produced a kivelly-skin flask from within the filthy folds of her clothes. "Take this, whatever filth they give you throw it away. One mouthful of my brew every day. Do that and you will continue to heal well and not die in the hagbower."

"You think they will poison me?"

"Not intentionally" — she sniffed, spat on the slate — "but few who go into a hagbower come out." She turned and watched the priests in the approaching boat. Black Orris fluttered down and landed on her shoulder.

"Arse," said Black Orris.

"My thoughts too, bird." Garriya turned, making her way down the deck toward the hatch and back to her place in the depths of the ship.

"Make sure you look ill, Joron," said Meas as the hagpriest's boat bumped against the side of the ship.

"I cannot help but do that, Shipwife," he said.

"I mean really ill," she whispered. "They must not suspect."

He nodded but did not reply, as now the hagpriests stood before them, harsh-looking women. Generally they were women from among the Bern who had not had children, not been desperate enough to risk the dangerous gamble of childbirth in exchange for power, so the priesthood was the next best option. Each had a bone knife at their hip, as if they could be called upon to sacrifice a life for a ship at any moment.

The leader of the four pointed at Joron. "This one is ours?"

"Ey, he is my deckkeeper, Joron Twiner. A good officer and one I want back."

"That is for the Hag to decide. Can he get in the boat on his own?"

Meas shook her head. "He took a bad sword strike to the back."

"The back, aye?" said the lead priest and her mouth curled up, making her look like a woman who had bitten into fruit only to find it rotten. "Well, I should not be surprised one of yours was running away." Meas ignored the insult, though Joron saw Farys, stood behind the priests, stiffen and her hand went toward where her curnow would usually be hooked; he was glad she did not wear it that day.

"We have rigged a crane to get him into your boat and, I say again, I want him back." The priests ignored Meas. Then ignored him as he was lifted aboard their ship, ignored him as they rowed back to the quay, ignored him as they placed him in a cart and as they moved up through the town, and if they had wanted to make him feel unwelcome they could not have done better if they had used harsh words and beatings. In turn Joron ignored them – they were stonebound after all, what did their opinion matter?

He studied the town. Bernshulme was different. It was as if the whole town was hungover, and more than that, it was like it had not only made itself ill through drink but spent the last of its wages on it and now wondered how it would eat. Flags were everywhere, coloured rags strewn between buildings – but they had clearly been there a while and were no longer bright and gay; instead they were dirtied, filthy, some missing from the strings so they looked like broken teeth in the slack jaws of the last fish in the market. In one square they passed through he saw what he imagined was meant to be an arakeesian but it had none of the wakewyrm's majesty; it was a sad thing, made of once-fresh varisk and gion which, together with the forests around the town, was now slowly melting. The people that thronged the streets of Bernshulme, as they always did, moved out of the way of the priest's cart and the strong men pulling it, but they had the air of people lost, broken, sad.

He wanted to ask why, but was sure these sour-faced and cold hagpriests would not answer. So he sat back and watched the dejected town as they passed through it. Had there been some huge loss of ships and deckchilder? Had the Gaunt Islands taken the upper hand somehow?

He did not know, could not. But curiosity burned within him and he would find out, he was sure of that. He was going to an officer's hagbower – there would probably be little else to do during the days but gossip.

Bernshulme's hagbower stood next to the Grand Bothy, and was an easy building to miss as its more glamorous sibling stole the attention of all those approaching on the Serpent

Road. Where the bothy was tall and flashy in its architecture, its dome rising far, far above, the hagbower was the opposite, low and old, its intricate stonework almost overtaken by green moss and white bird guano. Seagrass sprouted across the top of the hagbower and its roof was slowly being grassed over, helping to keep the heat in the long, low building. Meas had sketched out a map, showing how the hagbower was built into the island, and vanished within the rock. The rear of the building emerged around the curve of the island where its loading and unloading bay was out of sight of the town. "Better to hide the corpses coming out," she had said. "Hagpriests hate to admit failure."

His stretcher was pulled from the cart and taken inside, which was dark and thick with the scent of sickness; that sweet stench, uncomfortable and cloying, filling his nose with thick and sickly purple and yellow scents. It was hot too — a fire burned at the far end and wanelights had been placed along the walls.

The building was designed as one long corridor with rooms off each side. In the centre of the building it opened out into a larger space, lit with oil lamps, where a number of deck-keepers and deckholders lay around on couches. Each of them waxen or grey faced, depending on the colour of their skin — not one of them looked healthy or showed any interest in the new arrival. Then Joron's group were back in the corridor on the other side of the space and he was hauled past three closed doors before arriving at an open one where they stopped. The seaguard who had been dragging Joron helped him up, efficiently, if not kindly, and showed him into the room. Two beds, one occupied by a woman who stared sightlessly at the ceiling above her. Between the beds was a bath for cold water treatments.

"This is your room. Your companion is Deckkeeper Ashand, of the *Storm's Egg*." The hagpriest stared down at the woman. "She will not be your companion for long though. I would be surprised if she makes it through the night." Turning back to him, the hagpriest continued, "If she survives there will be a cold bath for you both at first light and one at last light, to drive the sickness from you and promote healing. You may sleep or use the lounge if you feel able. Meals are provided, you must eat nothing else outside of what you are given. Your people will be made aware that they may not bring you food from outside. If they do then visits will no longer be allowed. Should you die, the fleet will cover your funerary costs, even though you are from a black ship." With a glance, the hagpriest managed to ensure he knew his presence was a terrible affront to her. "By the head of your bed is a locker, please place your clothes in there and put on the gown folded on your pillow. Do you have any questions?" Joron shook his head, doing it slowly and managing to make it look like it took every last bit of energy he had. The hagpriest sighed. "Get his clothes off and redress him," she said to the seaguard. Joron shook his head.

"No," he said, "I must do things myself if I am to ever improve." He thought he sounded ridiculous, like the worst slatelayer trying to get out of an unpleasant duty, but the hagpriest did not seem to pick that up,

"Well, if you are prepared to work for it then the maybe the Hag will not take you." She stepped away from him. "May the Mother see you well and the Maiden grant you luck." With that she shut the door and left him with the glow of the wane-light and a dying woman. A chair stood by the foot of each bed and he lifted his foot, undid his boots then carried them to the other end of his bed and the small cupboard that could be locked and unlocked with an iron key. He opened it, put his boots in, removed the flask that Garriya had given him from inside his shirt and placed it in his left boot. No doubt the hagpriests that ran this place had keys to the lockers; he hoped they were not in the habit of searching them and that if they were that hiding the flask in his boot would be enough to stop it being found. Then he changed out of his clothes. Even in the dim light of the room he could see stains on his gown from the previous owner.

"Death is hard to wash away," he said to himself as he sat on the bed, staring at the shape of the woman under the blankets opposite him. She had lost a foot and he felt sorry for her, she was done in the fleet now. If she was lucky and her family had money maybe they would look after her; if not then whatever she had saved from her time as deckkeeper may keep her from the street for a while, but not forever. Life was hard in the Isles.

Her lips moved. He went to her.

"Water?" he said, finding a jug by the bed and pouring some into a cup. Her head rolled from side to side on the pillow.

"Don't," she said, "don't . . ." Sweat stood out on the dark skin of her brow and her hand fell from beneath the blanket that covered her. He took it. Held it.

"I am here," he said. "My name is Joron."

"Don't," she said again, and she turned her face toward him though she looked into somewhere else. "Don't."

They were interrupted by a hagpriest, much younger than the one who had brought him here. She carried a jug and two cups with her, smiled at him, and though she was young and showed no scars of birth, she was still attractive.

"Deckkeeper," she said, "I am glad you had the energy to dress yourself, we do not have as much help here as we may wish." He bowed his head, so she could not see his eyes and prick the lie from them.

"It was a struggle, but I fear my room-mate struggles more. She seemed in some distress."

The hagpriest nodded her head. "Her foot was amputated. It is a hard thing to go through and the wound now sours. But do not worry, she will not disturb your rest. I bring medicine." She lifted the jug to show him. Then she poured out a measure. "You should get into bed, Deckkeeper," she said. "while I see to Ashand here, then I will pour your measure." He did so, and the hagpriest lifted up Ashand's head. The woman kept saying, "Don't . . . don't . . ." but the hagpriest gently shushed her, like one would a child, and then managed to pour the liquid down her throat. That done she carefully wiped around the woman's mouth, blessing her in the name of the Mother. "Now," she said, pouring another shot, "your turn, Deckkeeper Twiner." She held up the cup. He remembered Garriya's warning, not to take the medicine offered.

"Please," he said, "leave it by my bed and I shall take it before I sleep."

She shook her head. "Oh, no, the Hagmother of the bower would not have that. I must watch you drink it, Deckkeeper." She smiled, then handed him the cup. "Please, do not make me call our seaguard. It is unpleasant when our patients are difficult." The smile again, and now he saw her in a different light, her beauty and gentleness a ploy to ensure he was likely to follow her advice.

Joron realised he had little choice, not at this moment and not if he wished them to believe he was really ill. And besides, what could one dose of medicine do? If he must take this so the hagpriest would leave then that is what he must do. Come true night he could find a way to escape from here and meet Mevans, Farys, Anzir and Hastir. He took the cup, knocked back the liquid – far more pleasant than the mulch Garriya provided for him. It was flowery, perfumed and sweet. Easy to drink and he finished the entire cup in one swig.

"Well done, Deckkeeper," said the Hagpriest and she ran a smooth cold hand over his brow. "Well done."

# 19

# The Sleeper

"D'keeper? D'keeper?"

A face. Skin like the rime of ice on a water bucket, wrinkling with each word, not like real skin. What face was that?

"D'keeper?"

From beneath the sea. From the cold to the warm. Up and up. Whose face was that?

"D'keeper?"

"Slap him."

"Anzir! I cannot, he is the D'keeper."

"I'll do it."

Those voices. Echoing down a tunnel, cascading from curved walls, losing form and twisting and twining until they were barely understandable and then, the song. He heard the lilting song of the windspire. The words reformed in his mind. The face remained in his vision and recognition came.

"Farys?"

"Ey, D'keeper. We thought you dead when you did not turn up."

"Dead?" Something was different in the room. What was it? "What time is it?"

"Skearith's Eye has just risen and those that worship go to the hagpriests."

He forced himself to sit up. Found it hard. The world swam; he felt as if he moved through clinging sand. Farys before him. Anzir and Mevans sat on the bed behind her.

"I have slept through the night?" A shard of pain in his back.

"Ey, you have, Deckkeeper," said Mevans. He seemed unable to keep still, shifting from side to side. "We took the gullaime to the spire yesterday, Had we known you was having a sleep we would have hit the taverns and the stews, but we waited."

"I am sorry, I did not mean to . . ." He remembered the hagpriest and the drink she gave him. And then nothing else, not even sleep. "I think I have been drugged and . . ." The bed. The empty bed.

Before he could frame another thought the young hagpriest came in.

"It is good you have visitors, Deckkeeper," she said, "but they must not tire you out. They cannot stay long."

"Where is . . .?" The name escaped him and his mind felt as if it were fogbound. He pointed at the other bed.

"I am afraid your companion died in the night, Deckkeeper," she said, "but do not worry, you shall not be alone for long. Now, you must take your medicine." She poured a cup of drink from the jug she held.

"I found it made me sleepy," he said, "that is not to my liking."

"That is the night drink, and it can make you a little woozy. This is day medicine, Deckkeeper," she said. "But your wound will make you sleep anyway, the healing of it, not what we give." She took a step closer and he shrank away from her.

"No, I do not want it, I . . ."

"Do not be difficult," she said, and her face hardened. "Do not make me call the seaguard."

"Ey, D'keeper," said Farys, "we want you well. Do as the priest says." He glared at Farys, saw that Mevans was grinning at her and Anzir was looking puzzled.

"I will not take orders from . . ."

"Let me help, priest," said Farys and she stood, reaching for the cup and then stumbled, managing to knock the cup and the jug from the priest's hand to smash on the hard floor.

"Oh!" said Farys, "I am sorry, priest, Mother's blessings on you, forgive me."

"Foolish girl!" shouted the hagpriest. "Remove yourself from here!"

"I's just trying to help, priest," said Farys. "Let me stay and I will make sure the D'keeper takes his medicine and—"

"You will leave!" The two women began arguing and behind them Joron saw Mevans elbow Anzir in the side, who looked at him, confused until Mevans nodded at Farys and Anzir stood, grabbed Farys, who started to struggle and fight like a wild bird in the claws of a sankrey.

"I will remove her, priest," Anzir said, "all our apologies. For the fuss."

The hagpriest stood back, straightened her robes, dark fingers against white material. "I should think so. Come, I will take you out the back way, so we do not disturb the other patients." The hagpriest left, taking Anzir who was carrying a struggling Farys. Mevans remained and when they were gone he crossed over and knelt by the bed.

"You chose well there, Deckkeeper," he said. "She's a clever one, that Farys. Stay strong and I will bring you some hurrock."

"Hurrock? I am not a man who cannot handle his drink, Mevans."

He grinned. "Ey, but I reckon that if hurrock stops a man getting drunk too quick it might slow whatever it is the hagpriests are doling out to you, dull its effects. I doubt they will let Farys back in to throw their poison on the floor again."

"Slowing is not stopping, Mevans."

"No, Deckkeeper, it is not. You will have to make yourself vomit, and not be found out. And we cannot return until tomorrow as these priests have more rules than a shipwife, so for today you must take their drugs."

"And hope I do not die in the night," Joron said, staring at the other bed.

"I suggest getting out of this room, Deckkeeper," he said. "Walk about. Too easy for the Hag to find a man who never moves." Joron nodded, and tried to stand, finding his body unsteady, as if there was a lag between him wishing his feet to move and them actually moving. He felt like an overladen ship, slow to the steering oar.

"You may have to help me, Mevans," he said. The man offered his arm and assisted Joron, who limped and hopped and stumbled out into the long, hot corridor. In the communal area in the centre of the hagbower, two women and one man were on the couches. Mevans helped Joron to an empty one and sat him down. He glanced at the others but they paid him no mind, did not even seem to notice him.

"What is he doing out of bed?" Joron's head slowly turned to see an elderly hagpriest, the same severe-looking woman who had escorted him from *Tide Child* to the hagbower.

"'Pologies, Priest," said Mevans, "only the Deckkeeper said he fancied a change of scenery and some talk so I brought him here to be among officers, for Mother knows I am not the type of man can talk to an officer fit to interest him. Can barely talk at all, for truth. My old mam, she were almost a Bern she were, only I 'ave a toe missing, see, and because I 'ave a toe missing she were not Bern, but that were good for me as I were the first child and if she were Bern I would be riding a ship as a corpselight, eh? Well . . ."

"Enough, deckchild," said the hagpriest. "I have no interest in your woes. Leave your charge there and stop flapping your mouth like a wounded bird's wing. I am sure your shipwife has duties for you." She pointed at the door and watched, stony-faced, until Mevans was gone. Then she strode over to Joron, pushed his head back by placing a hand on his forehead, used a thumb to lift his eyelid and stared at his eye. "Not had your medicine yet then," she said. "All that commotion was you, was it? Well, you will find I do not stand for it. You are here for a purpose and you will take your medicine. That is my word and that is what you will do." She managed to sound disapproving of both Joron and the medicine. "Hagsither," she said, "bring me a jug for Twiner here, let us give him his dose. I would not want him getting sick." Another hagpriest brought over a jug and poured a shot. *They can tell if I do not take it. And yet I must find a way not to*, he thought.

"Hagmother." The voice came from a woman across the small communal area. She lay on a couch, staring at the smoke rising from the pipe in her hand. "That fellow seems sparky enough. Would it kill you to hold off on the languor water so I can have a companion?"

"All patients are to be medicated, Deckkeeper Gueste, you know that."

"All, ey?" She turned her head to Joron and rolled her eyes. "Well, should you delay this fellow's medication for a short time, I am sure I can arrange some sort of stipend to the donation I pay your order, ey?"

A quiet fell then, the hagmother seeming wary of taking such an obvious bribe in front of Joron. Then she smiled at Gueste.

"Well, I would be foolish to turn down a donation to the bower. What do a few moments matter if it will help us care for all of those in our charge a little better?"

"Exactly what I was thinking, Hagmother," said Gueste, and then watched the woman walk away. "Knew she'd go for the money. Woman has two Kept in their own rooms in the town, thinks no one knows but everyone does. She sneaks them in here once in a while, she's a screamer that one. Fair wears them out." She took a drag on the pipe, watching smoke bubble through the water in the bulb. "Deckkeeper," she reached out a hand for him to clasp. "Alson Gueste, formerly of the two-ribber, *Spitewing*. Who knows what I am of now."

"Joron," he said. "Joron Twiner of the *Tide Child*."

"The black ship?" Her gaze seemed to drift away. "Truly the Maiden laughs every time I open my mouth. I pay for a companion and get someone unworthy of my station."

Joron wondered how Meas would reply to such rudeness, for he did not have the first idea of how to react. Gueste took another drag on the bubbling pipe then closed her eyes and turned back to him. "My apologies, Joron Twiner, that was rude of me." She laughed. "Truth be told, I should be on a black ship myself, instead I am here."

"Why?"

"Got myself pregnant by a deckchild on my ship. Lost the child, but too late in term to pretend it never happened."

"But you are not condemned?"

Gueste smiled. "My mother is a Tenbern, and just strong and rich enough to ensure everyone pretends it did not happen, though our family's fortunes wane. So I sit in this place to recuperate until the gossips find themselves a new scandal."

"And the deckchild goes to a black ship," said Joron.

Gueste shook her head. "Oh no, my mother had him drowned in case he talked. A pity as he was an athletic fellow. But let us not talk ourselves into the Hag's black moods – what brings you to this place, Joron? Some derring-do? Or did you fall over a spar and break your leg?"

"Took a sword blow to the back," he said. "We intercepted Gaunt Island raiders, didn't even know I'd been hurt until afterwards."

"You've seen action then?"

"Plenty of it."

"I haven't, just endless safe patrols. My mother has plans for me and a few years in the fleet are part of it. Then she'd like me to choose myself a few Kept and start on my way to being Bern." She was very young, Joron realised, maybe not even twenty yet. "I'd love to see more action, experience the glory and all. I'm a fighter not a politicker. I want to make myself a name."

"Careful what you wish for. The fight, when it happens, is terrible," said Joron. "And frightening. And people talk of skill but as far as I have seen survival is more about luck. I have seen seasoned deckchilder, fierce women and men, snatched away by bowshot, or cut down by a lucky strike. If you can stay on boring patrols then my advice is to do just that."

Gueste stared at him as if he had changed into some strange sea creature right before her.

"Indeed," she said, and went back to staring at the smoke rising from her pipe while silence squatted uncomfortably between them. It occurred to Joron that he could ask her just what it was Meas had done to get herself condemned to *Tide Child*, for as a daughter of the Thirteenbern Meas surely could have bought herself out as this woman had. He opened his mouth, closed it again as he realised that he would forever feel like he had betrayed his shipwife if he went searching for answers from others. And what would it say of him to Gueste? That his shipwife did not trust him enough to confide her sins in him? No, he could not ask, and yet he did not want this silence to last.

"Why is the town so morose?" he said.

"You do not know?" She frowned, puzzled, then tapped the stem of the pipe in the air making little Z's of smoke. "Of course, a black ship, you will know little. It is the arakeesians. Such joy when we heard they were back, such opportunity for glory when we have more ships. All those almost-forgotten industries coming back. The heart-burriers, flensers, bone softeners, and oil corers – so many trades ready to spring back to life." She sat up a little. "We had quite the celebration I tell you," she said. "Every woman and man thought they would never be poor again. I don't think anyone in Bernshulme was sober for a whole month."

"But?"

"Ey, always that isn't there? The Maiden loves her tricks. We had our party, sent out three ships, two three-ribbers and a two-ribber. Loaded 'em up with the best of everything we had, sent two brownbones after 'em, to tow the cargo back once they caught them." She took a drag on her pipe, a long one. Then let the smoke out slowly through her nose. "Only four people lived to tell the tale – three deckchilder and a deckholder made it back in a flukeboat."

"What happened?"

"They loosed the gallowbows and the creature wrecked them. It was the work of minutes. The only silver lining on the cloud was that our ships had been followed by a Gaunt Island fleet, four boneships they sent, and they fared no better."

"I thought the keyshans were hunted from towers?"

"Oh, it had passed through the towers, had a few big bolts sticking out of it but they didn't seem to slow it at all. Some say we need bigger bows," Gueste leaned closer, now whispering, "but the talk on the docks is of some forgotten magic that allowed us to hunt them, something we need to get back." Joron remembered the hiylbolts *Tide Child* had carried – rare and ancient weapons once used to hunt the beasts – and how they had cast them into the sea. Remembered how glad he had been that they had done that; not glad for all the lives lost protecting the sea dragon, but glad the keyshan swam free.

"Deckkeeper Twiner." He turned to find the hagmother stood behind him with her medicine. "It is time for your dose."

"Better do as she says," said Gueste, raising her pipe as if in salute. "Here's hoping you can do your bit toward bringing the Hundred Isles its glory, ey?" She grinned. "It's been nice knowing you, Twiner."

He took the glass from the hagmother and she watched as he drank. The liquid sweet and pleasurable as it slid down his throat. He had a moment where he considered what Gueste had said, the implied finality of it. Then his day dissolved into pastel shades and soft feelings and he lost himself in contemplation of the whirling stone that made up the roof.

"Deckkeeper? Deckkeeper?"

He awoke to a fog, the stinging slaps of a hand against his cheek barely registering through the thick blanket of numbness that surrounded his mind.

"Mevans?"

"Ah, you are back with us, D'keeper. Skearith's Eye is near to closing."

"What?" He looked about. Back in his room. So much time had passed. "How?"

"You have slept, D' keeper, and I could not waken you."

Joron tried to sit, and a searing pain ran down his back. Mevans leaned in and pushed him gently back onto the bed.

"Your wound has re-opened," he whispered. "I have bound it, but the hagpriest was not pleased." He lifted a cup. "Now, drink this. It is Garriya's concoction." He helped Joron to drink the medicine, it tasted no less foul than ever. When it was done Mevans produced a bottle from his coat and filled the cup with a milky liquid. "If you think her medicine tastes bad, D'keeper, she assured me this is worse. But she thinks it will protect you from the drug they give you. She thinks they are using sopweed."

"That is a poison."

Mevans nodded. "So is this," he said with a grin, and forced the cup against Joron's mouth. The liquid was acrid, stinging his tongue and burning his throat as he choked it down. Everything in him rebelled against drinking any more, but Mevans was having none of it and was far stronger than the weakened deckkeeper. When Mevans had forced the contents of the cup into Joron's mouth he placed his hand over it, pushing him down onto the bed, and with his other hand he pinched Joron's nose. "I am so sorry, D'keeper. Have me corded for this if you must but we cannot lose you. Garriya says one dose is all she dares give you, so you must find a way out of this place tonight. We will be waiting for you."

Joron swallowed. It felt like forcing hot coals down his throat and it burned into his gut. When the liquid was gone Mevans removed his hand.

Joron breathed. Swallowed anger bitter as any medicine.

"Where will you be, Mevans?" he said.

"Watching, D'keeper. Just get out, we will find you."

No shipfriends on the ship had she
"My Kept has all the love I need"
Dreamed every night of her return
Came home to find the island burned

She flew up high, she flew down low
*Heave on, crew, heave on.*
From north to south she flew the storms
*Heave on, crew, heave on.*
She flew to east, she flew to west.
*Heave on, crew, heave on.*
And always thought of home, hey!
She always thought of home.

"The Black Pirate" – traditional ballad

# 20

# What Is Found Within

Joron took his night dose of the bower's medicine, watched by the predatory eyes of the hagpriest, but this time the sopor did not come. Instead it was as if the drug from Garriya and the drug from the hagpriest mixed in his stomach to form a hard ball, a stone soaked in nausea and discomfort that squatted in his vitals, gnawing at him with the same fierceness as hunger.

But he did not sleep.

He sat in the darkness ignoring the churning in his guts and listening to the night sounds of the hagbower. When he looked out the small window Skearith's Blind Eye was rising, almost at its highest point. He heard noise, footsteps, doors opening deep within the bower where there should be no doors opening. After that, silence. He waited, watched the subtle shadows of the Blind Eye's light crawling across the tight sheets of the empty bed opposite him, and when he felt the silence was deep and long enough to signal that none walked the slate of the building he got up. Put on his clothes, grabbed his good boots and opened the door a crack.

Dark corridors: no one around.

He slid down the corridor, moving as silently as he could.

Used to finding quiet paths through decks full of sleeping women and men, easily doing the same on the solid floors. He stopped at the edge of the communal area, peering into the gloom, letting his eyes adjust, not trying to see a person but looking for movement. That was easier in the dark, to find movement rather than decode unfamiliar patterns of light and shade into something that may or may not be a threat.

Nothing.

Joron moved forward, padding through the space and then – *then* – a movement caught his eye. He froze, turned. Found Gueste there, dozing on one of the couches. Her eyes opened and the other deckkeeper watched him for a moment, then smiled and reached for her pipe before waving Joron on. He let his heart slow a little, carried on through the hagbower, down the corridors to the doors at the front. Found them unlocked, because of course, who would want to come in here?

The streets of Bernshulme were not busy, not at this time and not around the bothies. He saw lights in the lower town, and heard singing and shouting, voices drifting across to him on the still, cool air. A few of the Bern and the Kept strolled and Joron stayed in the shadows; he did not want to stay near the hagbower in case he was missed and a search began, but at the same time he did not want to go too far away as he knew Mevans would be looking for him. So he loitered in a crevice between two buildings, lacing up his boots and waiting to see a familiar face.

A hiss. A sound out of place in the Bernshulme night among the echoing laughter, song and shouting from the town below. A whistle. He looked around, saw nothing. The whistle again and this time he saw a group of figures loitering in the shadow of a bothy; one gave him a nod and he made his way over. Found the comfortable faces of Mevans, Anzir and Farys.

"D'keeper," said Mevans. "Glad you made it out."

"Ey, Mevans, and I am glad you found me."

"We have Hastir watching the back way, but all they bring in and out is carts."

"Back way?"

"Ey, where they bring in supplies."

"I forgot there was one, but then I have been asleep for most of my stay so it is little wonder. Come, we go to the Grand Bothy and to the chartmaster, Yirrid."

"Why him, D'keeper?"

"Anyone who wants to go anywhere will need charts."

"So he is the eyes and ears of the bothy," said Mevans.

"Well, he is definitely the ears, Mevans. Now, let us proceed as if we are fully entitled to be there."

"I am not sure anyone will believe that, D'keeper. Look at us."

And he was right – Joron felt that no more raggedy bunch could be found on the streets of Bernshulme. As they moved through the shadows, he remained, deep in thought, desperate for some clever plan, the type Meas would come up with. But nothing came to him and he had little time. Outside the Grand Bothy he could see two seaguard standing beneath burning braziers, keeping watch of all those that came and went.

"What would Meas do, Mevans?" said Joron.

"Walk right in, D'keeper. Ain't nowhere never kept her out."

Joron politely thanked the hatkeep for information that, if not useful, he at least knew was probably true. "Not an option for us, I think."

As he watched a drunk staggered past and shouted something at one of the guards. The seaguard immediately took a step forward but his friend restrained him. "He's eager," said Joron. Then he smiled to himself. "Farys, quickly – intercept that drunk, make it appear he has attacked you. With any luck it will draw that guard away, and maybe his friend."

"If it doesn't?" said Mevans.

"If it has no effect we think of something else. If it draws only the one man, then Anzir can make conversation with the other."

"Me?" she said.

"Ey."

"What shall I say?"

"Tell him how much you like his muscles, or something." She shrugged.

"They are good muscles, D'keeper."

"Well, go then," he said, and Farys walked across the road toward the drunk man. Joron had presumed she would have to start up some sort of commotion but the drunk man beat her to it, shouting at her and calling her filth. As soon as that started Joron and Mevans walked across the road further down, watching as the angry guard left his post to remonstrate with the drunk man again, his friend staying by the door. Anzir approached the second guard and engaged him in conversation. When his back was turned Joron and Mevans slipped past and into the building.

"That was easier than I thought," said Joron. "Come, I know the way from here." He led them quickly across the shiny floor of the bothy, eyes constantly scanning for any who may recognise them as intruders. There were people about, Bern and Kept and servants going about their duties, but they paid little attention to Joron and Mevans. He found the door Meas and he had used on their first visit, and from there led Mevans down into the tunnels which, as he remembered, all looked remarkably similar.

"I don't suppose you have ever accompanied the shipwife down here for charts, have you, Mevans?"

"I have indeed, D'keeper," he said.

"Then maybe you can lead us on from here?"

"Ey, rightly I can, if that's your order."

"It is," he said, slightly self-consciously. They made their way further into the bowels of the Grand Bothy until Joron saw a door he recognised. "Do you think the chartkeeper will be awake, Mevans?"

"Two chances, D'keeper."

"Ey, there is," said Joron, and he pushed the door open into the musty, dimly lit room, and walked forward.

"Hello?"

Nothing, just the faint echo of his own voice. He stood, listening, waiting. Did he hear the sound of shuffling coming from the back? Did he hear a low moan?

"Someone is hurt," said Mevans. Joron nodded and they headed into the back of the room, deeper into the gloom. As they passed they found the place a mess, charts on the floor, furniture thrown everywhere.

"Watch where you step, Mevans," said Joron quietly, "these charts are precious."

The sound from the far end of the dark room stopped.

"Who is there?"

Joron recognised Yirrid's voice, and yet also did not. The last time they had met, the chartmaster had been full of strength and humour, but now he sounded like an old man.

"Joron Twiner, Yirrid."

"Meas's boy?" he said.

"Ey, Yirrid," said Joron.

"Is she here?"

"No, they will not let her leave the ship."

The chartmaster came shuffling out of the darkness, a frail apparition. He walked slowly, scarred and burned face hidden by the curtains of his long hair. "What has happened?" asked Joron.

"A reminder, that is all." In the dim light of the wanelights Joron could see the shadows of old bruises on Yirrid's face, and the swellings of new ones around his ruined eyes. "I wondered why they came, but Meas being here – well, now it makes sense."

"What makes sense?"

"This reminder." He gestured around the room with a misshapen hand, then pointed at his face. "This gentle encouragement to forget."

"Forget what?"

Yirrid tried to laugh, but it turned into a cough and he grasped his chest. "Terrible things," he whispered. "I like to look through the old documents, boy, see what I can find. The

Maiden always curses the curious, and she cursed me as I found a thing." He turned away and Joron could just make out him muttering, "I should have destroyed it."

"Destroyed what?" said Joron.

"No matter," said Yirrid. "To mention it is to bring more misery, and Meas has enough." Mevans leaned over and picked up a chart.

"I could help put these away," said Mevans.

"No," said Yirrid, some of his old life as a shipwife coming through in his voice. "They are all marked in ways I can read with what fingers I have left. I have systems. And I have a boy who . . ." His voice faded away. "Well, they will send me a new boy I am sure. Now, enough, I am tired and hurt. What do you want?"

"We came across a ship, a brownbone, taking sick women and men and gullaime somewhere. We do not know where and the shipwife burned her charts before we could get to them. The ship was called *Maiden's Bounty* and the Shipwife named Golzin. Meas wants to know where it was going, and why. She thought you may know if charts had been requested by this shipwife, or charts for something you thought odd. She fears something terrible."

Yirrid's scarred face was fixed on him.

"So, it has started," he whispered into the darkness. "Get me my seat," he said. Mevans appeared behind him with a stool, and the old man sat. "Maybe the Mother sends you to help, maybe the Maiden sends you as a trick. Who knows, ey?"

"I feel it more likely the Hag follows our wake."

"Ever thus for the crew of a black ship," said Yirrid. "I cannot help you with where the brownbone was going. But with why it is going, though – well, sadly, that I know."

"Is that why you have been beaten?"

Yirrid nodded. "Ey, it is. A warning not to talk of what I know."

"Forgive me," said Mevans, "but if you cannot see, how do you find secrets in old papers?"

Yirrid smiled. "My boy read for me, I was training him to take my place." The old man sighed. "Now he never will."

"They killed him?"

Yirrid nodded.

"I am worth keeping, my knowledge is needed. The boy was only a Berncast child who knew too much."

"And what is it he knew?" asked Joron.

"Part of the secret to making hiyl, the poison for hunting keyshans."

"It is made from the keyshans themselves, is it not?" said Joron.

Yirrid shook his head. "No it is not. That I know." Then he repeated quietly, "It is what I wished I still believed."

Joron stared at him, mouth dry, feeling that he stood on the edge of some precipice, some knowledge that once passed on would never leave him, and would never be wanted either.

Yirrid lifted his head. "We always say that life in the Hundred Isles is harsh, but it is nothing to the way the old ones lived, nothing. The poison – the cost of making it? It is lives. The ancients spent hundreds of lives making hiyl, thousands even. It is a dark and poisonous process, that uses up bodies. That much my boy read out before they took the scrolls from me."

"That is why they want the sick," said Joron, and he found himself wishing for his own seat. "If you must expend life in the making of a thing, then use those who are expendable. But surely we are not that—"

"You think it cannot be, Joron Twiner? That we would not murder hundreds for a chance to hunt the keyshans once more?" He let out a small laugh, a wizened, bitter sound. "We sacrifice our own children to our ships, you think those in power care about the lives of the sick and the useless?"

"But so many?" said Joron.

"Ey, from the numbers, the process must use them up in days."

"And gullaime too?"

"Windtalkers? They are too valuable."

"What if they are windshorn?"

"Well," he shrugged again, "a worker is a worker, I suppose, and I have said too much. You must leave."

"You have no clue where these brownbones are taking these people?"

"What would you do if I did?" he said softly. "Take your black ship to save those who are dying anyway? I would not throw away Meas's life to save them even if I knew where they were taken."

"Then," said Joron, "are you any better than them?"

Yirrid chuckled, far from the reaction Joron expected to his insult.

"Of course I am no better, child." He heard the officer in the voice once again, the core of keyshan bone that ran through the man. "I was a Hundred Isles shipwife, boy. How many innocents do you think fell to my blade? Too many. You think I would throw away the one person I genuinely care about for those who I know nothing of? Those I care nothing for?" He shook his head. "No, never."

"She will hate you for it."

"But she will be alive to do it," said Yirrid.

Joron waited, trying to think of a way to convince the old man to help, but all he found was the churning in his gut of the twin poisons. The pain. He understood pain — his pain, and Meas's pain. With that understanding came words.

"There was a place, Yirrid, that was not as fierce as the Hundred Isles, or the Gaunt Islands. A place Meas helped create. But it does not exist anymore, and the people who lived there, who were not sick, or useless, or unknown to us, were taken from it in these brownbones. So if you truly care for Meas, then know she loved these people, not for who they were, but for what they stood for. A living, breathing sign of her peace. I cannot make you help, but you can be sure she will not stop whether you tell me what you know or not."

Yirrid tipped his blind face toward the chart-covered floor.

"Ah, Meas, you wish peace for all, but can you never be at

peace yourself?" he said quietly, before raising his head. "Charts for the brownbones go out en masse. They are bundled up and handed out by the chart office in the harbour. No doubt those for the brownbones you seek are removed before the harbour office sees them. Would not do to have the common folk know they are to be harvested, ey?" He chuckled. "If anyone knows which charts are for those brownbones, it is Indyl Karrad. Nothing happens on this island without him knowing of it. You must speak to him."

"I doubt he will want to speak to me," said Joron.

"Well, that is a problem for you, not me." He slid from the stool. "This place is a mess and I have work to do. I think you should go now."

"Ey," said Joron and he did, he and Mevans sneaking out of the Grand Bothy past the two men on the gate who, because they were leaving, did not even raise an eyebrow.

Outside they found Farys, Anzir and Hastir waiting in the shadows and the five of them made their way down the Serpent Road and into Fishdock, where Joron had visited Indyl Karrad before, though in the company of Meas. They wandered the streets, Joron conscious that time was running out and he must return to the hagbower before he was missed, until, eventually, they found a familiar building and Joron knocked on the door. A moment later the door was opened a crack.

"Too late for callers," said a voice.

"My name is Joron Twiner," he said. "I must speak to Indyl Karrad on behalf of Meas Gilbryn."

The door shut. They waited. The streets were starting to fill, though it was still dark. Bakers had begun their work and the smell of smoke as ovens were lit was chasing away the usual smell of rotting fish. The drinking holes had finally shut and the sound of brushes could be heard as floors were swept free of filth.

The door opened.

"Kept Karrad will speak to you, Twiner, alone." Joron nodded to Mevans.

"I do not like this," said Mevans.

"It is as it must be, Hatkeep."

He passed through the door. Behind it was a man, small and bent though there was something dangerous about him that set Joron on edge the same way he felt when around Narza.

"Follow me," said the man. Joron did, up the sumptuously lined stairs, and into Indyl Karrad's inner sanctum where the man sat at his desk. He still had the long, reed-woven plait growing from his chin, and he was still a finely sculpted and muscled man beneath the straps of material crossing his body that marked him as one of the Kept, but were there grey streaks in his hair that had not been there before? And was his musculature not quite as defined, and was the shimmering make-up around his eyes just a little thicker now, the better to hide the wrinkles there?

"Joron Twiner," he said. "I am surprised you have the tits to come to my house."

"I come on behalf of Meas. And I come with bad news."

"Are you are always destined to bring me bad news, Twiner? It seems to be your lot in life." Joron did not know how to answer. Here was the man whose son he had killed in a duel, and who in turn had made sure Joron was committed to a black ship. Though at the same time he was Meas's partner in peace, someone she trusted and the man who kept them supplied with both stores for the ships and information. "Well?" said Karrad, "speak then. I would have you here for as short a time as possible."

Joron took a deep breath.

"Safeharbour is gone." He searched Karrad's face for reaction but the man was a spy, his features betrayed nothing. "And worse, our people are taken, to be worked to death to make the poison for hiylbolts, together with some of the gullaime."

Karrad stared at him. "And you know this how?"

"There was a brownbone, name of *Maiden's Bounty*, under a shipwife called Golzin. We intercepted it but the charts were burned before we could find out where it went. Then we returned to Safeharbour to find it gone, and that brownbones had taken our people too."

Karrad continued staring at him.

"Meas has been busy," he said. "But you did not fully answer my question."

"And you do not seem concerned about Safeharbour."

Karrad tapped his desk. "As deckkeeper of a fleet ship, I thought you would know there is a time to grieve and a time to act." He took a breath, stood. "I have heard rumours, about disappearances on the streets of our towns and villages. I had put it down to people leaving to join Meas, but it seems it may not be so. Whoever is doing this is good at keeping secrets."

"The Thirteenbern," said Joron.

"Well," said Karrad, "there are few other suspects. I will find out where these brownbones are heading. You must come back tomorrow."

"I cannot."

"Why?"

"I am in the hagbower, they keep us drugged. I must leave there tomorrow or I may never leave at all."

Karrad chewed on the inside of his mouth.

"If Safeharbour is gone then it may be Meas will be discovered too," he said. "Go back to the hagbower tonight and have yourself discharged in the morran. They cannot stop you walking out but if you simply vanish it will raise questions. Tell Meas that I will leave her what information I can get on our island. She will know what I mean. Share this message with Mevans in case something happens to you, he can be trusted."

"I am not so easily overcome." Karrad stared at him, no expression on his face.

"You can go now," said Karrad. And Joron did, thankful to be away, pleased the meeting had been so short.

Outside he met Mevans and the others, told the hatkeep the message Karrad had shared with him. "Make sure this gets to Meas."

"Ey, D'keeper. Back to the bower now?"

"No, one more stop to make. Mulvan Cahanny."

"I told him you may call," said Mevans. Joron raised an eyebrow. "There are few in Bernshulme I do not know somehow," said the hatkeep, and he led them down back alleys, round through the darkest and foulest-smelling areas of Fishmarket to the drinking den named Boneship's Rest where Cahanny held sway. Just like on Joron's first visit there were two huge guards on the door but this time they did not turn the small group away.

"Mevans," said the woman on the left, "he's expecting you and the deckkeeper. The others have to wait here. Go straight to the back, the barwoman will let you into his sanctum."

"Do you want our weapons?" said Mevans.

"Cahanny ain't scared of you," said the man on the right as he pushed open the door.

When Joron had come here with Meas the bar had been full, now it was empty apart from a few obvious bodyguards scattered around the room. No braziers burned and the air was not thick with narcotic smoke, only the scent of spilled drink. Mevans walked up to the bar and Joron followed, as the woman behind the bar leaned against the barrels, watching disinterestedly. Then she walked to the end of her bar and opened a door, motioning Mevans and Joron to walk through with a jerk of her head.

The room inside was far nicer than the bar, panelled and with two padded chairs sat before the desk where Mulvan Cahanny waited.

"So," he nodded at Joron, "it's the man who stole my bird. Never thought I'd see you again if I'm honest, Birdman. The weak don't tend to last long on the black ships."

"Maybe I'm not weak," said Joron, and he took the seat opposite Cahanny uninvited. "Sit, Mevans," he said, "I am sure Cahanny would not mind."

Cahanny watched as Mevans sat; his little eyes sparkled and a small smile grew on his face. "Seems you've been learning manners from Black Orris, eh, boy?" He poured a shot of alcohol for himself, one for Joron and one for Mevans. "Drink," he said.

"I do not need a drink," said Joron and his stomach, that hard ball of pain and nausea, threatened to rebel. Mevans' eyes moved from one shot glass to the other. "Take them both, Mevans," said Joron and the hatkeep took a shot glass in each hand, knocking them both back with a grin.

"Thank you kindly, Mulvan."

"It's Cahanny to you, Mevans," he said.

"Whatever you say, Mulvan," said Mevans, and he held out his shot glasses. Cahanny shook his head and then filled one of them.

"You never did know when to stop. Now, let me talk to the deckkeeper. I cannot imagine he would come here without good reason."

"I do not," said Joron.

"You seem a mite less scared than last time."

"Let us just say, Cahanny, since last we met I have faced things far more terrifying than you."

Cahanny raised an eyebrow, then nodded. "I must be honest, I am seeing you more out of curiosity than anything else. I have no real wish to help you, Birdman." Joron watched him – he was not a big man and his burns and missing arm did a good job of masking his body language.

"Meas says nothing goes on in Bernshulme without you knowing about it."

"Nothing illegal, aye. Second to Indyl Karrad, I suspect I know more about Bernshulme than anyone."

"I'm looking for information on brownbones," said Joron, "and I have little time."

"Ey, you look a little peaky." Cahanny sipped from his drink. "I did not think it was my place to say."

"These brownbones would be outfitted strangely, with shelves within. The one we saw had its hold split into three. They may take on gullaime." Something shifted in Cahanny at that, some windchange in his face. "You know something?"

"It seems you really have grown under Meas, eh, Birdman?"

"Tell me."

"I give nothing for free," said Cahanny, "you know that. And as I reckon it you already owe me for stealing my second in command and fifteen of my men."

"Or you owe us."

Cahanny paused in drinking. Licked his lips and stared at Joron.

"And how do you work that one out, boy?"

"Do you know how we got your man, Coughlin, to come over to us? To stay on *Tide Child*?"

Cahanny nodded. "Some trick with beasts, I heard."

"Aye, exactly. Not a great trick either, and I cannot imagine it fooled him for long. He must know by now what we did. And yet he does not return to you."

"Probably feels foolish." Cahanny looked away. "I would."

"And yet," Joron leaned forward, "he holds no malice to the shipwife, serves her well even."

"Man needs a home."

"You wanted him gone," said Joron.

Cahanny leaned back. "I did?"

"He was too ready to believe you would double cross him," said Joron. "And I wondered, for a long time, why you would send your second in command and fifteen good men to guard a box of old keyshan bones. They aren't worth that much. So either he was planning to double cross you, or you him. Whichever, he must have suspected something was coming and so, when Meas pulled her trick, he was primed and ready to believe."

Cahanny tapped his small cup on the table, then he grinned.

"You're a thinker," he said. "If you ever run from the fleet, Birdman, I'd find you a place in my organisation." He drank from his cup, poured himself another. "How is Anzir?"

"Well," said Joron, surprised by the sudden change in Cahanny. "She protects me. Now, the brownbones, what do you know?"

"Little, Birdman. It is just the talk of the gullaime that pricked my ears. No ships matching your description have left Bernshulme, I can tell you that. But the refit you describe is the sort of change that could be done to a ship at sea – and if I wanted it kept secret I'd do it there and throw over the bonewrights." A grin, a flash of teeth. "There was an island, Birdman, it was used by those who wanted to move cargo that ain't generally allowed. Living cargo, you understand?"

"You mean slaves?"

"Human cargo, aye. Not much call for it here, if I am honest, but there are those in the Gaunt Islands who use slaves and sometimes I may have done some trade with 'em." He stared at Joron. "Do not dare judge me, Birdman. The fleets take children for the hagpriest's knives, and yet you would look down on a little slavery." Joron said nothing, only met the crime lord's gaze where once he would have turned away. "Anyway, the island was shut down, half a year ago. Not a shock really, those places are always transient."

"And you think these brownbones are operating out of there?"

Cahanny shrugged.

"I heard talk that someone was using them, and I heard talk they were smuggling gullaime."

"That happens?"

"Aye, but I have nothing to do with it. Generally that sort of thing is fleet, some bigshot Bern or Kept making illicit money. It's not worth my life to interfere in their business. I know my place."

"Where is this island? What is it called?"

"It is called it McLean's Rock, for a fellow who was gutted there, way back when," said Cahanny. He opened his desk, took out a sheet of parchment. "I shall draw you a chart and write directions. If it was simple gullaime smuggling it will not help you, but if you have no other option it may be worth a try." He drew on the parchment then slid it over the desk. Joron took it and rolled it up.

"Thank you, Cahanny," he said.

Cahanny nodded. "Whatever you are involved with, if Meas thinks it important, I reckon it matters. But I also reckon you owe me a favour."

"And what is it?"

"My niece is on your ship. Cwell, she is called."

"I know her."

"She is hard to like, but she is the only family I have left and precious to me. I only ask that you look out for her."

"I am always looking out for her," said Joron and he stood. "Now, I must get back to the hagbower before I am missed."

"Good luck to you, Deckkeeper," said Cahanny, and he watched them leave with bird-bright eyes.

In the lightening streets outside the hagbower Joron said his goodbyes.

"Tomorrow, Mevans, I will return to *Tide Child*. So be ready to cast off."

"Ey, D'keeper, you looks after yourself," said Mevans, then Joron slipped back into the heat of the hagbower.

As he walked down the dark corridor to his room he saw a figure appear from the shadows. Gueste.

"It seems you have been for an adventure, Joron Twiner," she grinned.

"Ey, but it is over now."

"Oh," said Gueste, "it surely is." She waved him past with a small bow. As he passed her he heard a whispered order, cloth brushing against cloth. Something flashed across his vision, and he felt a rough rope tighten around his neck, crushing his throat, choking off his airways and ushering him into a deeper darkness.

# 21

# A Tale in Three Parts

## How Joron Woke

It was early, the scent of fish filled his nose and worked its way into his stomach, awakening the burgeoning nausea. His head ached and his hands trembled in a way that would only be stilled by the first cup of shipwine. Then the pain in his mind would fade as the thick liquid slithered down his gullet, warming his throat and guts. After the first cup would come the second and with that would come the numbness that told him he was on the way to deadening his mind the way his body was dead, or waiting to be. Then there would be a third cup and then a fourth and then a fifth and the day would be over and he would slip into darkness.

No.

That was not him. Once him, not him any longer.

That was Joron Twiner the lost, Joron Twiner before Meas, before *Tide Child* flew the sea, before he sang a legend to the aid of his ship with the gullaime. That was not Joron Twiner the deckkeeper, that was Joron Twiner the broken.

He was Joron Twiner the deckkeeper.

The deckkeeper, Joron Twiner, tried to open his eyes,

experienced a moment of confusion when he realised that his eyes were already open. *Oh*, he thought. He closed his eyes. Opened them. It made no difference. All was darkness.

Panic.

What was this, some dream brought on by the medicine of the hagpriests? He tried to sit, choked, a rope around his neck. Ropes around his wrists, his midriff, his legs and his ankles. Walls, close on either side, a roof so near he could feel the warmth of his own breath bouncing off it as he gasped. He was in a box. Why was he in a box?

Struggling, pain. Pain in his throat. Bruising.

He tried to shout.

Nothing.

Only pain. A croak. That voice of his, that deep tenor his father had loved. The voice that sang up legend.

Gone. A creak, like a boneship catching the wind.

Light streaming in, blinding him, forcing his eyes shut. Some of that light still bleeding through. Forcing tears into his eyes. Blinding him.

"Joron." He knew that voice. "I'm sorry about all this, Joron. Just following orders, you understand?"

He let his eyes open, ever so slowly. The light was not bright, not really, not full daylight. Only lamplight, flickering and dim. But it still hurt. The air smelled of outside, the melting gion, old fish. A shadow loomed above him. He tried to speak, only a croak came out.

"Don't speak, my man was a little too rough with the garrotte, I am afraid. Don't be rough with him, says I. Joron is a good fellow, says I, but they did not listen. I imagine your throat will be sore for quite some time, though to be fair, it is the least of your worries."

"Gueste?" The name slipped out. His words both quiet and harsh, a rasp in his throat. "What?"

A finger on his lips. "Shhh, do not speak."

In the light, now the tears had flowed from his eyes, he could make out Gueste's face, sardonic, smiling still. The glimmer of Skearith's Bones in the sky far above her. "In a story, Joron Twiner, I would slip an old nail or a blade in for you, and you could use it to escape." A little light, a little hope because he was beginning to realise why he was in this box, there could only be one reason. He was to be sent aboard a brownbone to wherever those who were to be sacrificed in the cause of the boneships went.

To die, that he was ready for, had been ever since he was condemned. But to go into the foetid hold of one of those ships, in a box like this? No, that was more than he thought he could bear.

Gueste leaned in a little closer. "You Berncast fool," she said, and all hope died. "Take comfort that though you are a traitor, you serve a greater purpose. Your Berncast blood can do some good now, rather than simply dirtying up the deck of a fleet ship's rump. Even a dead ship deserves better than you." Joron tried to speak but his throat burned, his lips betrayed him. "You really think you can simply sneak out without being seen? You think you can meddle without others being aware?"

How foolish he felt — that he had thought he shared some kinship to this woman, sat and talked with her as if they could be friends. Not even considered that she may be there to spy upon him and all those in the hagbower.

"If you had any idea how much you are hated, Twiner, a Berncast officer raised on the whim of a disgraced shipwife, you would never show your face in this town, ever." She leaned in closer. "I know, you must be a little worried about your future, Joron. So let me give you a gift, a little positivity. I am born to the Bern, and born to the slate of a ship, and we guard our places jealously. There is nothing we hate more than an interloper, and putting you in this box has fixed more than a few bridges I may have previously burned. So, while you go to forward the cause of the Hundred Isles, in the best way for your kind, so shall I. I am to get my own ship."

"Gueste," he gasped out.

"Shh, shhh," said Gueste, "save your energy for the journey,

Twiner. You will need it. It is a kindness I do you, really, for I have seen the marks of the rot are already upon your skin." And then she withdrew and the lid was shut, locking him back into darkness. Joron struggled, straining his muscles against his bonds and more than anything he wanted to give voice to his terror.

But he could not scream.

He. Could. Not. Scream.

## What Mevans Did

Now Mevans was an old sea hand with all the experience and cunning such a thing brought. He knew many a thing, and one of those things he knew many things about was officers. He had particular, and very certain, beliefs about officers. He knew that when it came to directing a ship and directing a battle and formulating a tactic and such things, an officer was as fine as the Mother's breasts, but he also knew that without a crew to look after them, an officer was often likely to trip over some Maidentrick as would never gull a sensible fellow like Mevans. And as such, it did not sit well with him to leave his deckkeeper behind to make his own way back to *Tide Child*, as Mevans believed it entirely likely that his deckkeeper would fall off a harbour or some other such foolishness.

Though he had been given an order.

But Mevans was an old sea hand with all the experience and cunning such a thing brought. He knew many a thing and one of the other things he knew many things about was orders. He had particular and certain beliefs about orders. Now an order was to be carried out to the letter, and he had been ordered to take the information he had back to Meas and to wait there for the d'keeper. To many, this would seem a right specific order but Mevans was not so sure, and he felt it important that before he return to the ship, he clarify with his fellows just what they thought this order meant in the most exact way.

"I say," he said, drawing them into a dark alley by a small drinking hole that served the cheapest and fiercest shipwine in the whole of Bernshulme, "it does not sit right to leave the deckkeeper all alone in that place, not with knowing what it is we know."

"What is it we know, Hatkeep?" said Farys. Oh, he liked her, she were a quick one, with all the savvy a good deckchild needed to get ahead and make sure the ship ran fleet.

"The truth is, Farys, I cannot rightly be telling anyone what it is we know and I am not so sure it is a thing I should know myself. But it is as foul as the Hag all hungover, worse maybe."

"We was ordered though, by the deckkeeper," said Anzir. "To go back."

"That is indeed right and proper what we were ordered," said Mevans, for as said, he had particular and certain beliefs. "But he did not say to us that we should do it with all speed."

"Hatkeep," said Farys. "If what it is you know, and cannot say as it is right terrible, will the shipwife not be put out if we tarry?"

"Maybe; that can happen and I will handle her if it does. See, I reckon, Farys, that he has said, we must take the message back to the *Child*, and wait for him. And I also reckon, that as long as we are the ones to set foot on the deck first, then we will have obeyed that order, to the letter."

There was some chatter then, as Anzir, Hastir and Farys discussed the matter between themselves and Mevans, as the highest ranking, stepped away to let them talk.

"We have decided, Hatkeep," said Farys at last.

"And what is it you have decided?"

"Well, Hastir, who was once an officer, says we have been given an order and should follow that order and though she knows the d'keeper did not specifically say go straight back, that is what he meant and it being so that is what we should do."

"I see," said Mevans, for he did.

"But now, Anzir, she says it sits bad with her to leave the d'keeper for she is honour bound if he may be in danger to help, and she says we should go and check on him."

"I see," said Mevans, for he did. "Well, Bowsell Farys," said Mevans, "it appears you have the casting vote here."

"Ey," she said. "Well, though I have no doubt that Hastir is right and the d'keeper did mean us to go back, as it sounds like what it is you know is right important, I wondered if only one of us could go back?"

There were nods of agreement from Anzir and Hastir. But Mevans shook his head.

"No, that cannot be," he said. "For that is as good as saying we know what we was ordered to do and decided not to do it. No, it is an all-or-nothing deal, the interpretation of an order by a deckchild, see."

Farys gave him a short, sharp nod. She did indeed see.

"Well then, Hatkeep Mevans," she said, "I cannot in good conscience . . ." He felt a deep disappointment within at those words, that Farys was not made of the stuff he thought. But he had thought too soon. "I say," she continued, "I cannot leave the d'keeper if he may be in trouble." Mevans' disappointment immediately turned to elation.

"Shall we go and speak to the hagpriest then, Hatkeep?" said Anzir. "She will take us to Twiner."

"I fear she will not, good Anzir, not at all, for she has taken a right dislike to us. We must go in the back, through the bay where they bring in and out the goods. I am sure a few rough fellows like us will be right at home there."

"Can we not go back to Meas, and tell her we think the d'keeper is in trouble?" said Hastir.

"Ey, we could," said Mevans, although he knew, for him, even knowing what he knew, that he could not do that, for he had come to right like the new deckkeeper. And more, he had seen a brownbone drawing into the harbour under the cover of night, and had a terrible feeling – not a knowledge, just a deckchilder's feeling, the same way he knew a storm may be over the horizon – that he knew what that brownbone meant for those within the hagbower.

So they made their way, not to *Tide Child* as the deckkeeper had instructed them, but back to the hagbower which, although it appeared to vanish into the mountain did no such thing. It snaked its way around beneath the earth and emerged further down the mountain on the other side, in a small yard at the end of a long road which eventually ended at the harbour. Mevans, in the way he believed any good deckchilder should if they wanted to as much as call themselves fleet, had reconnoitred the area on the first day when his deckkeeper had not shown his face. And, in the way he believed any good deckchilder should if they wanted to as much as call themselves fleet, he had picked out places from which they could watch the small courtyard and all the comings and goings of the women and men who serviced the hagbower.

He led them through the town and out of it, until they found the rear of the hagbower and a vantage point in the vegetation above the loading bay behind. The first thing that Mevans noticed was that the place below was peculiar in its set-up. He took for granted that those with him also noticed, for they had not just walked off the stone and onto the deck of a ship that day and, truthfully, would he, Mevans, Hatkeep to none other than Lucky Meas herself, bring anyone with him who did not know their business?

No, he would not.

"There is a lot going on down there, but not many people doing it, Hatkeep," said Farys.

"Ey," he said, and oh, she was a clever one.

"Makes me think what is going on is secret," she said, and oh yes, she would go far.

"Ey," said Mevans.

"Is it not odd, Hatkeep," said Hastir, "that they are loading up something heavy, but not unloading nothing heavy from those wagons?

"Ey," said Mevans, and it was. Wagons, drawn by tall

gillybirds, were coming up the hill and rather than unloading barrels of food and drink for the sick they unloaded long, low boxes. As Hastir had pointed out, the boxes were clearly empty. The women and men carrying them did a poor job of pretending they were weighty as they took them in to the rear of the hagbower, but they were far more convincing when they brought them back out, stacking them two across two in little towers.

All except one box. Which was on its own to one side.

And it was this box that Mevans was most interested in. Not only was it stacked separately, but he'd seen a right stonebound-looking type, despite their fleet uniform, all full of her own swagger and of the type Mevans would have soon as thrown off a deck as trust on one, peering into that box for what was a peculiarly long time. Now, Mevans well knew how deckchilder became obsessed by the strangest of things: money, bone carvings, weapons; he'd even known a woman who collected the false legs of those she had killed. But something of that fellow's demeanour struck Mevans as right conversational. And he did not think a woman dressed like a cockbird in its best plumage was likely to talk to an empty box, or one full of weapons or bone carvings or money or even false legs. Though he knew it may have been a little bit of a stretch, he was willing to bet his own favoured stinker coat, the one that he would let no other wear, that his deckkeeper was – for whatever reason, no doubt a bad one– in that box.

"Right, my crew," he said. "That box down there, I reckon has our precious fellow in it, so before Skearith's Eye is fully risen it'll be bone knives at the ready and we shall go and get him. Do not be seen, do not raise so much as a chirp. Cut-throats is what we are tonight, and that will be our business." The faces that greeted him were all smiles, for his girls and boys knew their business and their business was getting the deck-keeper back. "Now, Anzir, I count four round those big doors that go into the hill. You and Hastir will deal with them and then shut and bar the doors while Farys and I find the two who are roaming around those carts."

So it was that four deckchilder, used to violence and danger and with all the skills that brings, tracked six women and men who were used to guarding carts and who were unaware that the pitiless gaze of the Hag had been turned upon them. And if the deaths were bloody, it can be said they were at least quick, for Mevans, Farys, Anzir and Hastir held no hate for these people; in fact, each was aware that given a twist of their tale by the Maiden it could have been them that guarded these carts. But they wished to see their deckkeeper put back in his proper place and would let no one stand between them. So knives were drawn, and flesh was neatly parted and the blood flowed.

When the deed was done the four deckchilder gathered around the box which Mevans had marked out.

"Well," said the jaunty hatkeep, "shall we see what lies within our chest of treasure?"

## And Joron Woke Again

There was no time within the box. No way of telling of the passage of Skearith's Eye except the slowly growing pressure in his bladder. He had tried to listen for signs of others, that someone may come to help, but the more he listened the louder became the sound of his own breathing until it filled his world and he could feel the edges of panic gnawing at his mind. With every bump and scuffle he heard outside he imagined it was those who would carry him to his berth on a brownbone, from then to go in misery and confinement to his death. His imagination magnified every sound into nightmares until he resolved to listen no more. He simply lay, trying to push his mind from his body into some other place, somewhere that was not dark and hot and miserable and sure to end in death.

He did not quite know when the visions started, as they crawled in around the edges of his consciousness in subtle incursion. Nothing concrete, not at first, simply flashes of white light in the foreground of his closed eyes. Then the light took on colours, and the colours resolved themselves into shapes and he saw the vast and terrifying shape of Skearith the godbird as the Golden Door opened in the storms that walled the world and it came to rest upon a mountain. He heard the songs that had been with him since he had taken the gullaime to the windspire, but different, louder and stronger, vast and twisting. He saw these images as scrimshaw, moving scrimshaw carved into the bones of his mind. He saw visions of the Maiden, the Mother and the Hag, massive and awe-inspiring, hovering above the thousands of islands of the archipelago, and every line of these figures was in constant motion, as if being endlessly carved anew, lines of white on yellow bone, and he could not shake the feeling that all three felt nothing but pity for their people, scurrying about heedless of those below. He thought he heard the Mother speak – though she spoke with a voice that sounded uncomfortably like Meas – "They threw the spear that killed a god, and have learned nothing since." He was overwhelmed by sorrow, the voice so loud and full of presence that it was forcing him from his own mind, crushing him away from sanity. He saw Hassith, who killed the godbird and shamed all men, as he threw his spear which pierced the eye of Skearith, loosing all sorrow.

He saw the hatching of the Maiden, Mother and Hag from the four eggs, saw the gift of the gullaime hatch from the fourth and something in him screamed that this was all wrong, and the song grew and grew in his mind until he felt sure he must go mad. The sore spots on his arms, legs and shoulders screamed into the night, linked through a burning fiery pain. Ghostly arakeesians carved in a white so bright they hurt his closed eyes now swum through the infinite darkness of his tight prison, burning their images onto the whorls of his brain and he knew no time nor awareness. He felt his mouth move, though he heard none of the words as he raved within his box, whispering words beyond understanding. He felt the cold of Garriya's knife against his neck, and thought he saw some truth but it was fleeting and lost to him before he understood it. Meas talked of change, and yet he had never believed that, only followed her. But now, here, and too late, he had heard the words of the Mother and knew change was needed.

Or was that just the desperation of the doomed?

Light flooded in. Unready for it, he turned his head away, so he did not see the smiling face of Mevans, and as he had resolved not to listen he did not hear the shout of joy from Farys and Anzir when he was uncovered.

"Deckkeeper! Are you drugged, Deckkeeper?"

What was this, some new hallucination? But this one lacked the bright colours, lacked the squirming lines of knife on bone. He found words, forced them past the rawness of his throat and, though he meant to say the name of the man who stood above him, he did not.

"Water," he croaked.

"Of course, D'keeper," and Mevans had it already, the liquid caressed Joron's lips, cooling his throat. Then it stopped. "Anzir, lift him from the box." She did, huge, strong and gentle arms reaching in, first to cut the ropes that bound him, then to lift him from the wooden coffin and lay him on the ground as feeling and pain flooded back into hands and feet denied blood for hours on end. Joron found himself growling, an involuntary action to ward away the pain.

"Ride it," said Mevans, "ride it Deckkeeper and listen to my voice." Mevans' hand took his, skin as hard as horn from hauling on ropes. Joron squeezed the hand tight as a wave of pain washed over him. "We must get you back to the *Child*," he said, "Anzir and Hastir will carry you. If any ask, we will say you have had too much anhir, so act thus, ey?"

"I told you," said Joron between sharp breaths, "to go back to the ship."

"Ey," said Mevans, his eyes opening wide in all innocence, "and we was indeed on our way when we happened to pass here and see a cock-fellow putting you into this box. And I said to Farys, we cannot be having that, can we. Farys?"

"No, said I, D'keeper," added Farys.

"Well you see, and with these other two, being of the lower ranks on the ship, well, Mother bless 'em, they 'ad no choice but to do as they was told, right?" Joron closed his eyes, gathered his strength.

"Thank you," he said. "Thank you." Raised his arm. "Others . . ."

"Tsk," said Mevans, "is only what is our job, you would have done the same. But, I am afraid time is not on our side, and well, we have made rather a mess so it is best we get away. Can you walk, enough to play drunk?"

"Others," said Joron again quietly. Mevans stared into his eye. "The other boxes."

"We are only four, D'keeper," he said. "Truly, I am sorry, but we must leave."

Joron nodded, knowing what they said was right, and breaking a little inside at the thought of any others trapped in the boxes stacked behind the hagbower. His little crew guided him through Bernshulme, apologising for their drunken friend all the way. The only odd thing that happened was as they went up the gangplank to *Tide Child*, Joron noticed that Farys, Anzir and Hastir hung back while supporting him, as if they wanted to ensure that Mevans was the first back aboard and Joron could not, for the life of him, work out why.

# 22

# Once More, To Sea

Joron woke to the familiar motion of his hammock and the ship beneath him, the bitter scent of rotting bones, the slightly repulsive stink of the water in the bilges and all these familiar discomforts served to banish the nightmares that had chased him through his dreams: tight spaces, the smell of his body the only company. But here there was the smell of so many other bodies, and above it all the welcome smell of the sea, his companion through so much of his life.

With that sixth sense she possessed, to know just when to appear, Meas opened the door of his cabin.

"I am glad you made it back, Deckkeeper," she said, her mouth twisted into something almost a smile.

"Thank you, Shipwife," he croaked.

"I knew it was dangerous, but not quite how dangerous. Had I known, I would not have sent you." He was almost shocked — did she apologise to him? Or as near as she ever could?

"I would still have gone," he said, and did his hand a shake a little at the thought of walking toward such imprisonment again? Maybe it did, but his resolve did not.

"Yes," she said, "I know. And now you know a little of the

horror which is given to our people, and as such why it is important that I pick up Karrad's message."

"We go to your island then," he said, "wherever that is."

But she shook her head. "I go there. I will take the larger of our flukeboats with Mevans, and a few others. You will take *Tide Child* and rendezvous with me. We cannot be careful enough. With your breakout from the hagbower any suspicions of my Mother's must now be confirmed. The island may well be watched. Easier to sneak in and out in a flukeboat than with a fleet ship."

"When?"

"Two days, then I will leave," said Meas.

"Then I should . . ." He started to lever himself up from the hammock but she stepped forward, putting her hand on his shoulder.

"Rest, Joron Twiner, that is what you shall do. Garriya said your wound opened while you were back on land, and what they gave you was poisonous and weakened you further. I will have you as well as you can be to command *Tide Child*, so rest until then."

"But I—"

"Will obey my order, Deckkeeper," she said. He nodded and lay back, thankful for her mercy and fretting about what he would do with the time.

"The gullaime has missed you," she said. That smile reappearing. "In fact it has made my life a misery and forced me to confine it to its quarters on some days. Following me round the ship, crowing 'Where Twiner? Where Twiner?' Prattling incessantly as if the passage of five minutes will change my answer." Now it was his turn to smile for she spoke of the creature with an undoubted fondness. "I think it would like to see you, if you can bear it." He nodded. Meas returned the nod. "I will tell it, so expect it very soon." She left, and barely a minute passed before he heard a commotion outside.

"Away go! Away go!" The harsh screech of the gullaime at its companion, of which it had clearly become no fonder. The door opened and the gullaime backed into his small cabin, pausing every step to stop and dart its head forward, hissing at the windshorn before using a foot to slam the door shut and keep the creature out. It turned to him, its head twitched to the side. It had repainted its mask in brighter colours.

"Jor-on Twiner," it snapped into the air.

"I am glad to see you, Gullaime," he said, barely able to raise his voice above a whisper. The gullaime reached down with its beak, snuffling about in its long robes, also now painted more brightly with long streaks of pink and blue, like Meas's hair. It took something from its robes with its beak and then hopped forward, placing the object on Joron's chest. A shell, a spiral of white calcite, veined with green and blue as it tightened toward the centre.

"A shell," said Joron.

"Good shell," said the gullaime. It preened a feather on its shoulder, pulling it from its plumage and Joron became fascinated by the play of light on it. What looked like white was nothing of the sort; it was a hundred colours, all different, all beautiful.

"Ship woman sent you away."

"It was my duty, Gullaime."

"Should sent me." It yarked, filling the room with harsh sound.

"I do not think they would have spoken to you, Gullaime."

"Kill them," it said. "Hurt Joron."

"They did, but if you had killed them we would not have the information."

"Bad things." It scratched a line on the bone floor of the cabin with its foot. "Bad things," it said again.

"Yes, and Meas will stop them."

"And Joron! And Gullaime!"

"Yes."

"And Farys, and Mevans and Solemn Muffaz and Anzir and . . ." The gullaime went on, joyfully naming the crew and Joron felt sure if he had not interrupted it the creature would have carried on until it had named everyone aboard the ship.

"Yes. All of us."

It hopped closer, its mask staring down into Joron's face.

"Even save windshorn?"

"Yes," he said, and the tiredness was starting to tell, his voice was retreating further. The gullaime continued to study him.

"Hmm," it said, cocked its head. "Hmmm."

"They took my singing voice, Gullaime," he said, and then he cracked, a single tear running down his face. "I used to sing with my father, and you and I, we sang the keyshan to us, sang a creature up to save us. But they took my voice."

The gullaime continued to stare down and then it reached out with its wingclaws, pushing the mask from its face and exposing the huge, glowing white eyes hidden beneath, their shared secret. And once more Joron saw the arakeesians flying through his mind, but not as dark, scrimshaw patterns; these were glorious, glowing things, creatures of magic and legend.

"Song not in voice, Joron Twiner," and though the gullaime said the words it was not quite its voice he heard, "song in here," and he felt the gullaime's wingclaws touch his chest. "Song in here." Then it lowered its mask again. "Sleep, Joron Twiner," it coughed out. "Joron Twiner tired." And it left, and as if commanded Joron slept, but this time it was a comfortable sleep, no longer haunted by nightmares of confinement.

The days passed quickly. Sleeping and eating. The ship creaking and groaning around him. Visits from the gullaime and the crew and Meas. Garriya brought him foul-tasting concoctions which, though the taste lingered like hate, he did have to admit made him feel better. Sometimes he heard Dinyl's voice, shouting orders on deck but he never saw him, the deckholder never visited. Some wounds could not be healed with medicine. When Meas finally brought Joron back on deck to reclaim his two-tailed hat, Dinyl clearly could not hide his resentment and turned from Joron to face the sea.

It was a beautiful day otherwise, cold but bright, and the sky as blue as Joron had ever seen it. *Tide Child*'s topwings were down and the wind was brisk, more than enough to push them through the waves at a good speed. The larger of the two fluke-boats was tied alongside and the crew Meas had picked – twenty in all, including Coughlin, Mevans, Gavith and ten of the seaguard – were loading enough food for a journey of ten days.

"Seven beakwyrms ride before us, Deckkeeper," said Meas.

"Ey," he said, "it feels like we make good speed." She nodded, stepped forward and spoke more quietly, for him alone.

"Look after my ship, Deckkeeper."

"I will, Shipwife."

"I know," she said. "Aelerin knows where to meet me. Ten days from now."

He wanted to say, And if you do not arrive? But he did not. He would not bring the Hag's gaze down on her.

"And when you have the information, Shipwife?" he asked.

"We will go and find our people."

He nodded. She made it all sound so simple.

The crew lined the slate of the deck and the pipes played as Meas went over the side. They watched the flukeboat raise its wing and catch the wind, becoming a smaller and smaller dot in the vastness of the ocean. When Meas was gone, swallowed up by the horizon, he gave the orders, crew went aloft, more wings were set, ropes were tied off and *Tide Child* creaked and moaned as he caught the wind and heeled over, slowly picking up speed.

"I think he'll fair fly today, Deckkeeper. Should pick us up a couple more beakwyrms," said Solemn Muffaz from his place before the mainspine.

"I think he fair will, Deckmother," said Joron in reply and he struggled to keep the grin from his face, for it seemed an age since he had stood here, the speed of *Tide Child*'s passage plucking at his hair. He had missed it. Behind Solemn Muffaz, vicious, cruel Cwell sneered at him as she pulled a rope tight. He had not missed her.

The days passed and *Tide Child* flew, his passage across the water unceasing, and Joron even began to worry that they may make their rendezvous with Meas too early, and that idea took hold and he filled his idle time on the rump of the ship with thoughts of the small things he could do for the crew, of the slacktime he could give them for work well done. Days passed in a haze of good winds and salt spray and not even the baleful looks from Dinyl and the cadre of ne'er do wells like Cwell, Sprackin and the rest of her clique could bring him down. His body was healing, his mind was healing. If only his voice would also.

Like all good things, it was not to last.

The storm came from the north, as the worst of them always do in the Hundred Isles. A slow gathering of cloud menaced the horizon, lines of rain as dark streaks against the sky.

"The Hag furrows her brow," said Solemn Muffaz to Dinyl, and the deckholder stared across the sea.

"Ey," he said, "and blood follows."

Joron stood on the rump and watched. When Skearith's Eye was at its highest the waves were swelling, pushing *Tide Child* up, then down into troughs that hid the world and turned all to churning water. Wind whistled through the rigging and Joron had the mainwings brought down. Still the clouds gathered; a short rain began to fall, icy needles that bit through clothing, that stung the skin while the crew worked. And they did work, as the higher the wind, the rougher the wave, the more must be done. *Tide Child* needed constant little adjustments, to the rigging here, to the wings there. Walking across the slate of the deck became an effort, sometimes like climbing a steep hill, sometimes like stumbling down a precipitous slope.

By night the storm had truly hit and all but the topwings were brought in. The wind howled and water washed over the ship in great plumes. Joron was constantly shouting, merely to make himself heard over the screaming gale, and he was constantly wet, his clothing soaked through. Worse of all for Joron, his wounds and his illness were showing and he knew it. He was not as fast, not as strong and not as hardy. He doubted himself, found himself giving orders and wanting to take them back a moment later. The shouting was taking a toll on his damaged throat; the rawness which had almost left after days of rest was coming back.

"Deckkeeper," shouted Dinyl over the howling wind.

"Ey?" he said, and had to strain his throat for even that one word to be heard.

"You have been on your feet all day, Deckkeeper," shouted Dinyl, water running down his face from the driving rain. "Maybe a couple of hours' rest may be a good idea? I can handle the ship for now."

His first instinct was to say no. But that was to feed the darkness between them, and he knew Dinyl was right. He was a capable officer who had weathered many storms, and Joron knew it was only a matter of time before his own tired body gave way. He nodded.

"Ey," he said again. Then he turned for his cabin. Once on his hammock, despite the wild motions *of Tide Child* and the screaming of the wind and the coldness of his damp clothes, like any seasoned deckchilder he fell asleep straight away.

A different kind of screaming woke him. At first he thought the storm still had them in its grasp, such was the commotion – and with the added fog of sleep it took him moments to realise the ship no longer bucked and heaved below him. He heard bangs and thuds and crashes and then more screams. What was this? Some attack? A banging on his door, a voice.

"Deckkeeper! Deckkeeper!" Anzir, and desperate sounding at that. He slid from the hammock. Pulled open the door. Found Anzir and he could make no sense of it, her face was slashed, blood ran down her cheek.

"Anzir?"

She opened her mouth, got as far as "Mut—" and then a sword blade thrust through her chest and her words turned into a grunt. Such confusion crossed her face, as if she could not understand how or where her death had come from. Then she raised her head and looked at Joron. "Sorry," she said, and fell to her knees. Behind her stood Sprackin, who had once been purseholder, small and angry and looking very pleased with himself.

"Told her I'd be avenged for that cording," he said, looking down at her, his face twisted in vicious glee. Joron took a step back, looking about for his own weapon, but before he moved more deckchilder appeared behind Sprackin, and every one of them Joron knew as slatelayer or troublemaker and every one held a weapon. Sprackin smiled at Joron. "I'd not move if I were you, the ship is ours now, Twiner," He put his foot on Anzir's still body and pulled his blade free. "And a new shipwife walks the slate." For a moment Joron could not speak. Overwhelmed. Anzir, huge, strong, always there for him and now gone. And Sprackin, so pleased with himself, but Joron found his voice. His confusion and the fear behind it masked with proper speech, fleet talk, polite as could be. Though why he could not fathom.

"And what is this shipwife's name?" he said. Forcing himself to sound calm, hoping his throat would not betray him.

"Cwell," said Sprackin with grin, "and she'll be wanting a word with you."

Joron stared at the man, taking in his glee, the sparkle in his eyes and thought to himself, *Well, I am sentenced to death long ago. Now it seems my time has finally come.*

# 23

## Before the Shipwife

Joron was tied, hands bound behind his back. The knots as unyielding as the bone of *Tide Child*'s hull, for if there was a thing a deckchild could do well it was to tie a knot. He was led through *Tide Child* and he had not seen the ship, his ship – *Meas's* ship – in such disarray since a time long ago, before the shipwife had come aboard. A time when he had, laughably, been called its commander.

This disarray was worse. He had simply been neglectful, this was the remnants of violence. The mutineers had taken Meas's loyal crew utterly by surprise. There were fewer bodies than he would have expected, and this filled him with hope – had most of the crew survived? – and fear – had most of the crew turned against him? Signs of violence were everywhere, smears of blood, stores and tools and ropes thrown about, and still being thrown about. Mutineers cackling with glee as they destroyed the ship's good order. Sprackin pulled him aside to allow four laughing deckchilder to roll a cask of good anhir past. Then he forced Joron up the stair and onto the deck.

Here he found his crew, tied and knelt before the mutineers' leaders, who stood on the rump of the deck. Cwell, he saw, and would have expected even had Sprackin not told him of her. By her stood Dinyl, and though he felt he should not be surprised, he could not pretend he was not disappointed. He had looked up to Dinyl, once, loved him even, once. Loved him for his talk of duty, for his devotion to it. A devotion that, at the last, he had evidently thrown aside. Once he had stood against Joron, Meas and the entire crew of *Tide Child* for what he believed was right and that had cost him his hand, hewn from his arm by Joron's blade. Other mutineers stood around the deck and he took in their faces; mostly those he knew had disliked him, who disliked the new regime Meas had brought to *Tide Child*, or those who simply loved to hate and had found an excuse for it in Cwell's words. Before them all knelt Solemn Muffaz, singled out, bound and on his knees, and it was to kneel by Solemn Muffaz that Joron was brought. He glanced at the deckmother, his face a mass of bruises.

"I failed you, Deckkeeper," he said miserably.

Joron shook his head. "We did not know this—"

"Quiet before your shipwife!" shouted Cwell. And there was laughter at that. "Who are you to speak on my rump without permission?"

"You are no shipwife," said Joron. And Cwell lashed out with her boot, catching Joron on the chest and sending him toppling backwards, the back of his head slamming into the slate, causing another round of laughter.

"Do not laugh!" shouted Cwell, and the laughter died down. "Do not laugh at our deckkeeper," she paced back and forth, "for he is an officer!" More laughter. "And besides, I would have him hear my judgement of the deckmother before he in turn is judged himself." Rough hands picked up Joron, righted him so he was looking at Dinyl and Cwell. Cwell had fashioned her own two-tailed hat, a thing of rag and bright colour. A deckchild appeared with Joron's one-tail, looted from his quarters, and gave it to Dinyl. He looked at it, but did not put it on, only held it. "Now, Deckmother," said Cwell to Muffaz, "the charges against you are that you have enforced the cruel and disloyal regime of the traitor shipwife, Meas Gilbryn. That you have visited cruel punishments upon the crew, and with much enjoyment, in her name."

"Never enjoyed it," said Solemn Muffaz, "not a once, never enjoyed it."

"That is fine defence," said Cwell, "a fine defence. And unlike the old shipwife, with her autocratic fleet ways" — she raised her voice when she used big words, as if to cow the crew around her with them — "I will not simply decide your guilt. No!" She raised her hands. "I am a fair shipwife, who will run a fair ship." She looked around, smiling. "So, I will ask my loyal crew to judge you." She turned and Joron looked over his shoulder; mutineers now filled the deck behind the kneeling and tied loyal crew. "Do you find the deckmother, Solemn Muffaz, guilty of the charges or not?"

From the mutineers went up the shout of, "Guilty!"

Cwell nodded her head, made herself look grave.

"Well, there you have it, Solemn Muffaz. It gives me little pleasure to pass sentence but I must do it, and it must be a punishment fitting the crime." She nodded to herself. "So, Solemn Muffaz, you will be tied to the mainspine, and every day, a member of the crew will give you ten lashes, until we have reached the amount of one thousand lashes."

"You will kill him," said Joron.

Cwell stared at him. "Well, that is the intent." She smiled at him, as if he was a dullard, short of understanding. "But hush your impatient noise, Twiner, we will get to you in good time, but first, the matter in hand," she gestured at the deckmother. "Now, my crew, who would give the first lashes to this sorry, wife-murdering man?" There was a commotion then, for not one of Cwell's mutineers was without scars from Solemn Muffaz's cord. But eventually the strongest of them put themself forward and Joron was forced to watch as Muffaz was dragged, with much jeering and shouting, to the mainmast, stripped of all his clothes and tied, face to the mast, arms around it. The cord was brought and the strikes were counted out, given with all the glee they had accused Solemn Muffaz of showing, though Joron had never seen a whit of evidence for it. Each cording cut deep, making a jagged map of blood on the deckmother's back.

When it was done drinks were passed around, jokes were told and Solemn Muffaz's torment did not end; he was not taken down and Joron noticed more than one deckchild, in passing, lash out and kick him. But this gave him opportunity to count the mutineers. There were few of them. Maybe thirty in all. Three had come from Coughlin's seaguard but Joron was glad he did not see Berhof, Coughlin's second, among them. He hoped the man was not dead. With so few crew he knew the mutineers would struggle to work the ship and maybe, when Cwell had dealt with him, those still loyal to Meas would find a way to escape and take *Tide Child* back.

Cwell wandered over to stand in front of Joron. Dinyl hung back, looking ashamed. As he rightly should.

"She will find you," said Joron to Cwell.

"We will be very far away from here by the time she realises what has happened," said Cwell.

"She will never stop looking."

Did Cwell pale a little at that? It did not matter; she stepped away from him and raised her arms for quiet.

"Now, my crew! We must deal with our next criminal — Joron Twiner, a fisherboy who styled himself as a deckkeeper, and before that, as a shipwife!" Laughter. "The worst shipwife we have ever seen, eh?"

"The drunkest!" shouted one of the mutineers, immune to the irony in the fact they were liberally passing around ship-wine.

"Now," said Cwell, "I have learned, from our dear Dinyl here . . ." She put her arm around his shoulders, and did Dinyl, up until this moment stoical and unfeeling, flinch at that? "I have learned many things, but most of all, I have learned that Joron Twiner did not even study at the bothies." Quiet on the deck. "Oh, and some aboard knew that, but plenty of us did not, ey?" Joron felt himself judged, not just by Cwell and the mutineers but also by the rest of the crew, those loyal to Meas who were tied and silent behind him. "He is an imposter. And I move to say we do not even need a vote on this one, for we have all suffered because of him. So I say, let us throw him overboard for the longthresh."

The word *No!* wanted to leap into Joron's mouth as he was grabbed by strong arms, but he held it back. He would not give them the satisfaction, he would not beg, he would not scream even as the longthresh ate him alive. Hag take every one of them.

"No."

That word from Dinyl.

"No, my deckkeeper?" said Cwell. "Do you gainsay your shipwife?"

"You promised him to me." An uncomfortable pause, "Shipwife. For what he did." Dinyl held up his arm, shortened by lack of a hand. "For this."

"Do you want to throw him overboard?" said Cwell.

"No," said Dinyl quietly. Joron could almost feel the mutineers turning against Dinyl for spoiling their fun. "I want to do far worse," he hissed. From the smile spreading across Cwell's face Dinyl's need for revenge was something she understood, would encourage even. "He took my hand, and that will be my starting point with him. But I want to do it on land. Where we have time, and space. Somewhere I can build a good fire to cauterise wounds. I do not want him to bleed out. I want to be somewhere I can make him suffer."

Cwell nodded. "Well, I would not be stood here without you, Deckkeeper," she said. "So he is my gift to you. At the first land we see we will stop, and you and your shipfriend over there," she pointed at Joron, "can put on a fine show for us." Dinyl nodded, glanced at Joron, still holding the one-tail hat in his one good hand. "But I feel we must give our crew a show now. For they have worked hard this day." A shout of appreciation went up from the mutineers as Cwell scanned the deckchilder knelt behind Joron. "Bring Hastir forward."

Two mutineers brought forward Hastir, who had once been a shipwife, once loyal to Cwell but no longer. A woman who was good at her job, a woman Joron had won over by giving her his trust. "You as good as spat in my face, Hastir, when you took up with that one." Cwell pointed at Joron. "You and I were once friends."

"If your creatures would bring me a little closer," said Hastir, "I will spit in your face for real."

Cwell let out a small laugh.

"You are spirited, I like that." She smiled, then shrugged. "But insubordination is punishable by death on my ship. Throw her overboard."

Hastir, kicking and struggling, was picked up by two of Cwell's mutineers and thrown over the side of *Tide Child*. All heard the splash and knew her lost. Joron, no doubt along with many others, said a silent prayer to the Hag to receive Hastir by her bonefire.

Cwell let a moment of silence pass. "The rest of you," she said to the women and men kneeling on the slate, "have a simple choice. Swear your loyalty to me, or join Hastir among the longthresh. I do not ask you to decide now, I am not unreasonable. Talk amongst yourselves and I will take your reply tomorrow. For now, I will have my crew take you all below to the hold." She paused. "Except Twiner. Lock him in the brig with the courser. I don't want him interfering with the crew's decisions."

It was a noisy and painful journey that Joron made from the deck of *Tide Child* to the brig, deep in the darkness of the ship's hold. Those who took him by the arms were not well disposed towards him, and they made sure that any mutinous crewmember who remembered a slight, or felt that Joron had treated them unfairly, got to pay back what they thought was owed, either with fists and feet, or harsh words – and so it was a bruised and bloodied Joron that was thrown into the small dark room well below the underdeck. There he sat alone, and time passed and passed. Once Joron tried the door, and found it just as sturdy and strong and impassable as the brig had always been. The walls around him as tough as any bone on the ship, the only view out through a small barred square at head height on the door. He had little to do but think about the pain he was in and how this was merely a weak echo of whatever Dinyl would visit on him when they hit land.

The brig consisted of three cells up in the beak end of the ship, reached by a ladder from the underdeck and locked away behind a thick door. Joron was surprised to find himself alone. He called out and there was no sound, despite Cwell having said he would share with the courser, Aelerin. The three cells were serviced by a small corridor that cut them off from the hold, and the armoury in the rump of the ship. As Joron nursed his bruises he listened. *Tide Child* sounded like a ship under way, but he also sounded different, subtly different. Was it Joron's mind that filled in an unhappiness to every creak and crack of the bones? Under this mutinous crew the ship was definitely more rowdy: more shouting, more laughter, though it was tinged with cruelty — and Joron well knew the sound of a cruel laugh.

Was it the Maiden he heard? Laughing cruelly at her trick, at Joron's fate — that he had escaped one small box designed to ship him to a horrible death, only to walk straight into another?

The Hundred Isles were ever cruel.

He heard a noise and stood to look through the small barred opening. The weak glow of the wanelight in his cell was joined by the weak light from a shaft of illumination creeping along the corridor toward his cell as the solid main door opened.

"Get in there. We'll come back for you when the shipwife needs you, or when we does." The last words a leer as the courser was roughly pushed forward. The door of the cell opened and they were thrown in with Joron — a flash of robes and they collapsed in a corner, clasping their stomach and curling up. Quiet sobs escaping their mouth.

"Aelerin," said Joron quietly. He had always wondered what

they looked like under the cowl. The hood had fallen away, but the courser's face was still hidden. All he could see was their scalp, covered in hundreds of tiny nicks where the courser had caught themselves with a blade as they shaved their hair to the skull. "Aelerin," he said again, "did they hurt you?" He knelt by them, put a hand on their shoulder. The courser looked up, then twisted their body away from him, pushing themselves further into the corner of the cell. He could just see their face. He had always wondered if they were male or female, always been half tempted to peek under the cowl but now he could see he was no wiser – the shorn hair, the young, smooth skin: boy or girl, he could not tell. All he saw in them was terror.

"I will not hurt you, Aelerin," he said softly, unsure whether to touch. Unsure whether that would bring the courser comfort or not.

"Why not? You do not like me," they said. Their lip was split, bruises around the eyes. How could he answer that? It was true, the courser made him uncomfortable. They were a person he did not understand, had never understood, never tried to.

"I do not know you," he said.

"And you do not want to," they said. In those words was the same tone he had heard once when the courser had spoken of the gullaime and of loneliness. He wondered how he could have been so blind.

"You are different," he said. "And I was raised in a way that did not expose me to different."

"Yet you befriend our gullaime." Was there betrayal in those big round eyes?

"Maybe," he said slowly, "there is only so much different I can take at a time." The courser continued to stare and Joron thought himself a fool. So much obvious pain and loneliness and he had chosen to look away. "Sometimes, Aelerin, I am wrong, and know I am wrong, and still I do not act because it is easier not to act." He moved a little closer. "But I am not the man who first came aboard *Tide Child*, and maybe I ignored you because it was easy for me to do so as deckkeeper. So many duties, ey? But here, in this place?" He shrugged, motioned to the small cell that contained them. "I am all you have, and you are all I have if we are to escape."

The courser stared at him.

"Escape?"

"Ey," he said, calm as he could. "Meas will be expecting this ship to meet her." He ripped a piece from the bottom of his shirt and moved to the back of the cell, finding a small pail of water and soaking the cloth in it. "Let me clean your wounds, Aelerin, and let us talk."

The courser continued to stare. Then they gave him a small nod and it was as if, for the first time, they realised they no longer had their hood over their face and they reached back. A sharp, panicked action.

"Wait," said Joron, "I will need to see your face to treat your bruises."

"It is not done," they said, the edge of fear in their voice. "It is an insult to the Mother."

"Well, Aelerin," said Joron quietly, "I assure you if there is a list of things that are 'not done' then losing your ship to a mutinous crew is probably more offensive to the Mother than me seeing your face, ey?" The courser stared more intently, and he thought he had lost them. Was it a foolish thing to say? Blasphemous to their cult, maybe? He knew so little. The coursers were so secretive. Then they nodded, closed their eyes and he approached, kneeling before them, trying not to block the weak light as he very gently began to clean the courser's face. Not only bruises there, but scuff marks. "They threw you about?" A nod. "What did they want from you?"

"Courses. Navigation."

"Dinyl cannot do that?" The courser shook their head.

"He can chart a course, but he cannot dream the winds, feel the storm's moods, no, he cannot do those things. And I do not think he charts a course well—*ow*."

"Sorry," he said, taking the cloth away, wringing it out before he set once more to cleaning wounds. "Why do you think Dinyl does not navigate well?"

"I have set the ship against a strong current, it will slow us considerably, Deckkeeper. And he did not seem to notice." Joron smiled.

"Brave of you."

"I am not brave. I am weak and I am frightened."

"You were in a room full of murderers who were beating you, probably threatening worse. Yet you had the forethought to slow the ship to help the Shipwife find us, even though you must know what they would do to you if they found out." He gently dabbed at a graze on their cheek. "You were chosen by Lucky Meas. She only chooses the brave."

"Meas will come for us," said the courser.

"She will," he said, though he, in that moment, was not as sure. The ocean was vast and *Tide Child* was small. Even going slow against a current, the odds of Meas coming across them, even when she realised what had happened, were vanishingly tiny. Still, the courser's faith in the shipwife was touching and he would not gainsay it. "But we must do all we can to help the shipwife when she comes." He moved back, placing the cloth in the small bucket to rinse it out. Then wanted to curse himself for spoiling their only drinking water.

"I do not mind drinking a bit of blood," said the courser. "Blood is part of our lives."

"Ey." Joron let out a quiet laugh. "You are right there." He went and sat close, but not too close, to the courser. "Did you notice any loyal crew?"

"They are all below, except Solemn Muffaz. They treat him most cruelly."

"He is strong, and he will weather it. He will consider it payment to the Hag for his crime, and he will be right."

The courser nodded. "He is always kind to me."

"What of the gullaime?"

"They have barricaded it in its room with the other one."

"It will hate that." Joron could not hide his amusement, and he was sure he heard similar in the courser's voice.

"It did not sound pleased." The levity fled. "They tried to force it to come on deck and it killed one of them."

"No better than they deserve," he said. The courser nodded.

"The rest of the crew," said Aelerin. "While I was there they brought their answer to Cwell."

"I have been in here all night?" he said, surprised that so much time had passed. The courser shook their head.

"No, their answer was a swift one. They did not need more than a couple of hours."

"And it was?"

"They serve the shipwife. Our shipwife." Joron let out the breath he had not realised he was holding. Felt a sudden sense of relief.

"I imagine Cwell did not like that?"

"She had their messenger beaten, then they held her over the side, so she could see the longthresh, and sent her back. Told them to reconsider."

"If the shipwife is coming I hope she hurries," said Joron. "Cwell strikes me as someone determined to get what she wants, and I do not think she will be patient."

# 24

# To Make Light in Darkness

They came next for Aelerin mid conversation. It was in the — morran? In the afternoon? The next day? The next week? There was no way to tell. Usually he would listen for the sound of the bells and the calls in response; Solemn Muffaz's sonorous voice tolling the hour of the watch: First watch, mid watch, middle watch, middle late watch, late watch, night watch, and on and on and round and round in the endless repetition of the sea. But under Cwell the bell no longer tolled, as if time had stopped when the shipwife's authority was taken from the ship.

His back hurt once more.

"Where is Anzir, Deckkeeper?" they had said, and in their voice was a tiny spark of hope. To Aelerin he knew Anzir must have appeared like a rock, this great immovable warrior. But even a rock was eventually reduced to sand by the sea. Pain deep within him.

"Dead, Aelerin. Sprackin killed her."

"But she was a warrior, and he is . . ."

"Cowardly, Aelerin," Joron had told them, and he realised that where there had been grief for the big, silent woman who had followed him around, now there was a deep anger at

Sprackin. "He struck her a cowardly blow from behind as she tried to warn me of the mutiny."

"I . . ."

"We will make him pay," and before Aelerin had asked the difficult question of "how" there was a commotion and the courser was whisked away, leaving Joron alone in the gloom once more, with sadness and dreams of vengeance his only company.

When Aelerin returned, they returned bloody and tear-stained. Once more Joron found himself playing hagshand, cleaning the courser's face. At first, they would not speak at all, but after gentle care and coaxing eventually words came from Aelerin's mouth, quiet as night waves on a long beach.

"I do not know how much longer I can hold back."

"What do you mean, Aelerin?"

"They do not know what I am doing, but I am sure they suspect me of something." They sniffed, wiped at tears and Joron noticed one of their hands was bunched tightly in a fist, as if they held something. "They threaten . . . they threaten . . ."

Joron put a hand on the courser's shoulder.

"You need not say. Women and men like that, they always threaten."

"Will the shipwife really come, Deckkeeper?"

"Yes," he said. To his own surprise he found that now he really did believe that. "She will. Somehow, she will." Aelerin nodded to herself. "What is in your hand, Aelerin?"

"I . . ." They looked down at their hand, almost guiltily. Then, slowly, the courser opened it. In their palm lay a small piece of parchment. "I . . . did not know whether to give it to you or not."

"Why?"

"It is from Dinyl." She held it out and Joron opened the note. Written in Dinyl's hand for sure, the words poorly formed as Joron had taken his writing hand. Just five words there but they made Joron's blood run cold: *I am coming for you.* He shuddered. Joron knew the sort of terrible pain one person could cause another, and knew how long such things could be made to last if a person had a mind to make them.

"Hag curse him, I should have taken his head not his hand."

"What does it say?"

"They threaten me too," he said. His hand shook a little, so he folded the note and put it in his pocket to give it something to do.

"It is strange, Deckkeeper. When they beat me it is not so bad as it is happening. It is the thinking of it I cannot stand. The thought of what might happen."

"Ey, so let us not think, Aelerin."

"How? How can I not think of their threats?"

"We must go to other places, Aelerin," said Joron.

"How?"

"Tell me your story. You know how I got here, I know nothing about you, or the coursers. I pride myself now on being able to spot a criminal, a violent person, and you strike me as none of these. How does someone like you end up on *Tide Child*?"

"It is not an exciting story, Deckkeeper."

"I will be the judge of that, Courser," said Joron.


How Aelerin came to the *Tide Child*

I was born one of five, fourth of those five, and my father said that was the luckiest number, for each of my sisters and brothers had a leg missing or an arm missing or a finger missing but, apart from a slight twist to my own leg, I was as near a perfect child as he had ever seen. Every laying night, when he would send out an older brother or sither, my mother and father would tell me how excited they were for me, how good it felt to lay with another and that if any of their children were likely to make it to the bothies and become Bern then it was I. But when they spoke of what happened on laying night, of the wild abandon and sharing your body with any other you meet, when my brother and sither came back and told stories of their laying, when they spoke of their hope to bring healthy children into the Hundred Isles, I did not feel the same excitement as them. I had no wish to share myself with another. I tried to explain this to my family but they would only become angry. My father would beat me and my mother would stand and watch, as if I deserved every bruise. Deckkeeper, I felt like I was as strange and alien to my family as a gullaime, and like all I was ever to be to them was a disappointment.

A year before I was of age for laying night I saw my first coursers, walking in a line through town. They were not all whole, not like you must be to be Bern or Kept. Some limped, some were missing fingers or arms, so being Berncast was surely no barrier to becoming one. As they passed it was as if silence followed them. All went quiet as they walked past in single file, heads bowed, hidden beneath robes so white I thought them sent by the godbird itself.

See, I was raised in a busy house where voices were always loud and shouting. I had never heard such quiet, Deckkeeper, it seemed like they were magical. So I asked about them, and my father had nothing but bad things to say. Called them witches, called them evil, performers of dark arts, neither man nor woman, a creature apart from good people. I remember those words, those exact words. "Neither man nor woman," and, "A creature apart from good people." And I could not help thinking that he spoke of me. And in the year that followed I searched for all I could about the coursers and it felt like the Maiden's hand guided me. They loved numbers, and charts, and pictures and quiet, and these were all things that I had taken to myself as comfort when my sithers and brothers had run to the arms of others.

Now, my father thought me some sort of hermit, cos I would take every moment I could to be alone and study what I could find on weather and currents and numbers. But that was not true. I did not for one moment long to be alone; in fact, my loneliness was as much a prison as this brig is. I simply longed for someone who would let me be as I wished to be. To this end, the coursers became my dream and I spoke of them so often that my father forbade talk of them. As my laying night drew closer, the more afeared I became, because it seemed my parents had begun to hate me for not being something they could understand. They had become cruel, as had my sithers and my brothers. All except the oldest, Fuller, who did not live at home any more and had taken up his job as a cobbler. Whenever he could he would bring me what he found about weather and the sea and navigation. Snippets taken from deck-childer who came into his shop. Sometimes he told me he would swap shoes for books to give to me, though my mother took the books away and sold them whenever she found them.

My father told me one day that he had been looking into coursers, and my heart leaped. Then he told me, with such a smile as I will never forget, that the coursers would only take those who had proven their commitment by staying untouched. That no courser could touch another woman nor man in passion and still expect the Mother to sing in their dreams. I wondered why he had suddenly gifted me this information. Then he sat and took my hand. He was gentle, like he had not been for years.

"After laying night, Aelerin, all this nonsense of yours will be forgot. You are the hope of us, most perfect of us. Likely to bear an unspoilt child, and your family will benefit from that, your sithers, your mother, your brothers, me." I did not answer, for I had no answer. "Now I know that you may be odd looking," he said, "but do not worry. I have spoken to the children of others, I have made sure you will not be lonely on laying night."

He had paid them, Deckkeeper. I choose to believe, still, that he was misguided, not malicious. I choose to believe he truly did not understand me, but nevertheless. He had offered a shiny coin to whoever lay with me, thinking that when the option of the coursers was removed from me, I would forget them. He could not understand that I saw the coursers as a place of refuge – they were not the cause of what he hated, they were simply a symptom of who I am.

On laying night, I begged my mother and father not to send me out. But they would hear nothing of it and threw me out of the tenement. A whole gang awaited me outside, male and female, for when you are strange those who are not mark you out, and cannot wait to visit their malice upon you. But they were drunk and I was not. And they were out for some fun. I was fighting to live, as I knew without the coursers I would surely take my own life, for I had none left there. So when they tried to take me, my ferocity took them by surprise.

I do not remember much of that night. I remember it mostly like a bad dream, the darkness full of fires, the air thick with the sweet scent of herbs thrown into those fires. The smoke which bent my thoughts in strange ways and filled the streets. Nightmare faces looming out of the dark, full of insane joy, laughing, shrieking, the sounds of passion. Coming across bodies twined together and moving rhythmically in alleys, doorways, by the docks. All the time I was running, running up the serpent road toward the courser's bothy. I got lost, somehow found myself in the lamyard, saw the gullaime in their spiked pens, heard them screeching and calling. I nearly tripped over a couple about the laying in the long grass. They swore at me and I ran on. Always running, it seemed I ran all night, and when I thought I could run no further, then I found it, the white door of the courser's bothy. I felt as if the Mother had guided me and I hammered on it, "Let me in! Let me in!" but the door did not open, and I believed that every moment I was about to grabbed from behind, dragged away by hands that wanted to earn my father's filthy coin.

But I was not. The door did open, and I thought my troubles over with. Here was the place I had dreamed of for so long. Here was a place that was quiet, and clean, so clean. White, everything whitewashed, and coursers walked everywhere, heads bowed. Undisturbed. Being who they were.

It seemed like another world, a paradise, compared to the

madness outside. Madness that I could still hear and I could not control myself. I spilled out my whole story to the courser who had met me at the gate. How thankful I was, how much I wished to be like them, how I had felt that, my whole life, this was where I should be. And the courser turned to me and said, "Become a courser? You? Some common Berncast? People like you do not become coursers."

My heart broke then. All this, for nothing. I must have been mistaken in what I saw, what I thought of them. But a single ray of light was provided. I thought then that maybe they remembered being like me, being an outsider, and that was why they did not turn me away, they took pity. Let me stay as a servant.

I found out exactly how hard it was keeping that place clean, keeping all those robes white. I did all the work they asked and when I had a moment I studied the books. I found out the lie behind them; there were many who were misformed and would usually be called Berncast, but all were the children of Bern. Hidden away, given a job and forbidden to talk of their lives before. After a year, I was made personal servant to a courser in training. They were not like me at all, they snuck out and proved what my father had said about a courser remaining untouched did not really matter if you were from the right family. But still, I found some friendship behind the white doors, among the lessers like myself, and even among some of the coursers. Many are truly committed to the mother, and the songs of the storm.

The courser I was servant to, Bralin, did not enjoy studying. When they realised I found pleasure in it they let me do their studying for them, and for the entire four years of their apprenticeship I had only joy. Bralin ignored me, went and enjoyed themselves while I did their work, learnt what they should.

It was to be my undoing.

Bralin passed for full courser, or rather I did, with flying colours. Among the best marks ever seen. He was sent to an important ship and I stayed in the courser's bothy, once more cleaning robes and floors. A month later Bralin returned in disgrace — he had almost run his ship into the rocks before it was out of sight of Bernshulme. When he was brought back it all came out. You would think that they would have hidden him out of sight, then moved me to a ship, maybe just a small ship. But I had, however unknowingly, embarrassed important people. The common Berncast, Deckkeeper, as you well know, are not meant to be capable or intelligent. We are meant to know our place.

And so that is why you find me here. On a ship of the dead. Telling you my story and wearing the robe of a true courser. This robe it is all I have wanted, it is my life's dream. However short that life may be.

When they finished their story, Joron stood. Unsure of what to say to the courser. He had wallowed in his own pity many times, but at least his youth had been one of joy.

"I have been a fool around you, Aelerin." He put out his hand to help the courser up. "You are as strong as any other on this ship. If you would have my friendship, I would give it." The courser looked up at him from where they sat. Then nodded, and took his arm, letting Joron lift them up.

"I am afraid, D'keeper," they said, "that our friendship may be a short one."

Joron was about to reply when he was interrupted by the opening of the brig door.

"Well, Deckkeeper," came Dinyl's voice from outside the cell, "I sent you warning, are you ready?"

"It seems you are right, Aelerin," said Joron, and the cell door opened.

# 25

# The Grim Business

"Are you ready?" whispered Dinyl. The weak glow of the wanelight gilded his face, turned his features into a monstrous landscape of gold and deep shadow.

"How can one ever be ready?"

"I did my best to prepare you." Dinyl held up a curnow, though he also had one on his hip.

"What?" Joron's confusion was absolute. Was this some trap? But why trap him?

"We do not have time for questions, Joron. Half of Cwell's crew are drunk or asleep, we must act." Joron stared at him, confusion making him mute. "Hag's tit's Joron," said Dinyl. "You know how canny Meas is. She saw this coming," he held up the stump of his wrist, "and saw this as the perfect way to put me amongst those she trusted least."

"You are on our side?"

"Of course," said Dinyl, "did you not read the note?"

"How can I trust you?"

"Mother's love, Joron, we do not have time for discussion." He glanced at the ceiling, and sighed. "I know that Aelerin has been slowing us and I have said nothing." He held out the curnow. "Now, will you take this and come?"

"You do not hate me then?"

"Well," said Dinyl, "I am not about to thank you for what you did, but I understand why you did it. Now come, before I am missed."

Joron took the curnow and it was as if a weight was lifted from his shoulders; the terror that had been in the back of his mind left, to be replaced by the familiar weight of a weapon in his hand. He would no longer die slowly, under a blade or heated rod. He may well die, but it would be with a curnow in his hand, fighting for his shipwife. All things considered, it was how he would choose to go.

"Thank you," he said. And it was as if the possibility of action chased away the pain that had been throbbing within the wound on his back.

"It is my duty," said Dinyl. Joron smiled wearily.

"Aelerin, stay behind us," he said. "If anything happens to us, claim we forced you to come and they will most likely keep you alive. You are useful to them." The courser nodded.

Dinyl led them forward and up the ladder to the underdeck. The deckholder could be seen by Cwell's mutinous crew and they would think nothing of it. Joron and Aelerin followed him through the darkness of the ship. In the dim light the curnow at Dinyl's hip glinted, and the white of his bone knife was the beacon that guided them.

"We must go through the main underdeck now, most will be sleeping," said Dinyl. "Then from there down into the hold to free our people."

"Ey," said Joron. Then he stopped. "No. One of us most go to the armoury and bring weapons. When we free the crew we will be found out — they will not be quiet enough for secrecy and if they are not armed then they stand little chance."

Dinyl stared at him in the dim light. "I will go to the armoury," he said. "If I go alone to free the crew from the hold they may tear me to ribbons before I get time to explain. You they will accept. So it must be this way."

"Ey," said Joron. "I suppose it must."

"Do you still not trust me, Joron?" There was pain in Dinyl's face.

"Go and get us some weapons." He put out a hand and Dinyl clasped it with his good hand. They shared a smile that Joron had thought was lost to him forever.

"When we meet again I will have weapons for as many as I can carry," said Dinyl. "There will be three or four deckchilder in the armoury but I am sure they will let me take what I wish. I have any number of good excuses prepared." He reached behind him and produced a ring of keys,. holding the ring in his mouth while using his good hand to remove one of the keys. "This is for the lock on the hold," he said, then he reached behind himself and replaced the keys, hand coming back with his bone knife. "This is in case you need it, for quiet work."

"Thank you, Dinyl," he said, and they made their way onwards through the underdeck. A few snoring bodies were in the hammocks and the smell of strong alcohol filled the air, as if it had seeped into the bones of the ship. Anger grew within Joron, a fury that he was in more danger of falling over some loose bit of rubbish and breaking his head on the floor than he was from running into a mutineer. Through the dark underdeck, to the hatch that led down to the hold and armoury. Rung by rung down the ladder into the pitch dark. There they split up – Dinyl heading one way, down toward the armoury; Joron and Aelerin toward the hold, where a wanelight glowed, showing him the way.

"Who is there?"

Joron froze. He recognised the voice – Coblin, one of Cwell's mutineers, stood before the door to the hold. Joron put his sleeve across his mouth and walked forward, muffling his speech.

"It is I, it is Gurant," he said, using another mutineer's name as he walked closer.

"Gurant? You sound terrible. Have you been at—"

But Joron would never find out what Coblin thought Gurant

had been at. Now within reach of the woman, his knife flashed out, finding her throat and silencing her forever. Then he was at the door.

"Hoy there," he said, as loudly, as he dared. "Hoy there, who listens?"

"Karring," came the reply.

"Well, Karring, wake those who sleep. This is your deck-keeper, and I have come to free you."

"Deckkeeper!" cried Karring, and Joron nearly jumped out of his skin.

"Quiet yourself, deckchild," he said, "we'll not want Cwell warned we are coming. Now wake the crew, I am opening the door."

He found the crew within. The hold ran almost the entire length of the ship, the thin corridor Joron stood in running down the side of it. Above was the large, double doored trap-doors that could be opened, a similar pair on the maindeck, allowing the hoisting in and out of goods. Over a hundred and fifty women and men were in there, trying to find a place to sleep amid bales and barrels and spars, wingcloth and staves. The place stank of too many bodies confined without fresh air.

"We did not give in, Deckkeeper," said Barlay as Joron stepped into the hold, her face badly bruised. "And when we get up on deck I have a special fate in line for traitors, especially the d'older."

"The deckholder is why I am here, Barlay," he said. "Dinyl is no traitor. He did Meas's work, getting in among the mutineers for she saw this coming. It was him who freed me." Behind her Berhof stood, his usually jovial face dark.

"Then why did he not stop them? Or warn us?" he said.

"I did not have time." Dinyl squeezed in through the door behind Joron with his arms full of curnows. "By the time Cwell had told me what she was doing the mutiny was well under way. All I could do was wait for my moment. Now, the armoury door is open but a few of Cwell's people are in there. We are bound to be heard, so must use these weapons to hold off any mutineers while the rest of you arm yourselves. Then we will take our ship back, ey?"

"Ey," said Barlay, and she took a curnow from him, passed it to Berhof before taking another and turning to Joron. "Where is Anzir? We could do with her arm."

"Dead stabbed in the back by Sprackin," said Joron and from the look that crossed Barlay's face he knew he should have been kinder, that the two women had been closer than he had thought.

"That will be avenged then," said Barlay, and she held up her curnow. "I will see to it."

"There are four in the armoury guard room, playing cards," said Dinyl. "We must take them quickly and quietly." Barlay touched the edge of her blade.

"I can do that," she said. "Berhof, Gulbry, Namd . . ."

"I would come too," said Fogle, the seakeep. Her face was covered in cuts and purplish bruises. "Cwell held me over the side and had me stare into the faces of the beakwyrms, would have fed me to them today. I would spill some blood for that."

"Ey," said Barlay. "I can well understand a need for vengeance."

"The deckholder will lead you," said Joron, but the noise in the hold was rising as the prospect of action grew. "Quiet!" he hissed, "or we will lose the ship again before we even have chance to take it. The mutineers will think nothing of Dinyl approaching, so be silent behind him. If you can kill them without the rest of Cwell's crew becoming aware then our bloody job will be all the easier."

They moved through the dark lower decks of the ships. If Meas was still in charge he knew there would have been more crew down here, but Cwell did not run a tight ship like Meas. Her authority came from giving the crew what they wanted, even when that was not what was best for the ship. Joron understood that now, in the same way every crew member that now moved silently with him through the belly of the ship understood. The ship was a machine, discipline the oil that allowed it to run. The anger within Joron burned hot. Anger that Cwell would try and take this ship from Meas, from him, from the women and men who had worked so hard to make *Tide Child* a ship as slick as any in the fleet. Anger that Cwell now put in danger something he had not understood at first, the idea of peace in the Scattered Archipelago – but it was something he now held dear to him. More dear to him, though, were these people; Farys, Barlay, Aelerin, Berhof of the seaguard who brought up their rear, even the gullaime. He was sure the anger that he felt radiating from the crew around him was that same anger.

Ahead, Dinyl stopped at the door to the armoury. Held up his fist and all became silence.

Life paused.

Dinyl looked to him, for the order.

Joron waited. Anger welling. Hatred.

"Wait," he whispered.

"What?" said Dinyl.

"I have been thinking like an angry man, not an officer." He turned, found Berhof and motioned him down toward him. "Berhof, take three of our strongest and go up the hatch of the underdeck. Hold that hatch. We have greater numbers, but if we are trapped here in a corridor it becomes meaningless. Cwell could finish us with crossbows. You must hold the way out."

Berhof nodded. "Aye, Deckkeeper," he said. "We'll hold it, no fear of that. I've no wish to die aboard a ship."

"Go, then, Berhof, take Barlay." He nodded and called out two more names, and the four of them pushed their way through the sweaty throng of deckchilder behind Joron. He watched, then waited quietly, though not silently, not really – such a large group of women and men could not be truly silent. He heard breathing, the brush of cloth on skin. The tap of feet as people moved their weight from one foot to the other. Over that, laughter from behind the door to the armoury.

Then he used his hand to signal for everyone to get as low

as they could. Namd and Fogle, with the last of the curnows Dinyl had brought, flattened themselves on either side of the door. Then Joron looked to Dinyl and nodded at him.

The deckholder opened the door.

"Have you come for more weapons, D'older?" There was no mistaking the sarcasm in the speaker's voice when Dinyl's rank was said, and Joron was sure it was Invar, one of Coughlin's men.

"Ey, Invar, I have."

In the dim glow of the wanelights Joron could make out Dinyl stood before the man, and three other deckchilder sat around a table. Behind them, the banded door of the armoury itself. Joron willed them not to look past Dinyl at the open doorway.

"A one-handed man like you, Dinyl, should be making gloves, not on a ship of war." Laughter. "What do you need all these blades for anyway?"

"What does a deckchild usually need a blade for?" said Dinyl, and his voice remained jocular as he unhooked the curnow at his waist. "Killing, of course." He ran the blade through Invar's chest. Before the other three could react Namd and Fogle ran into the small room. Blades rose and fell and the walls were covered with blood the way the base of the mainspine was spattered with paint. A roar went up from those behind them. Joron wanted to scream at them for quiet but knew it was no use. That bird had flown. He heard a shout from above.

"The prisoners are out! The prisoners are out!" On deck the bell started ringing, fast, strident and urgent.

"Weapons!" shouted Joron. "They will be on us quickly and those at the rear are not armed!" Inwardly he cursed himself, why had he not thought of this? If Barlay and Berhof did not hold the hatch above those at the rear would be first to fall. He looked around for Aelerin — he had feared they would be at the rear, easy prey to Cwell's raiders, but found the Courser in the thick of the scrum. Armfuls of curnows and wyrmpikes were being passed along. Joron pushed his way through the crowd to join those at the rear just as the first blades were being handed out among them.

Excitement in the air.

He heard voices raised in anger.

"Come!" shouted Joron to those around him. "Berhof and Barlay will need us on the underdeck." Then he was pushing through the tight corridors of the hold. Through the deck-childer. Up the ladder, all the time the sound of fighting getting louder where Berhof, Barlay, Jant and Fellin held the trapdoor. As Joron scaled the ladder to join them, going from the almost dark of the lower underdeck to the almost dark of the under-deck, he marvelled at Barlay and Berhof. Not all the mutineers were here, they had not had long enough to organise, but there were ten or more. Fellin, one of their own, was down, sat on the deck, hand around his middle, blood on the floor. And Barlay, Berhof and Gulbry were holding off the rest of them – though it was mostly Barlay and Berhof. Both held keyshan-pikes, the largest and heaviest of the many pikes held on a boneship, once used to hook the bodies of dead arakeesians, now mostly employed to push the ship away from the dock.

Barlay and the seaguard were swinging the huge and heavy pikes around themselves, creating space for Joron to climb into, helped up by Gulbry. As Barlay swung the gaff she roared, screamed at the mutineers around her to stop being cowards, while in counterpoint Berhof was silent. A woman rushed forward, brandishing a hand axe and Barlay's gaff came around, catching her in the midriff and spilling her entrails onto the deck – she screamed but it had no effect on Barlay who span the gaff again, shouting out her challenges.

The loyalists of Meas's crew boiled up through the trapdoor. Someone among Cwell's crew was screaming for bows to be brought, but the bows were kept in the armoury. Now they were in the hands of Joron's people, and as more of them appeared through the trapdoor Joron organised those armed with bows and crossbows into a line behind Barlay and Berhof.

The archers strung their weapons, and as women and men started to come down the steps from above arrows and bolts drove them back. Those without bows stood waiting, blades in hands. Joron let loose a roar.

"Into them!"

And those few of Cwell's rebels left on the underdeck could not stand against the ferocity of *Tide Child's* rightful crew. Just like the crew, that ferocity had been bottled up too long, and just like the crew it was thirsting for blood.

"The underdeck is ours!" shouted Joron, lofting his curnow and smashing the point into the overbones. "Now let us take back the slate!" Then they were running, Joron leading them, up and out of the underdeck and into the pale light of Skearith's Blind Eye. Before him, maybe thirty, maybe forty women and men, poorly armed, but arranged in a line by Cwell, her harsh voice shouting commands.

"Hold! Hold or die!"

But they could not hold against Barlay and her keyshanpike when she saw Sprackin among Cwell's troops. She roared, charged their line swinging the gaff, and the line broke before her. One of Coughlin's seaguard, probably the strongest of Cwell's rebels, tried to block a swing of Barlay's weapon and she nearly cut him in two. Another of the renegade seaguard tried to bring a curnow down on her and Berhof stepped in, running his pike through the man. Shouting, "Traitor!" and heaving on the pike, sending the attacker over the rail and into the sea. Cwell's mutineer's discipline fell apart and the fighting became vicious, little knots of deckchilder against deckchilder.

Joron swung about him with his curnow, no elegant straightsword work for him, and that thanks to Cwell. His world a nightmarish mix of faces. He swung at those he knew were with Cwell. He helped those he knew were on his side and avoided any he was unsure about. His fear of Cwell had gone. Where was she? Anger burning, a blade nicked his calf and he swung back, feeling the jarring in his wrist as his curnow hit bone. Where was she? His blade buried itself deep in another's gut.

Where was she?

Sudden quiet. Women and men standing about, confusion on their faces, blood on their hands.

Was it over?

Corpses on the deck.

He hoped it was over.

Was it over?

Where was she?

Not over.

Many lay dead. More wounded.

Cwell, still alive and bleeding from her face. She had retreated with the last of her mutineers. Joron thought them between fifteen and twenty. They had a line across the rump of the ship. Had pulled wingcloth and spars into a barricade. It could not save them. Joron knew it. They must know it too. But it would provide them some cover, stop Barlay and Berhof getting near enough to use their vicious weapons as easily.

Some of Cwell's people had bows. Slowly, as they got their breath back, *Tide Child's* crew were approaching the rump. Members of Cwell's group were leaning on their weapons as they too got their breath back. He saw Cwell's mutineers ready themselves. Knew every woman and man among his crew was gathering for the final push. He marked Cwell for himself. Looked about. Farys with him. Barlay with him. Dinyl with him. Berhof with him. The crew with him.

Cwell would die here. On his curnow.

He wanted that.

There would be a cost.

Wanted her dead.

At any cost?

Dead.

So many dead.

Deep breath.

Lower the curnow.

*You are an officer, Joron Twiner.* He heard it as if Meas was here, talking to him. Knew he had duty to his ship. They barely had enough hands as it was, every deckchild lost here would be sorely felt. And in Bernshulme he had given his word to Cahanny. Hag curse this life, he was no deckchilder who could take his vengeance as he wished. He really was an officer and bound by duty.

Joron walked up the slate to stand by the mainspine. Knowing himself an easy target should any of Cwell's archers decide to loose on him.

"Cwell!" he shouted. "Cwell, you have lost. *Tide Child* is mine once more. You cannot win and you know it. But there need not be any more death tonight."

"Why put it off?" Cwell shouted back. "At least this way I get a crack at you, and the traitor behind you, before I die." He looked over his shoulder and saw Dinyl, his face spattered with blood, a curnow in his one hand.

Joron hated Cwell. He had hated her since the moment he came aboard, and he had no doubt that she felt the same about him. But *Tide Child* needed crew, needed as many as possible. Corpses covered the deck. His need to get up there to her, to release his anger among the mutineers, was great. But he was not a free man, he served the ship. He served Meas. He was her officer and he had a duty to her before himself. He breathed in. Let go of the anger.

"What if I allow you to live?"

"Why would you do that?" said Cwell, and laughed.

"For the ship." He turned and used his curnow to cut Solemn Muffaz down from where he was tied to the spine. He expected, at any moment, to feel the searing agony of an arrow punching through him, to hear the whistle of the fletching cutting through the air. He did not. The only sound the groan from Solemn Muffaz as he slumped to the bloody deck. The only pain the deckmother's.

"Death is always the punishment for a mutineer," said Cwell. "Only the shipwife can defer it."

"True," said Joron, turning back to her. "But I give my word I will vouch for you, and tell her that, in the end, you chose to put down your weapons rather than kill more of her crew. I cannot promise she will let you live. As you say, it is her choice. But she may choose to let you off on an island or some such."

Silence.

Waiting.

Then Cwell spoke, very softly.

"That is death in all but name."

"It is your choice," said Joron.

The sound of the sea lapping against the hull. The chime of metal in the rigging. The tap of rope against wingcloth. The creak of the hull's bones.

"Put your weapons down," said Cwell and threw her curnow to the slate. "We are lost. Any hope is better than no hope at all."

"No!" This a roar from Barlay. "Many died, and died fighting, and that I understand. But Sprackin fair murdered Anzir, stabbed her in the back. And for that I claim blood as my right as her shipfriend."

Silence.

Waiting.

Then Joron spoke, very softly.

"I can order Barlay to stand down, Cwell," said Joron. "But I see Sprackin in among you. He took Barlay's lover from behind, no honest blow, and I see now he is the only one not bloodied from the fight." Cwell turned and looked at the man who, indeed, was not touched by a drop of blood. "What happens next is up to you."

Cwell stared at Joron, a smile on her face, and he felt he almost understood her then – she was fierce, and orders and discipline made no sense to her. But vengeance, that she understood.

"I have no time for cowards, Deckkeeper," she said, and for the first time he heard no sneer when she used his rank. She turned, grabbed Sprackin by the scruff of his neck and though he screamed for mercy she ignored him. Marched him forcibly forward and threw him over the barricade toward Barlay. Sprackin landed on his back, tried to rise. Barlay stopped him, stamping down with a meaty leg and smashing him to the deck. Then she raised her keyshanpike and silenced the screaming man, driving the blade through his chest.

"Good riddance," she said.

"Ey," said Joron. "Now bind the rest of them, lock them in the hold. And Deckholder . . ."

"Ey?" said Dinyl.

"Be good enough to make sure they are well guarded."

# 26

# A Ship as Fleet as Could Be

Joron felt despair: once the adrenalin had drained away, once the mutineers were locked below, once he was back on the rump of the ship. To see *Tide Child* in such disarray felt like he had travelled backwards through time and once more become the man he had been so long ago. This was his fault. Had he paid more attention, had he thought more, had he been more attentive then he would have stopped this happening. But he had not. He had let Meas down. Let the crew down. Let the ship down.

A hand on his back, a brief brush, the smallest breeze.

"It is not your fault, Joron."

He turned to find Dinyl, stood behind him at a respectful distance, the touch gone and his arms behind his back.

"I am Deckkeeper, Dinyl. It was my job to be aware and—"

"You were hurt, Joron. Sorely hurt, and then sorely tried. Meas does not expect miracles from us . . ."

"She deserves them."

"Well," he smiled, "she definitely believes that, but we cannot undo what is, Joron. We must work with what we have."

Joron took a deep breath. Surveyed the ship before him: the blood, the bodies, the badly stowed rigging, the gallowbows whose beautiful scrimshaw had been graffitied over by the mutineers, the bottles lazily rolling across the deck.

"Right, you slatelayers," he tried to roar, his voice betrayed him. But still, he was heard. "I'll not have the decks in this state for when we meet the shipwife, get you to work. Clean up the rubbish, swab the blood away. I'll have no sign of Cwell and her scum left on my ship." He glanced into the sky, at scudding clouds kissed bright red as Skearith's Eye broke the horizon. "Bring me the courser and bring me the gullaime. Set me full wings; we have a rendezvous with the shipwife and I'll be no later than I must be!" And immediately all was action, no complaint, no raised voices. There were smiles and activity and women and men doing as he ordered. He saw Farys collecting weapons and taking them down to the armoury, saw Karring bringing up mops and buckets and behind him came Aelerin, who had remained below while the fighting took place, as was proper for a courser. And behind Aelerin came the gullaime, yarking and snapping at the windshorn who followed meekly behind it.

"Deckkeeper," said Aelerin, "you wanted me?"

"Ey, Courser," he said and there was none of the curiosity, none of the discomfort he had felt around them before. "I require your expertise and I require it quick. Do you know where we are?"

"Not exactly, D'keeper." Was there enthusiasm, buried deep in their quiet voice? "But I have a good idea."

"And how long have we been under the sway of the mutineers?"

"Six days, D'keeper."

"So long," he said. "I did not know." A pain ran through him, a twinge from his back that caused an involuntary shudder and sweat to start from his forehead. It felt as though *Tide Child* lurched beneath him, but the sky continued to change slowly from red to pink and the black wings of the ship remained slack and windless.

"D'keeper?" said Aelerin, and he felt Dinyl stand closer, take his arm. He shrugged him off.

"Not in front of the crew, D'older," he said under his breath. Dinyl nodded, stood away and it was as if the coldest of winds wrapped themselves about him. "I am fine, Aelerin. How long for us to reach Meas? How late will we be if the winds are good?"

"Seven days at best, Deckkeeper," they said, "but I confess I dream only slight winds for us, and little hope of anything else."

Joron nodded, felt the short hairs on the back of his neck beneath the thick tangles of his hair stand up, as if caressed by an icy breeze.

"Gullaime," he said.

"Jo-ron Twin-er." That slow, door-opening creak of a voice. Then the gullaime span on the spot and snapped its beak at the windshorn who followed it, keeping so low to the deck as to be almost flat. "Not want! Not want!" The world felt as though it spun around Joron, took on pastel colours and he took a step — one, two — so he could lean against the rearspine. "Joron Twiner?" said the gullaime softly. It took a step toward him. He held up a hand.

"I am well," he said, but he was not well and he knew it. "Just tell me, how long can you keep us flying without hurting yourself?"

"Long on long," it said, the noise of the words strident and loud, its head tilting from side to side as it spoke. It repeated, more quietly, "Long on long."

"Good," said Joron. "We must head toward the shipwife." Was a storm coming? Was the world becoming darker? "We must meet her, she . . . She may need us." A wave, a black wave that washed over the ship, blocking out the light, and when it passed and light returned he was on his knees.

"Joron," said Dinyl, then he was shouting: "Farys! Barlay! Help me with the deckkeeper, call Garriya!"

Joron grabbed Dinyl's arm. "Keep *Tide Child* on course." Each word tore at his throat, his back burned, the sores on the tops of his arms itched. "Do not use all the gullaime has."

"I hear your orders," said Dinyl.

"Not orders," said Joron, the darkness closing in. "A request of my friend," he said. Then he knew nothing else.

"Caller?"

To move beneath the sea.

He dreamed unmoving beneath the sea.

Dreamed of a desperate want to glide through the water. Of frustration. Of being bound. He tried to fight, to punch his way free, to chew his way free, to escape the darkness which held him so tightly. Bound him so tightly. If sleep was the ocean he was drowning as surely as any deckchilder lost overboard in a storm.

"Caller!" A sharp sting against his cheek and the darkness receded, washed away like the tide down a beach, like water through pebbles. "Don't you run from me, Caller," said the voice. "I said events repeat themselves. Warned that you would find yourself here again. You have work to do, Caller, no running away for you." The claustrophobia receded, the sound of waves washing against a beach became the sound of his breath, wheezing in and out of burning lungs.

"Garriya. . ." the name creeping from his mouth.

"Aye, that is me." She mumbled to herself as she stared into his face, lifted his eyelids. "I have medicine for you to drink. All those fools and their foolishness opened the wound in your back again. All my good work undone. And you with so much work to do."

"How long?" So thirsty, the words a light breeze.

"Two, three days maybe? The ship moves, your windtalker squats on the deck day and night, bells ring and disturb my sleep." She moved away, shuffling across the white of the floor and only then he realised he was in Meas's cabin. Panic seized him and he tried to move. But Garriya was quick across the floor, her old, gnarled hands pushing him back onto the hard bed.

"No, this is Meas's . . ."

"Hush yourself, boy." She patted his cheek. "I needed the room to work and if you think she would mind then I reckon you do not understand the woman at all." Garriya stared down into his face. "She's a practical one, aye?" He nodded. "She needs you, Joron Twiner, and so you will lie back and drink this." She held up the cup and then leaned in close to him. "And I have other medicines for you, Caller, for I have seen the marks on your skin." Shame burned within him. "I cannot stop the keyshan's rot, boy; none can, nor its madness. But I can slow it."

He nodded. "Tell no one." The words burned hot in his mouth, brought tears to his eyes. "They will never trust an officer with the rot, will start to question every order I give if they know."

Garriya stared into his eyes, her face a road map of age, her eyes almost buried within the weathered folds of her face.

"Do not underestimate them," she said.

He grabbed her, his hand around her arm. It felt as thin and delicate as a bird's wing.

"Tell no one."

"As you wish, Deckkeeper," she said. "Now drink this and rest."

And he did, and he did.

When he awoke it was from a sleep so deep it had been dreamless, a loss of his entire consciousness to the deepest depths; and if he had seen the Hag, or drifted in that massive and powerful dream body, as he had done in dreams before, he had no memory of it. Neither did he have any memory of being moved to his own cabin, which had been whitewashed like the shipwife's, the bowpeek propped open so he could see the grey water that *Tide Child* flew through. He ached, but it was not the burning ache of infection and when he moved he did not feel as if his back may rip open at any point. Even the sores on the tops of his arms seemed to itch a little less.

He wore a white shirt.

It was rare to see white clothes on a ship where every

garment, no matter how colourful, seemed to exist on a trajectory toward the same grey as the sea. But his shirt was as white as the highest cloud on the warmest day – and just as soft. He slid his legs from the hammock, took a moment to test them, see how much of his strength had returned, and when he was sure they would take his weight, he stood. Groaned. Took a step.

The door to his cabin opened and Garriya stood there. Behind her in the gloom of the underdeck stood Farys and another deckchild, Karring.

"Up?" said Garriya. "About time." He saw Farys's eyes widen at the way the old woman spoke to him. "Well, will you laze about here or go check on your ship?"

"Yes," he said. "I mean yes, I must check on the ship."

"Your jacket, D'keeper," said Farys, and she slipped into the cabin, presenting Joron with his blue uniform jacket, pressed and scrubbed and sewn with new feathers that caught the light. She slipped it onto Joron, waiting patiently as her deckkeeper hissed, feeling twinges in his back as he stretched to get his arms into the sleeves.

"You're not good as new, Caller, so remember that," said Garriya. "But you'll heal now if you don't do anything foolish."

"I will try," he said. He looked around him in the bright white cabin, past the cabin door the gloomy underdeck, lit by flickering wanelights. He felt that something was missing. He touched his hip, the space where his sword had been, but it was not that. That was an annoyance right enough, a thing to be avenged. This was different, a gap within him. A space beside him where something was missing. "Anzir," he said to himself, and on saying it knew it was true. They had never really spoken much, never really shared anything of themselves. But she had always been there, like an arm, or a leg. Something ever present, but which you did not think about until you needed to use it. He coughed to clear the painful lump in his throat. "Farys," he said, "thank you for bringing my jacket, but I will also need my boots." Farys nodded. "And my trousers," he added with a small smile that seemed to take as much energy from him as standing had.

He made his way through the ship full of trepidation. How would he be received? He had shown weakness, made mistakes that had nearly lost the ship to mutineers, and had left loyal deckchilder dead or wounded. Then he had betrayed them all by letting Cwell live.

As he walked, with each difficult step, he thought of how he had proved Cwell right. He was no officer. He was simply a fisher's boy, out of his depth on the deck of a fleet ship. Ill and weak. A man who had failed. What would Meas be thinking now? As she waited, her ship not where it should be? Her running out of stores, cursing her deckkeeper for failing her?

Out of the gloom, and onto the slate.

"Officer on deck!"

The words rang out and all action stopped. No scrubbing, no fixing, no painting, no oiling. Every face on the slate turned to him. What shame he felt. Dinyl, who had called out those words, was stood on the rump with Aelerin. Solemn Muffaz before them, Barlay at the steering oar. Could Dinyl know what a mockery it felt like to hear those words? Did he do it in purpose?

Joron took a step forward. The topwings flapped and chains jingled, but all else was silence. Another step forward. The deckchilder to either side of him stood, rope axes in their hands. They brought their arms across their chest in salute.

"D'keeper," they said, heads bowed. And as he walked down the length of the ship their words and actions were echoed. Some avoided his eye. Some looked shy. Some smiled. Some looked proud and when he came to the rump Dinyl moved to one side.

"I have been minding your place, Deckkeeper Twiner," he said. "I am right glad you are back. The ship is yours once more."

He looked down the deck. Knew what Dinyl said was right.

This crew – oh, not as many as there had been, barely enough to work the ship. But, Mother bless them all, they really were his. He remembered how he had sworn once that he would take back command of this ship from Meas. Remembered the sand burning and cutting his feet. Remembered the shame he felt at having his command taken away. And as he stood there on the rump between Dinyl and Aelerin, he knew what Dinyl said was true. The mutiny, his wounds, these had not cost him respect – instead they had built him up. This crew would follow him. He was not sure when it had happened but he had become, in their eyes, a truly worthy officer, and though he searched for them, there were no sly looks, no sneers.

"Thank you, Deckholder," he said, and turned to the women and men on deck. "Well, what are you standing around for? I'll have no slatelayers on my deck. The shipwife is expecting us. Set all the wings, make all speed."

His words were met with a roar of approval and the crew sprang to their job. Black wings fell to catch the wind, the gullaime was called from below and it sprang onto the deck, yarking and calling and spitting at the windshorn that followed it. With the gullaime came more wind and a sense of purpose. Black Orris fluttered down to perch on Joron's shoulder.

"Arse!" called the bird and Joron found himself stifling a laugh as joy bubbled up within him and *Tide Child* pushed through the ocean, his beak cutting the waves as if he had found new life and new purpose.

# 27

# Reunion

The winds were, in the end, good to *Tide Child*. The Eaststorm was kinder than Aelerin had dreamed. Nine beakwyrms rode the wake and the ship pointed his beak forward, the seas parting before him. Joron stood on the rump, in his mind he saw their place on the ocean, and he knew from his conversations with Aelerin that they were late for meeting Meas by eight days. Despite the kindness of the winds he was tempted to ask the gullaime to bring even more, to push the ship harder. Once he may have done, foolishly worrying what Meas would think. But not now. Their gullaime was strong but it was not inexhaustible, and who knew when they would need it? Or when they would next set foot on land for the gullaime to visit a windspire? Not only that, but the stronger the wind the harder the ship was to handle and he was sore underhanded. What if he wore out the crew handling the ship under the gullaime's wind and then a storm hit?

No, though the itch not to let Meas down was worse than the itch from the sores on his arms, he knew he must trust her to look after herself. And if anyone could look after themselves it was his shipwife. He would bring her the ship and he would make sure that the ship he handed her was as ready for whatever she may need it for as it was possible to make it. She may feign anger at lateness, but she would rather have a strong ship than a timely one. So he stood on the rump and he pretended he did not feel, in every bone of his body, that he should be pushing harder and faster.

The crew felt his need. And Joron knew that. Solemn Muffaz had come back too quickly from the hagbower, his back so badly lashed he could not wear clothes and the mass of red, lacerated flesh was on show for all to see. Aelerin was constantly revising their routes, desperate to find some quicker way through the shoals and currents and islands. Dinyl was that bit sharper with those he did not think jumped to their tasks as quickly as they should. Every member of the crew worked that little harder, moved that little quicker and Joron wanted to say "No! Save yourselves for when it matters," and yet he could not. He could not steal this from them. They worked for her and they worked for him and he could not deny them that.

"We make good speed, ey, Deckkeeper?" said Dinyl.

"Ey, we do," said Joron. He felt a hand on his back. The briefest of touches.

"We can do no better," said Dinyl, quietly.

"I know. And tomorrow we should arrive at our rendezvous."

As the ranking officer on the deck of Tide Child Joron could not say, "I hope she is there." But it was what he thought.

Morran was yet to break as Tide Child arrived at his rendezvous in a huge and placid sea lake. A glass-flat expanse of water between four islands, where the placing of the land conspired to create a mere, a great body of calm water. The ship creaked and groaned as he was brought to a stop, the staystone dropped with a splash loud enough that the skeers on the far islands rose into the air, cawing and croaking in complaint at this loud intruder to their world.

The sea mere was empty of any other vessels.

"Topboys!" shouted Joron. "Tell of the sea!"

"Empty, D'keeper," came the reply. Joron took a deep breath. What now? Explore the sea around the islands? Or wait?

He decided to wait.

Meas would surely appear. In sea time nine days was not a great deal of time to be late by. A lost spar, an unexpected calm or any one of the many misfortunes that could fall upon a ship could delay a vessel by far more than nine days.

So he would wait. He could do nothing else.

And they did. The waiting was hard. Skearith's Eye crept across the sky and dipped beneath the skyline. Nothing changed. No wings breached the horizon. Joron found work for his crew, sent them rowing to the islands in the flukeboat to find water and food, set them to fishing. On the second day of waking, an eyefish rose from the water. A vast roundness, almost as big as *Tide Child*, and covered in white scales. Like Skearith's Blind Eye it glowed, its many diaphanous fins and streamers floating in the air as if in water and Joron heard echoes of the windspire song. The gullaime appeared on deck, hopping over to join Joron on the rump to stare at the eyefish. The windtalker seemed hypnotised and from its mouth fell a quiet, mournful song. Joron heard talk of hunting it from the deck, of the price its oil could bring, but he clamped down hard on that. An eyefish hunt was a hard thing, the creature able to spit burning oil, and many would die. With so many of the crew dead and the mutineers locked in the hold he needed every one of his loyal deckchilder. Besides, he had no appetite for the death of the creature. He would fill his stomach on its beauty, and he quieted the crew's dreams of filling their pockets with its bounty. The song of the gullaime died away and the eyefish submerged once more, vanishing beneath the waters of the mere to be on its way to wherever eyefish went. Joron silently wished it well.

"A good omen," said Solemn Muffaz, "to see an eyefish. That's what my old shipwife always said."

"And a shipwife is always right on their deck," said Joron, "so a good omen it will be." He turned to the deck and raised his voice. "Do you hear, my girls and boys? Solemn Muffaz tells me an eyefish is a good omen, and for the crew who does not hunt it? How much more blessed must they be? I reckon the Mother smiles on us and we'll see the shipwife any day."

But Skearith's Eye crept across the sky and dipped beneath the skyline and they did not see the shipwife, nor on the next day or the next. Joron felt he was running out of ways to keep his crew occupied. He dreaded hearing from his underdeck officers that questions were starting, of when the ship should move on, and where it should look for the shipwife next.

"Ship rising!"

Before the words were fully out of the topboy's mouth Joron was up the spine. When had his feet become so much surer on the ropes? Oh, he was no Meas, never that. But he no longer fretted that his boots would slip with every step as he scaled the spine. In the topboy's nest he found Karring, pointing in the gap between two flat islands.

"Over there, Deckkeeper," Joron wished he had Meas's nearglass, so much more powerful than the one he had. But he did not and must make the best of what he had, raising the nearglass to his eye, scanning the line between sea and sky.

"I do not . . . Wait, yes. There. A spine without doubt. And white wings." He felt cold. That was not Meas, that was a fleet ship.

Was *Tide Child* hunted now? Was that why Meas had not arrived? Was she caught? Oh, indecision was the Maiden's child. What to do? He watched through the grubby circle of the nearglass. The spines growing as the ship came over the horizon. A two-ribber, a few corpselights floating above, though he could not make out colours. What would Meas do?

Wait.

Something else in the circle of the nearglass. Smaller.

A flukeboat.

Wings up, running from the two-ribber but being reeled in as he watched. Hag curse this nearglass, the filth at the edges had hidden the smaller boat from him, and though he could not tell, for sure, in his gut he knew that it was Meas.

"Give me all the wings!" he shouted down to the deck. Immediately all was action and bustle and speed. Joron put the nearglass back to his eye. Hundred Isles flags on the two-ribber. He did not recognise the ship. He could not make out those in the flukeboat. "Clear for action!" But you could never be too prepared, he knew that. Then he was climbing down the spine, still a little wary going down, still overly careful about where he placed his boots, but as soon as he hit the deck he was shouting again. Feeling the words cut into his throat. "Bring me the gullaime!"

"Is it the shipwife?" said Dinyl.

"I do not know for certain." Joron stood on the rump, straightened his jacket. "It is a flukeboat, pursued by a fleet ship. It could be nothing of course. But if it is her I would rather be prepared to defend her than not."

"Ey," said Dinyl, "you chart the right course there." As he said it the black material of the wings fell from where they were tied and the gullaime joined them, hissing and yarking at its unwelcome consort.

"Jo-ron Twiner," it croaked.

"Ships coming from the east, Gullaime. I reckon it may be the shipwife and she is pursued. Can you give us wind?"

"Wind!" it shouted and crouched down on the deck, a shiver passing through its body. It lifted its beak and called out to the sky, a lonely shout. Warmth passed over the deck of *Tide Child* and the winds followed it. First soft, then harder and faster, filling the ship's black wings and pushing them through the sea. Clouds of skeers lifted from the islands around them, a thousand wings, beating against the air.

"Steer us east, Barlay!" The oarturner leaned into the steering oar and *Tide Child* groaned as he came about. Deckchilder pulled on ropes, making constant small changes, the better for the wings to catch the wind – and then, when the black ship was settled in its course and leaping forward in a shower of salt spray, Joron took his place upon the rump, arms behind his back. He watched the sails, the rigging, the crew. Seeing it all as one great machine focused on catching the wind and smashing through the waves.

"*Tide Child*'s got some speed on him, D'keeper," said Solemn Muffaz.

"He has indeed, Deckmother, now let us keep it. Let is see if we can outrun our beakwyrms."

"Ey, I'll cord any Hag-cursed who slatelays, I shall." And Solemn Muffaz made his way down the deck, his raw back still weeping, though he did not flinch when the salt spray washed over him.

"D'keeper!" The call came from the topboy.

"Tell of what you see, Topboy," shouted Dinyl, walking to the base of the mainspine. Joron gave a nod of thanks for that, for saving Joron's painful throat from more shouting.

"Ey, D'older, they're loosing at the flukeboat!" Dinyl looked over his shoulder at Joron and he knew they shared a thought. He gave a nod and Dinyl grinned back at him.

"Unfurl the flying wings!" he shouted. "Let's see what *Tide Child* can do if we really let him loose!" With that there was much excitement. The spars were extended from the mainspine right out over the sea on both sides of the deck and the flying wings, massive black squares of material, were unfurled on either side of *Tide Child*, and Joron felt the whole body of the ship shudder as if with joy, as he caught the wind and leaped forward.

"Seakeep, throw the rock! I'd know how much speed we make for when the shipwife is back aboard."

"Ey Deckkeeper," said Fogle and she scurried past, holding the rope with the rocks woven into it. She threw them over the rear of *Tide Child*, counting off as the water pulled them through her hands, watching the sand pass through the glass. Joron barely heard her call out the speed, barely saw Aelerin note it down. His mind was full of battles past, how he had watched flukeboats crumple and spill their crew into the sea with just one gallowbow hit. He tried to think of less drastic battles, of how a bolt could pass right through a flukeboat above the waterline and barely damage it. How the pursuing ship would have to slew to one side to bring its gallowbows to bear and how that would inevitably slow the bigger ship down. Unless they had rigged a gallowbow for'ard, but again, that would take time and such temporary riggings were never stable, never quite as easy to aim. And of course, if that boat did have the shipwife in it, she was Lucky Meas, beloved of the Sea Hag. Would the Hag have saved Meas from the knife all those years ago just to have her go under in an unimportant sea lake near some unnamed islands? No. Of course not.

But who could ever truly know the will of gods?

He turned to find Fogle grinning at him. "I said sixteen rocks, D'keeper." He nodded, pretended he had not been far away in thought and as so missed her first words.

"Sixteen," he said. "Well, that will have the shipwife in a good temper when she comes back aboard, Seakeep." He gave a fierce smile. "I do not think *Tide Child* has ever made such speed."

"I think he is eager to have his shipwife back," said Fogle. Then her face fell, as if she realised the insult she had just done her deckkeeper. "Not that you are not—"

"Peace, Fogle," said Joron, "I am eager to have our shipwife back too." He smiled and the seakeep turned, making her way down the slate of the deck to ensure all was as it should be.

"There they are, D'keeper!" The cry from the beak of the ship. Joron raised the nearglass to his eye, seeing through the dirty circle the two-ribber and the flukeboat. Some on the two-ribber's deck were pointing at *Tide Child* but the two-ribber, *Hassith's Spear*, was doing what he expected. Having loosed from its seaward bows it was now steering to seaward, the ship's beak tracking across the water as it brought its landward for'ard bows to bear, but in doing so it was losing water on the flukeboat.

"Too soon. Their shipwife is too eager," said Joron to himself. Then he closed the nearglass and raised his voice. "Barlay, steer three points to landward of that ship. I'll not give them a free loosing down our decks and I want enough room to swing *Tide Child* about and bring the landward bows to bear."

"You think that ship'll stand, D'keeper?" said Dinyl as he came to stand by him.

"Sense would say not; a two-ribber against a four ribber is a poor match. But we are a black ship and they may think that makes us an easier fight."

"They would be wrong in that," said Dinyl.

"Ey," said Joron, and neither of them spoke of how short-handed the ship was.

As the two-ribber grew, and the flukeboat grew, Joron walked down the slate deck, wind catching at the braids of his hair and the tail of his hat, until he found the gullaime. "You are well, gullaime?" It yarked at him. "Not windsick, friend?" It shook its head. The crest of feathers, a recent addition to its plumage, lifted a little, showing bright red and blue feathers below.

"Not tired. Not sick. Plenty wind."

"Good," said Joron, "but don't run yourself empty. That's not what we want from you."

"Eight," said the gullaime.

"Eight, Gullaime?"

"Eight of mine aboard that ship, sick and pained."

Joron put out a hand, rested it on the shoulder of the crouched gullaime, felt the thin and delicate bones beneath the robe. "I will do what I can not to hurt them if it comes to it, but *Tide Child* is not a precise instrument."

"Gullaime knows," it said quietly, and let out a mournful call. Joron was sure he did not imagine it, that the wind powering them along became a little brisker, a little colder.

"They're breaking off, D'keeper," came the call.

"Let them run, we concentrate on our people."

His gaze was pulled from the gullaime to the *Hassith's Spear*, coming full about now. As it did it loosed off all eight of its small gallowbows at the flukeboat. Not all hit, but at least three did. Two punctured the wing, which the wind then ripped apart, while one hit below the waterline. Oars sprang from either side of the flukeboat immediately, though the sudden loss of speed was notable. Someone aboard was bailing, water being thrown over the side but, even as Joron watched, the boat began to sit lower in the sea.

"It's sinking!" A voice from above.

"I think I see the shipwife!" came another voice.

"Gullaime," said Joron, watching the *Hassith's Spear* as it dropped all its wings and they filled with wind to drive it away from the larger *Tide Child*, "how exact can you be with our wind?"

The gullaime looked up, stared with masked eyes over the beak of the ship toward the sinking flukeboat. "Ship woman?" it said.

"I think so," said Joron.

"Exact," said the gullaime. The wind howled, forcing Joron to take a step back.

"Brace!" he shouted. "Brace!" The flukeboat was going down. Could he already see white shapes in the water? Longthresh in their incessant search for prey? "My crew! Get wyrmpikes and spears from the armoury, put ladders over the landward side and get ready to bring the ship about." He leaned in close to the gullaime. "If we get this wrong, we will crush them."

The flukeboat getting lower in the water. Growing larger as they sped toward it. Crew aboard bailing frantically.

"Not get wrong," it said. And just as quickly as the wind had come up, pushing the ship on, it fell away completely, and *Tide Child* was coasting forward. Joron watched the sinking flukeboat as it came nearer, and nearer, and nearer. Still *Tide Child* carried too much speed. He glanced up the deck.

"Barlay! On my mark, bring us round to seaward!" A nod from the oarturner.

"You get wrong," hissed the gullaime, "crush them."

The masked face focused on him. He grinned at the gullaime.

"Then I'll not get it wrong," said Joron, through a savage grin. Hag's tits, the boat was nearly under now. But he could not risk more speed or he would risk overshooting them, or smashing them beneath the hull. He took a deep breath. "Now Barlay!" he shouted. And *Tide Child* came about in a huge circle – not a violent motion, he was wary of stressing the hull too much – and when it seemed they would not make the turn the gullaime screeched into the air. Joron's ears hurt with the changing pressure as the wind came and the big ship heeled over, the turn becoming tighter. The wind died. *Tide Child* righted himself. And with another fierce call the gullaime brought the wind from head-on, bringing the black ship to a shuddering stop. Before he could congratulate the gullaime and his crew he heard the sound of boots on the hull of the ship as someone climbed it. A head appeared at the rail and he recognised the face, wanted to jump for joy despite how tired and angry that face looked.

But he was an officer.

So he did not.

Instead he stood as straight as he could, brought his hand to his breast in salute and croaked out the words:

"Shipwife on deck!"

# 28

# What Meas Did

*(Taken from the journals of 'Lucky' Meas Gilbryn. It should be noted that she had entirely stopped making navigational notes by this time. It is presumed she did this separately, and unfortunately those records are lost.)*

### Toilday

Weather – Brisk winds, south-easterly.

Cloud cover – Sparse.

Visibility – Good.

Swell – Small.

We left Tide Child and though the weather treated us well I feel as if I left Joron under the threat of a storm, and one he knows nothing about. I cannot doubt there are those who will try to take advantage of my absence. I hope Joron and Dinyl are ready. I have done all I can.

### Menday

Weather – Brisk winds, changeable.

Cloud cover – Thick.

Visibility – Middling.

Swell – Medium.

Four days. The winds are no longer kind to us and the motion of the sea is much magnified on this smaller boat. Coughlin is as seasick as I have ever seen a man be, but the rest of his men hold up well and are even beginning to understand the workings of this boat in a passable manner. They may even be decent deck-childer one day (though I would never tell Mevans that, he would be most upset). I cannot pretend I am comfortable doing such a journey in a flukeboat. It is a brittle thing and I long for the hardness of slate beneath my boots and the stout walls of bone – but I do not have them, and it is a fool who wishes for what they cannot have. I fear my estimates of the time this would take were overly optimistic. I have set the beak toward Skearith's Eye and must hope the Hag has no wish for my company.

## Maidenday

Weather – Winds, gusting, changeable. Constant thin rain.

Cloud cover – Thick.

Visibility – Middling to poor.

Swell – Medium, becoming large with some waves breaking.

Sink Karrad to the depths for sending me on this foolishness. Could he not simply have given Joron a clear message? He has always been overly careful, but that is what comes from dealing with spies. We have been beset by squalls and rain and if did I not know better I would say the Southstorm haunts us. This little boat has very poor cover for its crew and all is misery. Each time I am forced to take a voyage of more than a few hours in a flukeboat I rediscover my respect for the fishers who brave all weathers in these things to feed the stonebound. I would rather face off the Hag's Hunter again – without the wakewyrm at my back – than weather a storm in this. Where a fisher at least brings joy with a cargo of food, our cargo is only misery. We are all wet, we are all uncomfortable, we are all miserable. Faces are drawn and slow to smile. Except Narza – if she feels anything I have been unable to divine it; she sits like a rock in the belly of the boat, occasionally sharpening her bone knives. But for that, I would not know she lives. We are maybe a day away from the island. It is seldom visited by most but I am well familiar with that place.

The skies are grey. I feel sure they always used to be blue.

## Toilday

Weather – Light winds, changeable.

Cloud cover – Thick.

Visibility – Middling.

Swell – Small.

Hag curse my mother. And Hag curse Indyl Karrad too, so sure his spy network is impenetrable and so slow to listen to me when I say he underestimates her. If not for Gavith's keen eyes we would likely be locked in the brig of a boneship right now. Three of them are here, moored up in the harbour crescent of the largest island of the three here, though there is no true harbour to speak of, only a shallow area where the sand shoals gently down to water that is warm and good for swimming.

I do not recognise the ships, two-ribbers all, and I can only think that there are three because my mother suspects I may come here in Tide Child. This island has no strategic value. What I had hoped would be a simple case of landing, getting to the centre of the island and then getting out is now more complicated than I wish for. We dropped the spine on the flukeboat and rowed ashore, on the nearest to us of the two smaller islands, the other is slightly smaller, though flatter, and lies to landward of the main island where we need to be. Thank the Mother for lazy topboys as we were not seen. Then hours were spent crawling through greasegrass to the top of our island and slightly over, so we were not silhouetted against the skyline. While I watched these ships, I swear every creature that can bite has found its way to my skin and I itch like the filthiest bilge-laying deckchild, though I cannot let myself scratch in front of the crew so must bear it. I can only think the ships are sent to spring a trap, but they do it poorly. Were these shipwives mine to command I would break every one of them down to deckholder. What fools, bringing in their boneships for all to see – the spines are higher than the island. They make a racket landing their seaguard too, there is little discipline and much jollity. Had they a brain between them they would have loaded them all onto flukeboats and landed them at night, then I would have flown straight into their arms. Though it is just as likely that they are simply here for stores. Still, it is a chance I cannot take. If Karrad's network is compromised it is all the more important that I find whatever message he thinks so important he has to hide it all the way out here.

I took Gavith out with me today, his eyes are sharp and he is picking up good habits from spending time with Mevans here, and Barlay and Solemn Muffaz back on Tide Child. He talks of Farys often, I will have to watch that. They are of an age and it would not do to have to hang them if their friendship becomes anything more than that. They are both popular among the crew.

The boy scratches freely at his itches.

It is hard not to snap at him.

Mareday

Weather – Brisk winds, changeable.

Cloud cover – Thinning.

Visibility – Good.

Swell – Medium.

From another sojourn up the island (and another losing battle with whatever finds my flesh so delightful) it looks like two of the boneships are getting ready to leave. Coughlin is of the opinion that anything that may have been left for me is likely gone, and he may well be right. But I have spent long days on Indyl's island and know its paths and places as well as I know my own heart – those invading it (if they are) will not. I know the cabin at its centre well too and that it has many hidden places none would think to look. Ey, it is dangerous to go ashore and I have wrestled with this. I will leave most of my crew on this island and take only Coughlin, Narza and – though it pains me – Gavith. The boy's senses are better than any others and such a small group can move quickly and silently through the gion. I am glad that the gion and varisk is not dying here yet – we will be thankful of the cover.

Clensday

*Weather - Little wind. Rain.*

*Cloud cover - Thick, grey.*

*Visibility - Poor.*

*Swell - Small.*

*Two of the boneships left Indyl's island while we stayed on ours and watched. The first left early in the morran while the wind still held, towed out of the shelter of the island by its crew until its wings filled and it heeled around to head south toward who knows what. The ship was handled well and there was little I found to criticise in the way the deckchilder worked. Possibly it only goes south in hope of picking up the currents or kinder winds, possibly it had orders and must follow them. It was called Sorrowful Bird. Why I spent time wondering on it I do not know as there is little I can do, no matter what its course may be. The second left later and that ship caused me considerable trouble. If not for the speed with which Coughlin and his men can work with an axe - they may never be deckchilder but they have a different sort of strength to my crew and thank the Hag for it - all would have been lost before it began. It left slowly, towed out of the harbour like its brother-ship, and I saw its name - Hassith's Spear (if ever there were an unlucky sounding ship to serve upon then surely that must be it - who names a ship for the man that killed the God-Bird?). The wind gave it little energy and it moved with all the urgency of a woman in a warm bed heading for a cold bath.*

*However, the shipwife was clearly not pleased with this and all was action upon the slate, deckchilder running hither and thither (slovenly) and the coursers* (two of them) brought up while the officers set to screaming at the crew in a way that made me think it is not a happy ship to fly within (the deckmother was far too free with cord and club). Then gullaime were brought up and were it not for Gavith and his good eyes, well, I dread to think what would have happened. (Am I slipping? Am I?)

"Why does their shipwife spin his hands around, Shipwife?" he asked. Normally I barely hear his mumbles – he will not look me in the eye and is given to constant little complaints that I choose to ignore – but glad I am that I caught his words this day. Why indeed was their shipwife spinning his arms about and bringing the gullaime up?

Could be nothing, but more likely he intended to do a round of the islands just in case those he expected to turn up were hiding, as indeed we are.

Then we were squirming our way back and, as soon as we were over the brow of the hill, running for the little shelter we had made. We took the shelter down quickly and Coughlin felled a large gion in such a way it looked to have collapsed naturally, and that hid our boat. I do not know where he learned that but it is a useful skill and I will have him teach it to some of my deckchilder. Then we scattered across the island to hide in the brush which is where I write this and watch Hassith's Spear as it circles the island. Occasionally I catch a glint from the ship's deck as Skearith's Eye is reflected off the lens of a nearglass. I worry that they may choose to send deckchilder or seaguard ashore. If they do we are lost.

I remain a feast for insects.

Clensday – Night.

Weather – Blustery. Rain.

Cloud cover – Thick, grey.

Visibility – Poor.

Swell – Small.

That Hag-cursed ship is still circling even as night comes in. Clearly my mother knows something is up, even if not what. We have full cloud cover and Skearith's Blind Eye is closed. I cannot see the future or read fortunes in the eyes of a dead child like a hagpriest, but I think the shipwife of Hassith's Spear is the impatient type. Four times they have been round this island, the first two times far apart with sojourns to the other islands, the last two close enough for me to think they concentrate on us.

I feel sure they will land. I feel it in my bones the way I feel the rising of the sea. It is too late and dark now for them to do anything but send a flukeboat, and that would be foolish. Were it me I would wait until morran and come in close, land as much of my crew as I could.

We will leave here tonight on the flukeboat. All of us. We will make for Indyl's island, though it seems fool-hardy. This could get us all killed if we are caught between islands – there is not enough wind to escape and we cannot out-row a boneship powered by gullaime.

Should I wait them out?

Second guessing myself? That is no good and no use. I must act.

## Hagsday

Weather - Still. Unseasonably hot, like a storm is gathering his anger.

Cloud cover - None.

Visibility - Good.

Swell - Small.

We made land on Indyl's island last night and I will find a way to reward every woman and man who is with me. Not a complaint, not a moment when they did not jump to the orders given. I watched Hassith's Spear on its fifth journey round our island in the darkness. Then with all the energy we had we pulled the gion off the flukeboat and got it back in the water. We followed the course of Hassith's Spear and when we were in the channel between islands, and could see the rumplights of the boneship, we rowed for all we were worth for Indyl's island. Never have I been so sure I would hear the call of "ship rising" and see that boneship turning. But it did not (which speaks poorly of the crew of the Spear, but that is what happens when a shipwife is overly harsh). We made landfall at the rear of the island and hid the flukeboat once more under a gion cut by Coughlin and his men. We found plenty to eat (among the smaller plants some fine berries). I told the crew to get what rest they can. Coughlin has posted sentries. I have sent Narza to the quiet bothy on the east of the island. It was my and Indyl's most secret place and I do not want my crew trampling around in it. If the message is not there it must be in the larger shack, which is a pity as I suspect that will be well guarded.

The crew scratch freely at their insect bites while I feel close to madness.

Menday

Weather – Howling winds. A storm is coming.

Cloud cover – Thick grey.

Visibility – Poor.

Swell – High.

Damn Indyl. Narza found nothing. The weather has turned and the winds are fair set to rip the gion forest apart. I was right about Hassith's Spear, he has dropped his staystone by the island we were hiding on previously, if he lands crew I do not doubt he will find evidence of our stay. Narza has been to look at the shack and says there is almost an entire crew posted around it. Well, not posted, asleep mostly, but there is upwards of a hundred of them. I will not throw my life, nor the lives of my crew away trying to get into the place, but at the same time I cannot risk Indyl's message being found. I have instructed Narza to get in and set the place alight. Such things are as easy to her as climbing the side of a boneship is to me.

Things are not entirely bleak, though. The boneship in the island harbour is there for a reason – it appears to have lost its rudder and is going nowhere until it has a replacement, which is good. Once I am back on board Tide Child we will have little choice but to follow up on what Cahanny told Joron about the isle where gullaime are being sold. If nothing else we can wipe the place off the map, such places disgust me. (Ah Meas, and how many gullaime have you driven thoughtlessly to death?)

I must stop writing. Smoke rises above the gion.

Hagsday

Weather - Brisk winds.

Cloud cover - None.

Visibility - Good.

Swell - Small.

I thought our escape clean after days of empty horizons, but they have found us. Now it is a straight race, and one that we are sure to lose. Joron, I hope you have your keenest eyed topboy up the spine.

# 29

# The Consequences of Command

She had called him to her cabin. He wondered if she would take his hat from him. Oh, she had not obviously been looking at the state of the ship, seeing the scars from battle with the mutineers, seeing the depleted crew on the slate of the deck. He knew she had noticed these things because she was Meas Gilbryn. Even tired, even bedraggled, even looking like she had not slept for a whole week and had been cruelly treated by merciless seas; she would notice these things.

When she had come aboard, followed by her crew, all living but looking half dead, she had ordered they all be fed, and that somewhere dry and warm and quiet be found for every one of them to get a good long sleep, even if it meant the officers gave up their cabins and slept on the deck. Then she had vanished below. After her went Mevans, Gavith, Coughlin and each and every woman and man who had accompanied her, all looking as though they had lost everything. But not for one moment did Joron even consider that she may have failed in her task, for she was Lucky Meas, the witch of Keelhulme Sounding, and she did not fail.

His hand fell to his hip, where the sword she had given him should be but was not.

He failed.

So when the gullaime hopped over to him he barely heard its words.

"She is sad."

He did not understand why that would be. And when she called him to her cabin, he twisted it into worry about himself, about his shortcomings. Because surely she may be a little sad that she had chosen him and he had failed her. He had almost lost her ship. He had left her without enough crew to fight and crew it. What a poor commander he had been, and whatever judgement she had, he was ready for. So he stood before her desk, which stood in the long-worn ruts on the white floor. He stood and she stared into the pages of the small, sea-worn book she took everywhere with her, its cover tattered, filled with tiny handwriting in her own secret code. And had she been anyone but Meas Gilbryn he would have thought she swayed slightly in her seat because she was fighting sleep.

"Cwell finally made her move then," she said quietly.

"Ey," he said. "I should have—"

"Been told," she said, still in that quiet voice. "You should have been told." She stopped. Shut the book. "I should have told you. I have spoken with Dinyl already."

"It was not his fault . . ."

"You are right," she said. "It was not. And neither was it yours." She tapped a finger on the desk. "A shipwife can be too clever, you know, Joron. Too sure of herself. That you brought my ship to me at all, given what happened . . . well, it makes me wonder if the Mother has a special place in her heart for you." He did not know what to say. "How many do we have left? How many loyal?"

"Seventy-three, not including those you brought back, Shipwife."

She smashed her right fist onto the top of the desk, making him jump, making everything on the desk jump. Then she pulled her fist back, cradling it in her left hand, rubbing the edge she had slammed into the hard varisk of the old desk.

"It is not enough," she said, more to herself than to him. She looked up and he saw how tired she was. "You have been through much, but so have we. That ship, *Hassith's Spear*, pursued us without let-up or sleep. Had it not been wary about use of its gullaime we would not be having this conversation, Joron, I assure you. I used every trick I knew to escape. But I am here more through luck than any great skill and . . ."

"You should sleep, Shipwife," he said, and realised as he spoke that he was shaken. Because this was not the woman he was used to. Then, as if sensing his thoughts, that woman returned. He saw her temper and her pride rise up within, indignation that he had not only interrupted her, but seen fit to tell her what to do. And just as he braced himself for the squall of her temper, it vanished.

"Ey," she said quietly. "It is the duty of the deckkeeper to tell the shipwife what she needs to be told, even when she may not like it." Meas stood. "And you are right. I must sleep." She came round the desk and put a hand on his arm, looked up into his face. "The crew of that ship, *Hassith's Spear*, they saw me. My mother's suspicions cannot be confirmed. It ran and it has a start on us, right enough, but we must follow that ship, Deckkeeper, we must not let it escape." He nodded and she walked away from him, then turned. "Well? Why are you still standing there? See to it."

"Ey Shipwife," he said. And he turned to take his leave, stopping only at the door when she spoke again:

"Joron. I am sorry about Anzir."

He turned back to her, tried to smile. Failed.

"I did not realise how much I would miss her until she was gone."

"Ey," Meas nodded, "it is often the way. Now go."

They set course in the direction that *Hassith's Spear* had taken but Joron knew the likelihood of them catching the smaller ship was slim. As a two-ribber it was lighter and faster than *Tide Child*, unless the seas were particularly rough. The crew assured Joron, and had many upon many times, that *Tide*

*Child* was as fast as any in his class, faster even. He considered using the gullaime to speed them on but decided against it. *Tide Child* had lost precious hours getting Meas and her crew back on board and settled. It was likely *Hassith's Spear* had changed direction to lose them as soon as he was out of sight. Joron did not want to tire the gullaime on a wild chase for no purpose. Instead he set their course for the island Meas had escaped from, reckoning that the ship was most likely to head back there, and they barrelled through the darkening night and growing seas, and he felt the song of the windspires in his mind, growing in volume, and he wondered what that meant. When the night bell rang Dinyl came up so Joron could sleep.

"She is not happy, Joron," said Dinyl quietly.

"No," said Joron. "And half dead on her feet."

"Did she tell you what happened on the island? She did not tell me," Dinyl looked away, as if ashamed.

"She did not share it with me either, Dinyl, but I think it was nothing good. She did not seem . . ."

"Herself? No. And now she has us chasing this two-ribber with scant chance of catching it."

"You question her orders, Dinyl?"

The deckholder looked up, a hint of humour in his eyes at Joron's playful pretence at anger.

"I think she is tired, as are you, Joron. Go get some sleep."

"Ey, me and the whole ship."

"Well," said Dinyl, "I will shout at the topboys and threaten to throw them to the longthresh if they do not find me that ship. That should keep them busy."

"Careful, we do not want one falling asleep and out of the tops, Dinyl. I suspect Meas will be angry if she wakes and any more crew are missing."

"Well, then they had better stay awake," he grinned. And then he was striding down the decks, shouting, "Tell of the sea, Topboy! And if I think you're asleep I'll throw you overboard myself!"

\* \* \*

Knocking woke Joron. A gentle knocking on the door of his cabin and, as he forced open gluey eyes, he knew Skearith's Eye had risen. Diffused light was pushing in around the bones of the bowpeek. He took a great sniff of air, a moment to work out what was wrong.

They were still. No whistling wind. No water rushing along the hull. And the moisture he could smell in the air could only mean mist. Becalmed. Meas would be furious. But if they were becalmed then so was the ship they chased. There was that at least.

The knocking came again.

"Yes?" he said

"The shipwife wants us all on the slate, D'keeper." He recognised the cabin boy's voice.

"Very well, Gavith, give me time to get dressed."

"Shipwife is fair champing at—"

"I will be but a moment, and I imagine the shipwife will be even more angry if I go on deck without my trousers."

"Ey D'keeper," said Gavith. Joron heard him walk away.

It did not take him long to dress, and when he was decked out as he should be, in the blue jacket, one-tail hat and boots of the deckkeeper – a uniform to which he had added fine feathers from the gullaime and trinkets and memento mori of those slain, so he did not forget them – he made his way to the deck of Tide Child.

Oh, and what a solemn ship he found. Couched in mist, cocooned in grey air with every deckchilder loyal to the shipwife arrayed along the sides to seaward and landward. And all of them dressed in their best blues. At the far end of the ship, before the rump stood Meas, and Dinyl and Mevans and Solemn Muffaz. Coxward, Aelerin, Fogle, Coughlin and Berhof of the seaguard, looking a little green with seasickness, and all the petty officers of Tide Child, each in their best. Even eccentric Coxward had changed his bandages for less bloody ones than usual.

Above them, hanging from the spars of Tide Child, were

five nooses, dripping moisture collected from the mist. Joron took his place by Meas, on the opposite side to Dinyl, and he knew what those carefully knotted ropes meant. Meas had decided it was time to deal with the mutineers. When he was in place, Meas nodded to herself.

*Drip. Drip. Drip.*

"Deckmother," she barked. "Bring the prisoners up." And Solemn Muffaz marched down the length of the ship and down the stairs into the underdeck. And Joron heard his voice barking out orders. When he returned he brought with him those women and men who had betrayed *Tide Child* and those who had followed them. The group – Joron counted nineteen in all and was surprised, he had not thought so many had survived – were quickly flanked by Berhof and Coughlin's seaguard, again in their best clothes, and brought before Meas, where they were made to kneel on the deck. Joron hoped the cold damp slate beneath them felt like shame as water soaked through the knees of their clothes.

*Drip.*

Meas did not speak, not immediately. She let silence fall, let the mist envelop them. Let the ties that bound the wrists of each prisoner behind their back bite a little deeper. When she did speak he expected her to shout.

She did not. She spoke quietly.

*Drip.*

"A ship, a fleet ship, is a thing of trust," she said. She walked forward and stood before the kneeling mutineers. Joron picked out Cwell in the first rank and felt a prickle of hatred. "Every one of you has betrayed that trust. And every one of you deserves to die. And it is my right, as shipwife, to take your lives. There is no question of that, none at all. But I need crew. Now, I have no doubt that many of you were brought into this through weakness as much as wickedness. So some of you will live, though I will break those that do. You will have no rank until you earn it. You will be lower than stonebound on the deck of this ship. You will jump to the orders of Gavith the cabin boy. Any seniority you may have earned is gone. You come back to my deck as nothing." Such venom in that last word, somehow amplified by the fact she did not raise her voice. Not one woman or man who knelt before her raised their head. "You hear me? Nothing." She walked up and down the line of prisoners. "But I want the ringleaders," she said, and stamped her way back up the line until she stood before Joron. "You hear me? I want the ringleaders. Their necks, I will stretch. And their bodies will go to the beakwyrms and longthresh and the Hag will never receive them at her fire."

*Drip.*

"Shipwife," said Joron quietly, because he had promised some their lives and, though he partly regretted it, he could not keep quiet. But Meas held a hand out behind her back, a signal unseen by all but him and Dinyl that bade him be quiet, and so he was. Not because he was worried about speaking up, but because he knew he must trust her.

*Drip.*

"Speak quietly amongst yourselves," said Meas to the mutineers, "then give me five names." She turned away and came to stand by Joron. "I know of your promise," she whispered. "This is all about timing." She leaned in closer, "We will rid ourselves of Cwell once and for all here, and I will make sure you keep your honour about it." Then she turned to watch the prisoners as they talked amongst themselves, all except Cwell, her face badly bruised and swollen, who remained kneeling on the deck. Joron wondered why, then realised he knew. There was no point in her joining the quiet and intense discussions behind her, for what could she say? How could she deny her part in the mutiny, or that she had been the wellspring behind it?

*Drip.*

Then Cwell stood.

*Drip.*

"Shipwife," she said.

*Drip.*

"Ey, Cwell?" said Meas.

*Drip.*

"These fools" – she gave a jerk of her head at the women and men behind her – "could not organise a drunk in a hold full of anhir. Stretch all their necks or none, for they all just followed me in search of what they thought was an easy life." She took a step forward. "You are no fool, never have been. So you must know what the deckkeeper promised me, and I know you are too full of your own sense of right to go against it. So let us ignore this charade and I will make it easy for you." She took another step forward but it was to Joron, not the shipwife she went to, and she knelt before him. "My actions took your shadow, Deckkeeper." She looked up into his face. "You have no reason to trust me, I know, but I offer myself in the place of your shadow. And I also free you of your promise to me. Should you prefer me to hang, then stretch my neck and I will go to the Hag and suffer her judgement, whatever that may be."

*Drip.*

Joron stared at her. His mind awhirl.

*Drip.*

Was this some game she played?

*Drip.*

Was this what Meas planned? How could she have known? And what did she want him to do?

*Drip.*

Everything in him said Cwell must die. Everything. He glanced over at Meas but she stood, eyes straight forward, giving no clue to what she thought. Behind her stood Narza. Narza who generally took no interest in the doings of the ship. Narza who followed her shipwife and killed, or not, on her order. But now she was watching Cwell, watching as if some creature had suddenly appeared on the deck that she under-stood, and Joron was unsure why he thought this until he noticed her head was slowly nodding. Not as a signal to him, she cared nothing for him. Nodding in understanding, or maybe even approval?

*Drip. Drip.*

He touched the bone knife at his waist and walked around Cwell.

*Drip.*

"You do not deserve to live," he said. He drew the knife. "But it is fitting you give your life in Anzir's place." Then he knelt down and cut the ropes binding her hands and whispered into her ear. "Betray me, and I will hang you myself." Then he stood, making his voice as sure as sure could be while he felt nothing but confusion. "Now take your place at my back."

*Drip.*

Then he returned to the rump, Meas watching him before turning back to the mutineers.

*Drip.*

"There may be those of you, in among the prisoners, who plan revenge on Cwell for bringing you low." Her fierce gaze roaming among them. "Well, she has just bought all your lives, so you will not go anywhere near her." She raised her eyes, looking past the mutineers and at her loyal crew. "And there may be those among you who plan revenge on Cwell. You will do nothing to her because I order you not to. Now, all those knelt before me, you are on punishment duties, manning the pumps and cleaning the bilges until I decide you are worthy of something better. The rest of you must have some work to do I am sure." She gave them a nod. "This matter is done with. Now, return to your duties."

*Drip.*

*Drip.*

*Drip.*

Later, he went to Meas's cabin. He left Cwell on the slate, still uncomfortable with the idea of her at his back, through the decision had been made and he could not undo it.

"Come," said Meas when he knocked.

"How did you know, Shipwife?" he said. "How did you know Cwell would do that?"

Meas grinned at him. "No one, Joron, was more surprised than I at what happened on deck. I planned to get right to the point of stringing up the conspirators before I let you interrupt and then I would decide to maroon them on some island." She laughed. "Life is full of surprises, ey?"

She laughed but he could not.

"Why did she do it, Shipwife?"

Meas's laughter died away. She sat straighter.

"Why?" She closed her book. "I suspect there is not one answer." She moved the book, squaring its edge with the desk. "You beat her, I think is the feet of it. She had all the advantages, and you beat her. Then you offered her a way out that meant she didn't lose face, kept her pride and her life." Meas touched her book, very lightly, then smiled. "And, of course, if she was marooned with the rest of the mutineers I doubt she would last long. When food ran low they would eat her first." Joron searched Meas's face for some hint of a joke. Found nothing.

"How can I ever trust her?"

Meas shrugged, tapped on her desk. Moved the rock she kept on it.

"Look in the mirror when you return to your cabin. Ask yourself if people can change, ask yourself if people can surprise you."

"And if this is just a ruse on her part?"

"Then I am sure Solemn Muffaz will be all too happy to throw her overboard."

# 30

# A Change of Plans

The next morran Meas called her officers to her room.

"It has occurred to me, while we sit here becalmed, that we are unlikely to catch *Hassith's Spear*. It was well over the horizon, and we have no way of knowing if it is just barely out of our sight and becalmed, or far away on a strong wind. And when it comes to it, I have decided that freeing our people from whatever fate awaits them at the end of the brownbone's journey is more important than preventing my mother from knowing what I am doing. With that, I must let you all know what no doubt you already surmise. Whatever message may have been left by Karrad we could not retrieve. Ships were waiting for us. We must presume that Karrad's organisation is compromised somehow."

"Or he betrayed you," said Joron.

Just for the shortest moment her face changed – pain, like Joron had driven a knife into her back. But despite that he continued with his thought: "Why could he not just give me or Mevans the message in Bernshulme?"

There was quiet in the cabin, before Meas spoke.

"If he gave you or anyone else the message and they were caught, my mother would get it from them. It may sound overly cautious but it is how he has survived so long. Few outside our circle knew of our island."

"So he betrayed you?"

Again, the silence. Then she spoke again.

"Not in the way you mean," she said quietly. "If he walked up to my mother and came clean, offered me and all I have up to her, he would never leave the room. She has no stomach or pity for betrayal."

"So," said Dinyl, "if your mother knew about the meeting, she must know about Karrad. We have lost our only ally in Bernshulme."

Meas shook her head, a lock of grey hair with fading red dye through it stuck to the material of her uniform jacket.

"In all my life I have never met a man with a talent for survival like Indyl Karrad. My guess is he found himself in a position where he must give my mother something or be revealed himself."

"So he did betray you?" said Joron. Anger burned within him.

"He played the long game, gambled on my skill to get me away." She lifted a hand. "Before you get righteous, Joron, I would have done the same in his position."

"And what of the message?" said Mevans.

"He either never sent it, or had someone on one of those ships find and destroy it." She shrugged and the lock of hair was pulled free. "It makes little difference to us — the upshot is we do not have it."

"Where now then?" said Coxward.

"Joron visited Mulvan Cahanny while in Bernshulme," said Meas. "Now, he did not find out much. Only that a pirate isle that had once been trading in slaves suddenly cut off all contact. I know the place, it is named McLean's Rock — and breaking off contact is not strange in and of itself, but Cahanny picked up reports that gullaime were seen on the island. He thought they were being sold, but I am not so sure. I reckon either fleet ships are stopping there for some reason or it is more of these windshorn."

"Hate them!" screeched the gullaime.

"Thank you for your input, Gullaime," said Meas. And the gullaime preened the feathers sticking out of its robe. Joron made a mental note to explain to it, at a more convenient moment, that this was not actually praise. "So with that in mind we will go explore this pirate island, and if we are lucky enough to run into *Hassith's Spear* on the way then we will deal with him too. But that shall be our course, and we will call in at Leasthaven to pick up more crew, if they are there, and also Shipwife Brekir and *Snarltooth*. Even if McLean's Rock holds only pirates, it is still likely to offer resistance. Whatever we find, it will be better to go in mob-handed." She stood. "Well, I have told you what we are about, so get to it. Joron, Aelerin and the gullaime, stay a moment."

The three of them waited until the rest had left and they could hear the happy bustle of the ship working around them. "Aelerin, what chance of this calm lifting?" asked Meas.

"Little today," they replied. "Little tomorrow. But the winds are coming."

Meas nodded, then turned to the windtalker. Its masked face was lifted, as if it studied the ceiling. "Gullaime," she said. "It would do us well to leave this calm as soon as possible, but I would not leave you empty and in pain for only our comfort and speed."

"Plenty speed," it said, still looking up. "Plenty wind."

"Yes, but what about tomorrow and the next day? Can you tell how much of the magic is left to you? I do not know, even after all these years of dealing with your kind, how you work. And I would know. How can we tell if you are near to running out?"

Its masked face snapped back to Meas. "Cannot," it squawked. "I tell." Then it almost purred. "I feel."

"Well," said Meas, "I want you to keep plenty back. There is no windspire on Leasthaven but I have been past this pirate isle before and there is one there. We will need your skills more for battle than travel."

The gullaime nodded, yarked and bit at the air. "Can speed boat, ship woman," it said.

"I know, but you do not need to impress me or push yourself. Tell Joron when you have had enough." The gullaime nodded, and kept nodding as if lost in the motion. Then it spun around and headed for the cabin door.

"Done now," it said. "Done now. Move ship."

Meas watched it leave. Shook her head. "Courser, bring me your charts. Deckkeeper, go keep an eye on the gullaime and my ship."

On deck the gullaime crouched in the centre of the slate and brought the wind. Joron felt the familiar pressure in his ears and the heat across the deck and the song in his mind. His throat burned as *Tide Child* came about and he opened his mouth to shout, finding only a croak at first. Had to cough and clear his throat before the orders escaped his mouth and deckchilder were scurrying to get the ship under way. Once they were, he felt better and he walked among them, listening as they pulled on ropes and chanted songs. Was it his imagination, or had the song of the windspire somehow become part of this ship? Were those odd melodies winding through the shanties and chants of the crew? He felt sure they were, and wished more than anything to join them, but it was not appropriate for an officer to join the crew's shanties. Worse, he dared not as he did not believe his voice was there; it had been stolen by Gueste and a garotte back in Bernshulme. She may not have held the rope, but she gave the order, shouldered the responsibility. His hand twitched – he owed Gueste for that. Just as he owed a shipwife called Barnt and Cwell for a lost sword.

At that he glanced back. Cwell was there, silent behind him. Maybe that was all the vengeance he would ever have for the lost sword, that she served him now. Would he ever feel comfortable with that? He did not know, despite having searched his reflection in the polished metal he had used to shave his face that morran. Of course, he had changed, Meas was right. But Cwell? He turned to her.

"I could do with some water."

There was a pause, a brief stiffening of her entire body. Then she bowed her head and walked past him to the paint-spattered mainspine and the barrel below it. Filled the cup hooked to the side and brought it to him.

"Here," she said. And she held out the cup. He took it and she waited while he drank, then took the cup back from him and returned it to the hook and came to stand behind him once more. Skearith's Eye moved across the sky.

After three days the wind returned and the gullaime rested, seemingly untouched by its time driving the ship. It returned to its cabin, biting and sniping and cursing at its shadow. Soon after it had left Meas came onto the deck.

"We steer south," she said. "Aelerin says we'll find stronger currents and winds, and then we can turn for Cassin's Isle and Leasthaven to meet up with Brekir. From there we go to McLean's Rock, at worst to clean out some slavers. At best to find where our people are taken."

As the courser had promised, the winds picked up the further south they went, and though Joron could tell by the way Meas shouted into the tops that she was full of hope, they saw no sign of *Hassith's Spear* and it seemed that unluckily named ship was lost to them. From there it was only routine and the monotony of shipboard life as they flew the ocean, broken by occasional fights between those who had been mutineers and those who had been loyal, and whatever their position now it spared neither of them the bite of the cord at the hand of Solemn Muffaz. But, with time and tide and the gentle swell of an ocean so friendly even Berhof could not moan about it, the crew of *Tide Child* once more began to pull together. Resentments were not forgotten, but they were put aside in the service of the ship, and when the call came up – "Cassin's Isle rising!" – all the deckchilder hopped to their duties, eager that their ship should arrive in fine style, even though they must have known it would be many hours before they reached land. All the while, Joron worried with Fogle over lists of the crew and supplies *Tide Child* sorely needed before setting out for McLean's Rock, and the hope of finding something, anything to help them track down the remainder of Safeharbour's people.

The last true port Joron had seen was Bernshulme, and it would be true to say that Leasthaven on Cassin's Isle was a sad excuse for a dock compared to that, for it was not really a dock at all. The island shared the crescent shape of other islands, a slow slope rising from a long beach, eventually stopping with death-dealing finality at high cliffs which attracted skeers by the thousand to nest, fight and squawk. It was the long beach and deep bay before it that made it a good place for the small fleet – ships could drop staystones in the deep water and find some protection from the elements in the curve of the island. Joron counted five ships currently at rest, three black ships and two small brownbones.

Leasthaven town, barely worth the name, had no dry dock like the great ports, no cranes and cradles, but the long beach and lack of tides at this latitude meant ships could be pulled from the water and careened, lying lazily on their sides while weed was scraped from their bones and repairs were made. Two of the three black ships currently slouched on the pink sand, surrounded by crowds of women and men working on them. The dying season had come to Cassin's Isle, and the gion forest was brown, wilting and dripping to reveal the shanties and bothies of Leasthaven that had been built to store their meagre supplies. Had a ship come past these structures would have been seen straight away, but Cassin's Isle had its steep-sided back to the open water, and was one of many small isles of little interest to anyone passing. Meas brought *Tide Child* to a halt in the bay and dropped the staystone.

"I go ashore to see what supplies and crew we have available to us," she said. "I would love to have *Tide Child*'s bottom cleared of weed but I fear we do not have time. Joron, prepare my boat and accompany me. Dinyl, could you have Mevans ensure my cabin is prepared to receive Shipwife Brekir and her deckkeeper?"

"Ey, Shipwife." Joron and Dinyl said it in unison then looked at each other and shared a smile. Then Joron picked a crew to row, making giant Berhof's day by picking him and hearing him mutter, "Mother bless me, it will be good to have the world stop moving beneath my feet."

It seemed only moments before Joron was over the side and in the rear of the flukeboat while Meas stood at the front. Narza and Cwell sat opposite each other and joined the rowers and, though they never spoke, Joron felt that some understanding had grown between the two women — though he did not know whether that was something good or terrifying. Directly behind Meas, pulling on an oar with all his might, was the bonemaster Coxward; opposite him the wingwright Challin, behind them Berhof and Tarrin of the seaguard, and behind them Farys and three more Joron had favoured.

On land he took a moment to let his legs get used to the strange way the ground seemed to move beneath him.

"Hag's breath," said Berhof as he stumbled, "can I never escape the sea?"

Coxward clapped him on the shoulder. "Tis a gift, Berhof. The sea follows us on shore, but it will pass." Berhof nodded and grinned as Coxward turned from him. "But you'll have to work through your seasickness again once you're back on ship," he said, and walked over to Meas, cackling.

The shipwife dismissed the crew that had rowed them here, chosen from those who had been loyal to her when Cwell held her mutiny, with a harsh admonishment to remember they were her chosen and that any she found drunk on her return would be, as she put it, "a Hag's sight less chosen." From there they went up into the town, though town was hardly a word for Leasthaven. It was really only one street. Up close to the buildings he saw badly cured gion and varisk, cracks stuffed with dried mud and leaves. Coxward and Challin vanished up toward the warehouse while Meas headed for the largest building that was not a store house, the drinking hall.

Inside it was almost full, women and men lining the benches, and Joron marvelled that, no matter how rudimentary their billet may be, deckchilder always managed to supply themselves with alcohol. The noise of the hall, even from outside, was almost as loud as a battle. When Meas stepped through the door the noise stopped. Women and men held their breath as her gaze roved over them.

"You all know me," she said, with no need for her to shout. "Who here already serves on a black ship?" There were whoops and wails to that, drinks held up as if in toast. "Then kindly help me out, and go stand to seaward of me." This was done in a reasonably fleet manner – those too drunk to find their own way were helped by their comrades over a landscape of benches and tables that had become an impossible maze to their fuddled senses. "I will stand each of you a drink," she said. "For you are loyal and true and have given yourselves over to a new life and a better way, at much risk, and do not think I ignore that." A roar of approval. Meas had to quiet them with a wave of her hands. "Wait, my girls and boys, just wait. For I have a tale to tell, one of betrayal and sadness. For I have had mutiny aboard my ship." Gasps and whispers of "*No!*" "But do not worry – I had my good deckkeeper here," she put a hand on Joron's shoulder, "Joron Twiner. You all know him as a fair and kind man – maybe too kind I would say – but he put down those mutineers with such fierceness as I believe you have never seen." Joron felt a warmth within his chest at this praise, even though he knew she exaggerated the truth. "Yet despite his quick actions, the mighty *Tide Child*, largest ship of our brave fleet, our fleet that believes in better, newer ways, is sadly short-handed. Ey, short-handed, and at just the time when we have discovered a darkness that threatens us all. Brownbones that steal our people away. Take the sick and old to die, for who knows what foul reason?" More disbelieving exclamations from the deckchilder to seaward, and on some of those faces Joron saw smiles, excitement, for they knew what was coming. "Now I'll not force any woman or man to come to me. And I know," she raised a hand to those to seaward of her, "every one of you would gladly serve me, but I also know you are a fierce and loyal bunch, who would never walk away from their own shipwife." It was plain to Joron that this was not the case, but Meas's words reminded those thinking of offering themselves that they already had a duty – and if they were a little disappointed, he knew it was better that than the strife that would be caused should Meas steal crew from the shipwife of a warship.

A brownbone, though?

Well, that was another thing entirely.

"Now you," she said, "you crews of our brave merchants, those brought here who escaped Safeharbour, those who have come to us through many and varied other means, those of you dragged here by fate . . . Well, I have need of you. Oh, you need not know a warship to help me, need not understand the complex ways of my boneship. For I have many good people on board *Tide Child* and they will teach you, and Joron will teach you, and if you have the strength to pull on a rope or raise a curnow then you will be welcomed and put to good use on *Tide Child*. And you . . ." She let her voice fade away, let the silence of the room grow around her before speaking again. "You! Can avenge what was done to Safeharbour! You!" – she pointed at a woman missing a hand and dressed like a tailor – "Can help me stop what I believe is a great darkness! And you!" – she picked out another of those sat around, rapt and hypnotised by her – "Can help bring about a peace like our people have never known." Again, she let silence fall before talking again. Quietly, softly. "So what say you, ey? What say you all?"

A roar. An affirmative roar, and those on the landward of Meas were almost climbing over themselves to get to her. Now Meas had to shout to be heard.

"Wait! Wait, and quiet yourselves! Do not make your decision yet, for it is not a small one. Think on it. And if you still wish to fly with me then be on the beach as Skearith's Eye dips and report to my hatkeep, Mevans. He will speak to you and rate you and tell you your place aboard."

There was much chatter at this. A woman stepped forward.

"Shipwife Meas," she said. She was tall, thin and with long red hair that she brushed out of her face with a hand that had three fingers fused together.

"Ey?" said Meas

"I would ask a question."

"And what is your name?"

"Jennil, Shipwife Meas."

"Ask your question, Jennil." The room went silent, all the better to hear what was asked of the most famous shipwife on the Scattered Archipelago.

"I lost my child and man at Safeharbour, Shipwife, so if I join your crew, do you promise us action? For I thirst for vengeance."

Joron saw the smile creep across Meas's face.

"Oh Jennil," she said, "if you thirst then follow me, and your cup will overflow."

The room erupted into noise, and Joron knew that, by the time Skearith's Blind Eye rose above the bay, *Tide Child* would once more have a full complement on deck.

# 31

# What Sleeps Within

Brekir was her usual dour self at the meal held by Meas the next day. A new scar marked the right side of her face.

"So, we know no more than we did before but we have lost much-needed women and men, and Joron has a shadow likely to stab him in the back." She chewed solemnly on a tough bit of fish before reaching into her mouth, pulling out a bone and placing it onto her plate. "I almost choked. The beasts of the sea try and strike at us even from death."

"Admittedly," said Meas, "the loss of so many of my trained deckchilder is difficult, but I prefer to think of it as Joron solving a problem. Cwell is family to the crime lord Mulvan Cahanny. If I had executed her, and marooning was as good as, he would feel bound to avenge her. This way she lives but is removed from the rest of the crew. They see a shadow as apart from them, as you well know."

"Ey," said Brekir and she lifted her cup. Mevans stepped up behind her and filled it with shipwine then he offered the jug to her deckkeeper, Vulse, who followed Joron's lead by not drinking and covered his mug. Mevans offered drink to Aelerin. The courser gave a gentle shake of their robed head.

"Not drinking, Vulse?" said Brekir.

"Someone must make sure the shipwife gets back to *Snarltooth*," he said with a smile.

"Ten cordings for you when we return," she said.

"If you remember, Shipwife."

"Twenty," said Brekir, but beneath her miserable demeanour there was humour, though it had taken a long time for Joron to be able to read her.

"How do we stand, Brekir?" said Meas.

"Better than I thought if I am honest, and now I am let out of the dark and things are shared with me I can see how it truly stands." Meas was about to speak, apologise for keeping Leasthaven from Brekir but the dour shipwife waved a hand at her. "I understand the need for secrecy, fret you not. We have twelve black ships, five of the Hundred Isles and seven of the Gaunts — well, ten black ships and two pretenders."

"Pretenders?" said Joron.

Brekir smiled, a rare thing indeed. "It is what they have taken to calling the two 'white' boneships that came over. Their shipwives intend to paint them black, like criminals, because they think we do it from solidarity, not as we are all condemned, I gather. If more come across I reckon it may well become what we do."

"Don't let's do it yet though," said Meas. "A couple of white ships would be useful for slipping in and out of harbours if all black ships become thought of as traitors."

"Ey," said Brekir, "there is that. As well as the fleet ships we have nine brownbones and enough flukeboats to service the bigger ships and provide a steady stream of fish."

"So," said Meas, "it seems we have a fleet."

"Ey, we do, Shipmother," said Brekir.

"Don't call me that," said Meas. She snapped the words out, cold as the Northstorm.

"It is what is being said, Meas," said Brekir, "you may as well get used to it. We need a leader and you are seen as it."

"I'm no stonebound shipwife, Brekir, to command a desk and push supplies around a map."

"No one would ever suggest that you are," she said. "But after the destruction of Safeharbour our people need someone to look up to. None of the Bern Council escaped." Silence fell in the small room and it felt to Joron like a heaviness in the air, that a point had been reached where something had changed.

Eventually, Meas spoke: "I would not leave the deck of *Tide Child*."

"We would not ask it," said Brekir softly. Meas sighed.

"Very well." She did not sound in the least pleased at this promise of promotion. "But this cannot happen while so many of our people are missing. Once that is sorted I will take the name Shipmother and lead, though I will not do it alone. Maybe having our own Bern, even a council of them, was simply to recreate what we said must change. Maybe a council of shipwives should run us."

Brekir nodded. "I see no reason why that cannot be the case."

"Well, good," said Meas. She took a sip from her drink. "You know, Brekir, in this wish to name me Shipmother, I get the distinct feeling I have been outmanoeuvred and outmatched as surely as if my ship were sinking into the sea below me."

"I would never presume such a thing, Shipwife," said Brekir, but she hid her smiling mouth with her cup. "Now," she continued, once her usual seriousness was restored. "tell me of McLean's Rock."

"I know little about it. Aelerin has been studying it."

The courser nodded. "It is a crescent isle," they said, "like many of them are, but my charts tell me little of it. It is in temperate water where the dying season will either be under way or starting as we get there, and it is steeply sided, like a mound, with the sides falling away to beaches on all sides but to the north, where there are high cliffs. It has a windspire as well but that is all I can tell you. Information in our charts is scant."

"Thank you, Aelerin. How sings the weather?"

"A storm is coming, Shipwife."

"Well, we all know that," said Brekir.

"One other thing," said Aelerin, "and it may be nothing. The oldest of my charts had been scraped and written over. I did my best to recreate what had been there before – I think McLean's Rock was once called Sponge Island."

"A good place for fishing sponges once, do you think?" said Meas.

Aelerin shrugged. "I do not know, Shipwife."

"Is it just you and I to go, Meas?" said Brekir. Meas nodded.

"Ey," she said, "I will take *Tide Child* into the bay, drop the staystone and land everyone I can. I will need your flukeboats. We overwhelm those on the island then ransack the place looking for clues to where our people have gone."

"And if we find nothing, Meas?" said Brekir.

Meas looked at her, and there was something in her eyes that Joron had never seen before – a bleakness, a loss. He knew then that this was the last throw of the dice, that if they found nothing which led them to the people taken from Safeharbour then those people were lost and he shuddered, remembering his short time in the box. Joron bunched his fists, nails digging into his palms, as Meas spoke again, ignoring Brekir's words.

"I want you to bring some of the gullaime we saved from Safeharbour. They have made nests further up the hill from Leasthaven town. Bring plenty so you do not exhaust them if you need the wind. When we get to McLean's Rock, I want you to coast around the island and warn us in good time of any approaching ships. If something big comes, though I think it unlikely, stay out of range of it until we are back aboard *Tide Child* and we shall tackle it together."

"It sounds like a good plan."

"For however long it lasts, ey?" grinned Meas.

"Indeed," said Brekir, then the two shipwives stood and grasped arms while Joron put his hand to his breast to salute Brekir and Vulse did the same for Meas.

Above, *Tide Child's* deck was as full as Joron had ever seen it, old hands showing the newer ones how to pull on ropes without burning their hands, cranes rigged on the landward side of the ship to bring aboard water and stores for their journey. All was action – Solemn Muffaz walked among the deckchilder, face dark as a storm, while Coughlin, with a full regiment of his own seaguard, watched as the supplies were brought on, ready to lend an arm when needed. Joron wondered how Coughlin had replenished his numbers, then shrugged, presumed some connivance with Mevans and moved on. He passed Berhof, stood by a crane and looking distinctly sickly even though the ship only bobbed at his staystone. The man gave him a weak smile. Joron added his voice to the busy throng – a "Mind that barrel, Alvit," here and a "Tie off that rope, Mebble, or someone will lose a finger," there. Even if Joron had not known *Tide Child's* crew by name and sight he would have been able to pick out those who were new. Not because they worked less hard – Joron had never seen a crew go about their tasks with such single-minded purpose – but because the gullaime walked among them with its miserable follower. And where the regular crew of *Tide Child* took the windtalker's well-meaning curiosity in their stride, the newer members shied away from it, something met with laughter and derision by the more seasoned deckchilder.

"Ho mates, it's only our gullaime," said one.

"Well lucky our windtalker is, pay it no mind. And neither pay mind to Shorn, for it is the windtalker's shadow," said another.

"Ey, unless the windtalker gives you an order, for it is indeed an officer," said a third.

This last brought the most laughter and Joron smiled to himself, until the crew started to sing as they pulled on the ropes. The words were familiar, the chant familiar.

Bring the babe a-world.
Push, hey a push hey!
Bring it out in blood.
Push, hey a push hey!
Bring the babe a-world.
Push, hey a-push hey!
Be Bern girl and be good.
Push, hey a-push hey!

And Joron found his throat catching and his eyes damp, for he could not join in. He knew, from a few sad experiments in his quarters, that what he had once had, what had once been celebrated by his beloved father, had been stolen from him by a cord and an order from Gueste, and he would sing no longer.

"Jo-ron Twi-ner?" He turned, expecting to find the gullaime but it was not — it was the windshorn who acted as the gullaime's shadow.

"Yes, Windshorn."

"Smell sad, Jo-ron Twi-ner."

"I am . . ." But before he could explain what he was the windshorn was chased away from him in a flurry of sharp claws and snapping beak and shouts of "Away go! Away go!" And the windshorn cowered on the deck while the gullaime stood over it, the wings beneath its robe outstretched.

"Gullaime, please stop. Let the windshorn — let Shorn up," he said, as if giving it the name the crew had bestowed upon it gave him some power. The gullaime hissed and backed away.

"Made Joron sad," it said, swaying from side to side. "Bad windshorn. Bad."

"It was not the windshorn, Gullaime."

"Why Joron sad? Can smell!"

"Not in front of the crew, Gullaime."

"Ship woman? Ship woman made Joron sad?"

"No, Gullaime, anything but." He leaned in close. "It is simply that I can no longer sing. When I was strangled with a cord, it broke something in my throat, and my voice is gone."

But it was more than the loss of his singing voice, for Joron knew now that his voice had been more than just for song. He had hidden the events on Safeharbour in the back of his mind – none had asked about it and he had been nothing but glad of that. But where he had told himself the keyshan that had saved them from Meas's sither and her ship was simply coincidence, he could not pretend that the tunir rising from the ground to his and the gullaime's song were anything such. Together, they had brought them up, and that thought terrified him, but it also filled him with wonder, and sadness, that whatever had allowed him to bring that terrible creature out of the ground to his aid was lost to him now.

The gullaime took a step back, cooing and altering the inclination of its head as if it needed to refocus on him. Then it took a step nearer and reached up with its wingclaw.

"Come," it said, "come with Gullaime." And it walked away a few steps through the throng and the noise and it seemed to Joron as if all of the shouting and hammering and brushing and the creak of the rigging faded away. He followed the gullaime, down through the ship, through a haze as thick as the heaviest sea fret until they approached the gullaime's nest, and it was as if they walked in a trance together, unaware of anything else. Once in the nest-cabin the gullaime turned to him and it spoke, but not out loud – these words came directly into his mind and at the same time the creature reached out with a wingclaw.

"Song here," it said, and touched the temple of his head. "Song here," it said, and touched his chest above his heart. "Not here," it said, and touched his throat. "You sing inside, gullaime sing outside." He was about to say he did not know what it meant when it ripped the mask from its face, the eyes beneath blazing, shining white, the spiral pupils within slowly spinning. Joron felt himself pulled into those eyes, and forced into a communion with the windtalker. He felt the song rising within him, and realised how foolish he was to think that such a thing came only from his throat. This song was so much more than sound – he felt the archipelago stretching out around them, the metronomic beat of waves on rock, the melodies of the currents of air and sea, the way they twisted and shimmered around the islands, concentrating and chorusing around the windspires. And he felt the song within, the beat of his heart, the high-pitched passage of blood through veins, the cymbal-spatter of thoughts, the crack of muscles and the groan of tendons and it was beautiful. Behind it all was some meaning, and although he could not quite fathom it he felt sure of it, felt certain that this meaning was only a moment away from him.

Then the cabin door was thrown open and the windshorn entered.

It stopped.

Unmoving.

The melody of the world vanished as the door swung shut behind the windshorn. It stared at the gullaime, at its shining eyes.

"Windseer," it said. It sounded amazed, reverent. Fell to the floor, prostrate, gabbling and clicking in the gullaime's own language and Joron, knowing how precious the gullaime was about being seen without its mask, expected it to fly into a fury and attack the windshorn. But it did no such thing. The spirals in its eyes vanished, the heat within them also. Then it put the mask back, covering its eyes and the magnificent, beautiful and bright plumage around them. Then it hopped over to the prostrate windshorn.

"No windseer," it said. "Just gullaime. Stand. Stand."

"Windseer," said the windshorn, "have come to us. Windseer has come."

Once more the gullaime bowed its head.

"No. Not windseer. Only gullaime," it said. And Joron did not think he had ever seen a creature look so completely miserable.

# 32

# The Gathering Storm

*T*ide Child flew the sea and his crew pulled together quickly.
Most of those who had come aboard had served before,
and the ways of the sea were simply memories that needed
dredging back up to the surface of their minds, rather than
new skills which must be learned. And it was fortunate that
it was so, as only days after they left Cassin's Isle the storm
Aelerin had promised hit *Tide Child* and *Snarltooth*.

It was rare for the anger of the Northstorm to reach so far
up into the Hundred Isles, and Joron had thought they would
have had longer to prepare, but as the two ships passed through
a densely packed area of small islands he had recognised the
signs of its coming: a sharpness to the air and a thick band of
darkening cloud that stretched from horizon to horizon.

"That does not look good," said Dinyl.

"No," said Joron. "My instinct is to head for open water
where we cannot be smashed against these islands."

"I will call the shipwife."

"Thank you, Deckholder." And the call went out from Dinyl
to Solemn Muffaz to those in the underdecks, and a moment
later Meas wandered up the deck, like she had not a care in
the world, to take her place between her officers.

"Looks like a big storm, Deckkeeper," she said. "What are you planning on doing about it?"

"Heading for open water, Shipwife."

Meas nodded. "Good." She turned to stare behind at *Snarltooth*, and as the wind, already brisk, whirled the tails of her hat around she turned back to them. "Deckmother!" she shouted. "Signal *Snarltooth*, tell them I'd rather have them in one piece than in sight if it comes to it. If we get separated they know where we are heading."

"Ey, Shipwife," said Solemn Muffaz and he passed the order up the spine to the topboy and the topboy picked up his flags and sent the order. Meas watched *Snarltooth*, riding up and down the rolling waves, smashing through them in gouts of foam. They waited until an answer was returned and Solemn Muffaz nodded and walked up the slate to stand before his shipwife.

"*Snarltooth* says message received, Shipwife," he said.

"Well, I am glad of that," said Meas. "Deckkeeper, get us out of these islands and rig for bad weather. I will be in my cabin."

"Ey, Shipwife," he said.

It seemed to Joron that there was very little time between him giving his orders – to steer for open water, and to tie down the bowpeeks and get *Tide Child* all secure – and the time they entered the edges of the storm. A growing wind, a drop in temperature, a feeling in the ear that every deckchilder on the slate recognised as a coming storm, and a big one. The waves were growing, no longer undulating rollers but sharper and white-capped, the wind whipping their tops into froth and fury. Soon the wind was so strong that conversation could not be had without placing your head against that of whoever you wished to speak with, and a constant thin rain seeped through the old tears and found the weak seams in stinker coats, many times repaired on a Menday.

"If it is like this now," Dinyl shouted, "what will it be like when it hits?"

"Terrible," Joron yelled back. "Have no doubt of it."

He was not wrong.

The storm towered over them, huge thunderheads of grey, rising to black and shot through with flashes of lightning. Clouds became vast towers, lit from within by strobing light, and yet no thunder rumbled. Or maybe Joron could simply not hear it over the howl of the wind and the booming of the wings as they caught the air.

"Topwings only, Deckkeeper?" shouted Dinyl.

"Ey!" Then he turned, pushing his damaged voice as hard as he could. "Barlay, keep us beak on to the waves!"

And then the storm truly hit. A sheet of lightning whited out Joron's vision, followed by a rumble of thunder that sounded like wingbolts being fired into stone cliffs. Rain came, almost horizontal. No matter which way Joron turned his face was pelted with water. The ship began to judder as it was beaten by waves from all directions, and he turned to find Meas grabbing his arm.

"Double the teams on the pumps," she shouted. A wave crashed over them, freezing water covering the deck and, for a moment, it was easy to imagine *Tide Child* already sunk; then the water withdrew and the ship was rising up the face of a wave as sheer as any cliff. "The pumps, Joron!" He ran to carry out her order, gathering women and men to him as he went into the underdecks towards the pumps in the lower deck. He passed Coxward, the bonewright, his face dark with worry and his feet and lower legs black with bilge water.

"What is the problem, Coxward?" said Joron.

"Tis the lower bones, Deckkeeper," he said, as quietly as the creaking ship allowed. "*Tide Child* is an old ship and the bones move in harsh weather more than I would like. That breaks the seals and lets water in, but my girls and boys will keep on top of it. You just keep those pumps running." With that he was gone and Joron turned to the deckchilder around him.

"Well, you heard him – no one likes to be on the pumps

for it is fearful hard work, but it is you that will keep us afloat for the next two hours. I will have you relieved then."

"Ey, D'keeper," they said, and then Joron was running back to the deck. He took a moment to enjoy being relatively dry – though water ran in rivers through gaps in the deck and down the open main hatch – then he was back into it. Freezing wind, icy rain and waves that towered so high over *Tide Child* that it seemed impossible he would not be swamped, but the ship was as strong and stubborn as the crew that flew him and he faced every wave, climbing and climbing, then speeding down the other side while Barlay, Solemn Muffaz and Coughlin all fought the steering oar.

It seemed the storm would never stop. Joron lost all idea of time. The sandglass could not be trusted with the ship bucking so violently, despite that Gavith did his best to turn it when needed. Sleep was taken when it could be snatched, and it was never restful as the freezing water would not be stopped in its quest to drown the ship, sneaking in through every crevice and crack, waking those it found. Night and day came and went and the crew became leaden, but none gave up. And still, despite the discomfort and the danger, Joron felt himself grinning. This was the purest form of being at sea, this was when he and his father had felt most alive, when it was their frail human bodies and their boat fighting against the wind and the water to live. For Joron, this was what it meant to be Hundred Isles – not war, not sacrificing childer to ships, but to be one with the sea. If the Hag was to take them, let it be this way, let it be a great wave that turned his ship over and he would fight the water for his life all the way down to the Hag's bonefire.

"Joron!" It was Meas, her grey hair soaked and black under the hood of her stinker.

"Ey, Shipwife?"

"Get the gullaime on deck. I have faced stronger storms than this, but not longer, and the deckchilder are near spent. Aelerin says this storm is like no other we have faced – we have barely moved, we get near the edge and it drags us back in. We need the gullaime to push us out. Ask if it can." Was there worry there? An edge of fear?

"Ey, Shipwife," he shouted back and then he was heading for the underdecks, bobbing so he did not hit his head on the overbones, weaving between hammocks filled with fitfully sleeping bodies until he arrived at the door of the gullaime's nest. The damp windshorn crouched before it, looking even more dejected and miserable than ever, for though they were brought up on ships the gullaime as a species disliked the open sea, and hated rough seas especially.

"I need to see Gullaime."

The windshorn nodded its head and scratched on the door with a wingclaw.

"Away go!"

"Gullaime, it is me."

The tone of its voice changed immediately. "Come, come," it said, and he entered. The gullaime was crouched within its nest in a corner of the room. Joron could not recall if the nest was now in a different corner – it was moved and remade so often he barely paid attention now. Like the windshorn, the gullaime looked less than happy with the constant rough motion of the ship.

"The storm, Gullaime," he said.

"Not like!" it shrieked, and bobbed up and down on its bed of rags and feathers.

"None of us do." He had to steady himself against the wall of the cabin with a hand as the ship was buffeted. The lights swung on their cords, turning the gullaime's thin shadow into a pendulum on the wall and setting its strings of oddments swaying and rattling.

"Not right!" it squawked.

"Yes, I know but . . ." He hesitated. "What do you mean not right?"

"Listen Joron Twiner."

"I hear the wind and the sea and the rain."

"Listen inside."

"Inside?"

"Like song!" it hissed and turned away.

He did what it said. Closed his eyes, let the sound of his body fill him, but it was no different to the sounds he usually knew: heart, blood, bone and sinew all doing their job and why would . . . *No*. Not the same. Beneath it all another song, quiet, almost imperceptible, while at the same time furious, a jagged rising crescendo of squalling chords and drawn-out wails. A broken sither to the song of the windspires.

"What is that, Gullaime?"

"Killing, Joron Twiner."

"Killing how?"

"Sea sithers."

"The keyshans? How can they even . . ."

"Cannot. Have not. Not yet. But try. Sickness. Pain. So sad. So angry."

"We have not attacked them, Gullaime."

"No." It chattered its beak. "Like angry. Lash out."

"And we are caught in their anger?" Then his blood ran cold and he remembered the fate of the *Hag's Hunter*, plucked from the sea and crushed between the jaws of a keyshan. "Is one near, Gullaime? Are we in danger?" The gullaime yarked, making the noise sound like laughter. It shook its head and the shake moved down its whole body.

"Not here. Long way. Not here."

"Then why is the storm here?" The gullaime shook itself again. Touched its head with a wingclaw.

"Not know." It yarked again in strange half laughter. "Maybe remember us. Yes yes."

"Can you get us out of this storm, Gullaime?" he said. "If not, Meas fears we will be lost."

"Have to," it said. "Have to." It shook itself again and then spoke quietly to itself. "Plenty hard. Plenty hard."

"We will do whatever we can to help you, Gullaime," he said.

"Will need windspire after. Will be sick," it said quietly. "Is hard. Block angry song. Sing sleep."

"Can I help?"

It yarked again and hopped over to him. "Never," it said. Then it touched his chest. "Caller," it said. Then touched its head. "Not caller."

"Windseer?" he said. He half expected it to explode in anger but it did not. Only gave a small shake of its head.

"Not windseer. Not say that." It lifted its wingclaw to Joron's mouth. "Not say," it said again "Go now. Deck yes." He nodded, aware that there was something terribly sad in the way the gullaime spoke, but unable to understand why, or what, it was.

"Very well. I will stand by to do whatever you need me to do."

"When I say. Tell ship woman. Big wings."

He nodded.

"Very well."

The gullaime nodded once more then hopped past him to the door, pausing only to snap and hiss at the windshorn.

Once back on the slate, Joron had two deckchilder rig a cage of ropes around the gullaime, to ensure it was not washed off deck by the waves crashing across the ship. And as every woman and man they had available fought the wind to make the ship obey their shipwife's commands, Joron stood behind the gullaime, watching as it readied itself – stamping from one foot to the other, lifting its robes to show long scaled legs that vanished into heavily feathered thighs. Black Orris swooped down from the rigging, flying around in circles and chanting in a high voice that effortlessly cut through the wind – "Arse! Arse! Arse!" – and the gullaime yarked back. While it prepared itself, Joron dragged himself up the deck to Meas and warned her to be ready with the wings. Then he returned to where the gullaime waited before the mainspine.

"Be rough," said the gullaime, "be a rough arse. Hag curse it. Hag's tits." Then it squatted on the deck and went into a trance. Water broke over the deck and Joron tried to place himself between the waves and the gullaime, to protect it while it did its magic, and Shorn did the same. Then the gullaime stood, lifting its head and opening its beak, letting out a cry. And it did this, and it did it again.

At first Joron felt no discernible effect.

Then he felt the heat.

And then his ears hurt as if nails were being driven into them. And the gullaime was shouting.

"Big wing! Big wing!"

And then Joron was shouting — "Mainwings! Unfurl the mainwings!" — screaming it into a wall of water, tasting salt in his mouth. And Meas was echoing him, Solemn Muffaz echoing her and all that heard shouting out the words. And up above those bravest of all the souls on *Tide Child* were already arrayed across the crazily swaying mainspar, ready and warned by Meas of the coming order, and they pulled the ropes that let the mainwing fall.

The gullaime's wind came.

A gale howling into the face of the storm. A storm to meet a storm, to fight it. Winds ripping and cracking around the ship. Blowing deckchilder hither and thither. Winds that made no sense to any, never coming from any one direction for more than a moment.

"Brace! Brace!" shouted Joron, wrapping his arms around a rope as wind battered him, first his back and then his front. On the slate the gullaime shuddered, cried and squawked, raised its wings as if in supplication and, just at the moment it seemed the crew and the ship must be overwhelmed by the sudden violence, the winds stopped. For a brief moment, *Tide Child* existed in a little bubble of relative calm while the winds around it raged and fought. But that calm could not last, and with a squawk of rage something ripped in the bubble of calm air around them and wind came howling in from behind the ship, pushing *Tide Child* forward and through the storm. Forward toward battle and toward death.

# 33

# After the Storm

Meas jumped down from the mainspine, boots making solid contact with the slate of the deck and she stood for a moment, absolutely still. She became a statue clothed in blue fishskin and scintillating feather, staring out over the sea toward an island that could not yet be seen. Then, as if she had needed that second, to orientate something within her before she could continue, she moved again, walking up the deck to where Joron waited for her.

"I still see no sign of *Snarltooth*," she said. "But I can see McLean's Rock, and there is no sign of enemy ships so I suppose that is something to be glad of."

"The Hag takes and the Hag gives, Shipwife," he said.

"Ey, that is right enough," she said, words meant for herself and spoken so softly the lightest breeze could have stolen them. She took a step toward him, raised her voice. "How is our gullaime?"

"Garriya provided some sort of drink and it sleeps – fitfully, but it sleeps, Shipwife."

"Well, that is better than it moaning. At least it is free of pain while it sleeps." She stared out at the sea, blue and calm enough to make him wonder for a second if the storm had been a nightmare. He watched the crew about them work as Dinyl approached.

"*Snarltooth*?" he said.

"Nothing," said Joron.

"I fear him lost in the storm," said Dinyl. "There was something unnatural about it, and they had no gullaime the equal of ours to assist them."

"Brekir would be proud of such pessimism, Dinyl," said Joron, "but I have faith in her."

"Ey, Brekir is a wiley old bird," said Meas, "if anyone can survive such a storm she can, but it may well have pushed her far off course. What matters is that we are here alone." She walked to the rail, putting both hands on it as if to transfer the weight of command from her shoulders to the ship, even if only for a moment. "McLean's Rock, Joron, it is our last hope of finding our people. Faint as that hope may be we must continue, even if we only have one ship." She turned from the rail and looked down the deck, saw all was as it should be and nodded to herself. "We have done well with this ship, Deckkeeper, Deckholder." Dinyl gave a nod at this mention. "They have done well," she nodded at the deckchilder busy on the deck. "I am proud of *Tide Child* and I am proud of my officers and my crew."

"Rightly so, Shipwife," said Dinyl.

"And now, I take them into danger again," she said. "It is poor repayment for such hard work and commitment, that I may take them to their deaths." She stared down at the slate. Looked to the blue sky, looked to herself and took a deep breath. "But we have little choice."

He felt himself worried, puzzled at this crack in her usual demeanour. This was not the woman he was used to, not the strength that nailed down the centre of the ship and kept them all in place. But then something shifted within her, something that could not be seen only felt, and the brief glimpse of the woman, the person, the worries and the doubt that resided within even Lucky Meas, was gone.

"Do you believe the Hag speaks to us, Deckkeeper?" she said softly.

"And the Maiden and the Mother, if they so wish. Have you seen something, Shipwife?" He glanced about to ensure none listened too closely to them, for there were none more superstitious than deckchilder.

"Not seen, no, Deckkeeper. It is only that I feel as though we travel toward something terrible." She ran a hand through her hair where the bright red-and-blue streaks of command mixed with the grey, and it seemed that Meas grew just a little taller.

"The island will be in view to all soon. I saw no ships from the mainspine, nothing in sight. No people, though I suppose they could have been obscured by the gion – it is in full wilt but mostly still standing. The cages were apparent though, for the merchandise." This she said with such a sneer as he had never seen upon her face. "Even if we find nothing, it is a good thing to break all that is there and put a dent in the business of the people that run it. But we shall do a circuit of the island before I land anyone. It will take some hard tacking and be brutal work but it must be done. I shall leave you two to it, I will be in my cabin. Call me when we start to circle the island. I would look upon it with my own eyes."

So they started the job of taking *Tide Child* round in a great circle, plotting and planning with Aelerin so they did not get onto a lee shore and risk the winds pushing them onto the rocks of the island. Then making sure that when they must tack away to catch a favourable wind the island would not fall out of sight. The deckchilder were never still as they carried out these small tacks, constantly changing and finessing the rigging and the wings, and Joron was careful with his choice of crew. All the time aware that the same people currently running up and down spines and hauling on ropes had not long past fought a storm for days on end, and there was a good chance that they would have to fight women and men later on. Knowing that to take their strength now was to deny it later. So he forbade Coughlin and his seaguard from helping, tried not to smile at Berhof's look of relief at not having to climb the rigging. He set those he trusted least at his back to the hardest tasks, and reasoned that if he exhausted them now, they were less likely to cause trouble when left on the ship. He made use of Solemn Muffaz's great strength, knowing he would leave the ship in the deck-mother's charge when he, Meas and Dinyl went ashore. All the time he was aware, as all must be, how much easier this task would be if the gullaime was there to help. But the gullaime had spent all its energy fighting the storm.

And on thinking of the gullaime, another thought, one that had never been far from the surface of his mind bubbled up: *Windseer*. A name at once new to him but also so evocative it felt like a thing he had always known. Although, he did not of course, had no idea what it was. But he had never had the opportunity to explore it with the gullaime, first because of his duties, and then because it lay exhausted and insensible. Still that name would not leave him. *Windseer*. He wondered at the sadness when the Gullaime had spoken of it, and he wondered whether it was haunted by that word as it slept fitfully in the throes of windsickness, tended by the windshorn.

The windshorn.

Of course. What a fool he had been. What an unthinking idiot. The gullaime had hated the title windseer, swayed away from it when it was said. Even fully awake he doubted it would speak to him about it now. Only bite and snap and hiss and shout "Away go! Away go!"

But he could ask the windshorn.

And when the next tack was done and he knew *Tide Child* would fly free and straight for a little, he told Dinyl there was something he must attend to and slipped below decks, bobbing beneath the overbones, dodging slumbering bodies until he arrived at the gullaime's cabin. Inside he found it the same as always – the windshorn had been careful to preserve the nest just as it had been in the moments before the gullaime had ascended to fight the storm on deck. When he entered the windshorn was arranging the nest around the restless, unconscious body of the gullaime.

"Sick," it said.

"I know," said Joron. "There is a windspire on the island. We will make the gullaime better."

"Good, good." It turned away from him, pulled a small piece of old gion from the nest with its beak and placed it on the floor. Studied it. Then it moved it with a foot before picking it up again and placing it back in the nest. Once it was pleased with how it had been done it took a step back. "Good," it said again.

"Windshorn," said Joron. "I need to speak with you in my cabin." And the windshorn shied away from him, into the corner.

"Not hurt," it said. "Not hurt windshorn."

"No," said Joron and he put out a hand as if to take the creature by the wingclaw, and the windshorn pushed itself even further back into the corner of the cabin. He wondered what he had done to make the creature so scared of him. He looked at his hand, hard from working rope, blunt fingers, nails ingrained with dirt. Dark skin covered in nicks and scars – some shallow from working the ship, deeper ones from the swords and the knives and fights. These were the hands of a hard man, a violent man. He lowered his hand. "I will not hurt you. I only wish to speak with you."

"Speak," it said. And then it hopped past Joron, stopping in the doorway. "Speak," it said again. Joron followed it to his cabin where it stopped at the door. Waited for him to open it and go in before it followed, shutting the door behind itself then staying by it, as if ensuring an easy escape if Joron should go back on his word.

"I think you need a name," he said. "Do you have a name, one I could say?" It shook its head. "Then I will call you Shorn, like the crew do, if that is good to you?"

"Shorn," it said. Then coughed twice, "Good good."

Joron smiled. "Well, Shorn, I heard you say 'windseer' to the gullaime. What does it mean?"

"Nothing, nothing." The creature pushed itself back against the door.

"I know it means something," said Joron. He started to move

toward it and the windshorn cowered and shivered, making itself as small as possible. He stopped.

"Mistake is all. Mistake."

"I hear that word from you, Shorn." Joron crouched, bringing himself down to its level. "Windseer. And Garriya tells me I am the Caller and these words . . ." He touched his chest, as if to reassure himself that what he said was real. "These words, I feel them and . . ." He searched within for a way to reach the creature which had now forced itself almost flat against the floor. ". . . And yet, I do not know why I feel them so. When they are said, it is like they echo within me. Do you understand, Shorn?"

"Not say," it said, but so quietly Joron could barely hear it. "Say not say."

"I will not tell the gullaime, I promise." He waited but the creature said nothing, and then he remembered something Meas had done that had affected their own gullaime far more than any of them had expected. He took out his knife. The windshorn tried to vanish into itself, to make itself even smaller, curling up into a tight ball and making soft, fearful noises. "It is alright," said Joron. "It is alright." He took hold of one of the thick braids of his hair, one with a feather tied into the end and cut it off, holding it out to the windshorn. "For you," he said. "Part of me for you." He held it out and slowly, oh so very slowly, the windshorn came out of its tight ball of fear and misery.

"For me?" it said, looked at the braid. Then it stood. "For me." And it took the braid in its beak, tucking it away within its robes.

"Is it because our gullaime can see that you call it windseer?"

"See? Windshorn see. Bright eyes."

"Yes? But . . ."

It yarked softly as he spoke, not as brave or as raucous as the gullaime. Then used its wingclaws to push up its mask. Brown eyes, contained in a roundel of brown feathers flecked through with black, so much less impressive and colourful than the explosion of metallic colour that was the gullaime's feathers. Eyes far more human, less alien. And so very plainly afraid.

"Your eyes are not like the gullaime's."

"No. Not same." It pulled the mask down and once more looked through it at the world.

"Is it the brightness? That is what makes our gullaime special?" It nodded. "And what does a windseer do?"

"Lead us. Bring us free. Take us free. Away go."

"And the Caller?" It shook its head. "You don't know or won't tell me?" It shook its head again and before he could press it any further he heard the shouts from above that told him *Tide Child* was getting ready to tack again and bring them in close in to the island, which meant Meas would be going on deck – and if Meas was on the slate then he should be also. "Thank you, Shorn," he said. "I will keep your windseer secret, if you continue to tend the gullaime."

"Windseer," it said quietly and he nodded, then opened the door so it could hop out. As he left he found the old healer, Garriya, crouched in the shadows by the door.

"Were you listening in?"

"Garriya just stopped here to have a bite to eat, that is all, Caller."

"Why do you call me that?" he said, suddenly exasperated. "You have always called me that. What does it mean?"

She shuffled over to him. Looked up into his face and reached up, grabbing his cheek and pulling on it as if he was a child and she smiled into his face.

"It means change, Caller. Change is coming, you will see. The circle of storms turns, the winds blow and the Golden Door glimmers. We repeat ourselves and all changes and all remains the same. Fire and death or something else? Who knows? You will see though, oh yes, you will."

"What does that even mean?" he said.

"You will see," she said again, and then she shuffled off into the darkness of the underdeck, leaving him none the wiser, or any more comfortable.

# 34

# The Interloper

He returned to the slate of the deck, to the brisk wind, to the kiss of spray and the scent of the sea. To Dinyl on the beak watching the wyrms and Meas at the rump of the ship, staring at the brown and wilting island through her nearglass. She paid Joron no attention as he approached. He waited, squinting at the island and looking for movement among the dripping gion and varisk, but if anything moved he could not see it. If anything peered back at him it was well hidden. Occasionally he saw what looked like a building, hastily made, hidden within the brown vegetation, but as the ship moved on it vanished and he wondered if he had imagined it.

"Do you see anything Joron?" She lowered the nearglass.

"No." He squinted again. Skearith's Eye was rising over the island, half blinding him. "A building maybe, but no sign of any people."

"I saw nothing either." She handed him the nearglass. "Keep looking as we come around. The wind is with us now and I have stared so long I begin to doubt my eyes."

As they passed the island Joron watched it through the glass, searching for signs of movement. Once a shiver went down him as he thought he saw a tunir, striding through the wilt, but the ship moved on and he hoped it only a shadow. He picked out the spike of a windspire on the crest of the island; silhouetted against Skearith's shining eye it made it look like a slitted pupil. But he saw no sign of people, no sign of movement. Only the thick, decaying vegetation, and as *Tide Child* came back around to the inner crescent of the island he found himself humming the strange and twisting song of the windspire.

"See anything yet, Joron?" He shook his head. Passed her the nearglass back.

"Nothing."

"Ey," she said, and folded up the nearglass, placing it carefully within her coat. "And yet . . ."

"And yet?"

"I feel something is wrong."

"Why?"

She stared at the island, the wind twisting her hair, winding it into the fluttering tails of her hat.

"Because there is nothing there, Joron. No caretakers on the beach, no scavengers. Nothing."

"There are many islands, Shipwife. Some must be empty."

"Ey, but activity attracts scavengers, Joron. Always." She walked to the rail and leaned her weight on it. Staring out over the sea at the island. "Had we time I would wait in hope for *Snarltooth*." She sighed, bowing her head and staring at the water rushing along the hull. "But time is a luxury we do not have. Every day we pass is a day they have our people. A day they can put them to work to make their poison." Joron nodded, not wanting to speak in front of the crew of how short and lethal they knew that work to be.

"Shipwife," he said, coming to stand by her at the rail. "There is no guarantee there is anything on the island. Maybe we should take the time to wait for *Snarltooth*?"

She shook her head. "I close my eyes and see the hold of that brownbone, Deckkeeper. I cannot bear the horror." She did not look at him. Dropped her voice so her words were only shared between the two of them. "When I was young, Joron, there was little place for me in the world. So I was raised in one of the seacave houses."

"But they are for outcasts." He said it too quickly, without thinking.

"Ey, they are. For outcasts." She did not look at him, but he thought he sensed a certain bitter humour in her voice. "The woman who raised me, she had been a hagpriest, had spoken against me being sacrificed after the raiders took me and the sea returned me. They cast her out for it – it does not do to lose an argument among the hagpriests. After the waves saved me a second time, she took me in, as a babe."

Joron felt lost, unsure what to say.

"That was . . . kind of her?"

"There was nothing kind about Mabberlin, Joron. Nothing soft. Even the other outcasts hated us so we were in the very lowest of the seacaves. Shipshulme has very little tide but there is enough that twice a day our cave was flooded and the entrance . . . Well, even on a good day you had to crawl in, through a puddle of seawater. We slept on shelves that were usually above the waves, not always, mind. During the day Mabberlin would go out and beg food for us, leave me there while the tide came in. She said it made me safe, but when the water came it covered the cave entrance and the light went. That was my childhood, Deckkeeper. Long hours alone in the darkness, no explanation, little comfort and only the sound of the sea for company."

"It must have been frightening."

"Eventually I became numb. Mabberlin said I needed to be hard, but I do not think she could tell the difference between hard and numb." She paused, continued staring at the brown and wilting island. "When I dream of that ship hold, I hear the sound of the sea in that cave."

"We will find them, Shipwife."

She nodded. "We will." She stood, smoothed her jacket. "But we will not take *Tide Child* into the harbour and drop the staystone. We will take the flukeboats. You will command a small squad and take the gullaime to the windspire. I will take Coughlin and the seaguard and we will search the buildings in the harbour for papers or charts."

"Berhof will be glad to be off the ship, I dare say."

"Ey," said Meas quietly, but she did not laugh or smile. "*Tide Child* will stay out at sea under Dinyl. Solemn Muffaz is a good man, but if a ship turns up I want someone on deck who knows tactics." She turned, a gleam in her grey eye. "Have them spatter paint upon the spines and clear the ship for action, Deckkeeper. It is best to be prepared."

And the call went out and the drums beat and the bells rang and the deckchilder ran to their stations. Joron walked among them, choosing his people, his special few that would accompany him. And he set them to readying boats for both him and Meas. As *Tide Child* slowed to let them off – a brief clasp of arms with Dinyl, the sound of the bonewrights hammering as they took down the internal walls of the smaller cabins on the underdeck – he loaded the unconscious gullaime onto the boat. The ship was still readying for action as he stood in the beak of his flukeboat and Farys sang out a chant to time the oars that bit into the water, sending a million little fish scurrying for the depths and bringing them closer to the stinking, weeping island.

Meas's wingfluke was first to land, she jumped off the beak, followed by her ten deckchilder and Narza. Coughlin quickly followed, and then his second, Berhof and the rest of the twenty seaguard who helped pull the boat up the beach. A moment later Joron's boat jarred against the shallows and Farys and Cwell were over the side, quickly joined by the six rowers and four deckchilder they had squeezed in the rowboat, pulling it up past the tideline of broken shells on the wet pink sand. While their boat was dragged further away from the water, Joron pulled on the harness containing the gullaime and when he picked up the windtalker it felt dead in his arms. He was sure it was not, simply unconscious from drugs given to it by Garriya – drugs they had been forced to administer as the gullaime had fought and bit in delirium when they had tried to move it.

The windshorn fussed and tried to assist Joron, mostly just getting in the way, but he let it feel like it was helping, and once the harness was secure he hopped over the side of the boat, feet sinking into wet sand, and jogged up the beach with the wide-legged gait of one who suddenly felt the world moving beneath him. It was not just the change, sea to land, but the song of this place, shockingly loud.

"There are paths here, Deckkeeper," said Meas from the edge of the gion. "One leads up the island and the other away along the beach."

"I will take the gullaime to the windspire." He started to turn but she grabbed his arm.

"No, come with me. The gullaime sleeps, and I am unsure about this place. For now I would rather we stayed together as we moved through the forest. It is a ripe place for an ambush." She turned from him to Mekrin, one of her more seasoned deckchilder and a sturdy and sensible hand. "Stay here with ten deckchilder, keep an eye on the boats but if something happens do nothing overly brave."

"Ey, Shipwife." She turned from her.

"Coughlin, take the front with ten of yours, Berhof the rear with the rest, we proceed up the beach." They did, foot in front of foot, the straps of the harness cutting into Joron's shoulders and the curnow beating rhythmically against his thigh, and as he walked the song beat at his ears. Around him the gion wilted and the ground became slippery as the path wove in and out of the edge of the dying forest. He preferred to walk on the sand, the footing was easier and he had to concentrate less. A building appeared from the forest, the brown cured slats of its sides and roof difficult to see against the vegetation. Coughlin held up a hand. When everyone stopped he held up three fingers and went forward with three of his men into the building. A moment later he reappeared, wiping sap from his forehead.

"Empty, Shipwife," he said. "But you should come and look

in here." Joron moved to the side, feet slipping on rotten vines, so he could see through the door as Meas entered. Within the building it was dark, out here bright, though a chill hung in the air. Squinting, he watched Meas in the darkness of the building as Coughlin moved with her, talking and gesturing with his hands. She crouched down, touching something on the floor and bringing it up to her face. To see it better? To sniff it? He did not know. When she came out she looked troubled.

"Keep your eyes open," she said. "Someone has been here recently."

Joron hurried to catch up with her. "What did you find?"

"Nothing useful. The hut has been used by scavengers or to billet those trading slaves here. It is filthy and long abandoned, but there are signs that there has been someone there recently. Camping out."

"So not an army then?"

"A very small one, maybe," said Meas. "Looked like no more than one person." Joron felt an itch in the place between his shoulder blades, the one just out of reach of his hands and currently covered by the gullaime. In turn, this set the tops of his arms itching and he wriggled a little to try and alleviate the discomfort. "I doubt they are out there with a bow ready to pick us off, Joron. All signs are that they left in a hurry." She stopped talking, stared over his shoulder. Joron turned to see what it was that had stolen her attention. *Tide Child* had pulled up its staystone and begun its patrol of the waters. Wind filled black sails, and to an outsider it would have appeared they were being marooned, though Joron and Meas knew different. On the rump stood Dinyl and Joron saw him raise his good hand, as if in farewell. "I hope he takes better care of my ship than he did last time," she said. Then turned away from Joron. "Onwards. We follow the path."

They wound along the pathway up into the forest proper, making their gradual way in snaking single file. Joron inwardly cursed the constant soft noise of the dripping jungle, as it made good cover for hidden footsteps, or rustling bushes.

They broke into another clearing, this one with more large huts. Joron counted ten in all, though three were on the point of falling down, and four were not truly huts, only roofs over the bars of cured varisk making up their sides.

"The slave pens," said Coughlin.

"You have been here before?" said Joron. The big soldier nodded.

"Aye, Cahanny had more than a few dealings with these people. I had little appetite for it myself. Probably why he sent me. It hurts none to have your negotiator surly."

"He told me he had little appetite for slavery," said Joron.

"Of course he did, he knew what you wanted to hear," said Coughlin. "The middle cabin, Meas," he shouted. "That was where the headwoman lived. Calla, she was called. Hard as a bag of rocks, uglier too. If there is anything to find it will be in there."

"Set two thirds of our number in a circle around these buildings," she said. "I'll not have anyone sneak up on us."

"As you say," he said, and orders were quickly given. That done Meas gave Coughlin a nod and together with him, Berhof and Narza, she went into the main hut. Joron waited, listening to the slow breathing of the gullaime on his back and twice having to bat away the windshorn, who was trying to reach up and fuss over it.

"Leave it alone."

"Is uncomfortable."

"It is asleep, Shorn, leave it."

"Is uncomfortable."

"Leave it, Shorn." The smaller gullaime hissed at him and hopped back a few paces as Meas emerged from the main hut, looking as dejected as he had ever seen her. When she came within a few steps of him he heard her sigh.

"There is nothing there, Joron, the place has been cleared out." She raised her voice to the deckchilder around her. "Rip this place apart! Find me something." Women and men stood about staring at her. "Get on with you, I'll have no slatelayers.

Work, or I'll have Solemn Muffaz cord the lot of you when we return to *Tide Child*!" Joron was about to speak, to reassure her they would find something when she bit out, "And you. I do not give you permission to stand about either. Find me something that points to our people!"

"Ey, Shipwife," he said, stunned by her sudden bad temper, though he understood it. Since Safeharbour had been lost it seemed like the world was set against them.

As the nearest huts were already being ripped apart, Joron headed for those furthest away, still wearing the gullaime on his back and followed by the windshorn, Farys and Cwell. Something in him thought it was not sensible to head to the loneliest place with Cwell – he could not and did not trust her yet and no doubt she knew it. She kept her face straight, gave nothing away, but his wariness around her must be evident. Their relationship was as uncomfortable as it was new. So he kept his distance from her as they made their way around the farthest hut and comforted himself with the thought there were guards near, in the skirts of the forest. The building they approached was falling apart, one corner smashed by a fallen gion trunk, now slowly turning to slimy brown liquid and leaving a faecal smear down the side of the wall. Inside nothing but more mess, old blankets where women and men had slept, food so rotten and hard that even the vermin had decided not to bother with it. No sign of paper, no hint of charts. He turned to find Cwell stood in the doorway, a dark figure against the light. He flinched. Silently cursed himself for it and walked out. Wordlessly, she moved aside to let him pass and he headed to the next hut.

Out of the corner of his eye.

A flash of white.

"Did you see that?"

"What?" said Cwell. As much a challenge as a reply. Did she stay monosyllabic because she saw him as this nervy stonebound man, unworthy of more of her words?

"I saw something white, it went under the hut we just left."

"Animal?" said Cwell.

"I don't know."

She stared at him, gave a small nod and walked back toward the hut, four steps backwards, keeping his eye before she turned. Walked away, stopped by the front of the hut. Slowly she leaned over to one side, putting a hand on the crumbling wall to steady herself.

Something exploded from underneath the hut, knocking Cwell on her back and making a noise like nothing Joron had ever heard. He brought his curnow up – heart racing, breath rasping. The white thing, a ball of feather, mud and fury swerved away from him and toward the gap between the broken hut and its neighbour. The windshorn was there, behind it Farys, running toward them. The windshorn brought its wings up under its cloak, hissing and screeching and the thing turned around, finding Cwell on its other side. Then and only then did Joron realise that the filthy creature and the windshorn were making exactly the same noise, using exactly the same postures to make themselves bigger. But where the windshorn wore a robe and had its face hidden behind a mask, this gullaime did not. All it wore was a piece of dirty wingcloth wrapped around the tops of its thighs, exposing the dark scales of its lower legs, the huge fighting claws, a sparsely feathered, barrel chest and the stubby wings it held out from its body to try and make itself look bigger. It bobbed from side to side, snapping at the air, screeching and crowing. Joron was sure it was windshorn as it had eyes – or rather it had one; the other was a raw wound, bisected by a slash that had opened the creature's face to the bone and leaked a clear liquid that had left a yellow stain on the remaining feathers of its chest.

"We will not hurt you," said Joron. The wild gullaime screamed at him, a wordless, noisy fury that twisted and twined around the ever-present song in his mind. The creature made a dart for Cwell, trying to pass but she was too fast. Her sword and knife out, dancing through the air. The wild gullaime hissed and looked past Joron, toward where the rest of the crew were running toward them, then toward the forest where the guards Coughlin had posted were emerging.

"Not go back," it hissed, and made a dart toward Joron. He held his arms and curnow out, blocking. "Die first."

"Shorn!" shouted Joron. "Tell it we will not hurt it."

Shorn let out a stream of sound in the gullaime's musical language. The wounded creature replied, a darker counterpoint.

"Thinks we take it. Thinks we kill it," said Shorn. "Says make you eat sword."

"No," said Joron. He stepped back, his steps slow, his heart beating frantically. He spread his arms wide and slowly laid his curnow on the damp ground. All the time he kept eye contact with the wounded windshorn. He waited, let his heart slow. Took a step forward. The moment he did he knew it was a mistake. In his time on *Tide Child* he had come to understand the gullaime's body language, to know what to expect from its positioning and speed of movement and he knew this wild windshorn thought him a fool. That the way it held its head to one side, beak slightly open, meant it thought itself cunning beyond compare. It had no interest in his attempt to make peace. The creature was about to launch itself at him, its scythe-like claw extended to rip him open. Behind it Cwell, realising what it intended and already moving.

He knew he was lost.

"What is happening here?" The voice a roar. Like storm waves breaking against a cliff. All the power of a shipwife, of years of straining to be heard above wind and rain and battle pushed out into the air. It stopped the one-eyed windshorn right on the point of launching itself at him. Stopped Cwell on the point of defending him. Meas marched forward, jostling Joron to one side. "What is happening here?"

The scarred windshorn hissed at her.

"It thinks we want to take it away," said Joron.

"We do not," she snapped the words out. "We have questions though. Did you come on a brownbone?" said Meas. "Did they bring you here with others like you, and sick women and men?" In reply she received only hisses. "We are not those people. See who travels with us?" She pointed at Shorn, at the gullaime still sleeping on Joron's back. Her gaze rested on the supine creature for a moment and then she turned back to the tatty windshorn, now held at bay in a circle of blades as more deckchilder and seaguard arrived.

"Not go back," it hissed. "Die first."

"No one needs to die," said Meas. She reached up and took a feather from her sash, holding it out.

"I give you this gift, from me to you."

It blinked its single eye. Then screeched and hissed, and danced about in a circle making a racket, pulling its own feathers out by the beakful.

"What want feathers? Have plenty feather? Plenty feather!"

Meas took a step back, shock on her face, but behind it there was also amusement.

"Well, if we know what you don't want," she said, "what do you want?"

And the dancing and the plucking and the screeching stopped.

"What Madorra want?"

"Yes. Is Madorra your name?"

"Name name name," it said, and ran a long wing feather through its beak, pausing to bite at some itching creature on its skin. "Madorra want string."

"Well, I am Shipwife Meas, and on my ship, Tide Child, I have plenty of—"

"Want string now!"

It seemed there was an impasse. But Meas was not to be beaten so easily and she knelt. Unlaced her boot and pulled the lace free, holding it out. Madorra snatched it with its beak.

"Mine!" it said.

"Will you speak with us now, Madorra?" said Meas. "Will you trust us now?"

"Speak. Yes." The creature tucked the string away within its sparse breast feathers. "Trust, no."

# 35

# Women and Men of the Rock

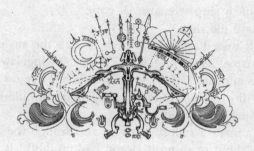

Madorra was one of the windshorn, but as unlike the one Joron had christened Shorn as possible: a mirror image. Where Shorn shied from them, Madorra hissed and spat. One deckchild took a nasty cut to the leg for going too near the one-eyed gullaime before it was ready. Meas then had to clamp down on her crew to stop them attacking Madorra. The crew had decided a fair while back that windshorn were not subject to the same rules as a gullaime, who could control the wind, who were useful and ship-like creatures to be born with good humour.

It took Meas and Joron and Shorn hours to gain even a little trust from the creature that called itself Madorra, or Mad Orra as the deckchilder called it when they thought none listened. Though it had accepted string from Meas it still swore at her and cursed her. Only when Meas offered food, a bag of dried fish scraps and salted kively meat, did Madorra finally decide to let its feathers down a little and stop trying to bite anyone who came near. From there, Joron and Meas accompanied the creature to the biggest of the huts, gave it the bag of food which it placed on the table with its beak. It sat on a stool, in a most human and very un-gullaime-like way.

"Madorra," said Meas quietly, standing in the open doorway of the hut with her arms behind her. "We need some information about the people who brought you here."

"All die here."

"Everyone is dead?"

"No, foolish ship woman. All gone."

"Who will die then?"

"You." It tossed a sliver of meat up into the air and caught it with a snap of its beak. "Them." It used a wingclaw to motion toward the outside. "Him." It turned its one eye on Joron and nodded. "All die. Only Madorra live. Madorra hide best."

"We found you," said Joron.

Madorra made a sound, blowing air through the nostrils on its beak without opening it. Joron had no doubt it was being rude to him.

"Let you," said Madorra.

"You did not," said Joron.

"Did. Hungry. Smell food."

"You were about to kill me."

Madorra paused, a long slice of kively meat hanging from its beak. It slowly reeled it in a little at a time.

"Ship man smell like food."

"It did not want to be found, Shipwife," said Joron.

"It hardly matters now," she said. "It is found."

"Maybe not kill you," said Madorra, "maybe kill that." It nodded at Joron and for a moment he was confused by its meaning, until he realised it talked of the gullaime on his back.

"The windtalker?"

"Spoilt, cruel, windchild," said Madorra, real venom in its voice.

"Enough," said Meas. "You can come with us, or stay on the island. It does not matter to me, but I need information from you as Hag knows there seems to be nothing else on this island." Madorra pitched its beak into the bag again and pulled out a whole dried fish, throwing back its head and swallowing it in a series of gulps. It turned its one good eye on Meas.

"Ask."

"How did you get here?"

"Ship."

"With other gullaime, and humans?"

"Stinking humans."

"And they offloaded you here?"

"Madorra escape. Madorra kill."

"So only you left the ship?"

"All left ship," it screeched. "Put in cages. Madorra kill. Escape. No cage."

"Very well," said Meas. She walked forward, picked up one of the fallen stools and sat opposite it. "Do you know where they were taking you, after here?"

"Not told," said Madorra, and stuck its head back in the bag. Meas closed her eyes, let out a breath. It was, to Joron, as if she breathed out disappointment, shrinking slightly as she did so.

"Madorra listen though." Muffled words from the bag. Meas sat upright on the stool once more. The windshorn slowly removed its head from the bag, the one eye blinking. "Madorra always listen."

"What did you hear?"

"Not matter," it said.

Meas leaned over the table and her words came out in single, sibilant hisses: "What. Did. You. Hear?"

The windshorn blinked at Meas.

Once.

Twice.

It pulled a piece of meat from the bag and gulped it down.

"Humans. Gullaime. They go other place. Go to rock island."

"'Rock island'?" said Meas, sitting back down. "They never called it anything else?" The windshorn shook its head. "Joron, we will have to ask Aelerin" — disappointment rose in her voice — "but if it is truly called Rock Island, there are hundreds so named. Although they tend to be small, not big enough for the amount of people on even one brownbone. And we can be sure there is more than one transporting people. So that may narrow it . . ."

"What," said Joron, whose understanding of the vagaries of gullaime speech was better than Meas's, "if it is not a place named Rock Island, but the island where our rock comes from?"

Silence in the small cabin.

"Sleighthulme?" said Meas. The silence fell again while she thought it through. "Brownbones coming in and out of Sleighthulme would bring no attention. It would be perfect but . . ." She tapped her hand on the table. "You may be right, Joron, but I hope you are not. The stone mined there is valuable, Sleighthulme is a fortress."

"Sleighthulme," said Madorra. "Rock island. Same same. Not matter."

"It does matter," said Meas. "Did they use the name Sleighthulme?"

"What say? Rock island, Sleighthulme. Same," snapped the windshorn. "Not matter."

"But they did say Sleighthulme?" pushed Meas.

"Yes, yes! Not matter!" it spat back.

"Why doesn't it matter, Madorra?" said Joron.

"Say." It snapped at the air with its beak. "Madorra say. All die here."

"No, they are taken somewhere else to die," said Meas.

The windshorn let out a screech.

"Not there. Here."

"They died here?" said Joron.

"No," screeched the windshorn. "Stupid human!"

"You mean us?" said Meas. "But there is no one here. How could we die?"

"Death in ground," said Madorra. "Waiting for ship woman. All die."

"I think the dead in their graves are past worrying about me, Madorra," said Meas, and she began to stand.

"Stupid ship woman," screeched the gullaime, then it put its head back into the food bag and continued to root around.

"Shipwife," said Joron. Something cold ran down his spine. "What if it doesn't mean the dead? Remember on Arkannis Isle, when we stormed the tower there? We went in underneath . . ."

"Through the caves," said Meas. "Hag's tits, Aelerin said this place was once named Sponge Island. I was not truly thinking. An island like a sponge, full of holes." She turned back to Madorra. "Do you mean there are people here, now, in the caves?"

"What said." It did not look up from its bag of food.

"Gah, bind me to the stone for a fool." She took off her hat and rubbed her forehead with the back of her wrist. "Joron, gather everyone and head back to the flukeboats. Madorra, you can come with us or stay here, it is up to you."

"What about the gullaime?" said Joron. "It needs the windspire."

"We will find it another. If they are waiting for us below ground then we must get away. Little use taking it to the windspire if we all die here." She put her hat back on her head. "Well? What are you waiting for?" Joron nodded, running from the hut to bring all the deckchilder together. As he left he heard Madorra cackling to itself.

"All die. All die."

"Everyone," shouted Joron. "Gather here, we return to the flukeboats. Be on your guard, we may not be alone."

The deckchilder and seaguard gathered. Many had small packs, now full of useful objects scavenged from the camp. Shorn came to hop around Joron and fuss with the gullaime on his back just as Meas came out of the hut.

"Listen close, my girls and my boys," she said. "Seems this island is a warren of caves, and my new friend in there" – she motioned back to the hut just as Madorra emerged – "tells me there are people hiding in them, waiting for us."

"All pity to them that come across Lucky Meas's finest," came a voice from those gathered before her. The breath of a smile passed across Meas's face.

"All pity indeed," she said. "But I do not want to visit

trouble on them if we can avoid it. I know where our people have been taken, and I'll need every woman and man of you to get them back. So we go quiet, avoid trouble." As she spoke Joron felt a movement behind him and turned, only to find Cwell coming to take her place. A shiver ran down him. If ever there was a time and a place to betray him this was it. A single shout when silence was needed was all it would take.

"Now, come," said Meas, "we make for the beach as quickly and quietly as possible, and if the Hag is looking the other way we may be gone before they even know we have been here." And there was much nodding and agreement to this. Then small conversations on how wise Meas was; because every one of them had the tits for a good fight but they didn't need to fight for no reason, and they were as sure of that as they were sure of Skearith's Eye rising on the morran.

Back through the dripping forest with blades bare and eyes and ears open for the slightest danger – though they found none. Joron started to believe that maybe the Hag was looking the other way today, and maybe they would simply make their way to the beach and slip away into the twilight to meet *Tide Child*.

But the Maiden laughs at a deckchilder's certainty.

Meas held up a hand, stopping the column as it approached the edge of the wilting forest at the far end of the beach where they had left their boats. Joron looked back, seeing the crew dappled with both light and liquid. Meas motioned him forward.

"This not good, Joron," she whispered, keeping down among the brown leaves, and pointing at the beach. He pushed a slimy leaf aside and saw three flukeboats lay on their sides on the pink sand, and with them were well over a hundred women and men. Among them walked an officer, and though Joron could not see their face there was something familiar about their movements. He looked to his side where Cwell crouched. She was watching the officer the way a predator watches prey. He wondered if she was calculating her chances – could she get away from him before she was cut down? For he was sure if Cwell made such a move the first thing Meas would do would be to end her.

"Narza," said Meas, "go and check on our flukeboats." The small dark woman nodded and it was as if the wilting vegetation simply swallowed her up. "Coughlin," said Meas over her shoulder. The big warrior came forward, "Any ideas?"

"We are forty in total, Shipwife," he said. "Give me ten of yours to add to mine, I reckon Berhof and I can hold them off long enough for you to get to the boats and get them down the beach."

"And what will happen to you?" said Joron.

"I serve on a ship of the dead, Deckkeeper," he said, then grinned. "My sentence will be served."

Meas looked at the ground, then back at the women and men on the beach. She bit on her knuckle then shook her head.

"No," she said. "If I am to take Sleighthulme I will need you, Coughlin, and every hand we have." She watched the movement on the beach in silence.

Narza reappeared from between two crazily slanted gion. "Smashed," she said quietly. "A thorough job done too." Meas let out a long sigh.

"Then we must take their boats from them," said Coughlin. But Meas shook her head.

"Forty against a hundred is too long odds. There must be a better way."

"Shipwife," said Joron. "Even if we can take their boats it may not help." She raised a questioning eyebrow. "The flukeboats must have come from somewhere. That means they have a ship. If we are on the open sea then . . ."

"But we did a sweep and we were thorough about it," she said. "And if there is a ship out there, then where is Dinyl? He should be engaging it to keep them away from us."

"Unless he has run—"

"No," she said, cutting him dead with sweep of her hand.

"No, he would not. Which means there is something we have missed." She rubbed her mouth. "Coughlin, bring me that bird."

"Mad Orra?"

She nodded, and a moment later he was back with the scarred windshorn. It took a bite at Shorn, who stood by Joron, and Shorn in turn snapped back, but before the conflict could escalate Meas grabbed Madorra's beak – a brave thing to do when it was likely to strike out with those vicious claws. Its single eye swivelled in its socket until it looked at Meas and then it blinked, twice, managing to make the action seem somehow mournful. Meas let go of its beak and it hissed, as if its anger escaped through its nostrils in a stream of steam.

"Madorra," she said. "These caves beneath the island. How big are they?"

"Big, big, big."

"Big enough to hide a ship in? The type we came in?"

Madorra shook its head.

"No, no no. Smaller. Whiter. Yes, yes."

"Hag take me for a fool," said Meas under her breath. "A two-ribber here, and hidden within the island itself."

"No one could have known that, Shipwife," said Joron and he felt some weight left from her at that. Then she began speaking quietly and only to herself:

"There is maybe a hundred on the beach. That leaves, say another seventy and presume my mother will have made sure they were well crewed. Maybe ten or twenty are left as guard on their ship. The rest probably roam the island, looking for us." She rubbed her temple. "Madorra, I take it these caves can be accessed from the island?" The windshorn nodded. "Do you know where from?" It nodded again.

"Shipwife," said Berhof, pointing at the beach, "if their ship is in these caves, and they can easily get onto the island, why come in boats?"

"To trap us," she said, "in case something on the island spooks us. Or maybe to catch us between two forces."

"That would be bad," said Coughlin. "We must act now, take their boats from them." He unhooked his blade. "It is the only way. Reinforcements may turn up at any moment."

Meas was not paying attention. She was staring at the figures on the beach as that strangely familiar officer rallied his deckchilder, forming them into some semblance of order. The worry that had dogged her seemed to fall away.

"Why only take their boats from them, Coughlin," she said, and a smile grew on her face, "when we could take their ship?"

# 36

# To Each a Calling

Madorra led them from the beach and up the incline of the island toward the place where the windshorn said the island's "big caves" could be accessed. It took them on a different, more winding path, and it felt to Joron as if the route not only twisted physically, but wrung them up within as well. Twisting the emotions of each of them into a tightness, tight like the wings of a ship under howling winds and ready to tear at any moment. When Madorra told them they were near the caves Meas took only Joron, Coughlin and Berhof forward to a place above where they could look down on them.

The entrance to the caves punctured a crumbling cliff face about halfway up the island, it was not big; a dark hole maybe just over the height of Coughlin. The rock of the cliff face around it had been white once, now it was stained with green algae from runoff water, brown ichor where the dying canopy had dripped onto it and webbed with climbing plants and vines. The opening was guarded by two seaguard, who stood beneath a lintel of ancient-looking cured varisk, and a group of about twenty deckchilder, sat about in the circular clearing before it.

"We can take them," said Meas.

"May I borrow your nearglass, shipwife," said Coughlin.

Meas nodded and passed it over. Coughlin scanned the clearing. "I do not gainsay you," he said. "But two good fighters could hold that entrance for long enough that we would be vulnerable from the rear. Twenty will be sure to, and the noise will attract every deckchild on the island."

"Hag curse them all," she spat. "Well, we must get them away from there then," she said as Coughlin handed the near-glass to Berhof, who stared through it.

"That entrance, Shipwife," he said, "looks like it was designed to come down easily. It was a thing we often did with caves for Cahanny, but I think this one was done a long time ago." He paused, still staring. "Usually you'd hammer out one end of the lintel but it looks jammed up with rock, I am not sure it could be brought down easily now."

"Well," she said, "at least they cannot keep us out, ey?" Coughlin nodded and Meas pointed back to where the rest of crew waited. Once they had re-joined them she crouched down with all around her.

"We cannot get to their ship just yet, my girls and boys, but here is what we shall do. Joron, you and half our number will take the gullaime to the windspire and hide there as long as you can. Once the gullaime is awake we have a weapon they cannot know about or prepare for. I will take the rest of our forces and we will light a fire, that should bring them all upon us, then we will double back once we have drawn them away from the cave. Joron, how long do you think the gullaime will need to lie within the spire?"

"I do not know. It does not seem dead, like it did before, but . . ."

"Hour," said Madorra.

"Not hour. Need longer," said Shorn, and snapped at Madorra.

"Not longer," snapped Madorra back. "Foul lazy creature. Hour do. Not true windsick."

"Longer," snapped Shorn. "Be sick again."

"Windshorn," said Meas. "We will take the gullaime from

here to the first island we find with a windspire, but we must live to do that."

The windshorn studied Meas then nodded its head.

"Hour may do. Hour may do," it said.

"It will have to," said Coughlin. "We will be lucky if we can remain undiscovered for that long."

"Then we leave now," said Meas. "Coughlin, you will go with Joron and build what defences you can around the spire."

"Berhof is better for that," he said. "He used to build houses."

"Aye," said Berhof, "I'm more use on the land than off it." Smiles were exchanged between the deckchilder, who no doubt agreed.

"Very well, Berhof it is. Once the gullaime is awake, we will want to be found and I want to draw as many of them as possible to us. We'll fall back to Berhof's defences at the windspire. It'll be hard and bloody work for a while but we only have to hold them. Then we break from the fight and we come back here. Kill whoever remains outside the cave and we take their ship. It's a simple plan, and I am sure I can trust you to carry it out, ey?" All around there were nods and smiles, for if it was Lucky Meas's plan then how could it fail? She was the witch of Keelhulme Sounding, the greatest shipwife who ever lived, and what a tale they would have to tell. Not only that they escaped a trap, but that they stole their enemy's ship right from under them and flew away in triumph to save their people.

There was no way of masking their tracks through the dying forest as they set off. But Meas's group would take a longer, winding path in the hope of leading off anyone who might come across their tracks. Before leaving, Meas picked out a particularly tall and robust-looking gion stalk, made sure all memorised it as a place to meet, and one from where they could find their way back to the right cave.

Joron led his crew up the island in a raggedy line that stretched out behind him. Though his women and men may

have seemed slovenly and lackadaisical, Joron knew that each
of them was as alert as it was possible to be, and twice as
fierce. A good thing, as he was distracted. Ever since he had
set foot on the island he had heard it singing to him, heard
the sound of the island as an alien melody in his mind, already
louder than he was used to. As they ascended toward the
windspire the song increased in volume, and he was sure he
felt the gullaime move against his back, followed by a low purr
near his ear. When he turned his head the gullaime appeared
asleep, though behind it Shorn was hopping from foot to foot
as if impatient, and Madorra plodded on as if uninterested.

The higher they went the louder the song became, an impossible volume contained within him, a vibration of his organs,
a heat on his skin and he wanted to sing out, but it was as if
his throat was blocked. As if his vocal cords, damaged by the
garrotte, had been tied in a knot that restricted the flow of
the music through him. The nearer they came to the windspire
the more he felt like he would burst.

Ahead of him Berhof was so covered in the brown sap of
dying plants that he appeared to be part of the forest. He raised
his hand and signalled them to stop. Then beckoned Joron
forward.

Before them was the windspire. Like the first one he had
seen, and all others since, it sat in a clearing of its own, as if
the forest had no wish to intrude upon its space. And like
each windspire it followed a similar form – a wide base with
a rising spine that bent forward to make a hook – and like
every windspire it was subtly different from all those he had
seen before. The carving was deeper on this one, the filigree
of holes more pronounced, making it an intricate web of
off-white bonework. He scanned the clearing.

"Seems clear. Do you see anything?"

Berhof shook his head. "No, but I will take Jasp and Kenrin
and circle round in case they hide. Wait for me to appear over
there." He pointed toward the far edge of the clearing and then
turned to gather his men. Joron waited, and as he waited the

song of the spire continued within him, increasing in depth and complexity. He glanced to his left and found Shorn staring up at him through its mask. On the other side was Madorra, staring up at him with one good eye.

"Do you hear it?" he said.

"Hear?" said Shorn.

Joron turned to Madorra. "Do you hear it?"

"Hear nothing."

"What hear?" said Shorn. As he turned back the windshorn shrank from him.

"The song," Joron said, and pointed at the windspire, "of that." Shorn made a sound, something in the gullaime's trilling language, then shook its head. When he turned back to Madorra it was studying him, the one eye rolling.

"Bad human," it said. Before he could ask anything else Berhof appeared on the far side of the clearing and motioned them forward. Joron gathered his crew and led them to the windspire.

"Help Berhof set up defences," he said to Jennil. "Find as much solid material as you can in the forest, make us barricades."

"Ey Deckkeeper," she said and drew her curnow, leading the rest of the crew out to forage as he approached the windspire. The song was even louder here, not the vicious gale of the first windspire he had approached – did this mean it was less powerful? – but more like approaching a giant tolling bell, a sound that drowned out all else to the point of pain. As he neared it he felt the gullaime stir on his back. It moved again as Shorn helped him take off the harness that held it, fussing and clicking and cooing as he lowered the gullaime to the ground.

"Careful. Careful. Not hurt windseer." Did Madorra, so carefully not being part of this, hear that word? Did it react? Did its one eye focus on them?

"We must get it into the spire's cave, Shorn," said Joron. All around the clearing was action, women and men dragging thick, wet stalks of gion into a rough square around the spire. He knew it must all be loud and noisy, but he could not hear them until he focused on their industry. His hearing had become oddly selective. What he fixed his attention on he heard, but all else was just the song. The beautiful, ugly, climbing, melodic, screeching, ascending and falling song, and it caught in his throat, scratching and biting as if it wanted to be free, making him cough.

"Come, Joron Twiner," said Shorn. "Come. Make gullaime well."

"Lazy bad bird," said Madorra, but when Joron picked up the gullaime, light as ever in his arms, Madorra hopped along beside him as he struggled over to the windspire's cave – head ringing, ears throbbing, throat full of spikes – to place the windtalker within the bottom of the spine. As ever, once he had it settled, and Shorn had finished fussing and messing with the cloths and clothes it had brought, stuffed into its robes, to make the gullaime comfortable, he stood back and felt only disappointment. Always he expected some reaction, some immediate change. But that was not the way of it. Something buzzed around his ear, a fly or something similar, and he turned. Found Cwell behind him.

"You should stay here," she said.

Shorn moved slightly, coming in front of him as if to protect him from her.

"What?" he said, standing.

"You should stay here, when they come." She looked at the ground so as not to meet his eye. "Deckkeeper."

"Why, do you think I am not able to fight?"

"You are able," she said. "But I am to protect you. And." She pointed at the gullaime. "We need that. It answers best to you, so it is best you stay near it. I will protect you and I will protect it." He realised it was the most Cwell had ever said to him without there being some obvious threat. Still he searched for some trick, and though her words made sense it rankled within him to simply follow her orders.

"We have twenty here, that is all, Cwell. Even with the defences I will be needed if they find us."

She stared at him, then nodded.

"Then I will protect you wherever you are," she said. Then added: "But you should stay here," before she stepped away and he wondered how he should react. Should he thank her? He could not bring himself to, so instead he went to look at how the defences were going. Gion stalks had been piled, then lashed together with what varisk vines they had found that still had enough substance.

"It is flimsy," said Berhof, wiping brown slime from his hands onto his clothes, "but it will disrupt a charge and it will stop an arrow."

"How long do you think until they find us?"

Berhof shrugged.

"Meas and Coughlin headed down the island, to turn circles about it. If we are lucky they will be found first and they will lead whoever finds them a merry dance," he said. "If we are really lucky they will not be found and she will light her fire and that will draw them all away."

"And if not?"

"Then the shipwife may wish we had attacked them on the beach."

"Well, let us wish for luck then," said Joron.

"The Hag seldom grants wishes, and the Maiden loves a trick," replied Berhof. "I have stationed people around us as lookouts. If they see the enemy in ones or twos they will kill them. If they see more they will alert us."

"So now we must wait." said Joron.

"Aye," said Berhof, "though if you will allow me, Deckkeeper, I will have the deckchilder and my seaguard keep looking for good gion. It will keep them busy and a few sharpened spikes in the ground around us would not go amiss."

"A good idea, Seaguard. Set them to it."

Berhof brought his hand to his breast in salute and went to work.

After that, just as Berhof had said, all was waiting. Joron walked, his feet displacing the mud, leaving furrows in the oozing brown floor to show where he had been. He stooped at the edge of the clearing, far enough away that the windspire's song did not overwhelm him completely, and he watched as his footsteps behind him filled with water. Almost as if something was displacing the water within the island, pushing it out. He thought of how Aelerin had described the island as a sponge.

"I hope it is not our blood it soaks up," he said to himself. Then he settled in to listen for any enemy, separating out the many sounds around him: the dripping of the dying plants. The chirp of insects. The screeches and growls and cries of the birds, and the song within him. He wondered if there were firash, angry and dangerous. He had always feared the fierce birds when he was younger, but no longer. He knew there were far more dangerous things — tunir, for one, and a shudder ran through him at the thought of them. If one came then he could not sing himself safe as he had before. Had that even happened? It felt like a dream, and no one had asked him of it, or even mentioned it. He put the thought aside and concentrated, as he knew far worse than imagined tunir lurked in the forest — the enemy. He had learned there was nothing more dangerous than his own kind. And nothing more likely to want to kill him. Even the myriad toothed and tentacled creatures of the sea's hatred were not as bad. At least their anger made a kind sense to him, for women and men invaded their domain, or pulled them from it, and killed them to eat, or just because they could. He took off his hat and ran a hand over the sweaty braids of his hair. Glanced at Skearith's Eye, beginning to sink behind the crest of the hill. If anything was to happen, he thought, best it happen now. To fight in the dark was the worst kind of fight. As easy to kill your own as to kill the enemy. He put his hat back on.

Sometimes it all seemed so pointless. The killing, for what? For their people.

For Meas.

He knew that.

In the end, the politics, the ideas, they were not what fired him, what drove him. Peace sounded like a wonderful dream, and right enough he longed for it, mostly. Though this place and what they did here felt far from it. On a lonely island, ready to die in a desperate bid to find their people. But that desperation did not matter. He would weather it for Meas. Because he believed in her, and she had believed in him, even when she should not have. And if he died here? Then he died and he would go to join his father at the Sea Hag's bonefire and he would enjoy telling his father stories of his time as a fleet officer. Of his time with Lucky Meas, the witch of Keelhulme Sounding.

"Hoy!" The call came from the forest. Joron stood, turned toward the wall of dripping leaves and stalks and the darkness between them. The call came again. "Hoy! They come!"

"Positions!" shouted Joron and he was still not used to that voice, the harsh croak that came from his mouth. Loud, right enough, but he sounded more like Black Orris than himself. "Take your positions!" he shouted again and the lookouts were breaking from the forest, running for the defences. Joron leaped over the gion and ran to the windspire, the song growing once more within him. The gullaime still lay within it, inert. Joron turned just as Meas broke from the forest, followed by her crew. He could not tell if any had been lost. Behind Meas came the enemy, and he did not need to count Meas's troops or add in his own to know that they were heavily outnumbered. He glanced once more over his shoulder at the windspire.

"Gullaime," he said under his breath, "now would be a good time to wake."

But the windtalker did not, and then he had no time to think about anything but the familiar weight of the curnow in his hand.

# 37

## What Berhof Did

**B**erhof felt it was good to fight on land once more. He understood this, it had a rhythm to it, an ebb and flow like waves — and Hag curse him, if he had not been with that ship too long. Now he thought in terms of the sea, in terms of the water and the cold and the damp that never left you once you had stepped on board the ship.

How he hated that ship.

This was honest fighting. Face to face. You saw your opponent, knew them. If they took your life then you could take them by the hand at the Hag's bonfire and talk of that fight. Or vice versa, and as Coughlin's second there were many that Berhof would talk to when he finally fell, many who he had hated in life, and many who he owed an apology to, who he had killed badly. But all was forgotten in the heat of the flame.

None of that on the ship. Just the knowing that, at any moment, you could be plucked from the deck by a bolt. The hours of manoeuvring and waves and nausea and water and a death that would never be seen, and the slowly tightening, slowly ratcheting tension. How could a man fight a ship? How could a shield stop a gallowbow bolt?

How he hated the ship.

The first battle of the windspire had passed and he still stood. It was easier on land. Oh, the deckchilder strutted about and cat-called the enemy like they had won a victory but Berhof knew different. On a ship there was only one battle; one terrible, all-or-nothing, no-quarter, screaming battle. And by the time you were in it, by the time you were coming in on them with your ship – the other sitting low in the water, spinebroke, maybe burning, blood running down the white sides – all that filled you was hate. Hate for the women and men who had been throwing bolts at you, hate for the officers on board who had orchestrated it. Hate for the ship that had hurt you and yours. By the time you were going aboard, swinging from ropes, mouth dry, voice hoarse with screaming, you knew inside that the battle was already won. That the other ship was wrecked, the crew broken. Which only made the fight all the more desperate and all the more vicious. Those left had nowhere to retreat to, had only hate for the damage done to them to fall back on. And those fights were like no other. They had a viciousness to them, a lack of order that Berhof hated. No battle lines, no real uniforms. You never knew if the woman or man by your side was yours or not. It was blind, like fighting in a rout, like the moment your troops broke and you ran from the battle and the enemy was amongst you, and you watched your brother hacked down but the fear was on you and you ran anyway. It was like visiting that moment again and again and again.

How he hated the ship.

They came again. He estimated their numbers at maybe a hundred, but he knew more would be coming. There was an officer among them – a deckkeeper, and he had seen a ship-wife on the beach but could not see them here. Berhof glanced over his shoulder at the gullaime in the windspire. No sign of movement. No help there. But a warrior could not look to magic for help, or those creatures, those strange and alien beasts. All his life Berhof had depended on the blade in his hand and it had never failed him, though he had failed it, and others that had depended on his strength to hold them safe.

But not here, not now.

"Hold! Hold!"

They came forward, a ragged line, deckkeeper and a deckholder now standing at the midpoint of it. Berhof looked over at Coughlin. They had set pairs of seaguard down the line among the deckchilder. Like rocks to hold the line, and he thought of the deckchilder as sand, as something malleable, but Coughlin's seaguard would not move, and the sand would gather around them.

Even here, he thought in terms of the sea.

Hag's guts, he hated the ship.

He caught Coughlin's eye, nodded at him, and pointed at the enemy deckholder. Coughlin grinned back. Take down the leaders first. Always do that.

And the enemy came on, feral, like firash.

"Ready yourselves!

Meas's voice. Harsh and loud and clear, and his muscles tensed then he let them relax as he watched her. Smaller than almost all of her crew and yet larger too, fearless. That straightsword held aloft, reflecting the dying light, and he didn't know how much of the blade's colour was from the last of Skearith's Eye blinking red on it, or the blood running down it. She had tricked Coughlin into staying aboard that Hagcurse ship, tricked him with lies. They had got drunk and he had told Berhof all about it. Coughlin would have killed for that once. But in tricking him she had somehow freed him, he said. Berhof did not really understand it.

Then they were fighting again and there was only what was in front of him, his shield held up, curnows biting into the hard edge as the enemy swung at him. Berhof's curnow still on his hip – not the place for it, this sort of fight. He used his bone knife. Holding back, waiting for his moment. Relying on Kenrin to protect his landward side, fighting how he had been trained. Oh, he screamed and he swore and cursed them in Hassith's name. In the Hag's name. In the Mother's name. In the Maiden's name. But inside he was cold. Inside he was calculating.

Gion chipped from his shield.

Duck to landward, see a gap.

Thrust.

Hit something, feel the give of parting flesh.

Feet slipping on the mud.

Feel the hot blood flow over his hand.

Not a scream in return but a sigh.

A sigh like disappointment. Like acknowledgement. He saw the face of the woman he had killed and she looked into his eyes. He looked into hers. They shared a moment. *I will see you by the fire.* And she fell backwards to be replaced by another, screaming, hacking, fighting. Blood and filth. Stink and spit. Anguish and triumph. Then the enemy are withdrawing again. The fight is tidal. Their enemy crashing against the rock of their defence and drawing back, leaving a line of broken bodies strewn across the ground.

All life gone from them.

Limbs at unnatural angles.

Dark zigzags of blood on the ground.

Down the line Meas's crew still stood, untouched by the enemy's blades so far. It would not last, he knew that. So far it had only been probing – testing the line, testing the defences.

"Shields!" That from Coughlin. Berhof, by instinct, crouched and lifted his shield to protect his head. Felt the impact of the arrows against it before he heard them. A cry from their lines where someone had not been quick enough and he looked – sudden fear. No, Meas still stood, as hard and sharp as the beak of her ship.

Oh, he hated that ship.

"Here they come!"

# 38

# The Last Push

Joron was bloodied. A glancing blow to his forearm had opened it up and now Farys, dear Farys, was working with needle and thread to bind the wound. Arrows were coming, but in the dusky gloom they were badly aimed, falling randomly. Meas brought torches, lit them and threw them out on the ground before their defences to confuse the archers' aim further.

"How is the arm, Joron?" said Meas. She had blood on her face. Not her blood.

"Well, Farys will never be a tailor but she does the job."

"Sorry, D'keeper," said Farys.

"There is nothing to be sorry for, Farys," said Joron. "I'll take quick over pretty." And he would – his heart beat fast and he longed to return to the fray, for the enemy to come at them once more. To pay back the cut to his arm many times over. Farys finished, biting the twine off and he pushed his way to the edge of the defences, staring out at the forest where it seemed a thousand torches burned.

"They light far more torches than there are deckchilder," said Meas. She raised her voice. "They wish to frighten us. But are we frightened?" A rousing shout of "No!" in return. Meas nodded in the dark, then leaned in close to Joron and spoke quietly. "They have nearly all of those we saw at the beach up here now, Joron. We can hold maybe one, two more attacks before they overrun us. How is the gullaime?"

"It still sleeps."

She nodded. "They will come at us with their full strength next. It will be a struggle to hold them but if we do then you must find some way to wake the gullaime before they come again."

"I do not know how, Shipwife."

"I did not ask for excuses." She glanced away as a roar from the enemy filled the air. "Unhook your blade, Joron, this will be a hard one."

It was a hard one, a vicious one. A screaming, crying, cutting one. The pain in his arm forgotten as he slashed, struggling to hold on to his small shield as a man grabbed it. Fighting to pull it away from him and let the woman by him in with her blade. Would have died had not Cwell saved him. Would have died had not Farys saved him. Would have died had not Tirof saved him. Would have died would have died would have died so many times. But his was a fleet ship's crew, and they acted as one, fought as one. Came together to plug the holes in the hull of their defences. Screamed in the faces of their attackers. Fought and fought and fought and in the firelight women and men became monsters.

He saw a face among the enemy in the flickering light, recognised it.

Saw a blade, knew it.

His blade.

Then moving through the fight, pushing through waves of violence down the line to reach the enemy shipwife. Shouting words only for them to be lost in the fray.

"That is my sword! My sword!" He saw it lifted, trailing a stream of blood and saw the face of the man who wielded it turn to him. "Barnt! That is my sword!" Then he was blocked by a man with a shield. A screaming face before him. A boarding axe swinging at him and he was fighting for his life.

Then fighting nothing.

The enemy had withdrawn once more. Joron's legs threatened to collapse. He was weak. Struggling for breath as the adrenaline drained from his system. Being moved back from the front line and into the clearing behind so fresher bodies could take his place.

"Joron." Meas striding over as arrows fell around them. "We have lost ten so far. They seek to tire us and wear us down with these short attacks and it is working. We need the gullaime and if you cannot wake it then we must make a break for the cave soon no matter what." He nodded. "When they come again we will hold them while we can, then draw back to the secondary defences around the spire to concentrate our line."

"Very well." He looked around for the two windshorn. Found them, stood together on the edge of the battle lines. Shorn's robe wet with blood. Madorra's feathers soaked in it. Even they had joined the fight. "You two, come, we must wake the gullaime somehow." Madorra nodded and Shorn jumped up and down on the spot, screeching and yarking before running over to Joron.

"Not wake! Not wake!"

"We must," said Joron. He strode toward the windspire, Shorn fluttering in front of him, holding out the wings beneath its cloak. "We will all die otherwise, Shorn."

"Make sick! Make sick!" it screeched. Then Madorra was in front of it, chirping something in the gullaime's own language and Shorn slowly lowered its wings, nodded its head. Cwell strode past him, her blade drawn and he grabbed her by the arm.

"You can help me more by holding the enemy at our defences than you can by being here." She stared at him, eyes full of defiance. Then gritted her teeth, turned around and walked back to where Meas stood with Narza, watching him.

"What did you say to Shorn?" said Joron to Madorra.

"Better sick than slave," replied Madorra, and it led them on, over the meagre lines of the secondary defence and to the windspire. As Joron knelt before the gullaime he heard the roar of the enemy advance, loud enough to be heard over the roar of the windspire's music in his head. Knew it would not be long before Meas withdrew. Within the windspire he hoped for movement but the gullaime only slept, curled up on itself. He turned to Shorn and Madorra.

"You can wake it?" Shorn hung back, but Madorra bobbed its head in acknowledgment.

"Sing awake," it said. "Not good. But can."

"Do it," said Joron. He glanced back. Saw the shine of blades in the firelight. Heard the screams of rage, of pain, of death.

"May not work," said Shorn, the creature sounded desperate. "May not—"

"Magic stop," said Madorra. "Wake early. Sometime no magic. Lazy gullaime. Bad gullaime. Minds weak."

"Do it anyway," said Joron. "And quick." Shorn bobbed its head in assent, then the two windshorn lowered their heads, lifted their wings and began to sing to the gullaime. This was not the song Joron was used to from the creatures – this was a strange, almost painful, discordant song. The windshorn did not harmonise, instead they sang across each other and within the discord Joron also heard the song of the island that had been a constant clawing in his mind. The gullaime, lying curled into a ball within the cave of the windspire, batted at the air with a wingclaw. Shorn glanced over at Joron. Was there some guilt in its body language as it opened its mouth once more to sing? Or was he imagining it? He could not tell. The song continued.

The gullaime's head moved.

"Hold them!" This call from Meas. Joron heard the furious roar as the attackers battered at the defences. He wanted to run toward the fight. To become a part of that fury and anger, but he could not. That was not his task. He turned back. The windshorn still singing.

Screams.

The beat of sword and spear on shield.

The gullaime moved again, its head twitched. Its beak opened and a thin stream of saliva fell from its mouth to pool on the floor of the windspire. Joron glanced over his shoulder. Saw their pitifully thin line, illuminated by torches. They could not hold much longer.

"Come on," said Joron under his breath.

"Not be hurried," said Shorn.

"We will all die if you do not," hissed Joron, but Shorn was no longer listening, it was once more singing that terrible discordant song.

"Break!" Meas's voice, cutting through the night, and at the same time the gullaime shuddered awake. Shook its head and lifted it from the floor of the cave.

"Away go," it said weakly. Then all was lost to noise as Meas, the remaining seaguard and deckchilder leaped over the defences, picking up the bows and crossbows that had been hidden under the gion stalks and immediately loosing arrows from the clumps stuck into the ground. It was enough to stall the attackers, but only for moments. At the same instant the gullaime sat upright, long legs stretched out in front of it, opening and closing its beak. Behind him the clash of weapons. Joron glanced over his shoulder. The fighting was fierce – a deckchild fell. A woman pushed through their lines and there was no one to stop her. She saw Joron, ran forward. An axe in her hand, but it was not Joron she was interested in – she looked beyond him at the gullaime and drew her hand back. Threw the axe. Joron could do nothing. It was too fast, too quick. The axe spinning through the darkness and he knew, from the look in her face, from the way the day had been going, that it was well aimed. The gullaime was still sat, as if in a daze, bereft of its usual fast reactions. It was an easy target and Joron was too slow.

Shorn was not.

The small, sad, loyal little windshorn threw itself into the path of the axe. The weapon hit it hard enough that it thrust the light body through the air, smashing it against the windspire. The woman ran forward, unhooking her curnow, and the fury that had been bound up within Joron, that fury which had been denied the fight, rose within him. He pulled himself up from the floor, unhooking his own curnow. The woman came forward, intent on the gullaime. He swung his blade, cutting into her side and felling her.

He turned. Shorn was cradled in the wings of Madorra. The axe had cut deep into its chest, blood ran from Shorn's beak and Madorra was cooing to it in their language. Then it turned to Joron, bright anger burning in its one eye.

"Why it do this?" it spat. "Why do this? Gullaime bad. Spoiled. Cruel." And Joron could not answer, did not know and could not argue against what Madorra said. The gullaime had treated Shorn badly at every juncture. Shorn reached up with a shaking wingclaw and touched Madorra's scarred face. Pulling it round so Madorra looked at the mortally wounded creature.

"Windseer," it said, and Joron was sure he heard happiness in its voice.

"No," said Madorra. "No."

Shorn nodded its head. "Windseer," it said and there was a definite satisfaction in its voice, as if death was welcome. "Protect, windseer," it said, and then Shorn's spirit was gone, flown to wherever gullaime spirits went when they left the creatures' bodies. Madorra opened its beak, as if to speak but was interrupted.

"Gullaime!" It turned. Meas stood above them. The gullaime opened its beak, shook its head as if to push away sleep. "We need your power and we need it now."

"Tired!" called the gullaime, then it fell forward on its face.

"What is this, Madorra?" said Meas, turning to the one-eyed windshorn, her gaze briefly resting on the body of Shorn and he saw her nod a little to herself, chalk up another corpse on her slate. "We need its power, we cannot hold them again." The scarred windshorn shrugged.

"Need hours wake properly," it said.

"What?" said Meas.

"Need hours."

"You did not tell us this."

"Sometimes does not happen."

"We do not wage war and risk lives on sometimes, creature," said Meas, and for a moment he thought she would lift the blood-smeared straightsword she held in her hand against the windshorn. But the gullaime spoiled her moment, dragging itself forward as it pointed a wingclaw at Joron.

"Caller," it said, then rolled over onto its back, letting out its yarking laugh. "Caller," it said again in a sing-song voice.

"Of course," said Meas. "Joron, is it true what they whisper of you? That at Safeharbour you called the tunir?"

He stopped, unable to think, the noise of the battle seeming to recede. Those events back on Safeharbour had felt so unreal, so dreamlike. He had almost come to believe it had not happened.

"Yes," he said.

"Then I need you to do it again."

He raised a hand, touched his throat. "I cannot," he said, the harshness in his voice betraying why, but Meas did not seem to understand. He ran a finger across the scar on his neck. "My voice, it is gone. Gueste's cord took it from me." Meas grabbed his shoulders.

"Listen to me," she hissed. "We are surrounded, Joron. They have brought nearly every woman and man they have against us. We need a distraction to get away." She stared into his eyes. "We have no time for self-pity. I need you to bring the tunir again."

"I cannot . . ."

"No." Their gullaime, seeming drunk, swaying before them. "Song not here." It touched Joron's throat. "Song here." It touched his chest. "Sing! Sing!" Then it fell over, yarking and rolling around as if had heard the most wonderful joke.

"Joron," said Meas. "We must try, do you understand? It is the only way." She leaned in, nearer to him. "My mother will want me taken alive. If you need time I may be able to hold them by talking a while."

"And our gullaime, Shipwife."

"What of it?"

"They want it also, or want it dead at least. The woman I killed came for the gullaime."

Meas nodded at that. "Well, maybe that is another chip I can bargain with. So you sing up death for me, Joron, for if you cannot we are all lost."

# 39

## The Calling of Joron Twiner

His throat hurt.

His throat hurt and they were all going to die.

The forest creatures filled the air with song and noise and they were all going to die.

The air was full of the thick, sweet and earthy smell of the gion forest decaying, the life leaving the forest like the life had left his vocal cords. Dying the way all those around him would die, because he could not do what was needed. It did not matter that he was unsure of exactly how he had brought the tunir from the ground that day, because the only thing he actually knew was that he had used his voice, his beautiful lost voice, to open the ground. And his voice was gone, no matter how the song may sit within him; that twisting, winding, discordant and yet strangely pleasing song. The one fighting to escape from within him and join the throbbing chorus of the windspire. He did not have the tools to air it. Maybe the gullaime sang without vocal cords. Maybe it just did not understand how humans worked.

But he could not do it.

So they would die.

Farys would die.

Meas would die.

Coughlin would die.

Berhof would die.

The gullaime would die.

Madorra would die.

He would die.

But what could he do? He was simply a damaged man among damaged people in a dying forest.

"Shipwife Barnt!" Meas's voice. Louder than anything else as she stood balanced on the defences, despite the slipperiness of the gion stalks. "Shipwife, come to me! Talk terms to me!" She was buying him time, but what use was time to him? Joron rubbed his throat, as if the pressure of fingers, calloused with years of work on rope and wing, could force his vocal cords into working again. "Shipwife!" It was as if Meas's shouts calmed and quietened the creatures of the dying forest, her last call echoing out into silence.

"What do you want of me, Meas?" A reply from the darkness. Joron squinted but could see no figure, became annoyed at this discourtesy, as discourtesy it was. To use her name rather than rank. And to remain hidden when a shipwife asked for terms was as much as saying you did not trust them, thought they may simply shoot you down if you appeared. It was to lump her in with raiders and brownbone shipwives.

"To talk," she shouted. Joron felt a movement by him, saw Madorra had picked up the gullaime and was helping it shamble toward him.

"Why should I talk with you?" returned the voice.

"Terms, Shipwife," replied Meas.

"Terms?" The tone amused, sardonic. "I think I need none. I think one more push and you are finished. The great Meas, beaten. And by a man at that."

"Or not. I'm well known for turning the tide, have been doing it all my life." Time, passing in the arrhythmic drips of the wilting forest. A figure emerged from the dark – tall and thin, well dressed in tight-fitting fishskin and a cloak of feathers.

"I think if you had some secret weapon or plan, you would

already have used it." Shipwife Barnt had a stick, a foolish affectation to drag through the forest. He also had Joron's sword. "But I have heard rumours of your gullaime's strength, and maybe that is why you try and delay my final push." Joron rubbed on his throat as the man spoke. The gullaime and Madorra shuffled nearer to him. "I tell you what, Shipwife Meas," said Barnt. "Bring me the head of your gullaime, and I will talk terms with you."

"Our gullaime? But why? Such a creature is worth far more to you alive."

"Do you think I hear nothing in Bernshulme, Lucky Meas?" He walked forward a step. "Do you think we know nothing of you?" Another step. "Do you think me a fool, Lucky Meas, the traitor?"

"I am no traitor. Our people are being taken to die and I would stop it."

"Your people are being taken? Well, traitors deserve all they get."

"You call me traitor," she said. "When you side with those who take the weak and sick from the streets, and the hagbowers."

Joron felt a pulling on his sleeve.

"A traitor," Shipwife Barnt raised his voice, "will say anything. Don't listen to her poison, my boys and girls. Sharpen your blades. Ready yourselves for the killing time."

Joron looked down, saw his gullaime, its painted mask angled up at him.

"Wait!" shouted Meas. "Do you not want me alive, to take back to my mother?"

"Right enough, a fine prize you would make." Barnt grinned. "But I have heard enough stories of you to know you would be nothing but trouble, Meas Gilbryn, so I'll settle for your head. Much simpler all round."

Joron listened while staring down into the masked face of the gullaime. It looked old, bent and frail, and it was clear that every movement hurt it. It reached up to him with a wingclaw.

"Very well," said Meas. "My fate is sealed, and every woman

and man who follows me knows what you do with traitors now, so they will not give up. The fight will be hard and to the last."

"Life is hard and to the last, Shipwife Meas," Barnt replied.

"Ey, that is true," she said. "May we sing, one last time, Shipwife Barnt? May I lead my crew in song, for they have been loyal to me, and they deserve one last moment of joy."

Barnt stared at her, then smiled and gave a small nod.

"What can one song hurt?" he said. And at that moment the gullaime's wingclaw touched Joron's chest.

"Song here," it said. "Sing, Joron Twiner. Sing for her."

And Meas lifted her shining sword and began to sing, a slow and low lament.

> For every one who left
> My dear
> For every one who flew
> For all aboard the ships
> My dear
> Lost, like me and you

And the crew joined in on the chorus:

> The Hag she knows no pity
> And the Maiden knows no love
> And the Mother only duty
> So I will be your warmth

The crew's voices fell away, leaving Meas's voice, loud and pure, to echo through the night.

> To each who met the water
> My dear
> For every one who flew
> To each who slowly sank
> My dear
> Lost, like me and you

And each and every crewmember stepped forward. To join their shipwife. And Joron felt a pain in his chest, a sharp wingclaw that pierced his shirt and cut into his flesh.

"Sing!" hissed the gullaime.

And Joron, with nothing left and no real hope of finding the tune, opened his mouth and tried. And what came out was not a tune, not a song. A single harsh cry. Like lone skeer flying over a stack of stone as the sea slowly beats away its base, inching it toward the moment it finally toppled into the sea and smashed apart in a last act of unwitnessed violence.

> The Hag she knows no pity
> And the Maiden knows no love
> And the Mother only duty
> So I will be your warmth

For the last verse no voices fell away but Joron's. What had come from his mouth had been a blow to him – worse, in so many ways, than what he had expected. Barely even human. He closed his mouth. Only to feel that sharp pain in his chest again.

"Sing!" hissed the gullaime. He stared at it. "Sing!"

And he did. Though it pained him, and forced tears from his eyes, he found himself unable to disobey. He sang.

> For all who man a bow
> My dear
> For every one who flew
> For who dies upon the slate
> My dear
> Lost, like me and you

"Sing, Joron Twiner." And was the gullaime's voice, deeper, louder, stranger and stronger than he had ever heard it before? Did it echo like they stood alone in a cave? Did it surround him like he was entombed in rock? It did and it did not and he felt dizzy and pained. He felt strong and weak. He opened his mouth and he sang once more.

> The Hag she knows no pity
> And the Maiden knows no love
> And the Mother only duty
> So I will be your warmth

The song ended and they were left in silence, looking to one another. The lament had affected Joron the same way it had affected every other in this filthy, muddy, smelly clearing around the windspire. How sad it was to die here, having come so far for such a grand purpose, to save lives. How terrible for those taken from Safeharbour, who must dream that Meas and the *Tide Child* would come for them, but that dream would die here and they would never know how hard they had been fought for.

"A good song, Shipwife Meas," said Shipwife Barnt. "An excellent choice for your last words, and I hope the Hag heard them." He paused, as if he heard something in the gion.

A shiver passed through the melting tops of the giant plants.

A huge leaf came down with a crash and the animals of the forest set up such a cacophony Joron could barely hear himself think, never mind hear what the enemy shipwife was shouting.

Was the man commanding a charge?

The ground shifted.

Joron almost thrown from his feet by the sudden and violent movement. This was not like when he and the gullaime had called the tunir. This was something altogether stranger, stronger. Something bigger was happening.

The ground shook again, staggering all those in the clearing and shaking the forest around them.

"Run!" Meas's voice. "All of you, run!"

"Don't let them escape!" shouted Barnt.

Joron scooped up the gullaime and ran for the edge of the clearing. Women and men had been scattered by the sudden tremor and many had fallen – another tremor came as they tried to stand and it was all Joron could do to keep his balance as he ran. A woman tried to stop him and Madorra flew at her, sharp claw taking out her throat in a shower of blood. A man came at him from the right and Berhof was there, taking his blow on his shield and lashing out. Joron did not see if the blow landed, for he was running, slipping and sliding into the brown vegetation at the edge of the clearing. Concentrating on going forward. Another woman before him and he heard Cwell shout, "Seaward!" He swerved in that direction. A knife flew past and took the woman in the chest. Then he was in among the dying gion, pushing through slimy vegetation. Glancing up, just by luck, or fate, he saw the huge gion Meas had made them all memorise, black against a sky smeared with the sparkling wash of Skearith's bones.

He paused.

Took a deep breath. Sounds of pursuit all around him. Bodies crashing through brush. Screams. Shouts.

He whistled. Heard answering whistles. Knew them for his people and he set off running again.

Beneath him the ground shivered and shook once more, as if trying to pull his feet from under him, making him stagger. He would have fallen but he had his crew now. Farys on one side, Berhof on the other, Cwell behind him and they steadied him, would not let him fall.

Shouting, all around them. The enemy. He glanced back and saw them, running pell-mell through the leaves, bashing them aside, whooping and screaming. There was joy in them. This was the killing time when your enemy were routed, when you cut them down from behind and lost yourself in blood and triumph.

"This way," shouted Farys, and led him landward, using her small body to push aside the brown vegetation.

Leaves lashing his face, vines slippery underfoot. They broke into a clearing. Five enemy deckchilder there who had somehow got ahead of them. They smiled, raised weapons. He stopped.

There was nothing he could do. The gullaime filled his arms. No time to drop it and draw his weapon. Then pushed aside, violently. Cwell, a fury of lashing blades and screaming anger as she ran past him, crashing into the group. Berhof joining her, Farys next and the enemy were down.

"Run on," shouted Cwell. "I will guard your back."

They ran, on and on until they burst through into the clearing before the entrance to the cave. Found a fight. Not a big one – most had been drawn away from here by the battle at the windspire. Berhof, Farys and Madorra ran for the fight while Joron hung back. He stood in the middle of the clearing, the gullaime comatose in his hands, fighting to keep his footing as the shuddering of the island increased, the rock moaning and creaking like a boneship caught in a storm. He turned, saw Cwell standing at the clearing's edge. As the cave mouth was cleared of its few defenders her gaze slid to the dark hole in the island. Then to Joron. She shifted her weight from one foot to the other, as if deep in consideration.

"Come on," he said, as more of *Tide Child*'s crew broke into the clearing. She stared at him. Held his gaze. Then shook her head and turned away, running back into the forest.

Hag curse her. He had almost started to believe she had changed. Well the Hag could take her then, and Hag pity her if he ever found her in a fight.

"Joron!" Meas's voice, calling from the cave entrance, flanked by Coughlin and Berhof. He ran, passing between them among the stream of *Tide Child*'s deckchilder. Watching Meas as she counted heads.

"How many made it?" he said.

"Not as many as I would like." She glanced over his shoulder and into the clearing and he turned. Saw enemy deckchilder emerging from the forest.

"Go," said Berhof. "With all this the movement of the island, I reckon I can bring down this entrance." He nodded at the lintel of cured varisk, now splintered and fragile-looking. The island rumbled and shifted again and the lintel creaked.

"It will crush you," said Meas.

"We can hold this passage you and I, Seaguard," said Coughlin.

Berhof smiled and moved the arm that covered his midriff, exposing a wound, and the oozing flesh beneath. Joron could smell the acid of Berhof's stomach, the sickly-sweet smell of ruptured guts, and knew it a killing wound.

"You go. I think I will stay." A smile crept onto Berhof's face. "Be glad not to get back on that Hag-cursed ship," he said. The smile fell away, replaced by lines of pain. "It has been a good fight, Coughlin."

"Aye," said Coughlin and he stepped forward, grasped Berhof by the forearm, and pulled him into an embrace. Joron heard quietly spoken words. "I will see you at the fire, my friend." Then they turned and were running again, down the tunnel beyond, into the island, and Joron did not know if the rumble he heard from behind was Berhof bringing the entrance down on himself or the island moving once more.

# 40

## In the Belly of the Beast

The twisting tunnels they ran down were dark and shivering. It felt as if the island were a huge, living and breathing creature and they were some unwelcome parasites, threading through its intestines. Walls wet with condensation were the tubes that hemmed them in, pulsing as they passed down the gullet of the island. The stone groaned and creaked as rocks, still for ages past knowing, rubbed against one another. Every so often there would be a crack, as if from a whip, and fragments of stone would tumble from the low ceiling. Joron quailed at the thought of the mountain coming down on him, entombing him here in darkness forever.

They broke from a tunnel into a huge cave, open onto the sea at the farthest end. Now Joron understood why they had not seen the cave when they circled the island. Its mouth, huge, yawning and obvious from this side, was covered by streamers of vegetation, masses of vines that fell from the forest above. But with the death of the forest, even just a night's worth, the curtain had become holed. Light from Skearith's Blind Eye, low in the sky now, shone through and illuminated a ship, sat in in a natural dock below them. The ship's corpse-lights gave the scene an eerie glow, and the pristine white boneship had been tied to a hastily built pier of varisk spars. Instinct had them all duck behind a low wall, just above the height of the ship's tallest spine. Joron looked ahead, saw the path that led to the enemy ship was steep and winding and open. "Give me?" said Madorra, and nodded at the gullaime Joron carried.

"Are you strong enough?"

"Madorra strong. Give me."

"Joron," said Meas, and she beckoned him down to her at the front of the snake of women and men. So he passed over the barely awake gullaime to Madorra, then counted his way down the line. Twenty-three of them. All that was left of the forty who had come ashore. He wondered if they would have fared better attacking the deckchilder on the beach, but that did not matter now. That time had passed and the time to advise that course of action had been then.

"Shipwife," he said. She did not answer immediately, only continued to scan the deck of the white ship below them.

"Two-ribber," she said, "named *Keyshantooth*. I recognise it."

"It was at Safeharbour," he said. "Its shipwife, Barnt, led them."

"Well," said Meas, collapsing the nearglass and placing it back into her coat. The island shook again, even more violently, and rocks rained down from the roof of the cave. Meas glanced up at the roof of the cave, almost twice the height of a woman from where they hid. "I feel no guilt for those I have killed then, only sadness I did not get Barnt." She gave Joron a weak smile and the ground moved, bucking and grinding and creaking, making her grab onto the rock before them. "I'd usually say, Joron, we go quiet and try and sneak up on whoever is on that ship." A huge painful groan. A crack ran across the ceiling and a massive chunk of rock fell from it, smashed into the path further down and rolled along it, turning and twisting, its trajectory altered by sharp protrusions, gathering smaller rocks and green plants as it bounced down the steep side of the cave, landing in the water with a huge splash. The panicked few on the slate of *Keyshantooth* began to untie the ship, better to take it out of the cave and to the safety of open sea. Meas had watched the giant rock's progress and when it had finished she turned to Joron. "I think speed will serve us best here." She gave him a wolfish grin. "Strange, is it not, Joron, to feel most alive when so close to death." Then she stood, and held her sword aloft, "My girls and boys! My glorious deckchilder! That ship was at Safeharbour, it took what was ours, now we will take it! To the blade, my crew! To the bloody work! Follow me!"

And she ran.

And they ran.

And he ran.

And the island trembled around them and the rocks rained down and the crew aboard *Keyshantooth* did all they could to free the ship of their improvised pier, but they were few and the sight of Meas and her bloodthirsty crew had put the fear of the Hag into them. As Joron fought the shaking path for his footing, he felt that Barnt must have left the worst of his crew here. For no arrows were loosed, no defences made. Only panicked attempts to cut the ship free continued. The time it took them to run down the steeply winding path should have been enough to free the ship but those left aboard did not manage it. Then Meas's crew were leaping the small gap between the varisk pier and the ship, feet landing on the deck, and the first thing Meas shouted, as she pulled a crossbow from her sash and sent a bolt down the deck into the body of a man, was, "No quarter! Give no quarter! Give no mercy!"

And there was a peculiar madness to them then. For this ship had been involved in the destruction of Safeharbour, and maybe those aboard knew something of the women and men taken from there, and maybe they should have been questioned, but that seemed not to matter. The night had been long and bloody and terrifying, and the shaking, disintegrating island magnified that fear, the ever-present knowledge the roof could come down and

all could die. And though Meas's remaining deckchilder were
evenly matched in numbers with *Keyshantooth*'s crew, there was
a supernatural fury upon them that none could stand against.
The killing on the slate was vicious, unrelenting – mercy was
called for but not given, sword and curnows and axes rose and
fell until there were no defenders left and Joron was left panting.
Hands on his knees, body bent over. When he straightened up,
blood ran down his face from his hairline but his fingers found
no wound. The blood was not his, it was splashed upon his face
and one-tail hat the way deckchilder splashed paint on a deck
for luck. All about him he saw similarly soaked faces – monsters,
madwomen and men, sick with bloodlust, eyes wild with fear.
Even Meas seemed shocked by what had happened, the thoroughness of it, the speed, the brutality.

"Well," she said at last, "what are you standing about for?
The place is not safe. Get the wings unfurled before the island
shakes itself to pieces." She strode across to where Madorra
had lain the gullaime upon the cold and bloodied slate of the
*Keyshantooth*. "Can it bring us wind?"

"No," said Madorra, "still broken," and Joron thought it
odd, that Madorra did not call it lazy or bad now. "But more
gullaime below," said Madorra. "Feel them."

"Get them up here," said Meas. "And hope to the Hag they
are not spent." She turned to Joron and smiled at him, a crooked
thing. "Maybe we sang too well, ey, Joron?" The island shook
again, hard enough to jolt the ship they stood on and even Meas,
steady and sturdy and sea-like as any woman or man who had
ever lived, almost fell. "Bring up those gullaime," she shouted.

Joron ran, followed by Madorra, into the darkness of the
underdeck, to the rump of the ship and the cabin that housed
the gullaime. In it he found four of them, terrified, huddling
together in a makeshift nest of stinking rubbish. These were
not gullaime as he thought of them now, not fierce and proud
and defiant. These were fleet gullaime, beaten and scared, blind
and featherless.

"Come," said Joron. "We need the wind." But they only

pushed themselves further away, huddling together in a corner at the sight of this blood soaked intruder. "If you do not come, we will all die."

"Confuse them," said Madorra. "Not need kindness." It leaped at them, screeching and yarking. Beating its wings in their faces. "Bad gullaime! Lazy gullaime! On deck. On deck. Listen to ship man. Do duty!" And it forced them past Joron, huddled together into a small flock, each with a wingclaw touching the body of the one in front as they moved. He followed them, and it was almost impossible to believe these creatures were the same as the one that he had slowly befriended over the last few years. "Make wind! Make wind!" screeched Madorra as they emerged to stand upon the slate, but the little group of four gullaime only huddled down, cooing and chirruping in their own language. "Say they are windsick," screeched Madorra, "But lazy. Bad. Should beat." Joron stared at them, and Meas looked to him, as the one with the most experience of their kind. The island rumbled and shook and rained down rock. He took a breath. The mountain seemed to breathe also, then let out its breath in another exhalation of falling stones, splashing water and cracking and creaking of rock under stress. Joron stepped forward.

"Listen to me," he said. "We are the crew of the *Tide Child* and we have taken this ship for ourselves——"

"No!" screeched Madorra, "only understand hurt."

"Quiet!" shouted Meas. "Let my deckkeeper work."

"If you are truly windsick," said Joron, "then I know you cannot bring the wind. But if you can bring us wind, any wind, we will leave here and if you do not wish it you will never have to ride the slate of a boneship ever again. Meas will not force you. But you must decide quickly." Another rumble from the stone around them, another shower of rocks, some splashing into the water, some bouncing from the decks. The roof of the cave cracked into a huge zigzag with a sound like lightning hitting gion. "Help us help you, or we will all die."

The smallest of the gullaime came forward from the group, staying low, subservient, but keeping its mask fixed on Joron.

"Ship human lie."

"Not this one," screeched Madorra. "Bad gullaime!"

"Why have windshorn?" said the gullaime. "Why beater and torturer?" More rocks, a shudder. Starlight shone down from above as part of the roof of the cave abruptly shifted and moved with a rumbling groan. Joron's heart leaped into his mouth, sure they would all be crushed. But the massive chunk of rock stopped, jammed in position against another. Joron knew it could not last long before the island moved again and they were all crushed beneath falling rock.

"We found Madorra on this island," said Joron. "We also have another gullaime, but we were forced by the crew of this ship to take him from the windspire and he is ill."

"Joron Twiner speak true." He turned to find their gullaime limping toward him. "Joron Twiner give string and dust and feathers," it said. "Will give to you. Bring wind."

A song, a quick trilling between *Tide Child*'s gullaime and the small and beaten gullaime before him. Then their timid speaker nodded and scurried back to the others. They raised their wings, made a circle and opened their mouths, singing out. Joron felt them as an echo of what it was to have *Tide Child*'s own gullaime work – not nearly as much power, but the power was there.

"Ready!" shouted Meas. "Unfurl the wings! We'll catch every bit of wind we can." And the deckchilder were rushing up the spines and along the spars, letting loose the wingcloth as the wind came, not a gale, not a howling current of air. The pressure change was something Joron only felt slightly in his ears, but it was enough. As the island continued groaning and crashing and tearing itself apart around them, filling the air with choking dust, *Keyshantooth* started to move. Slowly at first, then gathering speed, and as it went forward it was as if the island knew it was going, and had no wish to let this ship of bone and death escape. The cave began to collapse around them as they left, so it appeared that *Keyshantooth* was spat out of the island in a cloud of rock dust and a wave of churning water, as if the island had vomited out the ship as it destroyed itself.

Meas steered *Keyshantooth* out to sea, giving the oar over to Coughlin and taking out her nearglass, staring out to landward. "I have you," she said to herself. "Look, Joron, it is the remnants of Shipwife Barnt's people in their flukeboats. We cannot let them escape and take word of us living, or of what you have done here. If the island simply vanishes my mother may well believe we were all lost. To be thought dead could be to our advantage." But Joron was not watching the boats. He only pointed back the way they had come. When he did not answer her Meas turned, and saw what Joron could not tear his eyes away from.

Where the cave had collapsed a single stack of rock was left at the very edge of the island, towering over the sea. And on top of that rock was a figure. Meas raised her nearglass once more.

"Cwell," she said quietly. The figure on the stack of rock raised an arm, as if in greeting. Then it raised the other and dived from the tower. Joron felt a moment of terror, despite that he held no love for her, despite that she had run from the fight in the caves. Betrayed him. To be so desperate that she would leap into the sea from such a height, to throw her body into the water when it would find nothing but creatures of hate and teeth and stinging tentacles.

Meas swore under her breath. Then turned her nearglass to the flukeboats flying away from them. "Hassith's cursed spear," she spat, "but we do not leave our own behind." Then she strode forward, pointing at the flukeboat in the centre of the *Keyshantooth*'s deck. "Get that overboard and crewed. We have one of our own in the water and we are not so rich with people we can afford to lose them."

Then the boat was over and into the sea and a crew with it, and *Keyshantooth* was turning, their flukeboat rowing away and Meas was cursing and Joron could not for the life of him understand why she showed such loyalty, to Cwell of all people. But still he watched. Saw Cwell, between waves and she was small against the sea and the island breaking up behind her. No matter how much he had hated her and feared her, he found he could not wish her to die on the teeth of the fearsome creatures of the sea.

"Longthresh," said Meas, staring through her nearglass. She pointed. Joron held a hand above his eyes. Saw white bodies in the water making their way toward Cwell. What madness had gripped her? To run and then return? To throw herself into the sea?

"Swim, Cwell!" He turned. Coughlin was shouting. Another voice joined him. "Swim!" He looked back at the small body in the water, the white, sleek predators closing, the flukeboat crew rowing with all they had. And he understood why Meas wanted to save her. Why she did not pursue the enemy. Cwell was one of theirs, and she could not leave her to the sea, not when there was a chance of saving her. Then he found he was shouting too. "Come on, Cwell! Swim, Cwell!" All of them, shouting. And though it seemed impossible that the unwieldy flukeboat could outpace the longthresh, it did. Maybe the predators were confused by the violence of the collapsing island, maybe there was easier prey in the water, he did not know. But when they pulled Cwell from the water, soaking, but whole, he cheered as loud as any of them.

When the boat came back, when Cwell was on the deck, dripping and shivering, Joron expected Meas to say something to her. To berate her for abandoning them. She did not, only watching as Cwell walked forward to stand before Joron. In one hand she held a long package, wrapped in varisk cloth. She went down on one knee before him, holding out the package. He stared at her, expecting some trick, but when she did not move, did not speak, only drip, drip, dripped water onto the slate of the deck, he had no option but to take what she offered.

Unwrap it.

Find inside the sword that Meas had given him.

"This is why you went back?" he said. She nodded.

"It is yours," she said. "I should not have given away."

He dropped the sopping cloth on the deck, hooked the scabbard of the straightsword to his belt and drew the blade, watched as the pinking light of dawn shone along its length.

"Thank you," he said. "I truly thank you." Cwell nodded, but did not look at him, or raise her head. It was Narza who came forward. Who put a gentle hand on Cwell's arm and led her away toward the underdeck of the ship where there was some shelter from the freezing wind that was making Cwell shiver and shake like a dying gion about to fall. Joron watched them walk away, the sword in his hand.

"She may never like you," said Meas, "but you gave her back her life, and now she will die for you." She was not looking at him when she spoke and he turned, expecting her gaze to be fixed upon Cwell but it was not: it was Narza that Meas watched.

"I did not expect this," said Joron.

"I did not expect it either. But an hour ago I did not expect to survive at all," said Meas. "Today has been a day of wonders. Let us hope there are no more."

And then the call went up, shouted from the tops of the mainspine.

"Keyshan rising!"

# 41

# What Is Lost May Be Hard Found

The island was still ripping itself apart, massive tremors running through it, huge rock slabs sliding into the sea, their scale so vast that as they sheared from the island their collapse looked stately and controlled – until the moment they crashed into the ocean in a spray of violent white. It was easy for Joron to understand how some eye, far up in the top of the spines, could mistake that chaos for an arakeesian, a sea dragon. But Joron had seen a keyshan up close, spent months flying alongside it, had stared into its shining eyes, had shared its song and seen its terrible wrath. A keyshan was a creature of the sea, built and forged by it to be a perfect machine for riding through the waves, and under them. It was not of the land, of the stone, and if the untrained eye thought the island's destruction was a keyshan, well, yes he could, and he did, understand that mistake.

Then he saw the eye.

The white, bright, burning eye.

He saw the unmistakeable fire and found his mouth moving. At first hesitant. Then, as he walked up the slate, gathering speed, jumping on to the rail to look better at the crumbling island, the words coming, filling him.

"Keyshan rising . . . KEYSHAN RISING!"

Out of the stone, the crumbling rocks, the island crisscrossed by black lines with smoke and dust billowing around it, he heard it. The roar. The blast of noise that was both unbearable and beautiful as the head of the creature was fully revealed. As the keyshan raised itself above the island. Vast. The head as long as the ship they travelled in – no, longer. Far longer. A mouth full of teeth, each the size of a tall woman. Many branched horns sprang from the top of the head, and where the first keyshan – the wakewyrm – had been white and black, this one was red and bright purple.

It sounded again. And as it did more eyes opened on the huge head. He counted ten just on this side. Three big ones clustered together above the joint of the jaw, three that ran along the top of the jaw and four smaller ones in a quarter circle around the bigger eyes. The sound of its call had all aboard *Keyshantooth* covering their ears, all apart from Joron and Meas. The creature shook its massive head and the colours on its back changed; a rainbow flowed across it, like oil spilling on water. With a lurch and a roar the keyshan pulled itself up, exposing massive flippers ending in three huge claws the same off-white as the windspire that had crowned the island. All around the crumbling remnants of the island the water was boiling, giant bubbles coming to the surface and breaking in a white froth. The keyshan continued to fight, pushing itself from the wreckage of the island, claws raking at the rock, pulling it apart. Smashing, destroying, as if in fury at the foolish element that thought it could hold back one of the shipmothers of the sea. Between calls, and because the roars of the beast were so great and loud, it was almost as if *Keyshantooth* flew from the island in silence. Certainly, the gullaime no longer sang, the crew no longer talked. All stood watching the great beast as it struggled for freedom.

Did it see them? Those shining eyes called to Joron, the song, silent to all but him – it beat within, it sang within. A sound like the bellows of a forge, the lungs of the creature taking in great gulps of air, as if for one final titanic effort. All was still before one last attempt to free itself from the imprisoning rock. Dust settled, the massive boulders stopped rolling from the island. The wreckage revealed a jagged frame of broken white stone around the scintillating, shivering, colour-shifting body of the arakeesian. It shrank down a little into the rock, as if relaxing, opened its mouth and screamed. Then, with a final massive effort it threw itself free of its stone prison. Rising up and up, great flippers beating at the air as if it could fly, and when it seemed impossible it could go up any further, it kept going. And if the first keyshan, the wakewyrm, had been vast, this one was vaster. By an order of magnitude. As it reached a height – unimaginable for something so huge to throw itself up so far, and yet the body kept on going – until it finally let itself fall. Its sheer size defying sense and time, bending it, slowing the world as the keyshan toppled to seaward of them, its mouth open, shouting and screaming and bellowing as if outraged by the cold air as it descended. The remnants of the island crumbling beneath its great bulk – and then, more jointweight than all the combined fleets of the Hundred and Gaunt Islands smashed into the sea with a sound like nothing he had ever heard. If Skearith the godbird had clapped her wings together it must have sounded like this. Painful enough that Joron felt his ears must be bleeding.

The keyshan fell, but the ocean rose; a massive wave trying, and failing, to reach the great heights that the arakeesian had managed in its birthing pangs. Water roaring. Meas shouting.

"Brace! Brace! Grab whatever you can and hold on!" He knew they should bring the ship about, that the coming tsunami must be met beak-on or they were likely to be swamped. But they had neither the time nor enough crew for the captured ship. "Get below!" she shouted at the crowd of gullaime and, though the creatures were blind, they moved with plenty of speed, followed by Madorra and *Tide Child's* own gullaime. Joron looked about him, aware this could be the last time he saw some, any of his fellows. How unfair, that they had fought so hard, and won free against such great odds, only to be swamped by a creature he was not even sure knew they existed.

Meas grinned at him. Grabbed a rope and wrapped it round her forearm. He did the same.

"Hang on, Joron Twiner," she said. "For I believe this will be a wild ride."

Water fell upon them, the edge of the great watery convulsion caused by the keyshan's impact: but a deluge hard and thick as any storm. Meas turned to face the oncoming wave, a wall of water that Joron was sure must actually reach up and touch the sky. Though it was not this one that was to be feared, he knew that, but the next. And the next. And the next for sure as day followed night more waves would come.

Then he was rising. The ship climbing a mountain of green swirling water. But this was no normal wave, no giant wall of water generated by the sea itself. This was the wake of the arakeesian, and within the huge wave were maelstroms and currents. Smaller waves crashing against each other and making plumes of white water, whirling eddies and cross-currents. *Keyshantooth* rose and rose into the air and the water spun it around like a child's toy in a stream. First one way, then the other. The violent motions throwing Joron into the bonerail, bruising ribs and muscles. The ship slowed, stopped as it reached the crest of the wave and it felt to Joron as if it hovered there, as if he could, for that one single sparkling moment, look out and see the Scattered Archipelago the way Skearith the godbird must once have, the shining seas from storm to storm in all directions. Then, and with a great creak, *Keyshantooth* crested the wave and began to fall. Here was the danger – the ship was side-on to its direction of travel and too much speed would flip them over, capsizing the ship and drowning everyone aboard.

"Bring us round!" screamed Meas at Coughlin on the steering oar. The big man was fighting with all he had, Joron could see his muscles straining as he fought the oar, feel the ship tilting as it slipped down the steep water, each moment gathering a rock of speed, each moment leaning another degree nearer to the point where the ship would no longer be upright, where water would catch the slate of the deck, pull the ship over. Smash the spines and break them against the wave, drag the keel from the depths and throw the entire crew down into the Hag's embrace.

Faster, steeper, more frightening.

Then, when all aboard felt they must be lost – when they felt that the Maiden must be laughing once more at her cruel and deadly trick, letting them escape the island only to die here – the ocean, that greatest trickster of them all, took pity upon them. A vast ambulatory whirlpool moved across the surface of the wave they careened down, dragging all it touched into the black centre. It danced toward them, forward and back and side to side, Joron knew the terrifying power of such maelstroms, had seen small boats eaten whole by them, larger ships spinebroke and swallowed. But this whirling monster only kissed the hull of *Keyshantooth*, dragging the beak around so that the ship faced directly down the wave, and though the speed increased as *Keyshantooth* cut through the water, the deck righted.

"To the steering oar!" shouted Meas, and she and Joron and Farys and every other on the deck ran for the rump of the ship to lend their strength to Coughlin. "We must keep this ship head-on to the waves!" That shipwife voice of hers raised. "All wings furled!" she shouted. "Tie yourselves on if you can!" Then they were part of a press of bodies around the steering oar. All pushing on one another to keep the ship straight, to keep its beak aimed at the base of the next wave.

The sky was gone. All Joron could see, through a tunnel of bodies, was the deep green sea before them, and all he could hear, through the press of swearing, cursing, breathing deckchilder, was her voice yelling, "Hold on! Hold on!" The sea rushing up to meet them. The speed unlike anything Joron had ever felt.

Then they were rising, rising once more, up the face of the next wave, this one even bigger. And every woman and man at the oar was sweating and pushing to hold it straight as the ship climbed and climbed. Speed gradually being shed. Meas shouting. "Ready the wings! Ready the wings!" And up and up and up. All the time losing speed as if they steered into the wind, and it no longer became so important to hold the steering oar — there was no pressure against the tiller as the ship slowed almost to a stop.

And Joron felt despair. For the crest of the wave was so near, but not close enough.

Then Meas calling.

"Unfurl the wings!"

The wings dropped, but the wind coming up the wave was not strong enough. For a moment, the ship held its place and then it was as if they all felt the great jointweight of bone that made up *Keyshantooth* start to drag them backwards. "Wind," shouted Meas. "We need wind! Bring those gullaime up . . ."

"Wind!" A great cawing roar as their own gullaime, followed by Madorra and the four who were already on the ship, ran onto the deck. "Bring wind!" shouted the gullaime and it lifted wings. Screeched.

And the wind came.

Whatever malaise had beset the ship's gullaime had evidently fled before the spectre of certain death, and together with its companions they brought a howling gale. First holding the ship in place on the great wave, giving the illusion of movement as the ship did not fall down the steep side of the water below but the water still moved around it. A wing broke loose, flapping like loose skin in the gale that held *Keyshantooth* there. The deck was a steep hill before them, the water a steeper one. "More!" shouted Meas against the furious gale. "Gullaime, give us more!"

And more came.

A wind like Joron had never felt before. Its pressure against his back almost strong enough to push him, and every other at the oar, off it. The wings above, pristine white, bowing out tight as drumskins, and if they had not been the best wings, the strongest wingcloth only given to the whitest of boneships, Joron was sure they would have split under the great pressure. But they held. A rope snapped, whipping through the air. A scream and a body fell, cut in two and painting the deck in blood. And as if it had needed a spattering of paint for luck the ship climbed. It climbed and it climbed until it tottered once more upon the top of the watery world.

"Furl the wings!" shouted Meas. "Gullaime, stop the wind. Go below!" She looked around her at those on the oar, and grinned like a madwoman. "Hold him straight if you value your lives!"

And they fell.

Down and down another cliff face of freezing water, speed beyond knowing. Someone screaming. Someone shouting for the Hag's mercy. Some simply silent in the face of the ocean's fierce and implacable majesty, at the watery giants brought into being by the body of an empress of the sea.

"Deep breaths!" screamed Meas as they careened down the face of the wave. "Deep breaths! Hold tight!"

They flew toward the base of the wave. *Keyshantooth* had no space to come beak-up in the gap between waves. Or room to start climbing the next. The ship's beak sped toward the sea and Joron took great, deep breaths. Tightened his hands around the handle of the oar. Held on. Watched in horror as the beak of the ship, almost in slow motion, pierced the wall of the sea and then that wall came rushing on. Green and grey and freezing and noisy with froth and spume until it covered him.

And.

Silence.

Eyes open in not quite darkness.

Faces around him. Locked in panic. In wonder. In fear. In complacency. In acceptance. Swallowed by the sea. Distorted by the sea. Bound for the Hag. Hair waving. Bubbles forming around mouths, only to be whipped away by unseen currents. Stinging water in his nose. His mouth. His eyes.

There is peace here.

And.

Noise.

*Keyshantooth* rejected by the sea. Breaking from it in its own small mountain of waves and froth. Air rushing back in, freezing, screaming. So cold. The ship changed by its short passage through the water. Spines torn away and reduced to stumps, gallowbows ripped off. Corpselights gone. Crew missing and the ship sloughing off water in great runnels. Only the fact that this next wave was not of the great steepness as the others – shallower, larger but not as steep – saved them. Now the ship was uncontrolled. Rudder and oar broken. Spinning as the fallen spines caught the water and acted as seastones.

"Hold on!" shouted Meas, "It is all we can do now! Hold and hope the Hag takes pity on us!"

And they rose and span and twisted up the shallow wave until they reached the top and Joron saw that in a huge and growing circle around them was walls of water, brought up by the impact of the arakeesian's body against the sea. He knew those waves would move through the entire archipelago, messengers saying, "I am here! I am born!"

Below them, the vast body of the keyshan, purple and red and black and green and huge in its movements. Lazy in its progress through the water but faster than any ship could ever hope to be. As they drifted down the final wave, into the centre of the circle where the sea was relatively calm the keyshan raised its head and sounded.

The noise.

The music.

The beauty.

I am here.

I. Am. Here.

# 42

## Adrift

The day was cold and clear. The day was thirsty and hungry. Of the forty who had gone ashore on McLean's Rock only twelve humans had survived the battle and the birth of the sea dragon.

Joron dropped a stone over the side of the ship, and sent with it a prayer of quiet thanks to the Hag that she had not taken Meas, or him, or Barlay, or Coughlin, or Farys, or Jennil, or even Cwell. He watched the stone vanish into the green water, into shoals of fish that appeared and vanished, incorporeal presences in the cold waters. Then he raised his eyes to the sky. Not a cloud, only Skearith's Eye beating down. Not a breath of wind. It was like the violence of the keyshan's birth had sucked it all away

"Smile on your children, Mother," he said quietly. "For we have been through much."

But no reply came, though none was expected from such distant gods.

All that survived had suffered bruises and cuts. A piece of bone, splintered off from one of the rails, had stuck into Joron's lower leg, leaving a gaping wound. One of the gullaime had been killed outright as the ship had been thrown around, crushed against a bulkhead below. Another had been broken so badly it would never recover and Madorra — angry, fierce, and strange Madorra — had surprised Joron by insisting that it was allowed to nurse that gullaime toward the end of its life. In the moments he had passed by the gullaime cabin he had been surprised to hear Madorra singing a sad and sweet song to the dying creature. He had not thought the windshorn had such a gentle side. But there were to be many surprises in the coming days. Madorra's surprising gentleness was the only good one.

*Keyshantooth* held no spares: no wingcloth. No cord. No ropes. No bolts. No spars. No boneglue. No bone. No hagspit. Nothing. So they were reduced to salvaging what they could of the wreckage still attached to the ship. It was of little use, if any.

But worse news was to come.

No water. No dried fish. No dried meat. No grain. No food of any kind. And the only land they had been near, McLean's Rock, was gone.

What they did find, upon searching the ship, was a man named Anopp, locked in the brig and barely able to speak. The flesh had almost been whipped from his back and then left to suppurate. Meas had him cleaned and though Joron knew it must have been an agony he did not once cry out. But Joron watched his face, saw the pain in his eyes as rags soaked in salt water were applied to his wounds. Shared it in part as salt water constantly seeped through the bandages on his own leg.

"What happened here, Anopp?" said Joron, more to distract him as Narza applied the wet cloth. "Why is there nothing aboard this ship?"

"Our shipwife, Barnt, were a fool. I told him so, which is how I ended up in this state."

"You had a rank, to speak so to your shipwife?" said Meas.

"Deckmother. Had me own cord put to me back and those who I had dealt it out to, well, they were not kind in their revenge." He hissed as filth was cleaned from an open sore on his back. "I told him, said it were not done to empty a ship of all its stores when there may be a fight in the offing. What if we had to get away quick?" Anopp laughed to himself. "But he wanted the hull checked for leaks and said he'd have no such defeatist talk, that's what he called it. And when I pressed it, said we could move the stores about within the ship, he said it were too slow. And I argued and, well, now I lie here under the care of a traitor." His eyes flicked to Meas.

"Strikes me," said Meas, "you have the sort of mouth gets you into trouble, Anopp."

"Has been said before." He let out a long slow breath between his teeth. "Still, I am here now, so if you need me, I am yours."

"Well, I am not foolish enough to ignore good advice, or cord the skin off a useful man. We do things differently on my ships, Anopp, but call me traitor again and I'll put you off on the loneliest island I can find."

Anopp let out a small laugh. "You'll do for me, Shipwife Meas," he said. "You'll do."

Now, deckchilder are nothing if not inventive. Meas's crew built a small tent to catch dew and funnel it into a large barrel, though there was never enough water and some of the crew took to swilling out their mouths with seawater, which made them thirstier, but gave them a little moisture in return. Others swore this was a way to madness and stayed thirsty, but Meas said, quietly to Joron, that both methods worked and both were their own particular torture. He noticed, however, she took no seawater.

Useless ropes were unpicked and cord twisted into fishing lines. Needles, a thing no deckchilder was ever found without, were bent to make fishhooks. A small spine was rigged and on it was rigged a small and almost useless wing whose sole purpose, Joron thought, was to make the crew feel a little better as the wind remained shy of them, and all the gullaime were spent from their battle with the massive waves.

They drifted for a day. They drifted for two days. They drifted for a week. They drifted forever.

Lips became chapped. Skin flaked and wrinkled for lack of moisture. Wounds went bad, had to be constantly cleaned with seawater. Joron worried about the wound in his leg as it started to smell strange. Energy drained away and he shivered for lack of food when he did not burn with fever due to his wound. He was shocked at how quickly the human frame withered.

But all was not lost. The remaining gullaime demonstrated a previously unknown and unguessed-at ability to swim and to catch fish. In the water it was as if they became different creatures, gliding through it like they should have been able to fly through the air. White torpedoes flitting beneath the ship, quickly changing direction in pursuit of prey or to avoid the beakwyrms that prowled around the hull. Each time they returned to the deck they deposited beakfuls of fish onto the deck which the crew fell upon, eating raw.

As they squatted and ate another meal of raw fish, Meas stood.

"It is hard, my girls and my boys, I know that. To be adrift like this. To have no way of controlling our fate. But mark my words, mark what I say, for I am Lucky Meas, and you know I speak true and seawater runs in my veins. We have fought hard and it is not our destiny to die up in the waves like this. Under shot and blade? Ey, many will die that way, and I may be among them. But we will not die here, not like this."

There was a rumble of agreement, and then, as a line of women and men formed at the dew barrel to receive a meagre dribble of water, Meas took him to one side.

"This cannot last, Joron," she said. "We need more water, so if you find a moment to beg the Hag, Mother or Maiden for rain then take it, but do not let the deckchilder hear you."

"Ey, Shipwife," he said. Then the question that had been on his lips from the moment *Keyshantooth* had come to rest in this unnatural calm sprang to his lips. "What of *Tide Child*?"

"Dinyl is a good commander, and he knows the sea. With any luck they were further away than us when the waves hit. *Tide Child* is a strong ship, he will have ridden them easily. Though they may have pushed him far out, of course."

"We must hope he finds us soon. I feel myself weakening by the day."

She nodded. "Ey, me too." Then sniffed, making a face as much of distaste as worry. "How is your wound?"

"Clean."

She stared at him then nodded again.

"Good, keep it so. I fear the deckchild's disease will start soon. Old wounds will open, teeth will fall out, and without some vegetation there is little to be done."

"Ah, what I would do for a little good news," said Joron, and he did not say the wound on his back was already weeping a clear liquid that made his clothing stick to his flesh. "I am trying to find work to take my mind off our situation, but I find myself so listless."

"Well," said Meas, "think on this. If we are left in such a state by those waves then it is likely the flukeboats of those on the island were entirely destroyed."

"I know they are the enemy, Shipwife," he said. "But I can take no joy in the death of deckchilder on the sea when they are already beaten."

"Oh, I take no joy in feeding the Hag, Joron, do not read me wrong. But I have no wish for what you did on that island to be reported back to my mother."

"What I did?" Already, that strange haze had fallen over him, making the moments when he had sung the keyshan up dreamlike and unreal.

She stared at him, then peeled flesh from the fishskin she held in her hands and chewed on it.

"You raised a keyshan, Joron. You sang it into wakefulness."

"I did not."

But he knew it for a lie. He had forced the thought of it to the back of his mind. He had filled his thinking with their current predicament. Not with what had happened on the island. Not the swirling, spinning songs, the feelings of imprisonment that had haunted him for months, the feeling of waking. Of freedom. Of power. But they were not his, they were felt at second-hand and had the same nebulous strangeness as a dream. "I did not," he said, knowing it again for a lie.

"Well," said Meas, "that does not really matter. It happened and it is best my mother never knows that anyone may have such power."

"Surely it would make her leave us alone?"

Meas smiled, but to herself, not to him. The sort of smile a mother gives a child when it presents foolishness as wisdom.

"The power to destroy islands with a song, Joron? You think that would scare my mother? No, she will see it as the weapon it is." Meas threw her fishskin over the side and stared out across the empty sea. "And she will never rest until it is hers."

The next day they had their first death. She was called Mekrin, and had come on board *Tide Child* in the last influx from the prison ships at Bernshulme. She was neither the strongest nor the bravest nor the worst-behaved on the ship. Joron knew little about her, but he knew her name and knew she was quick to smile when given a good word, slow to anger and vicious in a fight. Given a little better luck, if they had been pushed toward *Tide Child* and found old Garriya in the underdecks, Mekrin may well have survived. Even if she had been a little louder, a little quicker to complain, then maybe something could have been done. Unlikely, but maybe. She had taken a wound on her arm in the fight on the island and kept quiet about it. The wound had soured and by the time she had shared her pain with a deckmate it was too late. They had washed the wound, done their best with all the same tools they had used on Anopp and his back, but bad food, little water and two weeks or more of drifting had weakened Mekrin. The flesh around the wound had become black and the poison reached past the shoulder joint, so they could not even remove the arm. That night, while she ranted and raved and sweated, Meas sat with her, a knife in her hand. And at the last, when Meas put the blade to the woman's neck Mekrin had a moment of lucidity, the pain vanished from her eyes and she met Meas's gaze.

"Do it, Shipwife," she said, "and I'll thank you at the Hag's fire." The blade bit, and Mekrin was released from her pain, later they wrapped her body and sent her to the Hag with all the honours the hungry, thirsty and tired crew could put together.

Two days later Jennil came to Joron, not yet comfortable enough to go straight to the shipwife, and she showed him her leg where many years ago a sword had caught her. The scar had reopened. Joron showed Meas but the shipwife could do nothing but nod.

"Hold on, Jennil," she said. "Help will come." But all knew the deckchild's disease was the beginning of the end. First wounds would open, then teeth would become loose and soon after would come the weakness of mind and body that led to listlessness and death.

Joron dared not ask anyone to look at his back, or at the sores on his arms, and he knew the wound on his leg was getting worse.

Soon after Jennil's wound opened, the days became strange, long and idly coloured. He remembered voices, and sweating and strange talk of legs and blackness. Somewhere inside he knew he was in dire trouble – a little voice, locked within him, called out for help. But the voice was swallowed up by an agony that quickly overwhelmed him.

So, when during the night Joron heard the sinister beating of wings, he was sure the skeers had come for him. That razored bills would eat him alive; eyes and tongue first, then ripping at his innards. And did he even have the strength to fight them off? He could feel a wind on his face as the bird beat its wings above him. He did not even steel himself for more pain. Could not bring himself to care.

"Arse."

He forced his eyes open. Saw the feathered face and the beady eyes of Black Orris inspecting him from the open bowpeek. "Hag's tits," croaked the bird and took off. He rolled his head to the side and there, coming through the water, lit by wanelights along his side and bright lanterns at front at rear, was the black-hulled form of *Tide Child*.

"Ship rising," he whispered into the night. "Ship rising."

# 43

## Aftermath/What Dinyl Did

The smell of the bilges — rotting food, sewage, brackish water — was like perfume to Joron. This was *Tide Child*, this was home. Deckchilder had carried the sick and failing from the deck of *Keyshantooth* and those hands, rough from years at sea, treated them as gently as any father takes a child to lay it down in bed. And that is what was done with every woman and man that survived. They were taken from *Keyshantooth* to their cabins and hammocks, there to be fed thin soup from the hand of Garriya. A soup she said would banish the deckchild's disease and bring them back to health.

And though it tasted foul, it did just that.

The gullaime had suffered far less than the humans, though Joron did not know why. He had a memory of the ship's gullaime's masked face above his own, singing to him in its own strange language as he had drifted in and out of consciousness. He was not quite sure whether that had happened on *Keyshantooth* or here on *Tide Child*.

But time had passed, and though he had been banished to his cabin by Garriya he felt his strength was returning and he would soon return to *Tide Child*'s deck. He had complained of being isolated and the hagshand had, only today, relented on his need for nothing but rest. Now he lay in his hammock and Dinyl and Aelerin sat with him in his small cabin.

"This is the second time I have been forced to my bed to recuperate, Dinyl," said Joron to the man sat beside him, "and I do not like it."

"Well, maybe you should avoid danger from now on, ey, Deckkeeper?" Dinyl glanced across at Aelerin and smiled at the courser. Joron felt a laugh bubble within as they all knew the chances of danger being avoided while on the slate of Lucky Meas's ship was almost none. But the laugh died in his throat because there was some seriousness there in Dinyl. Something unsaid between him and Aelerin. Or was there? His tiredness was such that it would be easy to ascribe feelings to others that were not there. "Now, Joron, do you wish to sit and moan about your lot or would you rather hear of our adventures?"

Joron nodded, which made pain radiate through his body from the re-opened sword wound on his back, and the gash on his leg. He hissed, but Dinyl ignored it and continued.

"Well, we dropped you off on the beach and I took *Tide Child* in a wide circle around the island. That was when we saw the boneship on the horizon. I was in two minds as to whether to stay or to follow it, but Meas had left orders that we were to keep others away." He shrugged. "Of course, Joron, we could not know it was too late for that."

"Of course," said Joron, and smiled for he knew that Dinyl told him this story in part to make sure he had not erred and was not likely to incur the shipwife's wrath, in part to distract Joron as he was confined to his bed by Garriya while she treated his wounds. How long had he had been in bed? Well, for a time. Did not want to think about why, or Garriya's worried face when she looked at his leg. Could not. Not yet. "You went after the ship. It is what I would have done."

"Ey, and the deckmother and Aelerin both agreed, as did Mevans. So we set the wings to make after it. My plan was to catch its shipwife's eye and then run with the wind and hope they chased us. When we were far enough away I could bring *Tide Child* to and let them board, feigning ignorance. Say I was chasing something over the horizon. As I am not important enough to be known to any roving shipwife – as far as I know, of course – we had planned for repainting the name, a fine ruse so they did not think us Meas's ship. I hoped to be back at the island in good time to pick up Meas and your good self. The only oddness was that Aelerin . . . well . . ." He shrugged. "I will let the courser tell you that."

"I knew another storm was coming," said Aelerin quietly, "but I also felt the winds were calm. This was not something I have ever heard sung by the storms before." Joron nodded, as he understood how one could feel two things at once. He was presently both hot and cold.

"And Aelerin was quite upfront with me about it," said Dinyl. "Yet still, I made the decision to approach the ship. The winds were brisk, I felt it a worthwhile risk to take if it would give Meas the time on the island she needed."

"As I said, Dinyl, you were right in your actions." The words seemed to fight being formed on Joron's lips.

Dinyl smiled once more. "Well, as soon as the ship saw us, it turned tail and ran, and it was only a two-ribber. Oh, thinks I, this is a mite suspicious, why would they run? And remembering how the shipwife had said she saw no one on the island, I thought, could they be bringing people for it, or orders? And I thought how much I would like for the shipwife to come back aboard *Tide Child*, having found nothing, and for me to present her a whole stack of orders telling her exactly where our people had been taken."

"I would not tell her you wished her to fail," said Joron. "Maybe just say you thought the ship curious."

"Well," said Dinyl, "ey. Maybe I should put it that way right enough." He made a note on the papers he held in his hand and Joron saw the shadow of a smile beneath Aelerin's hood. "But that is not the story – the story is we flew for the ship and it ran. And I spoke with Aelerin and Solemn Muffaz and Mevans and it was decided we would follow, for a while, and if we judged we were more than half a day from McLean's Rock we would turn back." He let out a long breath. "Had I only known, Joron, I would never have . . ."

"How could you, or anyone, have known," he said, his voice a whisper, like an old man's, "that they would hide a ship within an island. Not even Meas suspected it."

"I should have suspected a trap, Joron." Dinyl looked at the floor, and even though Joron did not think Meas would punish him, he felt Dinyl likely to punish himself far more than she ever could. "But I did not."

"Nor I," said the courser quietly. "Nor Solemn Muffaz or Mevans. None did."

"Thank you, Aelerin, but you were not in command." Quiet reigned then, and though Joron felt Dinyl punished himself for nothing he knew exactly how he felt. For Joron had been the deckkeeper among those who had gone ashore, forty in all. Of whom only a handful returned and those, like himself, badly wounded or in poor health. He felt keenly that he had somehow failed Meas and those who now sat with the Hag at the bonefire. He also knew that his guilt would be felt by Meas, but magnified a hundred times. Unlike Joron, who sat here, sharing failure with his friends, she had no such option. If she was well enough to stand – and he did not know how she fared as this was the first time he had been allowed visitors, and even this on Garriya's sufferance – he knew she would be standing at the great windows of *Tide Child*, staring out at the frothing wake left as the ship flew through the night. She would share her troubles with her only true compatriot, the dark and endless sea.

"So you turned back?" said Joron.

"Ey, we followed as we had said, and turned back. The ship tried to pull us further on, bringing in its wings, slowing. I cannot tell you how my heart fell at that, for it was then that I knew I had failed my shipwife, and fallen for exactly the same trick I had planned to play myself."

"We all fell for it," said Aelerin.

"And again, I say I was in charge," said Dinyl. He sighed. "We turned the ship, and started back, but it was hard work, tacking constantly and with half the crew we really needed. Worse, that Hag-cursed ship followed us, though it lost us during the night so there was at least that small sign the Mother smiled on us. As we were tacking back our topboy saw you leave the island. I almost had them corded, I thought they had lost their mind. A ghost ship exploding from within the island? What madness, I thought. But, of course, more madness was to come. We tacked away once more, thinking it for the final time and desperate to get back, unsure just what the topboy had seen and what this may mean for Meas and your good self."

"The d'older was fare beside himself," said Aelerin. "And still I felt the storm was coming, though there was not a cloud in the sky and the wind was poor. I doubted my sanity."

"And then it came," said Dinyl. "The islewyrm."

"That is what you have called it?"

"It is what the deckchilder have called it. And we were fortunate with the waves it brought. Our tack had taken us far enough out that we could turn *Tide Child* on to them, and there was space between them enough that we were not swamped. Still, we lost most of our tops as the waves passed."

"The keyshan was the storm," said Aelerin, "the islewyrm. I knew as soon as I felt it. I have never seen something so . . ."

"Magnificent," said Dinyl. He looked at the stump of his wrist. "I have hated you on occasion for what you did to me, Joron, to save the wakewyrm. But when we saw that keyshan breach, any hate I had left fled." He placed his good hand on Joron's good leg, squeezed gently. "Who are we to take such lives? How could I not have seen that back then?"

"The choices we make are never easy, Dinyl. You did what you believed was right," said Joron.

"And after the waves came the calm," said Aelerin, "and I can tell you there was nothing natural in that. Maybe it was an effect of the keyshan's birthing, I do not know. It felt like even the storms held their breath, to see such a creature loosed."

"Do you think they live in all the islands, Joron?" said Dinyl. But Joron did not know, though he suspected. He did not want to answer, and was not even sure he could. His mind was as full of clouds as the most overcast and drizzle-filled day.

"How did you escape the calm?" he said.

"Coxward, Mother bless him. Never has a man been more capable with scraps and spar. Given the calm, and that Aelerin felt it would last a long time, rather than replacing the tops he built flukeboats to replace the ones taken by you and the shipwife to the island. Now, you may never have seen uglier boats in your life, and I am certain that no more malformed and Berncast things have ever flown the sea. But they floated. It took us a week to put them together and make sure they would not sink. Then, as we had no gullaime, we had to tow *Tide Child* back towards the island, and of course it was gone. Though I found that hard to believe at the time and must apologise again, Courser, for my harsh words." He leaned forward, "I nearly had poor Aelerin corded when they said we were at the island and nothing was there."

"It is understandable, Dinyl," said the courser, "for it is not every day an island vanishes."

"Anyway, Joron, all who escaped McLean's Rock owe Aelerin their lives."

"And Black Orris," said the courser.

"Ey, true. But mostly Aelerin. I was sure all must be dead. But Aelerin said you were not. Said they would feel it the same way they feel the song of the storms if Meas passed, that you were tied in with them somehow. Once I had accepted their words, and I was almost mad with grief at losing both you and the shipwife, the courser did magnificent things, things I will never understand. Worked out positions from where we had been, how far away from the island we were when the keyshan breached, and the size of the waves when they hit. They set out a grid that we should search. And we did, the whole crew taking turns in those Hag-ugly flukeboats to tow *Tide Child* through the sea in search of you. We would find a place, sea anchor him. Then send the boats out to cover the area. For ever it took. It was Karring said they thought they had seen the hint of spine on the horizon during their search, but he struggled to be sure of where. So I sent Black Orris up. And he flew around and around before heading off east. When he returned, he called me an arse, and headed east once more. So we towed the ship after him and that is how we found you."

"And I am right glad you did. I am proud of you, Dinyl, and you, Aelerin." Joron felt his voice catch with emotion. "I thought us lost, finished. I had given up."

"That is the deckchild's disease talking, Joron. You were all in a very poor state. I have heard tell of what happened on the island." He smiled and put his hand on Joron's. "You never gave up."

"So many died, Dinyl," said Joron quietly. "And for what? I am not even sure we found anything useful."

"Well, let us hope you did. Coxward has rigged *Tide Child* back to fly and he has fixed the holes in the hull of *Keyshantooth* so we can tow it more easily. The wind is even picking up a little." He grinned and stood. Took the no-tail hat from where it hung on the corner of the chair he had sat on, knocked slightly out of shape by him leaning on it. "And now I must go make my report to the shipwife." His smile wavered a bit. "It seems she is once more on her feet." He punched the hat back into shape and placed it firmly on his head. "Be well, Joron. I am sure you will be needed again soon."

Joron smiled. "I hoped to be out of my bed before the shipwife," he said, and tried to sit up but his strength failed him and he lay back once more. "She will think I am making a habit of sickness." The words were hard to force from his mouth in a suddenly airless room. "And you know how she hates slatelayers."

"Ey," said Dinyl quietly, and he hid his face as he turned, opening the door.

"Dinyl," said Joron, closing his eyes as the world span around him. "I meant what I said. I am proud of you, and the shipwife – well, I cannot speak for her, but I do not see how she could find fault in your actions."

"She will find some," said Dinyl quietly, "I am sure of it."

"Well," said Joron, "that is her nature, but any fault will be small, for we all owe you our lives." He took a deep breath, opened his eyes and martialled his strength. Sat up a little. As Dinyl was about to shut the door Joron saw his sword, that beautiful thing that Meas had brought him, hanging from the handle of the door. "Dinyl!" He called out once more.

"Ey?"

"Did we lose any more – how is . . .?"

"Two more were lost," said Dinyl. Then he smiled. "But do not fret, Farys survived." Joron felt relief flood through him, because that was not the question he had been going to ask. That was a question he had been too scared to ask, as she had become dear to him.

"And what of Cwell, Dinyl?" he said, staring at the sword.

"Ah well, Deckkeeper," said Dinyl, "the news there is not as good, for I am afraid she survives also." And with that Dinyl left, puzzled by the smile he had seen on his shipfriend's face.

"I should go too," said Aelerin. "Garriya said we were not to tire you, that you are yet weak."

"I am fine," he said, laying back and knowing he was not. Aelerin put out a hand, touching his shoulder, then his brow – which, when touched by their icy finger, he suddenly became aware was burning, hot as hagspit, and covered with a thin film of sweat.

"I have said I am fine many times when it was not true, Deckkeeper," said the courser. "Rest. I will send Garriya to you." He tried to sit up again, to tell them he did not need the healer, but the stitches in his back pulled against the skin and a shot of pain ran through him, turning his dark skin grey, as if he were fresh pulled from a freezing sea. "It is time for the dressing on your leg to be changed. Garriya said you caught some bone it, from *Keyshantooth*."

"It hurts," he said quietly, the words coming unbidden.

"I will tell the hagshand," said Aelerin, and left.

Time passed, as time is wont to do, and Joron found himself unsure of how much had passed, for time had somehow become, to him, inconstant. He felt as though he were cast adrift upon its currents. One moment he knew where he was – in his cabin, on *Tide Child*, while Garriya looked over him. Other times he was sure he was back in the hagbower in Bernshulme, replaying his talk with Gueste, knowing the woman would betray him but unable to do anything about it. Going through the motions like a sleepwalker until he found himself once more imprisoned in a box and it was only then, awoken by his own shouting, that he would come back to the present. Find that he was in his cabin, wrapped tightly in blankets in his hammock as the ship rocked and fought the waves.

After his visit, events were fractured. One day he woke to find Garriya standing over him and the world moving. So much noise. His body full of pain. His mind suddenly clear. The old woman staggering from foot to foot in the small space as she tried to get some foul-tasting concoction down his throat.

"What is wrong with me?"

"'Tis just the deckchild's disease."

"What is the noise?"

"A storm, boy," she said. "That is all, and the ships weather it well, just as you shall weather yours."

He pulled himself up, grabbing Garriya by the front of her filthy tunic and pulling her down to meet him. Desperate to know . . . but to know what?

"Do not lie to me, Garriya. The deckchild's disease passes quickly with good food. What is wrong with me?"

She stared into his face – old and ugly maybe, but her eyes were bird bright and intelligent.

"That shard of old bone, some broke off, remained stuck in

your leg wound. It is out now, but the keyshan's rot, Caller – it complicates everything, weakens the body."

"Do not tell her about it."

"The shipwife? I would not tell her a thing unless you wish it, but you are fool if you think she does not know everything that goes on in her ship."

He was fighting for breath, his body suffused with pain that ran up from his leg and along every vein and artery and muscle.

"I am in much pain, old woman."

"You are very ill," she said. "But you will not go to the bonefire yet. I will not let you."

"No," he said, and felt the desperation within him, the need to live; while at the same time he felt something else, something akin to drowning, to slowly slipping away. "Do not let it take me. Do not. No matter the price."

"No matter the price?" she repeated, slowly.

"The fight is not yet over." He gasped those words out and fell back into darkness. The last thing he saw was her face, full of concern and care, and fear. "No matter the price," he whispered as darkness once more encroached.

# 44

# The Fiercest Battles Are
# Fought Within

The darkness. Trapped in the box.

Get me out of the box.

Agony. Searing, unbearable agony.

*Hold him down!*

Strapped in.

Unable to move.

The darkness.

This forever.

This his fate.

Mevans! Mevans! Get me out!

*Hold him down, for Hag's sake or I'll take the knife to you.*

Agony. Searing, unbearable agony.

There are borebones in the box! They have put borebones
in the box!

They are eating me alive. Please, Mevans. Come for me,
they are eating me alive.

*Hold him down, may the Hag take you if you can't keep him still.*

Agony. Searing, unbearable agony.

*Shhh, shhh, Deckkeeper, I am here. It is Mevans, I am here.*

Why is it so dark, Mevans?

Open the Hag-cursed box, I am being eaten alive.

Agony. Searing, unbearable agony.

*Hag curse you woman, hurry!*

The Shipwife! The Shipwife is here!

*Ey, Deckkeeper, she is. She will let no harm come to you.*

The agony. The searing, unbearable agony.

*Curse you woman, get the limb off, I could have done it more quickly myself.*

*Not and kept him alive, Shipwife.*

They are eating me alive. The borebones are in the box and they are eating me alive.

*Nearly done now, Caller.*

It is so dark.

So dark and so very painful.

Agony. Searing, unbearable agony.

*It is done now, Joron.*

*Rest.*

*You must rest.*

So dark. So dark and so very painful.

Agony.

Searing.

Unbearable agony.

# 45

# No Less of a Man for the Loss

"Will you be putting me ashore at Leasthaven?"

Meas looked at him as if he had sprung fully formed from the bones of *Tide Child* and claimed to be Skearith the godbird.

"What in all the islands do you mean by that, Deckkeeper?"

"You cannot have a deckkeeper with only one foot."

"Think before you speak, Joron," she said, plainly irritated. "Shipwife Arrin had most of one leg missing and it did not stop him."

"But he was Gaunt Islands. We are Hundred Isles, it is not what we do."

"Hundred Isles, are we?" said Meas with a laugh. She walked over so she stood looking down at him where he lay in his hammock. "I doubt my mother would agree. And, in case you have failed to notice, we do things differently on this ship." She stared at him a little longer and her hard, sharp face seemed to soften a little, like watching dawn light on a rock face. "Unless you wish to go ashore, Joron. There would be no shame, you have done much and—"

"Of course I do not wish to go ashore." He took a breath. "But I cannot walk."

"Well, then," she said, and straightened the sparkling blue fishskin of her jacket, "it seems we have a problem. You do not wish to go ashore, but I cannot have an officer who cannot walk."

"So I must be put ashore," he said, but she shook her head. "No."

"Shipwife, I have lost my foot, and part of my leg. I cannot walk."

"What nonsense, Deckkeeper. You have fought off what would kill most. Fought women and men, other ships and sickness. I am quite sure that if Arrin did it you can learn to walk also."

"He was born that way."

"So?"

"Well . . ." He realised he did not know how to answer her.

"Coxward!" she shouted. "Coxward! Come here!"

A moment later the bonewright bustled into the cabin. In his bandaged arms he held a bundled shape that Joron thought at first must be a sword. Then Coxward pulled the cover from it to show Joron a thing he was evidently very impressed with, but which meant nothing to Joron. One end was what looked like a cup with straps and rigging around it, and attached to this was a curve of white bone about as long as a man's calf.

"This is for you," he said.

"What is it?" said Joron.

Coxward's large round face fell a little at that.

"A leg," he said.

"It does not look like a leg," said Joron.

"Well, no," said Coxward. "See, I did make one that looked more like a proper leg – even had a foot, it did, but it was awful heavy. I have seen other men with peg legs, and even Shipwife Arrin could not move at any great pace and he were right fond of saying his leg was one of the finest ever made. Then, I were looking, see, at the leg of the gullaime. Which ain't like a human leg at all." He grinned and moved around, slapping his thigh. "All the muscle in your gullaime, it's up

here, see, barely any in the lower leg, that what you have lost."
He grinned, though Joron was not sure it was a thing to grin
about, but Coxward did not care, so lost in enthusiasm was he
for what he held. "Bottom of their leg is all tendon and spring.
So that is what I made, see. I mean, it ain't got tendon, but
it's made of laminated bone, has plenty of spring. So when
you walk, it'll push back. Give you some feeling."

"You cut the ship up for me?"

"Well, not quite," said Coxward. "*Tide Child* took some
damage, and I used some bone shed from there, and I used
your own, from what was cut off. So it's you and him see.
Mixed."

"Well, Joron?" said Meas.

He stared at the object, this strange totem that Coxward,
and evidently Meas, thought may give him back mobility. This
mixture of him and the ship, dead parts of Joron and dead
parts of a keyshan.

"Let me try it," he said, and was rewarded with a huge grin
from Coxward who started forward, only to be stopped by
Meas.

"Not yet," she said. "Garriya says your stump must heal
more, and that is at least a week away yet." Joron was about
to protest but she cut him off. "I did not enjoy watching you
have your leg sawn off at the knee, Deckkeeper, and I command
you to keep the rest of it. Leave that here, Coxward" – she
pointed at the bone leg – "and bring him a crutch for now.
Leave it by the door." The bonewright grinned, passed over
the leg and left. Meas put the leg down by Joron's hammock.

"We head back to Cassin's Isle and Leasthaven, to pick up
our fleet. From there we will go and take Sleighthulme. Free
our people."

"If they are there," he said. She did not speak for a moment,
let silence settle between them.

"They must be," she said, but it was hope, not surety that
filled her voice.

"Do you think they still survive?"

"If they do not, we will avenge them," she said, cold and hard as the ice in the north. "We will get our people, and we will destroy whatever is set up for making this poison for keyshans. Strike blows for peace." She nodded, looking sure and strong once more, "It is maybe four weeks journey, six if the weather is against us. I need you able to use that leg by then, Joron."

"Sleighthulme is a fortress, Shipwife," he said. "Our fleet is not big and even if it were, Sleighthulme has stood many a bombardment. The sea gates protect it."

"The sea gates will be open."

"How?"

"The *Keyshantooth*. It is theirs, it is known. And, Joron, you saved Anopp, its deckmother, who knows the codes and the phrases and the flags. I want you to take it in. I have been to Sleighthulme, I can draw you a map. You will take the ship in and take the gatehouse that controls the sea gates. From there, you will hold them long enough for the fleet to come in."

"But Shipwife," he said quietly, "I have lost half my leg. Send Dinyl, he is absolutely capable."

"Oh Joron," she said, and exasperation was a dark cloud on the edge of her words. "You are right, he is utterly capable. But able to think on his feet?" She hesitated, aware of what she had said. Joron laughed, unable to stop himself.

"He at least has feet, and he is able. He is . . ."

"By the book, is what he is, Joron."

"The minute they see me, they will know I am not what I pretend to be." He nodded down the hammock, at the space where his seaward foot should be.

Meas seemed to deflate. She turned from him and for a moment he thought she would hammer her hand against the wall of the cabin.

"Hag curse me for a fool, you are right," she said. Did her voice waver? Was there some emotion there? Was her frustration rising like a wave, to break over him?

"I have been so long among people who think differently I

have started to take it for granted." She turned back, the mask of shipwife back in place. "You are right, it must be Dinyl."

But now she had talked of letting him go, the thought was filling Joron's mind. He heard an echo of Garriya's voice: *When you will just repeat all you have done and return here, under my knives all over again . . .*

"No, Shipwife," he said. "I am wrong. You are right. I should go."

"Why?" she said.

"Because I am wounded. A boneship being chased by traitors? Its shipwife sorely injured? They will throw open the gates and let me rush onto the docks with my people. It would be expected that there would be chaos, raised voices."

"They would think you helpless," said Meas. He nodded.

"So I must make sure I am not. There will be no repeat of what happened on Bernshulme." He shuddered, at the thought of Gueste and being locked in that box.

"Indeed," she said, and paused for a moment, letting silence settle around them like sediment in water. "The gullaime wishes to see you. I have kept it away for as long as I can – I did not want you tired and Hag knows that creature can be tiring. But I think it worries."

"I would be glad to see it. Only . . ." Meas raised an eyebrow. ". . . Maybe give me an hour alone, first?"

"I will send it after the third bell, when the crew have eaten."

"Thank you," he said, and she left him in the cabin. Alone with his thoughts. For the first time he felt truly awake. Whatever drugs Garriya had been dosing him with were fading, leaving an ache where his foot and lower leg should be, and a space in his mind, as if whatever part of him had controlled that missing piece of flesh and bone had also been neatly excised.

He had not yet dared look under the blanket. He dimly remembered Garriya coming in with unguents and water and cloth, and the pain that ensued. But he had looked away when she had pulled back the blanket. Pushed the reality of it to the back of his mind, sure that with the loss of his leg came the loss of himself and everything he had become.

But that was not to be.

He stared down the hammock, one side a whole leg, the other a rumpled blanket from just above his knee down. He pulled the covers up, up and up, revealing his foot, then the leg of the dirty and stained trouser he wore, had worn since the island. Then the stump of his missing leg, the end of the trousers neatly folded back over and held in place with a bone pin. He reached down, shards of pain lancing through him, and with shaking hands pulled out the pin. The cloth of his trouser had been slit so it could be folded back and opened. He gently did so.

The stump of his leg had not been bandaged, or if it had Garriya had chosen to take it off now. It was smoother than he had imagined, a flap of skin neatly sewn up and over just where his knee had been. It seemed somehow unreal. His thigh looked the same, and then his lower leg was gone. But he could still feel it. If he closed his eyes it was there and he was sure he could reach out and touch his toes.

But when he opened his eyes it was still gone.

So much gone.

His leg, his father; friends, enemies. Lost. Taken by the eternal war machine that was life in the Scattered Archipelago, bodies ground up between the Hundred Isles and the Gaunt Islands. He stared at the space where his leg should be and felt a desolation within. Empty. As arid as a waterless island. Something within him shook, and grief erupted like the keyshan from McLean's Rock, smashing through the desolation, shaking his body, and he clasped his arms around himself. Keening silently for all that was lost, to him, to everyone.

And for what?

For what?

*. . . you will just repeat all you have done and return here, under my knives all over again . . .*

Sleep took him, eventually, a deep and exhausted sleep he had been denied by the cocktails of drugs he had taken, and outside his cabin, unseen and unheard by him, the deckchilder did all they could to remain as quiet as it was possible to be on a boneship, with its many duties and never ending jobs, for they knew the deckkeeper had been though much. And if they heard him weep a little, did they care? No, they did not, for what did it matter to them if a brave man wept? It did not make him any less brave, and had they not all wept at some point in their lives? So they smiled to themselves and went on with their jobs, never to mention it again.

When he woke it was to the familiar hot smell of the ship's gullaime. He opened an eye, crusted with sleep and dried tears, and stared around the dimly lit cabin. He had slept through the day and into the night. He heard a late bell. Knew that Skearith's Bones would be twirling overhead. There were two gullaime – *Tide Child's* own windtalker, and Madorra – squatting like statues in opposite corners of the cabin. As far from each other as it was possible to be without leaving the small room. Madorra barely covered, a mass of white feathers and pink skin, one brown eye glinting from an unmasked face. The gullaime, its robe coloured and adorned with trinkets and dye, its mask surrounded by feathers it had stuck all over it and which now almost entirely covered its face. It looked like some fierce priest of its race, some demigod of bird people.

Its head turned, the beak pointed at him. Opened.

"Jo-ron Twi-ner." It stood, squatting to standing in one move, and hopped over. "Joron Twiner awake?"

"Yes."

"Not dead?"

"No. Not dead."

"Good. Good." Its head passed down his body, stopping at the empty space below his stump.

"Leg gone."

"Yes."

"Hurt?"

"Yes." With that admission the pain came flooding in. He gritted his teeth. Closed his eyes. When he opened them again the gullaime's face was in front of his.

"Shorn gone," it said.

"Yes," he said, and once more those tears threatened.

"Why?"

"He gave his life to save yours."

The gullaime did not move.

"Why?" Through the mask Joron could feel the unwavering gaze of those glowing eyes.

"It thought you were important."

The gullaime's head slowly moved backwards, away from him. Then it turned its beak, looking down his body, coming back to his face.

"Leg gone," it said again.

"Yes."

"Hurts."

"Yes."

"Shorn gone," it said.

"Yes."

"Hurts," it said. Then it opened its mouth and made a sound so quiet Joron was sure only he could hear it: the lonely call of a skeer, riding the wind above a cliff without any of its fellows. The shout of a deckchilder as they slipped beneath the waves. The cry of a babe as the blade fell and the ship took its soul for a corpselight. "Not know why." It said it so quietly it was barely even a whisper. "Did not know. Hurts."

"I am sorry, Gullaime, but know it died happy, sure it had done the right thing."

"No," said the gullaime. "Not right. Not right. Not want. Not want hurt. Not want this."

"What do you mean, 'this'?"

"Windseer." That from Madorra. The windshorn bird stood. "Windseer," it said again, then its single eye focused on Joron. "Caller."

"No," said the gullaime.

"Caller," said Madorra again, voice gathering strength. "Is Caller. Is Windseer. Is true."

"No," said the gullaime once more. And took a step back from Madorra as it slowly advanced.

"Show face."

The gullaime shook its head, such a human motion.

"Show face."

"No," it said, and for the first time ever, Joron felt that there was real fear in the gullaime's voice. It was not fear as would be heard through a human's voice – no shake, no tremor. But it was, recognisably, fear. Madorra lunged at the gullaime, a wingclaw catching the mask and ripping it from its head. Beneath the mask the gullaime's eyes were screwed shut; around them the beautiful feathers that caught even the tiniest bit of light and reflected it back in myriad colours. The gullaime backed away, eyes still tightly closed.

"Open eyes," said Madorra.

"No."

"Open eyes!"

"No!"

"Open. Eyes," said Madorra once more and, as if the gullaime was unable to fight the command in the windshorn's voice, it obeyed. First, just a crack of white light in the centre of the lids. And then the eyes opened fully. Burning orbs, black corkscrew iris spinning into being.

The effect on Madorra could not have been more dramatic. The windshorn's posture went from one of aggression and authority to one of abject submission. It fell to the floor, body pressed as hard as could be against the bone boards, thinly feathered wings spread out. "Windseer!" it said. And where Joron had heard fear in the gullaime's words he heard awe in Madorra's. "Windseer is come." Awe – and was that calculation? Was it cunning? Or was he ascribing things to the windshorn's voice he only imagined as he did not like the creature?

"No, no, no," squawked the gullaime and it retrieved its mask, placing it back over its eyes. "Not want. Not want."

"Is!" said Madorra. "Is!"

"No," said the gullaime quietly and, even in the dimness, he was sure its wingclaws were shaking.

"What is the Windseer?" said Joron. "What is the Caller?"

Madorra sprang from its prone position on the floor and hopped over so its scarred and ruined face was in front of Joron's.

"Windseer is freedom of gullaime. Caller is freedom of gullaime."

"Windseer is death," said the gullaime quietly. "Is death. Is destruction. Is end." And as it spoke Madorra was nodding its head. Joron saw in its eye the same light he had seen in the hagpriests as they cut open the throat of a babe, the unwavering belief of the fanatic.

"Yes, yes," it said. "Windseer and Caller. Bring back sea sither. Then Skearith reborn."

"Fire and blood," added the gullaime. "Death to all. The burning door."

"Yes, yes," said Madorra, as if the idea of death and fire and blood was nothing but an inconvenience. "All gullaime die, all reborn free."

"Not want!" said the gullaime.

"Stupid bird!" shouted Madorra. "What want no matter. What is. Free people. Fire and death and—"

Joron's hand shot out, grabbing Madorra's beak and holding it closed. For a moment he thought the windshorn would lash out. It did not. The single eye only rolled to look at him.

"And my people? And all else that lives on the isles?" said Joron.

"All dead," said the gullaime, and there was a weight of sorrow in its voice despite how its people had been treated.

"You believe this wholeheartedly?" said Joron to Madorra, and he felt the windshorn nod its head by the movement of the beak in his hand. "So you will protect the gullaime? Even with your life, exactly like Shorn did?" It nodded again. Joron removed his hand from its beak.

"All gullaime will," said Madorra, more calmly.

"You cannot tell the others what you believe," said Joron.

"Windseer is importa—" it began, but once more Joron held its beak closed.

"What do you think will happen if your people talk? If this crew, if humans in general, find out that the gullaime here, your Windseer, is their doom?" The single eye rolled to look at Joron once more. "They will kill it, Madorra. Then they will kill you and it would not surprise me at all if they went from there and killed every gullaime in the Hundred and the Gaunt Islands." He stared into that single eye. "Would such actions surprise you?" The eye blinked, as if in agreement, and Joron let go of its beak. "You can tell no one."

"Told you," it said.

"I can keep a secret," he said. "Now go."

Madorra turned and hopped across the cabin, opening the door. While it did the gullaime shuffled over to Joron.

"Not kill all," it said quietly. "Windshorn mad. Gullaime not do it."

"I never thought you would kill us all, Gullaime," he said, and the gullaime bobbed its head and followed Madorra out of the cabin.

Joron looked down at the space where his leg should be and the desolation within him ruled once more. A vast emotional wasteland where, even though he was not sure he believed in prophecies, he could not help feeling that if Madorra was right and the gullaime was this Windseer, this harbinger of the end for humanity, then maybe it was for the best.

# 46

# First Steps

They were days and weeks of pain and frustration and stumbling. They were days and weeks of much kindness and support.

The bone leg, that thing that was part him, part ship, was uncomfortable, and for days he bore it until the stump started bleeding and Coxward chided him.

"It is easier to fix a lump of bone than a man, Deckkeeper. It will not fit straight off. We must work together to find your comfort."

And they did. Not just Coxward either. When he slipped and tripped there was Farys or Mevans to help him back up. When he sat, exhausted, on the slate deck, sure he would never master it, there was Solemn Muffaz or Gavith with a story of how they had failed and come through some trial in their lives. When he ached there was Garriya rubbing salves into his stump, into his bruises. When he thought he could go no further and the crew's will for him to succeed was an almost physical force. When he was determined to carry on and Dinyl gently took his elbow and told him he must rest. When he thought all was lost and he would never walk again and Meas was there, silent but full of surety that he would.

And he did.

Step.

Two steps.

Then three steps.

And then four steps.

Then once he had mastered that success came in a wave — this sense of balance, this knowledge of how the bone spur moved with him, of how his body would react. Oh, he would win no races. He still fell and swore, often joined in that by Black Orris, but by the time the call of "Land rising!" went up and *Tide Child* hove into view of Cassin's Isle and the waiting fleet, he no longer felt like a burden. He could stand on the rump of the deck with Meas and Dinyl, he could haul on a rope and he could pace up and down the slate picking on those who took a moment to slack. And when he did pace the deck, if his gait was marked by a slight limp from the pain where his spur attached to his stump, then what of it?

Often, when he walked, the gullaime would follow him, mimicking his walk, putting on a limp of its own. "Good leg. New leg. Good leg," it would call. If he stopped it would lower its head to examine the false leg, tapping it with its beak and screeching out in glee, "Like mine! Like mine!" There was much joy in it, though behind the gullaime was always Madorra, who made something cold run through Joron in a way that Shorn had never done. A dark and ascetic cloud to the riotous colour, noise and joyous curiosity of the gullaime.

When the other shipwives were brought on board Joron stood with his shipwife to welcome them. And if they noticed he was missing a leg they said nothing, and never once was his ability questioned or doubted. For he was the choice of Lucky Meas and they had named her shipmother of the small fleet, and for all she pretended not to want it and commanded they not use the title, she could not hide her pride from Joron, who knew his shipwife's moods as well as he knew their ship.

Five shipwives came aboard. Brekir, Meas had asked for, and the remaining four had been chosen as the most senior of those gathered, because no more than five could be fitted into *Tide Child's* great cabin. Had this been Safeharbour, reflected Joron, they would have all met together on land. But it was not, and Safeharbour was a ruin now, its ashes long grown cold, and Leasthaven had nowhere large enough for them all to meet. So Meas must either bring them here in dribs and drabs, or tell a few of the most senior and let them spread her plans, and it was the latter she had chosen to do.

In her cabin they sat, around a thin spread of food that was the best Mevans and the cook could put together, though none seemed bothered by the meagre spread and they ate with the same relish they would have shown if it was a true feast.

"Brekir," said Meas. "How many ships do we have?"

"Those of the five shipwives here are the largest of our fleet. Though none are as large as *Tide Child*, Adrantchi's *Beakwyrm's Glee* is almost as big, even though it is only a two-ribber."

"Less of the only, please, Shipwife Brekir, for the *Glee* is a fine ship and he has done his crew well." Adrantchi was a solid man, with thick black eyebrows that gave his face an imposing, serious and fierce look that Joron had heard was more than deserved. He ruled his black ship with a hand of iron, though his crew loved him for it.

"The shipwife is right," said his deckkeeper – a tall, thin woman who they called Black Ani, despite her skin being unnaturally white and her eyes pink. It was commonly held the two, in defiance of the Bernlaw, were lovers and Joron could believe it. They sat just a little closer than was right for a shipwife and deckkeeper. But how a shipwife ran their ship was their own business, and Adrantchi and Black Ani were from the Gaunt Islands – they did things differently there, so Joron gave it no more thought. "The *Glee* will fight as hard as a ship three times his size and our crew will outloose any other."

"I in no way disparage you," said Brekir, "I only tell Shipmo—" She caught herself, looking as miserable as ever. "I only tell Shipwife Meas the technical aspects of our fleet. I speak not of their fierceness." Adrantchi nodded and used a knife to take a piece of rubbery-looking fish from the serving platter and place it before him.

"You said you loose faster than any other," said Shipwife Turrimore, dark-skinned like Joron, and of the Hundred Isles, though she was far thinner than Joron, little more than bones beneath her tight purple fishskin. She had no deckkeeper with her, only her deckmother, a huge woman that Turrimore did not bother to name and who sat behind her, glowering silently. "Only, Shipwife Adrantchi, if you are sure of the speed of your loosing, perhaps we could make a small wager? For I reckon the *Bloodskeer* looses faster than any." She grinned, showing she had no teeth at all in her bottom jaw, some congenital defect that let Joron know she had risen to shipwife on her black ship through fury and strength, not birth.

"There will be no betting," said Meas. "This is a council of war. Not a games room." Turrimore leaned back in her seat with a shrug, then gave Meas a small nod of assent. "Brekir, please carry on."

"Well, back to our numbers. We have five of the shipwives gathered here. Then seven more, though *Bonebore* lacks a shipwife – and, of course, the ship you bring, *Keyshantooth*, though it is in poor repair."

"Twelve warships. It is a fleet," said Sarring of the *Hag's Maelstrom*, one of the two pure white boneships that had come across from the Hundred Isles fleet. By her sat her Deckkeeper, Lellyn, a woman so small that Joron suspected her family must be extremely rich to have kept her in among the Bern. She was barely over the height of Joron's hip.

"Albeit a fleet of the dead," said Chiver, shipwife of the *Last Light*, the second of the fleet boneships that had come over to Meas. His deckkeeper, Tona, sat beside him. He still wore the leather straps and sculpted trousers of the Kept and he nodded as he spoke.

"A black ship fights harder than any pretty fleet boneship," growled Adrantchi. "Pretty lights above the deck do not make a fighting ship."

"No, they do not," said Chiver lightly. "It is about discipline, about having the Bernlaw on the deck and following it and—"

"Enough!" shouted Meas. "Chiver, stop talking afore you drive your beak into the sea and drown in your own words. You chose to come join us, so your ship is black in all but paint, for now." For a moment the threat of violence filled the room, then Chiver nodded.

"Ey, you are right." His words were almost a sigh. "I am a fighting shipwife. I suppose it is in me to fight and this is not the place."

"Save it for those set against us," said Meas.

"Ey," said Adrantchi, "it will be a hard fight, and we will need all the fighting shipwives we have."

"We also have five brownbones," said Brekir. "Big ones."

"That is good," said Meas, "we will need them."

"For what?" said Chiver. "That is the real question."

"To take our people back."

"You have found them then?" said Adrantchi. "I am glad. It will shut the mouths of those who doubted you." He glanced at Chiver but the shipwife ignored him. "Do they use them as slaves?"

"In a manner," said Meas. "It seems that hiyl, for hunting the keyshans, is not made from the beasts as we thought, but the process of making it is so poisonous it kills the workers in a matter of days."

"And this is what they take people for?" said Turrimore. "It makes a certain sense I suppose. Why look after them well when they are destined to die so quickly?"

"It is barbaric," said Brekir quietly.

"We will take our people back," said Meas, "and more than that, we will destroy my mother's ability to make hiyl."

"No hiyl, no keyshan bone," said Brekir. "No bone, no ships. No ships, no war."

"They will only set up again somewhere else," said Chiver.

"That is a problem for later," said Meas. "This is a wound we can make now, and it will be a deep one."

"Where though?" said Turrimore. "That is the question. I hope it is not Bernshulme, as I doubt twelve ships will be enough." She grinned, and her joke was met with smiles and laughter.

"No, not Bernshulme," said Meas. "Sleighthulme."

The laughter stopped.

"Sleighthulme cannot be taken," said Adrantchi. Meas shook her head.

"No, Sleighthulme has not yet been taken, it is different." She looked around the table, serious faces considering her words. "*Keyshantooth*'s deckmother, Anopp, had been sorely treated by his shipwife. He was more than glad to tell me what he knew of Sleighthulme. It was not much but it is enough. He knows the signals needed to get inside."

"I doubt they will open their gates for a fleet of black ships, Meas, no matter what signals we have," said Sarring. "And good though you are, Sleighthulme is a natural fortress."

"A fortress is only as strong as its doors," said Meas with a grin. "Joron will fly in *Keyshantooth*. We will be chasing him, and it will look like he is seeking safety. Then that night he will take the gatehouse and open the gate for us. That is how we take Sleighthulme."

"Surely they will know the crew of *Keyshantooth*," said Black Ani.

"Anopp assures me they never landed, only escorted the brownbones to the island then left and I do not think he ever knew what horrors were aboard. The ship is all that is familiar to them."

"What if it is a trap?" said Chiver. "What if that man was left for you to find?"

"The man was half dead when we found him."

Chiver shrugged and Joron wished Coult, the fierce shipwife he had fought with at Safeharbour, had come instead of this fleet shipwife. He was beginning to dislike Chiver. But Coult had been out on patrol and was not back yet.

"You think a shipwife would not throw a man's life away if it meant victory?" said Chiver.

Silence.

Faces around the table.

Some blank, hiding their opinions.

Some angry.

Some thoughtful.

"Maybe a poor shipwife would," said Meas, "but my mother would not risk an entire ship to set up a trap. How could she know we would take it?"

Chiver kept Meas's gaze for a fraction too long, then nodded.

"How indeed," he said, breaking off his stare.

"Can you bring the keyshans, Meas?" said Adrantchi. "To help us?"

Meas glanced for the briefest second at Joron, then tapped the table.

"What makes you think anyone can do that, Adrantchi?"

"Oh come, we've all heard it. When you fought *Hag's Hunter*, and then at McLean's Rock, the keyshans come when you need then. We all talk of it, even Brekir there, but no one else will say it. I think we should put all we have on the table and it is a mighty weapon, to have the sea dragons come when you ask."

Something in Joron ran cold at this. And yet, he was strangely glad that they had put their expectation on Meas, who had never raised a sea dragon, and not on him, who he was very sure had, even if he did not really know how.

"They do not come when I ask," said Meas. "I just happened to be where they were, that is all. We can bank on no arakeesians as allies." Adrantchi nodded, as if he had thought this all along but Joron could sense the disappointment that hung in the air.

"If that is all then?" said Meas. No one spoke. "Well, we leave in the morran. You have tonight to load what you need on to your ships. Chiver and Sarring, we can do nothing about your corpselights but you are to paint your ships black. You are of us now."

Joron expected argument from the two fleet shipwives but

they simply nodded and the meeting broke up. Only Brekir hung back, making an excuse of a personal matter and waiting until the others were over the side of *Tide Child* and on their way back to their commands.

"What is it, Brekir?"

"I only wish to say two things, and I did not wish to say them in front of the others."

Meas gave her a curt nod. "What is the first?"

"The two fleet shipwives. They only left because they felt they could get nowhere under your mother. They came to us not knowing Safeharbour was lost, thinking they had a future. I am not sure they can be trusted."

Meas picked up a knife from the table and ran the tip along the bone surface, making a long scratched line.

"Were it only Chiver, I would agree. He has a mouth and a temper on him. But Sarring is the more forceful personality between them and I know them both from Bernshulme. Chiver's family are poor, and owe their place to Sarring's. Sarring's family, in turn, owe their own fortunes to the family of Lellyn, Sarring's deckkeeper. Now that family, were it not for their vast holdings, would not be counted among the Bern for many of their children are smaller than the hagpriests would say is right. I think it is Lellyn's family that both of them serve, and our way would be good for them. So, we trust them for now. It is politicking — those two boneships are someone's outside bet. We will watch them, though, do not worry." Brekir nodded. "And the second point, Brekir?"

"A harder one, shipwife," she said quietly.

"One does not become a shipwife by making easy decisions." Meas smiled as she spoke.

"Ey, that is ever true." Brekir took a deep breath. "We must be very sure of what we do next, Shipwife Meas." She licked her lips, chapped by salt winds. "These ships we go to Sleighthulme with, they will carry all we are. All our women and men are needed to crew them, and as the children cannot be left alone they will be brought along in the brownbones.

We leave none behind at Leasthaven. If we fail, Meas, all we are is finished."

"We are that badly depleted?"

"Ey," said Brekir, "We are."

"Well, Brekir, and I tell you this as a friend not a commander, we have no choice, do we? We cannot leave our people to die."

"It has been months, Meas. The growing is finally upon us again. No one may even have survived this long from Safeharbour."

"I cannot believe that, Brekir. We cannot fail our people so fully. What are we if we do not even try?"

Brekir stood for a moment, as if lost. Then she put out her arm and clasped Meas by her forearm as one does an old and respected comrade.

"We are nothing, Shipwife," she said. "If we do not try we are nothing. You are right there. Better to lose it all for what is right than to live in fear."

As Brekir left Joron went to follow her, his movements slow and careful on the bone spur; one hand ever ready to reach for something to steady his walk.

"Joron, stay a moment," said Meas. "I would speak with you."

He nodded and once more took a seat at the table. "If it is about what Brekir said, then you are right. We cannot leave our people."

"It is not about what Brekir said," returned Meas. "You look troubled, Joron, and I would know why."

"It is only the coming action – and, well . . ." He glanced down, at where the table hid his leg and that which had been severed from him. Meas held up a hand.

"Do not tell me it is fear of action, for you have seen plenty. And do not say it is only your leg. You have made great progress in the past weeks and I am not a fool." He nodded. "Something else weighs on you, and it has weighed heavy on you for a while now. So, tell me what ails you."

He leaned forward and sighed. Tried not to look at her, for whenever he put what he had been told into words it sounded like a madness.

"Do not make me order you to speak, Joron," she said, a familiar hardness in her voice, though when he looked up that hardness was not in her grey eyes. "I can, of course, if it would make speaking easier."

"No, you need not do that." He leaned against his chair. "Have you heard Madorra, and before that, Shorn, refer to our gullaime as Windseer?"

"Ey, on occasion I have. It is some gullaime thing, I have heard others of their kind say it before. What of it?"

"It is a name of power to the gullaime, a name of prophecy. They believe the Windseer will come and free them all."

"And that is no bad thing for them to believe. They will fight harder in our cause for it."

He leaned forward and whispered to her.

"The Windseer frees the gullaime by killing everything, Shipwife. Everything. Fire and blood, they say. Humans and gullaime all die as the world and Skearith are reborn."

"And you believe this?"

He stopped. Did he? Under Meas's cold grey gaze he was not as sure. Was it only superstition and was he being as foolish and gullible as a deckchild fresh off the slate?

"Our gullaime is like no other," he said, his words slow. "We know that. And now the keyshans return just as the gullaime believe they will." Meas sat back. "Our gullaime says it will not do this thing Madorra believes in. But if the prophecy is real, what if it has no control?"

"Have you told anyone of this, Joron?"

"No, and I have sworn the gullaime and Madorra to secrecy."

"Will they keep this secret?"

Joron thought for a moment and then nodded. "Ey, our gullaime wants nothing to do with being the Windseer. And Madorra, well, it is a fanatic and will do anything to protect the gullaime. We should be careful of it, I think."

"Fanatics can be useful Joron." She paused. "Do you believe it?"

He shrugged. He did not know. Silence, gently resting between them in the cabin.

"Do you know the story of the Tide Child, Joron? That this ship is named for?" He shook his head. "Of course not. It is not a story my mother or the Bern before her have ever wanted told. But I will tell it to you. The Tide Child is a babe brought to land by the sea, a lost daughter of a powerful family. Unable to die on land, or by the blade of woman or man. She sweeps all foes before her. Sound familiar, to you, Joron?"

"It is you," he said, in wonder, and fear — a tide of fear, washing over him. "Do we live in an age of prophecy?"

She smiled and shook her head. "There is more to it, yet. Eventually it is said the Tide Child will unite Gaunt and Hundred Islander in peace. War will end."

"It really is you," he said. She chuckled, shook her head.

"Do you see any sign of war ending, Joron?" Meas stood, walked to the back of the cabin where the great windows looked out on the bleak sea. "I believed it once: Lucky Meas, the greatest shipwife who ever lived. But look at us now, Joron, struggling for enough crew to fly our ships. Outcast and outlawed. And even if it were true, then how could this prophecy and the windseer prophecy be true at the same time? Ey? They cannot. They are all lies. Stories to make children feel good about themselves, to give hope to the lost."

"But it is true, Shipwife," he said.

"What?"

"You have united Gaunt and Hundred Islanders in peace, on this ship, in our fleet. Among our people."

"That is only a small thing, Joron." She looked down at the white boards of the deck. "Maybe that is the true nature of prophecy — we can only change what is within our reach. So do not worry about the gullaime, do not worry about their prophecy. Hold close those you care for. Worry only about tomorrow, and the day after. Think not on the day after that for we fly a ship of the dead, and the Hag calls us all. To plan far ahead is to ask for the Maiden to thwart all you are. We live in the now. We fight for what we believe is right. We can do nothing else."

He nodded, struggled to stand, the unfamiliar bone leg working against him and he almost tripped. But she was there, a steadying hand. "Thank you for telling me, Joron," she said softly. "Thank you for trusting me."

He nodded, unsure how to reply.

"Send Dinyl to me," she continued. "It has been a bleak day and I would put a little joy in it. *Bonebore* needs a ship-wife, and it is about time Dinyl was rewarded for his loyalty." And with that glad news, Joron left her cabin a little lighter of heart.

# 47

# The First Command Is the Hardest

It was a bright day, and some of the bite had left the wind so it was easy to believe the dying season had really ended and the growing time was about to start. Though for those who trod the slate decks of the Hundred Isles' fleet ships the dying season never ended – the green shoots of growth began, only to be cut down by gallowbow or curnow or straightsword.

This was the hardest time in the Hundred Isles: the stores of crops and food were running out, and the ground was not yet yielding new grain or roots. Fish had gone deeper to escape the cold currents coming from the north and south storms, and the only sea creatures that could still be hunted were the hardiest, largest and fiercest. But there was hope now – in the cleared ground and the fixed and cleaned nets that lay drying on docks; in Skearith's Eye which shimmered on the wavelets, making the deckchilder and the officers squint against the brightness, promising that the heat and the growing would come.

Joron may have been physically diminished by the constant fight, but he had grown in other ways and now, as a result of that growth, he stood on the rump of his own ship. Oh, it was not a permanent command, the ship was not nearly as grand as *Tide Child*, not as great, as well kept or as loved. This ship was a patched-together wreck, but the *Keyshantooth* at least had spines now, sheeted with white wings taken from *Hag's Maelstrom* and *Last Light*, done under sufferance of their shipwives, who had already suffered the indignity of painting their ships black and being told to bring up the rear of the convoy. This so the corpselights floating above the ships did not give away that they were fleet ships, as for Meas's ruse to work Sleighthulme must believe one of their own ships was in danger from a whole fleet of attackers. If, as it seemed, it was known in the Hundred Isles that the black ships no longer served Thirteenbern Gilbryn, then Joron's ship must appear to be running from those same black ships.

His crew was not large, but enough to keep the ship running. Farys was here, and Mevans, to act as his command crew along with Aelerin, who had hidden themselves away with charts below. Jennil stood as deckmother and somewhere the gullaime, accompanied by Madorra, gave full rein to its curiosity and explored the dark bowels of the ship. Meas had also sent Coughlin and his seaguard aboard as she foresaw most of Joron's fighting would be done on land. Despite the sad state *Keyshantooth* was in he flew well, was a well-made ship, if small as most modern ships were. Beside them flew *Tide Child*, like the shadow of the white ship. Behind them *Borebone* with Dinyl – full of joy at his new, and permanent, command. No doubt also complaining of a headache from the late night of drinking that, despite Joron's warnings, he had indulged in to celebrate their new positions. Joron could still hear Dinyl shouting, "Join me in a drink, to celebrate!" as he had thrown an arm around him. But Joron had been too deep in thought about the coming action, too desirous of a clear head and had instead only promised to join his delighted shipfriend in a drink when they returned from Sleighthulme.

"Joron!" Meas's shout came from the rail of *Tide Child* as the bigger ship came closer, white water rushing along the hull. "How does it feel to wear the two-tail, Shipwife Joron?"

She was grinning as she stood on the rail, one hand on a rope, the other holding on to her hat. He strode across to his own rail, a little less steady and with no intention of testing his nascent skill with his bone leg by trying to balance on the rail when he could not always successfully balance on a deck. Like her, he had to hold the two-tail hat onto his head – not because he stuck his head out into the rushing wind, but because he was uncomfortably aware that the hat he wore barely even fit him. It was an old misshapen and much mended hat of Brekir's. As ill fitting as the rank of shipwife felt to him..

"Good, Shipwife Meas," he shouted back, "I would wear it longer, maybe?" He said it as a joke, but there was nothing of the joker on her face when she replied.

"A shipmother needs a shipwife, Joron, for she cannot be both. So maybe start thinking about saving for a tailor, eh? And who you will choose from Handy Alley to make your uniform?" She gave him a wave and jumped from the rail, returning to her deck and shouting orders that were whipped away by the wind, *Tide Child*'s . . . deckchilder jumping to action around her. Wings were dropped and the flying wings put out to grab the wind as the bigger ship peeled way, splashing the deck of *Keyshantooth* and all on it with salt water, much to the hilarity of all aboard.

"The shipwife is in fine spirits." Farys paused, scratched her head under the one-tail that she wore, then added, almost apologetically, "Shipwife Joron."

"She is indeed. Perhaps it is better if you call me deckkeeper still."

Farys looked troubled by that and Jennil turned from where she stood before the mainspine, the cord held in her hand. "Maybe, Shipwife," she said, "it is best if we get used to calling you that so mistakes are not made once we are within Sleighthulme."

"Ey, she has a point, Shipwife," said Mevans, who had chosen to play the part of deckholder. Joron did not quite understand why, since Mevans was by far the most senior deckchild — but he had let his people choose their own roles and would not question them.

"Well," he said with a smile, "then shipwife I will be while it lasts." He grinned and stepped forward, feeling the rub of his bone spur against the stump of his leg and fighting not to wince. "It seems Meas and *Tide Child* think the Mother gives them all the speed of the storms — well, let us see what *Keyshantooth* has to say to that!" A cheer from the deck and his own sparse crew were running up the spines and letting down wings, pulling on ropes to tighten the sheets, and behind them Coughlin leaned in to the steering oar, veins standing out on the muscles of his arms as he fought to keep the ship on the line that best caught the wind. *Keyshantooth* clearly liked the attention for he leaped forward, cutting through the cold grey waves toward the horizon and the shout came from the front: "Nine beakwyrms ride our waves, Shipwife!" And Joron felt pride swell within him at that, for this seemed right and proper and how things should be.

A pity only, that they flew toward death and despair and destruction.

But he could enjoy the flight, enjoy the brisk winds against his skin that whipped the braids of his hair around his face, that twisted the two tails of his hat, filled the white wings above him, that stole the words and the breath from his mouth, lifted the water into choppy waves that the beak of the ship smashed through. Salt water rained upon the deck, making him laugh with joy. His joy was infectious, it ran through the ship and touched every woman and man on the slate or up the spines. As *Keyshantooth* cut through the sea, his beak a blade, neatly parting the water the way a butcher flenses meat from the bone, the crew began to sing and then the call came from up the spine.

"Keyshan rising!"

With that came another level of excitement in the deck-childer around him. "Where is it, topboy?" shouted Joron.

"Two points of the for'ard shadow, far on the horizon!"

"Steer us two point to shadow, Coughlin," shouted Joron, "I do not think Meas will begrudge us sight of the beast."

He knew she would not. His crew, all the crews, would enjoy seeing a keyshan as the beasts had brought them nothing but good fortune so far, to their way of thinking. Maybe he should have wondered if his topboy could have been mistaken, and maybe another commander would have but Joron did not. He had felt a strangeness in the world, a vibration within him, a blueness within his mind and a sense of freedom that made no sense until that call went up. Of course there was a keyshan – it touched every part of him, and as if in answer, as if in affirmation, the gullaime hopped up from the underdecks, yarking and calling, dancing across the deck in circles with its wings outstretched.

"Sea sither! Sea sither!" it shouted. And behind it came Madorra, joining the song. Joron noticed that the gullaime, though it seemed to be dancing in a joyous and carefree manner, was also very careful to never dance with Madorra. So the windshorn circled the gullaime, the way Skearith's Blind Eye circled the world – together, but always apart.

"Keyshan rising!" This time the call came from the beak, and Joron stumbled and limped down the ship, taking the old and battered nearglass Meas had given him as a present for his first command and raising it to his eye.

There!

Oh wondrous beast, oh creature of legend. Somehow, he had expected it to be the one that had destroyed McLean's Rock, but the creature he saw in the nearglass was, even at this distance, entirely different. It swam away from them, towards the north, with its head out of the water and the wings on its back raised to catch the wind. The head was massive and blocky, giant branching horns sticking up. Even at this distance Joron fancied he could see the light of its eyes, like blurs around the beast's snout. Its mouth was open and it was bearded with hair like seaweed. Behind the great head a stretch of sea and then the body, rising like an island and studded with wings. The overriding colour of this one was blue, dark and rich.

He heard the shouts from the other ships – "Keyshan rising!" – echoing joyfully back and forth among them, until all he could hear was voices mixed in with the sound of the water as if the sea was whispering to him – *rising, rising, rising* . . . The creature tilted its head back and sounded, though Joron did not know that, not at first. It opened its mouth and he felt a thrill run through him, from the top of his head to the tips of his toes, both the ones he had and the ones he had lost seemed to vibrate. Then came the sound, even at this distance like a wall of a hundred thousand different screams and pitches and harmonies that shook the water and the ships upon it. In return a cheer went up from them. Behind him he heard a similar noise to the call and turned to find the gullaime and Madorra calling back to the keyshan, wings stretched out beneath robes, heads extended, beaks open and their throats distended so he could see the bright red skin between white throat feathers.

There was something unbidden amongst all this joyous noise that made Joron cold. For if this keyshan was not the one raised at McLean's Island and not the wakewyrm, then had another island broken open? Had it been inhabited? Had hundreds gone into the sea amid broken rock and collapsed buildings? Had thousands?

*Windseer. Fire and blood.*

"Put us back on course now, Coughlin," he said but he could not keep the sudden worry from his voice.

"One comes. More come," said Madorra. "The sither will rise."

Had he done this? Had he started this all that time ago by singing to the wakewyrm? By waking the islewyrm had he sent some signal out across the islands that would bring them all crashing down?

"Not rise, Joron Twiner," said the gullaime quietly as it came to stand by him. "Not rise. Come when called. When needed. Not destroy, not kill," it whispered. "Not want."

"No," said Joron, "not want." The gullaime called again as the ship heeled over, catching a stronger breeze as it slipped back into its original course and the arakeesian once more vanished over the horizon. The ship danced across the waves and felt to Joron as if it moved as swiftly and smoothly as the white clouds passing through the sky, while within him all was turmoil. The mood aboard the ship now joyful at the sighting, though Joron could not help feeling less so, for he was the only one who saw some worrying portent in the fact that this keyshan swam away from them.

"Farys, the rump is yours," he said, and from there he made his careful way down into the ship to find Anopp, *Keyshantooth*'s old deckmother. He now haunted the underdeck, trying to find a place he could lay comfortably while his back healed under the supervision of Garriya in what would have been the deckholder's cabin. As Joron approached the cabin the door opened and the ragged old woman slipped out.

"Caller," said Garriya in a whisper – which surprised him as she was never usually one to mind her voice – "do you wish to speak to my charge?"

"Ey," he said.

"Well, that is good. He is lucid now."

"Lucid? I thought he was healed?"

She stared at him, piercing eyes beneath a mop of filthy curls, in a way she reminded him of Meas. "Keep your voice down. A great part of healing is to believe you can heal."

Joron did not talk immediately, instead chewing over what that meant.

"I thought he was well, that he was up and about."

"Aye," she said. "He was, but you have the skin removed from your back and see how you fare. I chase the filth from one wound to another, but always something is leaking or suppurating. Sew him up, open him again." She shrugged. "It is a race I am losing."

"Does he know?"

She shrugged. "I have not told him, but in his heart, inside, somewhere, he must feel the Hag draws near. Be gentle with him, Caller."

"I will be."

"Good," she said. "Now I must eat. Never enough food on these boats."

"Ships," he said quietly, "they are ships," but Garriya did not care and was not listening.

In the deckholder's cabin he could smell the souring wounds on the air, but Anopp was sitting up, wrapped in a sheet that had been soaked in salt water. Wanelights burned along with a small brazier, making the room stiflingly hot after the fresh winds on deck.

"You are a shipwife now," said Anopp, his voice a croak.

"Not for long."

"Yet you find time for me," he said. "I can tell you no more. I have given your courser all the information I have, all the codes I know."

"It is not why I am here," he said.

"Then why are you ?" He stared at Joron and in his eyes Joron saw pain, a pain he recognised. A shared experience of agony beyond that which most would ever feel.

"Only to say you are not bound to us. We shall tell no one where we got our information from. If you wish to be left behind on Sleighthulme when we leave, I will arrange that for you."

Anopp laughed quietly. "Go back? To that Hassith-lover who whipped me? No, from what I see you have it better on your ships. This is a happier place than I have ever known."

"Then you are welcome to stay," said Joron.

"I think we both know I will be staying," he said softly, "whether I wish to or not." And Joron felt the shadow of the Hag over them and, despite the brazier, he was suddenly cold in the small room.

# 48

## The Killing Time

The killing started early. The rise and fall of knives, the blood, the bodies falling to the deck, and still there was more to do. Every kivelly in Meas's fleet had been rounded up, caged and brought to *Keyshantooth* for execution in the name of Meas's plan. And, though there had been much grumbling about the coming lack of eggs, the butchery of the kivelly was viewed as a game more than anything. The small birds had been running round the deck, squawking and fluttering in panic while laughing deckchilder pursued them. Several were lost over the side only to be quickly snatched from the water by hungry beakwyrms. Despite Joron's shouting the games had carried on until he had threatened the crew with the cord, then they had calmed and the butchery of the small frightened birds became a production line.

Pull them from the cage.

Cut off the heads.

Hold the twitching body over a barrel to drain the blood from it.

A team of pluckers, spreading white feather across the deck like snow.

Slit 'em and gizzard 'em.

Pack the bodies in salt.

Occasionally the gullaime would dart in and grab one of the kivelly corpses, gulping it down whole while yarking to itself as deckchilder chased it away, and this was also seen as a merry game until Joron spoke severely to the gullaime. Though it complained at being told to stop, it did not complain too hard and sloped off to its cabin to sleep. Joron thought it had probably eaten too much and made itself feel ill, as the gullaime was not a creature that usually took well to being told no.

How odd it must seem, to those unaware of the ruse to be played, that the morran before a battle they spent it butchering birds for food. Though, of course, it was not the flesh they really wanted. It was the blood.

When Aelerin quietly came on deck and whispered to Joron that they neared their destination, the barrels of salted kivelly were put over the side onto waiting flukeboats, to be distributed among the fleet, and on the last boat Joron sent Aelerin and the gullaime with Madorra, back to Meas on *Tide Child*, as he would not risk them within Sleighthulme. Then all that could be done was to fly before the brisk wind, order his deckchilder to chase every feather from the deck, and wait.

Wait while they pulled ropes and tautened wings.

Wait while his stump throbbed.

Wait while the blood thumped through his body.

Wait while he tensed and slackened his muscles, all the while appearing to stand still and calm.

Wait while a feather whirled around the deck, rose into the air and escaped the ship.

Wait through those moments of inaction, pressed between fear and flight.

"Sleighthulme rising!"

He sent Farys up the spine, not ready to go up himself yet. Probably never would be. His leg ached and he could feel dampness in the cup that held his stump. No matter how thickly he wadded it with material it was never truly comfortable, and he hoped that dampness was sweat, not blood.

Though, given their plan, it might be that blood would serve him well.

"They'll see us soon," said Farys as she jumped from the bottom of the spine.

"Very well," said Joron, then he raised his voice. "Prepare the ship, loosen the wings, make us fly a little ragged." Wings were furled and new ones let down, these prepared with holes and cuts as if the ship had been under shot. This together with a ship already damaged from its escape at McLean's Rock made *Keyshantooth* look a sorry state, but not sorry enough, and it was to complete this illusion that Joron's crew had spent the morran killing. "Bring out the blood!" he shouted, and the barrels of kivelly blood were rolled up. Two barrels, the blood of the birds diluted with seawater and with dye and a little ground seed to keep it thick. When forming this plan, Joron had briefly wondered if dye alone would be enough to create the illusion they required, but Farys had pointed out that one taste by someone on land would give lie to their ruse, so kivelly blood it had to be. Once the barrels were on deck Jennil and two chosen deckchilder took buckets and scooped blood out, pouring it over the side of the ship as if the Hag had cast her eye over *Keyshantooth*, bursting bodies and taking her due. When Jennil was satisfied with her work she came to Joron.

"It is your turn now, Shipwife," she said, standing before him with her bloodied bucket.

"Ey," he said, "I suppose it must be." He reached down to undo the buckles around his leg, but before he could start Cwell was already there.

"Let me, Shipwife. I will keep the spur close for when it is needed." And though he still felt uncomfortable with the woman so near to him, he nodded, knowing it would do him only good for the crew to see the woman who had once tried to overthrow him and Meas now acting as his servant. Once the spur was unbuckled – he felt strangely naked before the crew – Cwell carefully unfurled the rolled-up end of his trouser, that he had cut ragged with his bone knife, and helped lay him on the deck. Then she produced a thin birdleather cord and wrapped it around his leg above the knee, tight enough that it appeared to be a tourniquet. That done she looked up and nodded at Jennil who artfully splashed blood around him on the deck, then, with an apology, over his clothes, spattering them with the mixture of blood and seawater. *What better to baptise a shipwife*, he thought, *than with the two elements that would soak their command.*

The fleet of black ships fell behind and *Keyshantooth* cut through the sea. Joron had them untruss the gallowbows, had crews standing around them as if ready for action. Two bows had been smashed escaping McLean's Rock and they were left to swing wildly. Some of the deckchilder lay on the deck around them and, though Joron was sure it was partly an excuse for them to do nothing, it added to the illusion of a ship badly mauled.

And he lay on the deck.

And he lay on the deck and waited.

And he lay on the deck and he waited to see Sleighthulme rise.

Up it came, from the water, breaking the horizon with staggered, vicious promontories – black claws scratching at the sky and sucking in the light of Skearith's Eye. Sleighthulme was nothing like the other islands of the Scattered Archipelago. No white rock, no windspire, no varisk or gion growing on it. The only native life was the cruelly beaked skeers which fed on carrion and the helpless. As he lay on the deck and watched the pyramid of basalt grow from the sea he wondered how it had come to be, this lonely black island ringed by white breakers and sharp rocks. The only other place in the archipelago like this was Skearith's Spine, and it was as if part of the Spine had been picked up and thrown, to land here in this cold and lonely part of the sea. And though Meas and every ship and every woman and man that followed her was behind Joron, and though he was surrounded by those loyal to him, he still felt cold and lonely himself as they raced toward Sleighthulme.

Nearer he could see the smoke, columns of grey rising straight up from the settlement at the bottom of the mountain only to be caught by the wind, pushed against the rock to crawl up it in runnels and webs of grey. It was as if filthy water ran up the mountain to escape what happened below, where the slate was cut and the ore was smelted. Closer still he could see the castellated harbour walls, built from the same black stone as the island. Two huge and round towers, even higher than the tallest boneship, and between them sat the bonegate, a sea gate made of two giant pelvis bones from ancient arakeesians, the thickest and strongest bones bound together with boneglue and rope and precious iron, into a barrier that could be raised or dropped to allow ships to pass in and out of the harbour. On top of the towers fire burned, and Joron was sure he could see the outline of the great gallowbows mounted there to protect the precious resources that Sleighthulme produced.

"Farys," he shouted, and she came running to squat beside him. "Get up the spine, start making the signals for help. Remember the codes and do it yourself. I trust no other like I trust you."

"You do not trust Mevans, or Gavith?" she said.

"Of course I do," he said, "but I trust you more."

"Yes, Shipwife," she replied. Then he heard the whistle of something cutting through the air and heard a splash as a bolt landed in the sea by them. Specks of water wet his face.

"Well, it has started now." Another whistle and splash of water over the deck as a bolt from the black ships behind them was launched. "I knew Meas would make it look real," he said, "but that was closer than I would like, Farys."

She grinned at him.

"Best we escape then, eh Shipwife?"

"Best indeed," he said, and watched her as she turned and ran up the rigging as if she had not a care in the world.

The island before them grew, gatehouses like jutting teeth,

and he could see the town beyond through the holes in the gate. In the town was a distant shape he recognised, and yet could not quite understand. He went to reach within his jacket but remembered he no longer wore it — it had been taken off at Mevans' insistence, the better to look like he was wounded, and because, as the man said, "Blood is the very arse to get off, Shipwife."

"Cwell," he said, "bring me my nearglass." She vanished, returning quickly and passing him the instrument. He brought it to his eye. A flash of the white bone of the gate, a flash of the black stone beyond. Trying to keep the nearglass still to see through the gate while the ship moved up and down on the waves was almost impossible.

White.

Black.

A glimpse.

The smooth roundness of bothies — some small, some huge. Blocky buildings that must be foundries, belching smoke. Some spines of ships in the harbour — a huge space, quarried out of the island. Cranes for unloading and . . .

White.

Black.

A glimpse.

There!

White.

Black.

A glimpse.

What was it?

White.

Black.

A glimpse.

A tripod, taller than the bothies. Something like a crane but not a crane. Hoisted into the air on it was a huge block of rock, but for what purpose? Why would such a great weight be hanging in the air in the very centre of the town? And behind the tripod a fire, a huge fire.

White.

Black.

A glimpse.

"Shipwife," said Cwell, "what do you see that concerns you?"

White.

Black.

A glimpse.

"Mangonel," he said quietly, lowering the nearglass. "A massive one, a siege catapult of the like I have never seen, Cwell. They must have scrapped an entire boneship to build it." All that he was wanted to race up the spine and signal Meas behind him – *Retreat! Scatter!* But he knew he could not: physically could not, his body would not let him; and if he did such a thing, then all would be for nothing as it would betray their ruse to Sleighthulme. It would ruin the illusion of a ship pursued by enemies entirely. All he could do was raise the nearglass, watch through the jerky lens.

White.

Black.

A glimpse.

Movement near the bottom of the giant catapult, shadows in the fire.

White.

Black.

A glimpse.

The great block began to fall, a slow motion. The arm rising, pulling behind it the rope and the cradle for the burning missile, up and up.

White.

Black.

A glimpse.

And it launched. The arm swung lazily forwards, though he knew there would be an army of women and men at the bottom, ready to fight with ropes to bring it back under control.

White.

Black.

Lowered the nearglass.

Something roared overhead, a fiery star that lit the deck of *Keyshantooth* as if Skearith had opened a second eye and stared down at them. He waited, holding his breath, listening for the splash and a hiss as the sea extinguished the flame of the missile, swallowed the projectile.

A crash.

Screams.

He knew what it meant, and could not help – though he should lay still – rolling over to see the damage. The fleet splitting in two behind them. It looked so orderly, as if every ship knew its place, but he knew it would not be. Every woman and man would be scrambling to put space between them and the giant catapult.

Between the two arms of the fleet was a burning wreck. Prone as he was, he could not see well enough to recognise the ship.

"Was it her?" he said, barely able to breathe.

"It was not *Tide Child*," said Cwell from by him.

"Who then?"

"I am sorry, Shipwife," said Cwell, and at that moment he knew he could trust her, as he heard his coming pain echoed in her voice and there was no joy there. No gloat nor sneer. "It were the *Bonebore*, Shipwife."

And he nearly broke in that moment, was nearly overwhelmed by emotion. That Cwell, of all people would recognise his loss. Hag's mercy, he hoped it had been quick. Hoped that Dinyl had never seen the missile, never had time to think about it before it hit. To cover the wetness in his eyes he lifted the nearglass once more, found the gaps in the gate.

White.

Black.

A glimpse through tears.

The mangonel was already wound halfway back down.

"Hag take you all," he said under his breath, rubbed at his

wet eyes. "I'll send every single one of you to her if I have to send you myself."

"Will they loose again, Shipwife?" said Cwell.

White.

Black.

A glimpse through tears.

"Yes." He rolled on the deck, looking back at the ships now heading away. "But I imagine Meas will have the fleet out of range by the time they do."

"Signal, Shipwife!" was shouted down from the tops, and did he imagine it, but even in that shout did Farys sound a little gentler than usual? "They say, 'Hove to outside the gate'."

"Cwell," he said softly, lowering the nearglass. "Have Farys reply that we will. I would do it myself but I find my voice is not as strong as I would wish." And with that order *Keyshantooth* came about, slowing to a stop before the great gate while all those they knew, trusted and loved flew away, or sank beneath the sea, never to be seen again.

"What do you want here?" was shouted from the tower. And Farys, dear Farys, shouted back:

"Entry and help. My shipwife lies broken upon the deck." And Joron – a lancing pain in his heart and the fading image of Dinyl, stood in his shipwife's finery upon the rump of *Bonebore* while the fiery missile came down – thought that she spoke even truer than she could know.

# 49

## The Enemy Within

There was much toing and froing, much exchanging of codewords and much anger that *Keyshantooth* was here when the Bern of Sleighthulme did not think it should be. At one moment Joron was sure they would not be let in, and there were many questions as to why Shipwife Barnt was not in command. The agreed excuse – that he had moved to a bigger ship – was given by Farys. Joron was introduced as Shipwife Tinner, a name near enough his own to forgive any slip of the tongue amongst his crew, but also the name of a rich family back in Bernshulme, which would more than explain the rapid rise of a shipwife they had never heard of. Eventually, grudgingly, it was decided that *Keyshantooth* should be let in and the great bone gate was lifted from the sea, its bottom thick with green weed and encrusted with shells. Two pilot boats rowed out and were swiftly tied on to the front of *Keyshantooth* so he could be towed into the harbour. Joron was pulled from his place, leaving a smear of red on the deck, so he sat against the bottom of the mainspine in among spatters of red and blue paint. From there he could watch the harbour and town of Sleighthulme and the giant mangonel that sat wreathed in the smoke of Sleighthulme's foundries.

While he watched the hateful machine Joron found that if he took the icy, gnawing pain within and twisted it up as hard as he could, like a deckchild drying their clothes on washing day, he could wring out the pain and distil it into hate, and it was that towering siege weapon that he aimed his hate at. The weapon, and those that operated it. It sat at rest now, long throwing arm in the air, the sling hanging down, pushed slightly from the stained bone of the arm by the wind. Two thirds of the way down it was the axle which it moved on, and below that the huge weight that gave the projectile its power and range.

"That'll have to go," said Coughlin as he came to stand by Joron.

"Ey, and it will give me great pleasure to see it fall." Then he took a breath, and pushed back his hate. "But Meas may think it worth weathering its shot to have it intact when we take the island, in case Sleighthulme is the trap some fear." Coughlin shook his head. "You disagree, Coughlin?"

He bit on his lip and nodded. "Were it I in command of that giant, Shipwife," he said, "then I would know exactly how to aim it at the gate we just passed through. Wreck one ship in the gate and you as good as block it."

Joron nodded, absorbed the sense in his words.

"Then the weapon must come down," said Joron. "That makes our job harder. Where is the map that Anopp drew for us?"

Coughlin took a beautifully drawn map of Sleighthulme from inside his robe and passed it to Joron. "Aelerin embellished it," he said.

"Then we should thank the courser. Now, see here," said Joron, and he pointed at the map. "We are here, coming through the gate and just passing the infirmary of Sleighthulme, built into the same building that gives access to the landward tower and the winding mechanism for the gate."

"That is often the way," said Coughlin, "to put those worth least as a buffer against the places a besieger would be sure to attack."

"Well, you are right, but space is at a premium here and as

no one has ever managed to get in, maybe they do not think it will ever be a problem?" He gave Coughlin the sort of grin a longthresh would give a drowning deckchild. "Now, Anopp tells us that their gallowbows are built in such a way that the weapons cannot be turned on one another. They are confident they will only ever be loosing outward. I had hoped to take the bow on our side and use it on the other."

"There will be a way," said Mevans. "There always is."

"Well, Mevans, when the time comes, that will be your job. A race between your expertise on our side and their knowledge of their own weapon on the other. It must come down or it will do fearful damage to the ships coming in."

Mevans nodded and turned to a deckchild. "Tell one of the bonewrights, we will need saws and hammers on land."

"Now . . ." Joron took a stick of charcoal from an inner pocket, and wondered what it looked like to those on land, so many gathered round him. They must think him close to death. "Here is the town centre where they have built the mangonel." He drew an X on the map and his voice became quiet, the words dying in his mouth. *Dinyl*. He took a breath. Fought back the sudden pain in his throat and tear in his eye. "There are many entrances to this square. If they have enough deckchilder and soldiers taking that catapult will be hard."

"I will take a look when we are on land," said Coughlin. "It is still your plan to wait until night?"

"It is what Meas wants. Unless we are forced to move before then we will stick to her timetable. We will need to find a way to send her some sort of signal too."

"I'm sure there will be a way," said Coughlin.

"Let me through," said a voice, "all you big ones barring an old woman from her charge." Garriya pushed into sight past Coughlin and Mevans. "Would you have us killed before we even land? To have a wounded shipwife unattended by a hagshand? What sort of ship would that be?" She groaned as she squatted by Joron's stump and produced some bloody rags from the healer's bag she carried.

"What is that?"

"Subterfuge," she said. "A kivelly's corpse. Managed to stop that Hag-cursed gullaime eating this one. I cut it and mangled it, so it looks like bloody flesh and bone." She pulled off the rags and showed him the wet red-and-white mess in her hand. "See? Now I just need to attach it to your stump." She pulled at the ragged trouser leg. "You have not been keeping this clean enough."

"I have had a ship to command."

"No excuses, there are ulcers. Don't look after it and I'll end up cutting more off."

*Foolish to argue with her,* he thought, and it was plain on the faces of those around him they agreed, for no woman or man aboard had ever won an argument with Garriya.

"It will look like a fresh wound?"

"Aye — to those who just glance, anyway."

"And those who look deeper? I am sure their hagpriests will not leave us alone for long."

"There's many a healer would be fooled by this," she cackled, tucking the cold flesh around the end of his leg. "But the hagpriests, Mother curse them, well, they tend to look a little closer." She looked up, her eyes suddenly intense. "We may have to kill them, Caller."

*A fire descending from the sky.*

"I have no qualms on that front, Hagshand."

"Good," she said. "We should kill a lot more hagpriests, make the world a better place, I say." She shuffled back so she could admire her handiwork, then returned, tugging and pulling on the corpse attached to his leg before she was finally happy. "I'll keep them from you as long as we can. But you have taken an important name, and they will want their important priests to look at you, Caller. Nothing I can do about that in the end. Fierce as I can be, would look strange if I did not eventually comply. Me being a lowborn know-nothing and all." She cackled and backed away.

"No plan survives contact with the enemy, Garriya," he said. And she chuckled once more.

"Let's hope we survive though, aye? Garriya may be old but she'd like to see a few more years out yet." Then she was gone, back into the depths of the ship and Joron was forced to wait and feign illness as *Keyshantooth* was towed into the harbour.

From there a small force of seaguard came aboard and he was picked up, moaning and groaning. His pain brought curious looks until he let a different pain rise up, let grief overwhelm him, and the sobbing began. Such pain in a shipwife made the seaguard about him far less curious, and they turned away in embarrassment. He was put into a hammock that was swung over the side by a hastily erected crane into a waiting fluke-boat. Mevans, Farys and Garriya accompanied him to the quayside and from there he was carried through gloomy streets to the hagbower.

Everything within him wanted to scream. Here the bothies were built close, and the tenements were built close, and when you moved between them, through the streets, the light of Skearith's Eye was blocked. It was like being once more imprisoned within a box. He found it hard to breathe, found himself panicking. Found his mind going down dark paths: imagining Dinyl, thrown overboard by the missile from the mangonel, sinking into black water, drowning, while the many and varied toothed and tentacled beasts of the sea circled and—

He felt a hand on his arm.

"Calm, Caller, calm. The pain will be over soon. You just breathe for old Garriya, you breathe."

He did. Focusing on the in and out of air through his lungs. And while he did that his thoughts calmed a little, and he concentrated on the stones and blocks that made the buildings, on the shadows formed by Skearith's Eye above and he told himself he was not within the box. Told himself that the obstruction in his throat was not swelling from the garrotte but something put there by his grief. When his mind had quietened a little more he noticed something else about this place, this bleak and black island – it did not sing to him the way the others did.

Silence.

He had not felt a silence in his mind ever, now he thought on it. The song had always been there, and it had only got louder since he had met the gullaime — when the creature was about, the song ran on and on in counterpoint to the many other melodies in his mind. Now it felt as if some vast hand had dampened the constantly vibrating strings within him. This silence felt as dark and as oppressive as the shadows, as waking within the box with his voice crushed from him, as being held down by unseen hands and powerful drugs while they cut off his leg. The panic started to rise again.

A cold white hand on the warm brown skin of his arm. He felt a song within him, a quiet one, only a whisper of the greater melodies that had always been there, but enough.

"Be calm, Caller," said Garriya. "This dead island taxes us all." And he tried to breathe and listen to the quiet song of his blood and his body. Garriya kept her hand on his arm for the rest of the short walk to the hagbower. That place also held its terrors for Joron, as it was in a hagbower where mind-numbing sedatives had been fed to him and he had come close to joining those taken away, stowed in tight racks on dark ships.

"Be calm, Caller, be calm."

It did not take long before they were installed in a small room within the hagbower. The priest who escorted them was a young-looking Bern and though she was quietly insistent she "see the shipwife's wounds", she was quickly seen off by the old woman's sharp words and talismanic use of the Tinner name. Though Garriya was also forced to make concessions, and both Mevans and Farys had to agree to leave. Farys went first, turning the wrong way out of the door and hurrying away as fast as she could further into the building, quickly followed by the hagpriest.

"Deckkeeper," the priest called after Farys, "that is not the way! Deckkeeper!" But Farys paid no attention. Once they had gone Mevans turned to Joron and gave him a grin.

"I better go have a look around," he said, and vanished, back the way they had come to explore the building.

"While they are gone," said Garriya, "I will clean the ulcers on your stump." She removed the kivelly carcass and his dressings and began to treat where his spur had rubbed his stump. He hissed with pain as she applied one of her salves. "If you had looked after it properly, Caller, then it would not be hurting, aye?"

"Ey," he nodded. "I cannot argue—" And then his words were cut off by a lance of pain so severe it was bite down or scream out, and he was a shipwife now, even if only a temporary one, and if there was one thing Meas had taught him it was that shipwives do not scream.

At one point the hagpriest looked in and Garriya snapped at her, in a voice that carried all her foul temper: "Out! Can you not see I work on the Shipwife? If you would be useful bring me food."

When the wound was clean and covered and the bird's corpse reapplied, Garriya turned, pulling over a stool and taking a piece of bread from the basket the hagpriest had eventually delivered. "Now you wait, eh Shipwife? And then you plan."

"Yes," he said, his nerves still jangling with pain.

"Best be a good plan too, aye? No keyshans to come save you here. All you have is all you have."

"I know," he said. "Maybe that is a good thing. I would not want to . . ."

"Bring down another isle?"

"No," he said, but he was not sure he meant it, as when he closed his eyes he once more saw that fiery projectile arcing overhead, Dinyl falling inexorably into the deep. And he wondered, would it be so bad if he could raise a keyshan from under this place? Bring the black basalt crashing down on all?

"Meas believes your people are somewhere here, Caller," said Garriya, interrupting his thoughts.

"Ey," he said. Sat up a little. "And we must find them."

"Many will be dead," she said.

"You know this how?"

She stared at him, and the eyes within her face seemed infinitely sad.

"Because," she said, "it is always so."

Before he could ask what she meant, the merry face of Mevans appeared at the door.

"Shipwife, Garriya," he said. "The hagpriest will only let one extra in at a time now. Coughlin is here and also waits to speak to you."

"What did you find, Mevans?" Joron levered himself up so Mevans could come closer and speak more quietly.

"They are lax," he said. "No more than ten guards for this whole tower. Most of our crew are in the town now, though we are not allowed to leave it. The island is much bigger than it looks. The place goes right back into the rock, but the mines are out of bounds."

"How many troops are in the town?"

Mevans usual smile vanished. "I reckon a lot, but best ask Coughlin. A true estimate of strengths is more his arena, Shipwife."

"Then why did you not simply send him?" he said, then realised how tetchy he sounded, and knew that Mevans did not deserve that. But the hatkeep seemed more amused than offended by his outburst.

"Ey, you are right, Shipwife, foolish of me to waste your time." And that familiar grin slipped back onto his face once more. "Best I send in him in, ey?" he said as he left the room.

A moment later Coughlin appeared. "Shipwife," he said.

"How is it in the town?" said Joron.

"I have fair and foul weather to report. The fair is that these people are fools who are too sure of themselves."

"What do you mean?"

"I mean they are fools," he said again. "They are so sure they are safe they have become lazy. They pile their hagspit around the base of the mangonel so it is easy for them to get to. One spark and the machine is gone."

"Good, I will be glad to see it fall. But what is the foul weather you speak of?"

"They have a fair-sized garrison around the thing."

"Enough to hold off our crew?"

"Not forever, but they have more soldiers in the mines they can call on, and I imagine they could hold us off long enough for them to come to their aid. The square has multiple entrances and there's no way we can block them all without being seen."

Joron nodded, wondered what Meas would do.

"But I have an idea." said Coughlin.

"Tell me."

"When you take this place and the tower, let all our crew in, but either let a defender escape or make such noise it will draw attention. That should bring the garrison from the mangonel. I will hide in the town with some of my seaguard, and when the guard around the catapult is gone, we will attack it."

"But you may end up trapped, Coughlin."

"No plan is perfect, Shipwife."

"You may die."

"I will do my best not to."

Joron felt sure that if Meas were here she would have thought of some clever way out of this. But she was not here, he was. And he had no clever answers.

"Stay alive, Coughlin," he said, "I have lost one good friend today, I would not lose another."

The seaguard paused, for the smallest of moments. Then nodded. He was about to stand when a voice, imperious and used to being obeyed, spoke outside the room:

"Who is it that denies my priests their Hag-given right to tend the ill? I shall not stand for it."

*Well*, thought Joron. *Now it begins.*

# 50

# The Taking of the Gate

Garriya eyed up the taller woman, swaying from side to side as she did, like a bird guarding its nest, puffing up her layers of ragged clothes.

"I have dressed the wound, and done good work. To disturb it will not help the shipwife. What he needs is rest."

The new hagpriest pushed back the hood of her robe. Joron almost gasped, a tide of shock washing over him. She had Meas's face – oh, not as scarred by sun and wind and age, but the same face nonetheless.

"I am a hagmother of this island, old woman," she said and now he had seen her face he heard echoes of Meas in her voice. "And though it may seem to be nothing but a cold and lonely rock, it is a place of high honour, higher than you know. I do not change dirty bandages or look over deck-childer's wounds, there are others here for that, though you saw fit to send her away. But worry not, I will have your work checked as all know the work of ship's hagshand leaves much to be desired. For now, I only wish to talk to your shipwife."

"He is sleepy with drugs, and—"

"Did I ask your opinion?" said the hagmother. She had the

same quality of voice as Meas, commanding, powerful. Garriya bowed her head, turned to Joron and leaned over him.

"Take care," she said, and he felt her hand slide under the covers and push the familiar shape of a bone knife against his thigh. Then she stood, gave the hagmother a glance, a sneer, shrugged and muttered something Joron did not catch, before leaving the room.

Beneath the thin cover Joron wrapped his fingers around the hilt of the knife.

"Shipwife Tinner," the hagmother said, and pulled over a seat so she could sit by him, folding her hands in her lap.

"Hagmother, you have a look of Meas Gilbryn."

Something cold passed across the her face.

"I saw her once at a parade," Joron said.

"I do not talk of the coward, Meas, nor claim any kinship." Her voice had all the icy chill of the Northstorm "But I am of the Thirteenbern, and the stamp of her strength is on the faces of all her daughters. You are honoured to be in my presence."

"Indeed," he said. The bone hilt warmed in his grip.

"Though of course," she said, "I call you Shipwife only as a courtesy, for we both know that is your position no longer." She pointed at the space beneath the covers where his lower leg should be.

"Then to what do I owe this honour, Hagmother?"

"Well," she leaned forward, "yours is an old and powerful family, Shipwife Tinner. They, and you, have given much honour to the Hundred Isles. I would have you think about your position."

"My position?" he said.

"Let us not be delicate, for we are not a people of delicate places and do not live delicate lives." She put her hand on his thigh, just above where his leg had been severed. From experience, Joron knew that had the wound been fresh, her touch would have been agonising. "A shipwife without a leg is not a shipwife, and as a Tinner you can hardly go back to

Bernshulme and find work on Hoppity Lane making shoes, can you? It would not be fitting."

"No," he said. "Of course not."

"And it must gall such a man as you that you cannot serve on a ship, and you will never be one of the Kept now either. So you must throw yourself on your family's charity." Her eyes searched his face. "I do not mean to be cruel. I only think it is best I am honest with you. Truly honest, as few people will be." She leaned in closer. "But you have chosen a life of honour and service, Shipwife," she said. "What if I were to tell you that you may continue to serve, that you may make a sacrifice? And though it may sound great, it is simply the same one you have already agreed to."

"What do you mean?" he said.

"Death," she replied.

"You threaten me? I am a Tinner and—"

She lifted a hand to stop him talking. "It is not a threat," she said. "You are free to leave this island and return a cripple to live off your family, if that is what you wish."

"Why would I take your offer?" he said. "Death is a poor reward for service, and my family would find me a place." He knew the reality was that there was no family and nowhere for him to go, but they felt like the things a man in his position would say. A proud man. A man with a heritage.

"I am sure your family would," she said, and sat back. "If a life in a corner being disregarded is what you wish for. I offer you a chance to do something that will resonate throughout the Hundred Isles for lifetimes." He stared at her. She leaned further forward, gaze intense, burning into him. "I offer you a chance to change our world, to hand the entire archipelago to the Hundred Isles. To crush the Gaunt Islanders."

"How?" He said it in a whisper, and though he suspected what was coming, what she would say, he was entranced by her words. He felt the power of them, like she wove some strange magic about him, and he could not help thinking this was something she shared with her sither, Meas. This magnetism.

"You have heard," she said, "that the arakeesians have returned?" He nodded. "Small numbers. Only two have been seen so far. But whoever can hunt them will rule the Scattered Archipelago."

"Surely our ships are already out there?" he said. She nodded.

"Oh aye, they are indeed. But hunting keyshans is not like hunting longthresh. You cannot simply fill them with harpoons. We have learned this to our cost." She shuffled nearer, smiling. "But there is a way."

He knew, of course, but could not say it, played the fool.

"You would have me hunt them?"

"In a way."

"In a way?"

"There are old secrets, buried within the records in Bernshulme that tell us how these creatures must be hunted. There is a poison that kills them quickly. Using it will save thousands of lives."

"And?"

"Sacrifices are needed in the making of it." She stopped, her mouth slightly open. He saw the tip of her tongue touch her front teeth. "It is not a kind process. We need help." He recoiled – even though he already knew, he recoiled. It was not even the words, or the horror of it. It was that she did not feel it. That she was inured to it, seemed almost entranced by it. "Oh, I know how it sounds," she cooed, like a mother with a babe. "I do know how it sounds. But if we do not do it, the Gaunt Islanders will, eventually."

"So I escape death on the sea, only to find it here," he said.

"The recipe we have found is old and incomplete. So we make batches of the poison, and even that uses up bodies faster than we can find them. Then we send out a ship to try it. And of course, they must first find the keyshan. Then a report must come back from the companion ship on whether it worked or not before we go into production. It is a lengthy process, Shipwife," she said, then sat back.

"You want me to help make this poison of yours, which uses people up so quickly?" he said.

Her eyes widened. "Of course not. You are from an old and honoured family." She leaned in a little closer. "But we need crews for those ships, see? Experienced crews. Oh, it is dangerous work, I will not lie. Often not even the companion ship makes it back. But when you are not at sea you will live here. In luxury. You will want for nothing. We will inform your family you died on your ship, and you will, in necessary secrecy, provide a service that will ensure the strength of the Hundred Isles for generations." Her eyes searched his face, looking for understanding.

"What of my crew?"

"We are always in need of soldiers and deckchilder. Though, of course, it is likely they will find out about what we do here. Some struggle with it. And I am afraid they cannot be allowed to leave. You understand. The Berncast may not understand."

"Of course," he said. She smiled.

"Well?"

"May I have some time to think about it? It is a lot to take in," he said.

She stood. "I will give you an hour, then return for your answer." Though of course, he knew what she did not say. That he was as doomed now as any Berncast, and that this hour was simply a courtesy.

Once the hagmother had gone Garriya returned. "What did she want?"

"My service," he said. "Send word to Farys, Mevans, Coughlin and Cwell. We have an hour to prepare."

But they did not need an hour. Mevans and Farys and Coughlin and Cwell had long been ready: seaguard and deckchilder had been moved around the town until they were all in the places it was judged best they be. The majority of them in or around the tower and the infirmary. Coughlin and a few volunteers hidden within the town, as near to the great mangonel as they could get. So, when the time came and Garriya hissed at him, "Be ready, Caller. She comes," he was entirely ready. It felt like every sinew and muscle in his body was wound tight, waiting for the moment. And when the hagmother once more came into his room, this time followed by the younger priest who had been first to attend him, his hand was around the warm hilt of the bone knife beneath his covers.

"Shipwife Tinner," said the hagmother. "Have you come to a decision?"

He nodded. "I will take your offer," he said as she sat down by him. "But tell me truth. Once you had told me of what you do here, I had joined those who would never leave, had I not?"

She smiled at him, that mouth, so similar to Meas.

"Yes," she said and leaned in close. "It is good you chose to serve. You would not have enjoyed the alternative."

He nodded. Hand tightened on the blade.

"Neither will you," he said. With one hand he grabbed the back of her head, and with the other brought the knife up, still with the thin sheet wrapped around it. A white wave rising from the bed. That wave only to be crowned in red, slick and wet, as he drove the blade beneath it into the side of her neck. Never giving her time to scream. Pulling the blade out. Thrusting it back into flesh. Never giving her time to shout. Pulling the blade out. Thrusting it back in. Never giving her any time at all. Behind her Garriya held the younger hagpriest, her sharp hagshand's blade at the girl's throat.

"And this one, Caller?"

She was young, terrified.

*The fiery projectile coming down on Dinyl's ship.*

"No quarter, Garriya."

Garriya's blade bit. The girl's mouth opened in a perfect "o" as if she were simply surprised by the sudden turn of events, and as the sheet of blood spilled down the front of her white robe, Joron could almost believe it. Garriya's blade was so sharp he thought the young hagpriest may not even have felt the blade bite home before life fled from her. He tried to believe it, as he had given the order which took her life. He tried to believe it as she looked so young.

But he knew the pain of the blade.

He knew you always felt it, eventually.

"Come, Caller, you'll need your leg and your sword." She pulled them from his pack under the bed and started fixing the leg on to him. Practiced hands moved quickly as she clamped the leather and buckles around his thigh. He felt the familiar pain in the stump of his leg as he moved his weight off the bed. Then Garriya was buckling on his sword belt and he found himself staring at the bodies. The hagmother he felt nothing for, despite that her blood was drying, bright red to russet brown, on his hands, but he could not tear his eyes away from the girl's body.

"Feel no pity, Caller," said Garriya, "what happens here is monstrous, and all who support it are monsters. We both know that."

He pulled his gaze from the dead girl.

"Let us leave this place."

Outside he found Farys and Cwell waiting for him. And behind them almost the entire crew of *Keyshantooth* filled the corridor.

"Mevans has wandered up to the room used by those on guard here," said Farys, "with Jennil and Jirrid. When we arrive they will attack."

"How many are there?"

"Ten in the room now, and another ten up the tower. I will leave Panir here with twenty to barricade the doors and hold the rear, though I think five could hold it."

"Better to be sure, Farys," he said. "Once they realise what we are about, then they will throw everything they have at that door."

"My deckchilder will hold it, Shipwife," she said.

"I know they will," he replied, and clapped her on the arm.

"If the congratulations are over," said Cwell, "there is plenty killing to be done."

"Ey, that is true." He drew the sword from his scabbard. "Now come," he said to the others, "Mevans awaits us."

With that his crew ran ahead, leaving Joron behind. He knew how they were used to shouting and whooping when battle came and felt inordinately proud that not one of them made a noise as they made their way, barefoot and almost silent, through the infirmary. At the corridor leading to the guardroom they stopped. Joron pushed through the throng of warm bodies, peered around the corner. Saw Mevans sharing a drink with the guards. Laughing. Occasionally he would glance down the corridor and when he saw Joron they shared a look. Mevans gave him a short nod. Joron breathed in a deep breath. Shouted, "Now!" Attacked. Closely followed by Cwell. Closely followed by Farys. Closely followed by Camin and behind her another and another. Running down the corridor. Now was the time to shout and to scream and to make a noise. Before the guards could close their door Joron was through. A straight lunge took a woman running at him in the throat. Cwell passed him, going to landward. Farys went to seaward, cutting out with her curnow, slashing and hacking. With a roar, Mevans attacked. Blood flew. Death came quick, and these were women and men they killed, not girls who were little more than childer themselves. And then they were done. Finished. Breathing heavily, the smell of blood hanging in the air, blood sprayed from cut arteries like paint left for luck on the walls. Mevans grinned at him.

A figure appeared in the arch at the bottom of the spiral stairwell that lead up into the tower. A look of shock, almost comically exaggerated as he stared up the room toward where Joron stood. One of Cwell's knives flew across the room. Not quick enough. The knife hit only stone as the observer ran back up the spiral.

"After them," shouted Joron.

"I will lead," shouted Jennil, "I am landward-handed, easier for me to fight up a spiral stair." Then they were running again, up the tight spiral, feet slipping on worn stone steps until Jennil met resistance at the entrance to the next floor. The clash of arms. Shouting. Pushing. A curse from Jennil and she fell back, a nasty cut to her arm.

"Have Garriya see to that," shouted Joron, and he pushed himself past on the stairwell, straightsword held out. The enemy clustered in the doorway, pushing him back down the stair. As he stepped back he sensed something above him. Cwell, using a deckchilder's trick in a tight space to move up the low, curved ceiling, arms and legs wedged against the curved stone. The defenders of the tower were not deckchilder, and were unprepared for such tactics. All eyes were on the man before them, not on the woman who appeared from above. This furious, spitting, screaming, fighting creature suddenly among them. The space she made gave Joron room to advance and he pushed forward, then it was as if a boneboard in a ship's hull had broken and the deckchilder were water, rushing in, cutting and killing until another room fell silent. "We do not stop," shouted Joron. "We do not stop until the top of the tower is ours."

They met no more resistance — everyone had been pulled down into the tower by the noise of the attack, and all that waited for them at the top was the giant gallowbow. Across from them was the other tower and its crew, gathered around their own bow. Alert, waiting. Aware something was wrong. When Joron's women and men appeared on the top their tower a shout went up: 'Enemies, on the seaward tower!' Then he saw furious industry and they started to work on their gallowbow.

"Mevans!" shouted Joron, "we need to bring the bow around!"

And Mevans was there by him. Standing back, rubbing his chin and looking at the great bow.

"Problem is the track, see, Shipwife," he said, pointing at the wooden rails the bow sat on. "Ey, that it is. See, it don't go far round enough to target the other tower."

"I do not want an explanation of the technicalities," said

Joron, "I want a solution," and he heard the echoes of Meas in his voice.

"A solution, ey?" said Mevans. He scratched at his cheek. "Well it does happen, Shipwife, I reckons I have one."

"And it is?"

"One moment," he said, and vanished back the way they had come. Joron glanced at the tower opposite where much shouting and pointing was happening around that gallowbow, then he ran to the door, shouting down the twisting stair to Mevans. "Will you hurry on, Mevans? They're hardly sat idle and waiting our leisure on that other tower."

"Don't worry yourself, Shipwife," he shouted back, "for we have a great advantage over them." He appeared around the curve of the stair.

"And what is that, Mevans?"

"Well, Shipwife, they will want to take care of that weapon. And us?" He grinned as he pushed through the doorway and held up a great hammer. "We have no such concerns." He ran over to the gallowbow and starting enthusiastically smashing away the bone and stone around the end of the track. On the tower opposite voices were raised, there was more pointing and Joron heard the sounds of hammering drifting across to them.

"Seems them lot have caught on." Mevans glanced over his shoulder, "Well," he said to the other deckchilder, "push it round, we'll need everyone spare to catch it at the end of the track and handle the thing into position." Then it was all about who was the quickest, which deckchilder were more efficient, and as Joron stared at the other tower it became clear there was little in it.

"Come on!" shouted Mevans. Shoulders put to the weapon. Grunts and groans as they pushed the bow around. All mirrored on the opposite tower.

With a crash the gallowbow came off the track, and then with much swearing and cursing of the Hag it was made stable and pointed at the opposite tower.

"Spin!" shouted Joron, and he heard his word echoed from across the gate. "Spin for your lives!" And they did. Two towers, mirrors of each other, two great bows inching back cords, filling them with violent intent. Two sets of loaders struggling with stone wingbolts.

There could only be one winner.

The warmoan of the bow.

"Loose!"

Stone smashed into the great bow, scattering those around it, throwing them out into the empty air. A shout of triumph went up from those around Joron while he sent up a silent prayer of thanks to the Mother that Lucky Meas had trained her bowcrews so well. There were none faster and he was well glad of it. He pulled his nearglass from his jacket, a brief look at the ruined bow opposite, the dead scattered around it. Then swinging the nearglass so he looked out to sea.

"Where is the shipwife?" said Mevans.

"I do not know," said Joron, "but get a team down into the winding room and lift that gate. And another team to drag this bow right around, so we can loose on anyone in the town who tries to get a ship out."

"We need some sort of signal," said Cwell.

"Ey," said Joron, and he looked around, and seeing the great brazier for signals, but either the crew were lax or deliveries had not been made yet as there was no fuel for it. "We must think of something."

# 51

## What Coughlin Did

There is little to please a warrior more than a plan well carried out and an enemy surprised by that plan, and so it was that Coughlin found himself well pleased. He sat, with eight of his, in the ruin of a house by the harbour. He did not know why it was ruined, and he was not curious about it as he was not a curious man, or a man who was interested in the world around him. Not unless it directly affected the now, for the now was where Coughlin lived and the now was where Coughlin was safest. He lived by the blade and when that was your profession the now was the only guarantee you had, for the future may not exist, as it no longer did for poor Berhof, and the past was a place full of sorrows and lost friends.

The air around him had the faint tinge of fire, and the stonework of the building was blackened by it. Maybe there had been some great calamity here that still carried ill luck, as the people of Sleighthulme seemed to avoid the ruin. All the better for Coughlin and his.

Before them was a town square, mostly filled by the base of the giant mangonel, and between him and the siege weapon barricades had been erected. Within those barricades sat and slumped the women and men meant to be guarding it. *Not seaguard*, he thought. They were a motley mix of deckchilder, who at least would know how to look after themselves, and civilians who looked uncomfortable with the weapons they held, despite they must be Hundred Isles raised, and familiar with such things. The two groups kept to themselves. Coughlin was not surprised – he well knew how deckchilder thought all those who did not tread the slate of a ship were somehow less than them. He had been on the end of that disrespect for long on long until, at some point, he had not been, and now he was one of them. Without even realising it he looked now upon the armed civilians and thought them fools, unable to tell the beak of a ship from the rump.

What was behind those civilians and deckchilder worried him more. Ten figures only, and the man who must be leading them, dressed in the straps and embroidered trews of the Kept. They were seaguard, keeping themselves separate from the civilian and the deckchilder and, he was sure, considering themselves as far above the deckchilder as the deckchilder considered themselves above the seaguard.

Such was the way of things in the Hundred Isles.

The mangonel – he had learned it was named "Skearith's Wing" – was the largest he had ever seen. Four thick legs rising to a swivel joint and axle that allowed the great arm, rising higher than a boneship's mainspine, to throw its burning payloads right out into the sea. He had seen such weapons before. Knew there were multiple ways to take them down, most temporary. Cut the ropes, smash the winders, unhitch the arm somehow. Though if all else failed then the fools of Sleighthulme had done his job for him, packing the hagspit used to put fire to the projectiles around the base of the mangonel in a makeshift hut of dried gion. If all went his way, he could present Meas with a working mangonel and she would be pleased at that, and though he did not entirely understand why that was so important to him, he knew that to please her would please him. So he would not skimp or stop in his efforts to take the giant weapon. But at the same time, if it came to it, it was more important that it be put out of action or the shipwife may never even make it into the harbour.

Coughlin, in his life, had done many terrible things, hurt many people, but he had always had what he believed was a good reason for it. Those poor souls trapped within the belly of the *Maiden's Bounty* haunted him. He could see no good reason for what was done to them. None that he would agree with. Kill someone for wronging you, even make it hurt if they wronged you enough. That made sense. But this machine of death and misery? That did not sit right with him. And it did not sit right with his shipwife. So he would do his bit.

And so would his men: Varin, Porran, Lamba, Chil; his new second, Lossick – who had been with him a long time and was the last of those brought over from Mulvan Cahanny's criminal enterprise back in Bernshulme; and Rassa and Bers – who were both women but he still thought of them as his men, since seaguard were always men and that was the way things were done.

He looked them over, proud of his command and realised he had changed much since he had come aboard the black ship.

He would never fall for the trick with the bonebores now.

A noise. He turned, taking out the bone knife he wore strapped to his thigh, ready to silence whoever may have come upon them unawares. Every. Muscle. Tensing. Then relaxing as he recognised Chiff, one of the deckchilder.

"Farys says an hour, at most. And it took me a quarter of one to get here, so tell me you are ready?"

"Ey," said Coughlin, for the deckchilder did not say "Aye" like normal women and men, "we are ready. You may stay and join us if you wish?"

"Fair little chance of that, Seaguard," said Chiff. "I reckon my chances much better on the tower than they are going up against all 'o them." She pointed at the soldiers before the giant catapult.

"If you do your jobs right," said Lossick, "all o' them won't be there."

"Well," said the deckchild as she melted back into the building, "let's hope we all do our jobs right, ey?"

Then they settled in to wait, to let time wash over them like sea over rocks — though time was even more dependable and relentless than the sea. He watched those around him settle, for up until this moment it had always been possible — if you really wished to believe it — to tell yourself the fight would not happen, but now they were committed and a place in time existed, not far in the future, when the terrible red work of war would start. They knew, as each and every one of them had been bloodied many times before, that they were most at risk — their position was the furthest extended and most susceptible to counter-attack. If the deckkeeper and those in the tower succeeded they could barricade themselves in, but if Coughlin and his men succeeded then they had no such succour. They must hide themselves and hope that Meas arrived in time to save them from those within the town. Coughlin had accepted this, and sat waiting, bone-straight and stiff. Varin and Porran had cleared a patch of ground and were playing some form of dice game. Lamba was sitting with both hands on the hilt of his curnow, the blade propped point down in the dirt, staring morosely at something only he could see. Chil appeared to be asleep. Rassa and Bers spoke quietly to one another and Lossick was carving something into a stick of bone.

And they waited and time ebbed away, leaving only the dry mouths and hollow stomachs of women and men about to pit their skill and strength against the skill and strength of others. Women and men knowing if they were not the more skilful, or stronger, or luckier, then these would be their last moments before they met the Hag.

"They are going," said Lossick quietly. Though it was needless. A woman had run in to the square, shouting about the tower and an attack. In answer it seemed every woman and man rose up, grabbed the nearest weapon and ran from the square. Though it was not all − the Hag did not love *Tide Child*'s crew that much. The seaguard remained, their officer stood behind them. Lossick made to move forward but Coughlin grabbed his arm.

"Wait," he said. "It would only take one of these deckchilder to glance behind and see us and they'll all come rushing back, then we are lost before we even start. So wait." Lossick nodded. In his mind Coughlin counted out the seconds the way he had heard the shipwife do when she stood on the rump and threw the rock to gauge *Tide Child*'s speed. When he reached thirty-two, he judged it a good amount of time, partly because he knew how twisty the streets were around here, and that those who had run must be out of sight by now. And partly because that was as far as his numbers went. "I am not one for speeches," he said, and wished he had listened to the things the shipwife said more, "but let us avenge Dinyl and the *Bonebore*." And there was no rousing shout. Only a shuffling of feet and small smiles that, though small, he knew were those of women and men who had heard something they liked.

It was not hard to cross the square, and it was not hard to pass through the fences that had once housed the ragtag mixture of deckchilder and armed civilians. They did this at speed, with curnow by their side and small shields held across their chests. And those defending the catapult, the paltry group not much bigger than Coughlin's, were almost unable to believe what they saw, this small armed group running toward them. But they were seaguard, and their surprise did not last. At a single shout from their leader they arranged themselves into a thin line, bristling with spears. Something soared within Coughlin. This was what he was, this was why he was here. This was what made him worthwhile to the shipwife. This was his purpose.

He saw the leader of the seaguard shouting as they ran forward. The line of men drew back their arms and threw spears.

"Shields!" shouted Coughlin. And shields came up, spears deflected, digging into the ground.

And they ran on.

Except Coughlin.

Who did not.

And he did not understand why.

He had the will.

He was not afraid.

Anything but afraid.

Never afraid.

But in pain. Pain in his stomach, like someone had punched him hard, and kept on punching him. He watched his troops smash into the line of seaguard, curnows rising and falling. Saw the line pushed back as the charge hit. He was on his knees. Which was not in his plan. Not his intention at all. He was going to lead. He was going to kill the leader of the other seaguard. He could see them. Slashing back and forth with their curnow.

Why was he kneeling on the floor?

Looked down. 'Oh,' he thought. A strange disconnected thought. 'Oh,' because the pain made sense now. A spear, through his gut.

He watched Lossick die. Cut down by the leader. Saw his people were losing, being pushed back. But they were fighting, hard as they could to hold their ground. To one side of the fighting was a gap in the bone wall barricade around the mangonel. Through that gap was the hagspit.

The spear in his gut, the spear was a problem.

He wrapped his arms around it and was about to pull when he noticed another spear lying on the floor. It had vicious barbs on it. No hope of pulling out such a thing. So he pushed it instead, driving the handle of the spear through his body. The pain was immense, furious. But his screams were lost in the screams of those fighting and like all things, it was eventually over and then he was lying on the floor. Sweating. Hurting.

The gap called to him.

His legs would not work.

But he had strong arms. Dragged himself forward. Women and men died. Forward. He tasted blood in his mouth. Forward.

The stinging scent of hagspit in his nostrils. Forward, only forward. Crawling through a slime of mud and hagspit that had leaked from the barrels. Shadows falling round him. Nearly there. His eyes watering with pain and the acrid fumes that gathered in the small hut. There. Here. Made it. Behind him a noise. He rolled over. Pushed himself up so he sat amongst the barrels. One hand scrabbled at the pouch by his side, finding his flint and sparker. A figure silhouetted in the entrance to the hut. Coughlin held up the flint and sparker. The figure drew back their arm, ready to throw the spear they held.

"Stop," said Coughlin.

The figure did.

"You are their leader," he said.

Coughlin nodded.

"My people," said Coughlin through a mouthful of blood. "They are all dead?"

The figure nodded in return.

"They took all my men with them, though. They fought well."

"They were good, my seaguard."

"As were mine." The officer hunkered down a little, getting ready to throw. "Do you think you can make the spark before I can kill you?" There was no threat in the question, only curiosity.

"Whether I do, or do not, I will toast you at the Hag's fire," said Coughlin.

"And I you," said the seaguard commander. Coughlin gave him a small salute, drew the flint across the scratcher and the seaguard threw his spear. Coughlin felt the point pierce his chest as the shower of sparks from the sparker multiplied and changed colour, taken up by air thick with hagspit fumes, and his last thought was how very, very beautiful the flame was.

Across the harbour, on top of a tower, watching desperately out to sea for the ships of his shipwife, Joron Twiner no longer had to worry about how to make a signal. Behind him, the giant mangonel was no more, engulfed in a huge green flame that sent up a plume of black smoke. One he was sure would be seen even by those in Bernshulme, far, far over the horizon.

# 52

## The Calm Before . . .

With the gate open, and the huge mangonel fallen, the end was quick. Sleighthulme's army was too used to living in a town that was untakeable and had never truly expected to fight. When presented with a fleet of boneships crewed by angry deckchilder and commanded by the famed Lucky Meas, who glared about her as if she could bring the whole island down around her ears, they capitulated. There was no fight left in them after the mangonel's destruction. Joron was returned to his shipwife, greeting her on the docks with Mevans and Farys as she alighted from *Tide Child*'s boat.

"Well done, Deckkeeper," she said. "How many did you lose?"

"Seven deckchilder," he said. Then looked down at the floor, avoiding the eyes of those around him. "And Coughlin. He and all his seaguard gave their lives to destroy the mangonel." More deaths on his slate, more friends lost and he had to fight back a sudden upswell of emotion. Meas nodded, looked away from him and bitter experience let him recognise something in her he never had before; how keenly she felt her losses. How hard she worked not to show it.

"He was a good warrior. He will be missed." She stared over his shoulder, past the forest of ship spines and through the closed gate out to sea. She stepped closer, and spoke only for him. "Joron, I am truly sorry for your loss out there." She put a hand on his shoulder and was about to say more, but whether she realised he was near to being overcome by the pain of his grief or was feeling it herself he did not know. She simply nodded. Smiled a small sad smile, bit on her bottom lip and changed the subject. "So, you have the island's commander?"

"The island was led by a hagpriest." A pause. "She is dead."

"What are you not saying?"

How to answer that?

"She was your sither. I had to kill her. I have laid out her body and—"

"I have no sithers." Said just too quickly. Meas straightened the cuffs on her jacket, any trace of feeling gone from her face. "And no need to see the body. Have it thrown off the walls for the longthresh."

"Yes, Shipwife."

"Where is her next in command?"

"In the largest of the bothies, where all those who lead this island await us."

"Then we will go there," said Meas. She stared at the black hill. "But first we go to the mines."

"The mines?"

"Do you think you work people to death out in the open, Joron?"

"They could be anywhere," he said, but she shook her head.

"You wish to do something dark, Deckkeeper, then you do it in darkness." She looked up the winding serpent road. "I have given this much thought while I waited out to sea. Besides, I would find my people, and know what crimes their captors are responsible for before I talk to them." With that she strode away from the dock and he followed, after commanding Mevans and Farys to stay and make sure the ships were well cared for and the brownbones made ready to take on whoever they should find.

If anyone.

He followed her through the streets, Narza and Cwell behind them. It was an ugly town of blocky buildings put up quickly to house the miners. The ugliness was màde worse by the stink of hagspit from the still-burning mangonel. He wondered what made Meas so sure about the mines, though he questioned her decisions less and less as they passed through the town. There were fewer people here than he would expect. Many of the buildings were plainly empty once they were away from the harbourside.

"Where are the miners?" he asked as they walked.

"Curious, is it not," she said, "for a mining town to be so quiet? Almost as if they did not wish people in the mines, ey?

"Well . . ." he began.

"Come, Joron," she said, and they turned the corner, the black arch of the mine entrance before them.

"Should we bring deckchilder with us?"

"Narza and Cwell will do for now," she said, and strode forward, leaving him little choice but to follow.

To enter the mines of Sleighthulme was to move into a different world: as different from the world of land as was the sea. As damp and cold as the underdecks when traversing the north – but more alien than any ship could ever be. It was so still, the air becalmed and full of moisture without the wind to whip it away. It engendered a nervousness in Joron, for he also felt becalmed, and at the same time entombed. Like he was once more locked in the box back in Bernshulme by Gueste. The panic rising within him as the darkness grew. Meas passed him a lantern, and used a wanelight to light the oil within. Then passed lanterns to Narza and Cwell. That done she touched his arm, a brief squeeze, but in that one touch was so much understanding – *I know this is hard for you, I trust you to be strong.* And so he followed her down into the depths and he knew that wherever she went he would always follow, for she was his shipwife.

In the light of his lanterns he saw the scars of work on the mountain, years and years of quarrying for slate to deck the ships, and stone to build the bothies. The caves of Sleighthulme were vast, the mountain above little more than a shell and as they made their way downwards, four small lights carefully picking their way down hundreds and hundreds of stairs, he felt a sense of awe at what had been done here. That once this had been solid rock, and women and men had changed that with little more than their hands, rocks and iron tools.

The further they descended the more oppressive the air became. He heard a sound like great lungs breathing, in and out, and remembered McLean's Rock, torn apart as the keyshan shook itself loose. But what he heard could not be a pair of vast lungs. Sleighthulme was dead, it did not sing.

"Pumps," said Meas. "Mines always have pumps running."

Further down.

Deeper.

And.

Deeper.

Under the sound of the pumps another sound. It reminded him of wind sighing through the ropes of a ship – it had that same mournful sound, like rigging in the darkest part of the night when even Skearith's Blind Eye was closed. What was mournful started to become heartbreaking the louder it sounded.

"Shipwife," he said, and something about this vast oppressive space made him whisper, even though he was sure if he raised his voice it would still barely be heard. "It is voices."

"Ey," she said. "It is voices."

And down.

And down.

And deeper.

Until they found the pens.

Here, in this black and dank place were pens, of the type that were used to cage the gullaime back in Bernshulme. In these pens were not windtalkers and windshorn, lit by guttering torches, but people.

Here were those who had made the trip in the confines of

the brownbones and survived: sickly looking, many missing legs and arms or sporting some other imperfection that marked them out as women and men never destined to join the Bern. Many had the marks of disease, of keyshan's rot.

Joron looked away.

Felt the tops of his arms itch.

Opposite the pens was a small cave, barred by gion. Joron walked away from the pen containing people, full of horror and revulsion at what had been done and at the raw stink of humans penned up and suffering. He stared past the gion, into the cave: inside were windshorn, huddled together as far from the entrance as they could get. He turned away.

"Shipwife?" The voice was weak, almost broken. Then it spoke again and it was filled with joy, like Skearith's Bright Eye breaking a horizon. "'Tis the Shipwife, I knew she would come!" And a body pressed themselves against the bars. Joron expected more to do the same but it was as if the others, so many others, in the cage had been leeched of all energy. They did not even look up. Meas crossed the space, looking at the face and in the firelight Joron could see that she struggled to find familiarity in the emaciated features.

"I do not . . ." she said.

"Oh, you do not know me, and I only ever saw you from afar," they said, "I built bothies for the proud Bern of Safeharbour once. They are all gone now. They went first."

"What is your name, builder?" said Meas gently.

"Lavin, Shipwife, Herat Lavin." She looked like she was about to burst into tears. "I never dreamed I would see you before I was taken through the door."

"The door?"

Lavin nodded. She had been a handsome woman, but now her hair was matted and the scars of childbirth on her belly had been obscured by dirt.

"Over there." She pointed at a pair of varisk doors. "Those who go through never come back. I have heard our keeper talk of the vats, but do not know what they are."

"The work they put them to," said Meas, "it is harsh, from what we have discovered. Few would survive long. Now, Lavin, I must go through there. But I will come back, that is a promise." She brought her hands up and her face close to the bars. "A promise, you understand?" Lavin nodded. "Now, brave Lavin, how many of ours remain?"

"From Safeharbour? A hundred maybe, no more than that. We were stronger, so have survived longer than the poor wretches scoured from the streets of Bernshulme and the other islands. They take the weakest first, before the life runs out of them." She tried to smile. "Or those who have offended them, my daughter," said Lavin, "she could not stay quiet . . ." Her voice died away. Her grief all too plain on her face.

Joron found himself shaking, anger and horror warring within him at what had been done here. To take those least able and use them so sorely and foully. To rip families apart. If ever he had doubted Meas's wish for change it would have fled on seeing these people, caged and waiting to die.

"She will be avenged," said Meas. Then added under her breath, "This is the Hag's work."

"No," said Lavin, "The Hag, Mother and Maiden are not at work here. What is done in this place is done by the hands of women and men."

Meas took Lavin's hand through the bars, grasped it tightly. Behind Lavin some of those in the cage were coming forward now, wide frightened eyes in skeletal bodies. Many others did not move and Joron felt sure, more by smell than sight, that a good few corpses lay among the unmoving. For a moment his mind was cast back to the hold of the storm-wracked boat that started all this. The stink, the foulness, the inhumanity.

"I will return soon." Then she let go and turned. "Come Joron, come Narza and Cwell," she said, and he heard the tremor in her voice, how near she was to being overcome with fury. "And bare your blades. If there is anyone on this island most likely to be worthy of its edge I expect to find them in there." She drew her own sword and pointed it the doors.

They went through.

It smelled like the butcher's street back in Bernshulme, and behind that cloying scent was the choking stink of smoke and fire. The space was big, but not cavernous like the rest of the mines, more like the hollowed out inside of a grand bothy, many times the height of a tall woman. The room was filled with huge stone vats three times the height of Joron, blackened around the bottom by fire and grey at the top.

Joron stepped forward and something cracked beneath his feet – a piece of varisk or gion, he guessed. Then he looked down. Not varisk or gion – bone. It had rolled from a huge pile of bones that had been heaped against the wall, the carelessly collected remains of hundreds: skulls, shoulder blades, thighbones.

"Meas," he said, "what is this? They do not even bury them?"

"Joron," she replied, and took him by the arm. "Come away from there. We cannot help the dead. Let us see if any living remain further in." He did as she asked and they ventured deeper into the vat room.

A noise.

A voice.

Begging for life. Suddenly silenced.

The familiar squeak of rope and pulley.

They came around a huge vat to find a scene of nightmare.

A hagpriest stood before them, her robe pristine white, glowing in the darkness. She spoke under her breath, whispering the names of the three goddesses, asking for their favour as she pulled on a rope.

"Maiden look upon my work. Mother look upon my work. Hag look upon my work." And the squeak of the rope around the winches.

Joron's gaze followed that rope. From her hands, to the pulley, up to the high ceiling where it ran around another pulley and down to the end from which hung a human corpse. It was being lifted above the vat, blood dripping from a cut throat. Already hanging above the vat were two windshorn, slack, dead and dripping. By the base of the vat were stacked various herbs and plants. Some had been measured out and placed on the table, others were in sacks, sagging on the floor. Joron did not know what to do. Did not speak. Did not move. Meas similarly frozen by the scene before them. The hagpriest acted as if they did not exist. Simply kept pulling on the rope. When the corpse was fully hoisted the hagpriest turned.

"Who are you?" she croaked, "Can you not see I am busy working? And if you come from the hagmother to tell me to work faster then I cannot. This is not mere slaughter. There is ritual, and herbs before I flense away the flesh for the hiyl. It is not some simple stew." She turned away, bent over a book on the table, noted something down and muttered to herself.

"Where are your workers?" said Joron.

"There are none," said Meas, her voice flat, dead as the corpses above the vat. "Are there?" she said, walking forward. Joron thought it obvious to any who watched her stiff-legged walk that she was furious beyond any reckoning.

"Of course not, Reas," said the hagpriest, squinting into the gloom. "Though I would like them, but you trust none with the recipes, do you? As if anyone could get off this island." She stopped writing and stared at Meas, squinting her eyes as if she had difficulty seeing. She was young – from her voice Joron had expected her to be old, jaded. But she was not. "Why are you not wearing your robe, Reas?"

"Because I am not Reas Gilbryn," she said. "I am Meas Gilbryn. Sometimes called Lucky Meas, sometimes called the witch of Keelhulme Sounding. This island is mine now. I have taken it by force where no other has ever succeeded."

The hagpriest shrugged. "Why?" she said. "The recipe is not yet perfected, maybe five, six more trials. Though we may hit upon it sooner if the Mother smiles upon us." She grinned, and what shone in this woman's eyes was a bright excitement, and at the same time it was something darker than anything Joron had ever seen. "So I hope you have brought me more supplies, Lucky Meas Gilbryn, witch of Keelhulme Sounding. For if you have not, even if we do hit upon the recipe soon, then we will not have enough material to produce it in any great amount."

"Material?" said Meas.

"Yes," she said, and that dark light in her eyes, Joron realised he knew it, the same as the look in Madorra's when it had talked of the windseer, the gleam of the fanatic. A mind that teetered on the edge of madness. "I need more of them for my work. The dregs, the worthless who through this great task will find worth, just as they did in the old days."

"You will die for this," said Meas, no emotion in her voice, and the hagpriest only then realised the danger. But she did not seem afraid, more confused.

"Why?"

"Can you not see the horror you perform here?"

"Horror?" The hagpriest smiled. "Every time you walk upon the deck of your ship, Shipwife, you walk upon the bones of those sacrificed by our foremothers. Did you ever wonder why we sacrifice children to our ships? Simply for corpselights to shine prettily above them? No. It is in memory of the great sacrifices made to hunt the arakeesians." She stepped forward. "This"– she pointed at the vat – "is what the Hundred Isles' greatness, and what the Gaunt Islanders believe is their own, is built on. Corpses." She walked forward, standing before Meas. "It is not just our ships that are built of bones, Shipwife." She smiled, as if everything she said was entirely reasonable. Made perfect sense. "Without my work, all we are falls. All you are becomes worthless."

"Worthless?" said Meas.

"Aye," said the hagpriest. "All your warrior spirit and honour will be meaningless without ships to fly, and what do you think of that, witch of Keelhulme Sounding? You need me."

Meas stared at her, and it seemed she did it for an age. The only sound in the cold damp air of the cave was blood dripping from the opened neck of the corpse and into the vat.

"And you are the only one that knows this recipe," she pointed at the corpse, "this secret?"

"The recipe, aye. The rudiments are known by some of my sisters. But the subtleties that will ensure success? They are mine alone."

Meas nodded.

"In truth, Hagpriest, if all my honour and warrior spirit were to become worthless, I would welcome it. I long for peace, but life in the Hundred Isles has forced me to become a killer." She smiled. "That is what I am, and I have come to accept it."

"Good," sad the hagpriests, "I am glad you are able to accept that."

"Glad?" said Meas. "You should not be." Her blade flicked out, flashed across the neck of the priest. Blood sprayed across them both. Meas did not flinch as the hagpriest fell back, clutching at her throat and gasping. "Yours is a quick death," said Meas, looking down at her, "and you should be thankful, for I believe you deserve much worse." She turned and walked away. "Come, Joron. I have seen enough. We return to the surface."

He followed her back into the main room and Meas walked over to the pens, using the hilt of her sword to smash the lock on the door. "Joron, open the other pen, and the cave holding the windshorn." He did, hearing Meas speaking to Lavin. "Do what you can for your fellows, Lavin. I will send women and men with food and stretchers to get them out of the cave. We have ships to take you away from here. But I have business on the surface now." Then they were going back up the stairs, so many, so steep.

"What will you say to those of Sleighthulme, gathered in the bothy and waiting?" he said. Meas stopped on the stair. Turned to him.

"Say?" she said. "I will say nothing." She was shaking, anger held in a tight knot within her. "For what has gone on here a price must be paid. The horror of the ships bringing people here, keeping them caged. Murdered in pursuit of a poison to hunt keyshans. Every woman and man who let this happen will hang from a rope. I will make a charnel garden of them and I will start with the hagpriests. Every trace of this poison, every clue to its creation on this island must be destroyed. Whether it be in a book or a mind." He had never heard her talk so, never seen such utter hardness but at the same time he could not argue with her. What could be said?

They broke into the light, left the dark moistness of the cave and headed toward the Serpent Road that led to the bothy, where those who had governed Sleighthulme waited, unaware that sentence on them had already been passed. A voice stopped their passage. A shout from the towers in the harbour, loud enough to be heard across the entire town.

"Ship rising!" Then a space. A gap. "Ships rising! A whole fleet!"

Meas looked to him.

"Well," she said, "there always was the possibility this was a trap," and she changed direction, heading toward the harbour. "Let us go and see what we have sprung."

# 53

# The Storm that Never Was

The wind plucked at their hair, twisted it into tangles with the tails of their hats while they stared out to sea. Meas's fifth visit to the tower that day. A cloud of white wings on the horizon, all making for Sleighthulme. Meas closed up her nearglass and placed it in her coat. Black Orris, who sat upon her shoulder, flapped his wings and shouted "Arse! Arse!" at this disturbance.

"More ships now. I make out ten – eight two-ribbers, a four-ribber the equal of *Tide Child* and a ship that may be a four- or a five-ribber, I can't quite tell."

"That's overkill, four ships is enough to blockade us," said Joron.

"Sleighthulme is rich," she said, "and she will not want what she was doing here to get out. She will want to make sure of the outcome."

"How did she know?" said Joron.

"If she knew what I was looking for, then it would not be hard to work out where I would end up. She could have had a watcher out there" – she pointed to the sea – "well, it is almost certain. As soon as the mangonel went up I knew it would attract attention." She shrugged. "That, or one of the spies among us managed to report back."

"You knew this would happen," he said.

"My mother is many things – ruthless, devious, but most of all she is clever." She sucked on her teeth. "I thought we would have more time, hoped we would be able to get out before her ships came. It seems we do not." Meas glanced back at the town. "What I would do to still have that mangonel in working order, but the Maiden plays her tricks, shows us the tools we need for the job, and lets us choose which ones we are left with." She turned to Solemn Muffaz, stood behind her with his body rigid, eyes staring straight ahead.

"Go down into the town, Solemn Muffaz," said Meas. "I need to know water sources, how much food we have, and how many mouths we must feed."

"Ey, Shipwife," he said, and started to turn away.

"And Solemn Muffaz," she added. He paused, waiting for her words. "You do not need to count the townspeople among those we must find food for. I have no pity for any of them." He nodded and made his way down into the tower. As he left through the small door the gullaime pushed past, followed by Madorra. It hopped up onto a crenulation, splendid and glittering in robe and feather, and stared out to sea.

"Bad ships," it said. Meas took out her nearglass once more, annoyed Black Orris once more, and looked out to sea.

"Can you bring up a storm, Gullaime?" said Meas. "Can you smash them all against this island?"

It yarked, shook its head then its entire body. "No, no, no," it said. "Gullaime on board ships. Bad gullaime." It spat the words out. "Bad bad. Maybe wreck one. Maybe two. Then tired."

"Well then, hold on to your strength, Gullaime," she said, staring at the ships as they grew in the lens, "we may need it. What of the keyshans? Can you sing us up a sea dragon, gullaime, you and Joron there?"

"Sea sither not come," said the gullaime. "Not like Black Orris. Not hear name, come."

As if to repudiate the idea that Black Orris came when called, the corpsebird shouted "Arse!" then lifted from Meas' shoulders, launching itself into the air above the tower.

"Well, it is bleak for us then, Joron," said Meas. "They can stand off and resupply for as long as it takes to starve us out."

"Can we not run? They are a way out still."

She turned her nearglass on to the town, down onto the docks where a steady stream of her crews were loading the women and men from the mines onto the brownbones. They would be moved in little luxury, though in far better conditions than the ones they were brought in. Even so, many fought rather than be taken on board, many cried and the deckchilder, no matter how well they wished to treat these poor unfortunates, were forced to be rougher than Joron, and Meas, would have wished.

"No," said Meas. "We will not have them loaded in time, and even if we had, the brownbones are slow and the fleet ships are fast."

"Then we go out and fight?" he said. She shook her head. "But we have more ships."

"True in numbers, Joron, but our ships are small and they are mostly damaged and badly supplied. What gullaime we have, and they are few, are tired and have no access to a windspire. Those ships" – she pointed out to sea – "will be fresh and well supplied with gullaime and all else they need. Numbers will count for little, I expect. And if the shipmother of that fleet has anything about them then the moment we open the gate they will have their gullaime drive a fireship through it. Then we are ruined. Were it just us, I would take them on still." She closed up the nearglass again and glanced into the town. "But it is not. Those poor wretches have only just escaped captivity. I won't put them back into it." Meas took a deep breath. "No, fighting is our last option and I am of a mind that we pursue a more peaceful one first."

"You have a plan?" he said. She nodded, but did not meet his gaze. Instead she turned to Narza, standing still and forgotten, just like Cwell at his side.

"Narza, go find me Mevans." Narza hesitated, clearly unwilling to leave. "I am unlikely to be hurt on top of this tower," said Meas. "I am sure Cwell there can protect me from the skeers."

She watched Narza go and spoke, more to herself than him. "They will not want a siege, they will want the island back. It has stone and iron, and they will want all the knowledge they can salvage of hiyl." She stared out at the ships. "Some prizes, Joron, are worth sacrifices."

Mevans and Narza emerged from the tower door.

"Shipwife?" said Mevans.

"Put up the flags for a parlay," she said. "Then wait here with Joron and he can escort whoever they send down into the infirmary. I'll see them there. I want them to see as little of the town as possible." Mevans nodded. "And also, Mevans, you can explain to me what so many of our people are doing around the bottom of that mangonel. I gave no orders to fix it."

He grinned at her, irrepressible as ever.

"And it is a good job you did not, Shipwife, for it is never going to be fixed. But I reckoned you may talk to whoever comes, and if there was a parlay on the cards, I thought it may be good for us to look as though we thought that mangonel may indeed be fixable."

"Well," she said, stepping forward and putting a hand on his arm in a curiously familiar gesture, "I cannot fault that. But I will also have our people build gallows along the harbour. Take down the buildings if you need the materials." She stared out to sea once more then turned to Joron. "I will see you in the infirmary. I do not expect I will have long to wait."

Once Meas was gone and the flags were up Joron sat with Mevans, while Cwell stood, and they had little to do but watch the incoming ships grow bigger. One split from the main group and made for the gate, going much faster than the fleet behind it. Mevans stood on the wall, squinting down at it.

"Flying the flags for parlay, and working his gullaime hard," he said. "They must have brought plenty." Joron joined him and watched as the two-ribber flew toward them, eventually coming to stop below and letting down its seastay. A flukeboat was put over the side, filled with women and men from the ship and the unmistakeable form of an officer, stood in the beak of the little boat.

"Mevans," said Joron, "bring up some deckchilder and a boarding chair. I doubt their officer will want to climb the outside of the tower." Mevans nodded, returning quickly with small group of deckchilder and they used a hastily rigged crane to lower the boarding chair over the side of the tower just as the small boat was drawing up to it.

"Take the strain," said Mevans. And when the rope became taut he shouted, "Pull!" And they sang as they pulled on the rope.

> Hard it is the deckchild's life
> *Heave up, heave on.*
> *Heave up, heave on.*
> Obey commands of our Shipwife
> *Heave up, heave on.*
> *Heave up, heave on.*
> Deckmother has a heavy hand
> *Heave up, heave on.*
> *Heave up, heave on.*
> We'll know no peace till we hit land.
> *Heave up, heave on.*
> *Heave up, heave on.*

"We could drop whoever it is they send," said Mevans, "by accident."

"I suspect the shipwife would frown on that, Mevans," said Joron.

"Ey," he said, "she has never been too fond of a joke, right enough."

But when the chair crowned the tower, and the officer,

dressed in the finery of a shipwife, stood before them Joron wished, more than anything, they had dropped the woman to be smashed among the rocks far below them. He knew this elegant, louche woman. Those same elegant hands that handed over her sword and crossbows were the same ones that had locked Joron into a box, and given the order that broke his voice so he would never sing again.

"Why, Joron Twiner," said Gueste, "I did not expect to ever meet you again." She glanced down at his bone spur. "Though I see you are not quite the man you once were, ey?"

"And you have a new rank," he said. "You have been well rewarded for your loyalty."

"*Painful Loss* is a small ship, but he is mine. More apt for you though, with a name like that." She grinned at him. "Now, I believe I am to be taken to speak to your shipwife, ey?" Joron nodded and watched as Gueste made a show of looking over the town. The gallows that were growing along the docks, the women and men working on the mangonel. Joron's blade came up, a hiss as it left the scabbard and he held it before Gueste's eyes.

"You're here to talk, not spy," he said.

Gueste smiled at him then reached out, gently pushing the blade down.

"No doubt," she said, "but I suspect I see nothing Meas does not want me to, ey?"

"You and I," said Joron, "have a score to settle."

"We do, but on another day. Now, will you escort me or not?"

He did, taking her down through the tower and into the infirmary where Meas had found a desk and set herself up behind it. She had provided no chair for Gueste.

"Leave us please, Joron," she said, and he could not help but feel slightly offended that she did not want him there. But she was the shipwife, and he the deckkeeper, so he did as he was told and waited outside the door.

They talked for a long time.

When they emerged from the makeshift office Meas had a deckchilder take Gueste back up the tower and bade Joron come into the office. She went to the side and pulled over a chair, putting it by the desk, motioning for him to sit. At no point did she smile, or talk or share a joke. When she sat down, she waited, as if something within her needed to give time for Gueste to leave the island.

"A price has been struck," she said.

"And what is the cost?"

"The brownbones can leave, unmolested."

"And what is the cost?"

"The fleet also."

"And what is the cost?"

"You are to take command of my fleet, Joron. I will speak to all the shipwives. There will be no argument."

And he said the words again, even though he knew what the cost must be, because she had spoken to him of sacrifice, and he had misunderstood her then.

"And what is the cost," he said quietly, "of all this?"

"I am, Joron." She smiled a sad smile. He went cold inside.

"You knew that before Gueste set foot on Sleighthulme."

"I suspected it may be the case, yes."

"Your mother really wants you that badly? Enough that she will let the rest of us go with tales of the horrors we found here?"

Meas laughed, though still there was little humour there.

"No, it is not really me she wants, Joron." She rubbed the top of the table with her palm, round and round. "It is you she wants, but she does not know it. She knows we raised a keyshan from McLean's Rock and she wants that power. No greater weapon exists in the entire archipelago." She sat back in her chair. "But the idea a man could be the one that raised a keyshan? Well, that is clearly too much for her."

"But you cannot raise keyshans for her," he said.

"No. And I would not if I could."

"You should send me, Shipwife." He was suddenly near to

panic. "You are needed. You are the one who sets the course. You are the one who knows the way."

"Joron." She leaned forward. "The pain she will be prepared to inflict to get what she wants, no one could stand up to it. My mother, she does not know pity, only ambition. You have seen that, here. On this island."

"And you think you will bear it better?" he said. "I have become well used to pain."

She shook her head.

"No one is immune to torture, Joron. I say I would not do what she wanted if I could." Another smile, one that quickly fled. "That is bravado. All give in eventually, and so would you. It is no dishonour. But me? Even when I break, and I will, I have nothing to give her."

"You cannot do this."

"I have already done it."

"No," he said, standing. "This is not right, this is—"

"An order, Joron," barked out. Then more softly, "It is an order. From me." She stared up at him from where she sat behind this desk. "You will be allowed to leave and I have said you will return to Cassin's Isle and Leasthaven. Gueste promises me that my mother will leave you alone. When you have arrived, you must leave the two newer warships to the Hundred Isles, but you may take their crews. That is what has been agreed."

"And you trust her?" He could not hide the anger he felt.

"Of course not." Her voice barely a whisper, then stronger, recovering her familiar shipwife tone. "Once you are out of sight of their fleet, turn our ships and head for the Gaunt Islands. They will take you in, I am sure of it."

"What is to stop them destroying us as soon as we leave Sleighthulme?"

"I am, Joron," she said. "I will stand atop the tower and watch you go. And if so much as one of their ships makes to go after you then I will throw myself into the sea. I am the prize my mother wants. They will not risk losing me."

"This is not right," he said, and he wanted to beg her to change her mind. "There must be some other way."

"If there is, I cannot see it."

"I will not do it," he said. "I cannot do it."

Then she stood, and he expected her to shout once more. She did not.

"I am putting my trust in you, Joron Twiner, to look after my people. Our people. They have been treated sorely here." She came around the desk and put a hand on his arm. "What I must do is hard enough, do not make it harder." She looked away from him, and did her voice crack when she spoke the next words? Did the cold grey facade of the shipwife fall away? "Obey my order, Joron. Obey it, please. For it is harder to give than you know."

Silence, filling the room, swelling until it became unbearable.

"Of course," he said. "I will do as you order, Shipwife."

"Thank you," she said, and returned to sit once more. "Thank you."

# 54

# The Black Pirate

Skearith's Eye was falling behind Sleighthulme as the fleet made its way from the island. And he could still see her, through his nearglass — her nearglass — a small figure on the battlements of the dock gate, hair streaming in the wind as she watched her fleet leave. He told himself the tears streaming from his eyes were because of the wind, and the crew of *Tide Child* must have known it was so because they did not comment on it, nor make a ribald joke behind their hands. Behind him stood Cwell, and Narza, who Meas had commanded to go with him.

Farys stepped forward. In her hands she held something which she lifted up, showing him the same two-tailed hat that Meas had taken from his head so long ago on a beach on Shipshulmé Island.

"The shipwife," she said, and wiped a tear from her eye, because the wind was awful unkind on that hard deck. "The shipwife said I were to give you this when we were out of sight of Sleighthulme. Said you are the shipwife now and we must treat you as such." He stared at the hat. Raised the nearglass and glanced back at Sleighthulme, at the figure so small on the tower of the island silhouetted by the burning eye of the godbird.

"No," he said. "You keep hold of that, and you call me deckkeeper, Farys, for that is my rank. It is a deckkeeper's job to safeguard the shipwife and keep the ship in good order for her return. And that is what I will do. She will stand on this slate with us again, Farys."

"How, Deckkeeper?" she said.

"I do not know," he said. "Not yet. I only know it is my duty and I shall see it done."

"And I also," said Farys.

"And I," said Mevans.

"And I," said Solemn Muffaz, and the call of "and I' went around the ship and even those who could not know what Joron had said joined it, because they did not care. They only knew that their shipwife believed in the deckkeeper, and that he had proven worthy of her. And so he was worthy of them. And whatever he promised, well, they would promise also.

Joron knew he should have felt thankful for that belief. But did not. Because there had been so much pain, so much loss in the name of the Hundred Isles. His mother, his father, his lover, his leg, his voice, his shipwife. He felt that pain as a raging, furious hate for those who blew wind into the wings of this eternal war, and he understood now his shipwife's burning desire for peace. And though he did not know how he would return Meas Gilbryn, Lucky Meas, the witch of Keelhulme Sounding, to the deck of *Tide Child*, he knew he would do anything to make it happen.

Anything.

There would be no quarter.

No surrender

No mercy.

He would do anything.

And within him, a powerful song became louder.

Such fury on her face they saw
Would see that hate forever more
Raiders all on land had taken
Her Kept would never be forsaken

She searched up high, she searched down low
*Heave on, crew, heave on.*
From north to south she flew the storms
*Heave on, crew, heave on.*
She searched to east, she searched to west
*Heave on, crew, heave on.*
With no pity in her soul hey!
No pity in her soul.

No love she had for woman or man
Once on her quest she had began
"My Kept you must return," she said
And all she left behind were dead

She searched up high, she searched down low
*Heave on, crew, heave on.*
From north to south she flew the storms
*Heave on, crew, heave on.*
She searched to east, she searched to west
*Heave on, crew, heave on.*
With no pity in her soul, hey!
No pity in her soul.

From "The Black Pirate" – traditional ballad

*The story will continue in book three of the Tide Child trilogy.*

# Appendix: Ranks in the Fleet and the Hundred Isles

**Bern** The ruling class of the Hundred Isles consisting of women who have birthed children well-formed and unmarred.

**Berncast** Second-class Citizens of the Hundred Isles. Those who are born malformed or whose mothers die in childbirth proving their blood "weak".

**Bonemaster** In charge of the upkeep of the ship's hull and spines.

**Bonewright** Specialist crew member who answers to the bonemaster.

**Bowsell** Head of a gallowbow team. A bowsell of the deck is in charge of all the gallowbows on each deck of a boneship.

**Courser** Ship's navigator and holder of the charts. Although all officers are expected to be able to navigate, the sect of coursers are specialists. They are believed to be able to dream the coming weather and hear the songs of the storms.

**Deckholder** Third officer, generally known as the d'older. Larger ships may have up to four deckholders, who are known as the first d'older (most senior), the second d'older, and so on.

**Deckkeeper** Second to the shipwife and speaks with their authority. Larger ships may have up to three deckkeepers, who are traditionally known as the d'keeper (most senior), the keepsall and the decksall.

**Deckchild** A crew member who has proved themselves capable of all the minor tasks required in the running of a boneship.

**Deckchilder** A generic term for the entire crew of a ship below the rank of whoever is using it.

**Deckmother** In charge of discipline aboard a boneship. A traditionally unpopular rank.

**Gullaime** Also called windtalker and weathermage. An avian race of magicians able to control the winds and as such invaluable to the running of a boneship.

**Hagshand** The ship's surgeon, who works in the hagbower. Few who go under the knife of the hagshand survive.

**Hatkeep** Steward to the shipwife. A post often given to a deckchild who has proved particularly loyal or clever.

**Kept** The chosen men of the Bern.

**Oarturner** In charge of steering the ship.

**Purseholder** In charge of the ship's funds, weapons and food supplies.

**Seakeep** A seasoned deckchild with thorough knowledge of a boneship and how it should be run. The seakeep is expected to run the ship if there are no officers on deck and often acts as a go-between should the crew wish to communicate something to the shipwife.

**Shipmother** Commander of the fleet. There are five shipmothers. The ruler of the Hundred Isles is the most senior and has four deputies. These are named for the Northstorm, the Eaststorm, the Southstorm and the Weststorm. Shipmother of the North, Shipmother of the East, etc.

**Shipwife** Master and commander of a ship. The shipwife's word is law aboard their ship. To disobey is punishable by anything up to being sent to a black ship or death, depending on the shipwife's whim.

**Stonebound** The lowest rank on a ship. Used as an insult or as a quick way of denoting that someone does not really understand how the ship works or is not fleet.

**Topboy** The lookouts posted at the top of a ship's spines.

**Wingmaster** In charge of the wings and rigging of a boneship.

**Wingwright** Specialist crew member who answers to the wingmaster.

# Afterword and Acknowledgements

In fantasy, we often deal with huge and world-changing events. Even when the focus may be, like in my own writing, largely on the way it affects people on a more personal level, there's still big history-making events happening. So it feels strange that I should be writing this afterword while living through an event that will doubtlessly be written about in the history books of future generations. Of course, being stuck at home because of the coronavirus isn't hugely different for me, I'm generally at home anyway. But it's amazing what a creature of habit you can become as a writer. Monday to Friday when there's no one about is writing time. But there are people about, and even though these are people I dearly love it's not normal and I can't quite settle. But it seems that "not normal" will become the new normal for us all and, just like you in your life, I'll have to learn to get through it. However, it really cheers me to see hundreds of small acts of kindness happening. I hope we don't forget how much we need each other once this has passed.

By the time you are reading this, I will have finished writing the saga of Joron, Meas, the gullaime and *Tide Child* and moved on to something else. Such are the ways of publishing but it seems really odd that you'll be partway through when I am finished. Anyway, I hope you've enjoyed the second part of their story and I must apologise for leaving things on a – literal – cliffhanger. It's always a thing I've said to myself I would never do, but I am also an incredibly contrary person who absolutely cannot be relied on to do as I say, and anyway, it was what the story needed.*

* The author's favourite excuse

In *The Bone Ships* we saw Joron built up from nothing, and in *Call of the Bone Ships* we see Joron, quite literally in some ways, taken apart again, going through the pain and the loss that we all have go through at some point and in the end losing the one thing he has depended on the most. In fact, this book is about loss and sacrifice in many ways. Now Joron must strike out on his own without the person he has relied upon for so long. This cycle of growth seems to be one that fascinates me as Girton, in the Wounded Kingdom books, went through a similar process. We all grow and change; it is our nature, and the more elastic you can keep your mind and ability to change the better really. Or so I tend to think.

As ever, when I write I am supported by my wonderful wife and (somewhat) helped by my son and definitely given no help at all by our cat. There's also my very patient early reading group, Fiona, Richard and Matt, who very kindly give up their time and probably get a massive headache from reading very early versions of these books. They also offer me some invaluable cheerleading which every author needs now and again.

One of those little-known facts outside the publishing world is that writers write, but other people make us look good, or at least a lot less foolish than we really are. So thanks to my agent, Ed Wilson at Johnson and Alcock, for making sure I can afford to eat, which is always useful. My editor, Jenni Hill, who is wonderful, and the team at Orbit; Joanna Kramer, who helps make sure I don't take YEARS to bring you these things and put them out riddled with errors; and my copy-editor, Saxon Bullock, who really locked into the style of these books and made the usually onorous task of doing the copy-edit, well, if not fun exactly than at least less onorous.

I owe a lot of authors a thank you for supporting me and these books with kind words and, probably more importantly, friendship: Robin Hobb, James Barclay, Adrian Tchaikovsky, Pete McClean, Tasha Suri, Sam Hawk, Devin Madson, Melissa Caruso, Evan Winter, Chaz Brenchly, Steve Aryan, Anne

Stephens, Nicholas Eames, Luke Arnold, Rowenna Miller, Alix Harrow, Jenn Williams, and oh my there is so many of you I would run out of ink. You know who you are and you are all brilliant.

I suppose I should also thank Tom Parker for his interior art and the astounding work he's done on the special edition hardbacks from the lovely people at Anderida Books. Even though he is TOO FAMOUS to read books now.

I'd also like to thank Austin Farr and Chris Shrewsbury who talked to me about what it is like to be an amputee, and the process of getting used to being without a limb and what that feels like. I've tried to stay as true as I can to what they were kind enough to share with me and any errors are mine (though I will of course claim they were forced upon me by the requirements of drama and plot*). But thank you ever so much for being generous enough to share your experiences. I'd also like to thank Wilfred Berghof who made a very generous donation to the Worldbuilders charity in exchange for having his name appear in this book. I did say you wouldn't make it out, Wilfred. . .

As ever, thanks to probably the most important people of this entire process: you, dear reader. For reading, leaving reviews, talking about the books and helping put me in a position where hopefully I'll get to write more.

I'd like to share one last thing, and it might seem a bit trite but I promise you it's true. Be kind to others whenever you can be and it will reward you. You'll see "be kind" said a lot, and sometimes it's hard to think the best of people when our own situation is tough. But if you can try, if you can always meet a stranger and presume the best of them, then you will be one of the people out there making the world into a better place. Maybe sometimes you'll be let down, but that's on them not you. More often than not you will be rewarded, often in very small ways. Sometimes you won't even know about the

* Or maybe this is

good you've done, or how you've made someone's day a little bit better just by sharing a smile. But you will have done it, and you will carry that with you. The world is a strange place right now, and it's a little bit scary, so try and go through life making it a bit better. Cos even a bit better is a step in the right direction, and sometimes a tiny gesture on one person's part is a huge gift to another.

Life is hard, look after one another.

RJ Barker
Leeds. March 2020

# extras

orbit

# about the author

**RJ Barker** lives in Leeds with his wife, son and a collection of questionable taxidermy, odd art, scary music and more books than they have room for. He grew up reading whatever he could get his hands on, and has always been "that one with the book in his pocket". Having played in a rock band before deciding he was a rubbish musician, RJ returned to his first love, fiction, to find he is rather better at that. As well as his debut epic fantasy novel, *Age of Assassins*, RJ has written short stories and historical scripts which have been performed across the country. He has the sort of flowing locks any cavalier would be proud of.

Find out more about RJ Barker and other Orbit authors by registering for the free monthly newsletter at www.orbitbooks.net.

# if you enjoyed
## CALL OF THE BONE SHIPS

### look out for

# THE RAGE OF DRAGONS
## The Burning: Book One

#### by

## Evan Winter

*IN A WORLD CONSUMED BY ENDLESS WAR
ONE YOUNG MAN WILL BECOME HIS
PEOPLE'S ONLY HOPE FOR SURVIVAL.*

*The Omehi people have been fighting an unwinnable war
for generations. The lucky ones are born gifted: some have
the power to call down dragons, others can be magically
transformed into bigger, stronger, faster killing machines.*

*Everyone else is fodder, destined to fight and die in the
endless war. Tau Tafari wants more than this, but his plans
of escape are destroyed when those closest to him are
brutally murdered.*

*With too few gifted left, the Omehi are facing genocide, but
Tau cares only for revenge. Following an unthinkable path,
he will strive to become the greatest swordsman to ever live,
willing to die a hundred thousand times for the chance to
kill three of his own people.*

# CHAMPION TSIORY

Tsiory stared at the incomplete maps laid out on the command tent's only table. He tried to stand tall, wanting to project an image of strength for the military leaders with him, but he swayed slightly, a blade of grass in an imperceptible breeze. He needed rest and was unlikely to get it.

It'd been three days since he'd last gone to the ships to see Taifa. He didn't want to think he was punishing her. He told himself he had to be here, where the fighting was thickest. She wanted him to hold the beach and push into the territory beyond it, and that was what he was doing.

The last of the twenty-five hundred ships had arrived, and every woman, man, and child who was left of the Chosen was now on this hostile land. Most of the ships had been scavenged for resources, broken to pieces, so the Omehi could survive. There would be no retreat. Losing against the savages would mean the end of his people, and that Tsiory could not permit.

The last few days had been filled with fighting, but his soldiers had beaten back the natives. More than that, Tsiory had taken the beach, pushed into the tree line, and marched the bulk of his army deeper into the peninsula. He couldn't hold the ground he'd taken, but he'd given her time. He'd done as his queen had asked.

Still, he couldn't pretend he wasn't angry with her. He loved Taifa, the Goddess knew he did, but she was playing a suicidal game. Capturing the peninsula with dragons wouldn't mean much if they brought the Cull down on themselves.

"Champion!" An Indlovu soldier entered the command tent,

taking Tsiory from his thoughts. "Major Ojore is being overrun. He's asking for reinforcements."

"Tell him to hold." Tsiory knew the young soldier wanted to say more. He didn't give him the chance. "Tell Major Ojore to hold."

"Yes, Champion!"

Harun spat some of the calla leaf he was always chewing. "He can't hold," the colonel told Tsiory and the rest of the assembled Guardian Council. The men were huddled in their makeshift tent beyond the beach. They were off the hot sands and sheltered by the desiccated trees that bordered them. "He's out of arrows. It's all that kept the savages off him, and Goddess knows, the wood in this forsaken land is too brittle to make more."

Tsiory looked over his shoulder at the barrel-chested colonel. Harun was standing close enough for him to smell the man's sour breath. Returning his attention to the hand-drawn maps their scouts had made of the peninsula, Tsiory shook his head. "There are no reinforcements."

"You're condemning Ojore and his fighters to death."

Tsiory waited, and, as expected, Colonel Dayo Okello chimed in. "Harun is right. Ojore will fall and our flank will collapse. You need to speak with the queen. Make her see sense. We're outnumbered and the savages have gifts we've never encountered before. We can't win."

"We don't need to," Tsiory said. "We just need to give her time."

"How long? How long until we have the dragons?" Tahir asked, pacing. He didn't look like the man Tsiory remembered from home. Tahir Oni came from one of the Chosen's wealthiest families and was renowned for his intelligence and precision. He was a man who took intense pride in his appearance.

Back on Osonte, every time Tsiory had seen Tahir, the man's head was freshly shaved, his dark skin oiled to a sheen, and his colonel's uniform sculpted to his muscular frame. The man before him now was a stranger to that memory.

Tahir's head was stubbly, his skin dry, and his uniform hung off a wasted body. Worse, it was difficult for Tsiory to keep his eyes from the stump of Tahir's right arm, which was bleeding through its bandages.

Tsiory needed to calm these men. He was their leader, their inkokeli, and they needed to believe in their mission and queen. He caught Tahir's attention, tried to hold it and speak confidently, but the soldier's eyes twitched like a prey animal's.

"The savages won't last against dragons," Tsiory said. "We'll break them. Once we have firm footing, we can defend the whole of the valley and peninsula indefinitely."

"Your lips to the Goddess's ears, Tsiory," Tahir muttered, without using either of his honorifics.

"Escaping the Cull," Dayo said, echoing Tsiory's unvoiced thoughts, "won't mean anything if we all die here. I say we go back to the ships and find somewhere a little less . . . occupied."

"What ships, Dayo? There aren't enough for all of us, and we don't have the resources to travel farther. We're lucky the dragons led us here," Tsiory said. "It was a gamble, hoping they'd find land before we starved. Even if we could take to the water again, without them leading us, we'd have no hope."

Harun waved his arms at their surroundings. "Does this look like hope to you, Tsiory?"

"You'd rather die on the water?"

"I'd rather not die at all."

Tsiory knew where the conversation would head next, and it would be close to treason. These were hard men, good men, but the voyage had made them as brittle as this strange land's wood. He tried to find the words to calm them, when the shouting outside their tent began.

"What in the Goddess's name—" said Harun, opening the tent's flap and looking out. He couldn't have seen the hatchet that took his life. It happened too fast.

Tahir cursed, scrambling back as Harun's severed head fell to the ground at his feet.

"Swords out!" Tsiory said, drawing his weapon and slicing a cut through the rear of the tent to avoid the brunt of whatever was out front.

Tsiory was first through the new exit, blinking under the sun's blinding light, and all around him was chaos. Somehow, impossibly, a massive force of savages had made their way past the distant front lines, and his lightly defended command camp was under assault.

He had just enough time to absorb this when a savage, spear in hand, leapt for him. Tsiory, inkokeli of the Omehi military and champion to Queen Taifa, slipped to the side of the man's downward thrust and swung hard for his neck. His blade bit deep and the man fell, his life's blood spilling onto the white sands.

He turned to his colonels. "Back to the ships!"

It was the only choice. The majority of their soldiers were on the front lines, far beyond the trees, but the enemy was between Tsiory and his army. Back on the beach, camped in the shadows of their scavenged ships, there were fighters and Gifted, held in reserve to protect the Omehi people. Tsiory, the colonels, the men assigned to the command camp, they had to get back there if they hoped to survive and repel the ambush.

Tsiory cursed himself for a fool. His colonels had wanted the command tent pitched inside the tree line, to shelter the leadership from the punishing sun, and though it didn't feel right, he'd been unable to make any arguments against the decision. The tree line ended well back from the front lines, and he'd believed they had enough soldiers to ensure they were protected. He was wrong.

"Run!" Tsiory shouted, pulling Tahir along.

They made it three steps before their escape was blocked by another savage. Tahir fumbled for his sword, forgetting for a moment that he'd lost his fighting hand. He called out for help and reached for his blade with his left. His fingers hadn't even touched the sword's hilt when the savage cut him down.

Tsiory lunged at the half-naked aggressor, blade out in front, skewering the tattooed man who'd killed Tahir. He stepped back from the impaled savage, seeking to shake him off the sword, but the heathen, blood bubbling in his mouth, tried to stab him with a dagger made of bone.

Tsiory's bronze-plated leathers turned the blow and he grabbed the man's wrist, breaking it across his knee. The dagger fell to the sand and Tsiory crashed his forehead into his opponent's nose, snapping the man's head back. With his enemy stunned, Tsiory shoved all his weight forward, forcing the rest of his sword into the man's guts, drawing an open-mouthed howl from him that spattered Tsiory with blood and phlegm.

He yanked his weapon away, pulling it clear of the dying native, and swung round to rally his men. He saw Dayo fighting off five savages with the help of a soldier and ran toward them as more of the enemy emerged from the trees.

They were outnumbered, badly, and they'd all die if they didn't disengage. He kept running but couldn't get to his colonel before Dayo took the point of a long-hafted spear to the side and went down. The closest soldier killed the native who had dealt the blow, and Tsiory, running full tilt, slammed into two others, sending them to the ground.

On top of them, he pulled his dagger from his belt and rammed it into the closest man's eye. The other one, struggling beneath him, reached for a trapped weapon, but Tsiory shoved his sword hilt against the man's throat, using his weight to press it down. He heard the bones in the man's neck crack, and the savage went still.

Tsiory got to his feet and grabbed Dayo, "Go!"

Dayo, bleeding everywhere, went.

"Back to the beach!" Tsiory ordered the soldiers near him. "Back to the ships!"

Tsiory ran with his men, looking back to see how they'd been undone. The savages were using gifts to mask themselves in broad daylight. As he ran, he saw more and more of them stepping out of what his eyes told him were empty spaces among the trees. The trick had allowed them to move an attacking force past the front lines and right up to Tsiory's command tent.

Tsiory forced himself to move faster. He had to get to the reserves and order a defensive posture. His heart hammered in his chest and it wasn't from running. If the savages had a large enough force, this surprise attack could kill everyone. They'd still have the front-line army, but the women, men, and children they were meant to protect would be dead.

Tsiory heard galloping. It was an Ingonyama, riding double with his Gifted, on one of the few horses put on the ships when they fled Osonte. The Ingonyama spotted Tsiory and rode for him.

"Champion," the man said, dismounting with his Gifted. "Take the horse. I will allow the others to escape."

Tsiory mounted, saluted before galloping away, and looked back. The Gifted, a young woman, little more than a girl, closed her eyes and focused, and the Ingonyama began to change, slowly at first, but with increasing speed.

The warrior grew taller. His skin, deep black, darkened further, and, moving like a million worms writhing beneath his flesh, the man's muscles re-formed thicker and stronger. The soldier, a Greater Noble of the Omehi, was already powerful and deadly, but now that his Gifted's powers flowed through him, he was a colossus.

The Ingonyama let out a spine-chilling howl and launched himself at his enemies. The savages tried to hold, but there was little any man, no matter how skilled, could do against an Enraged Ingonyama.

The Ingonyama shattered a man's skull with his sword pommel, and in the same swing, he split another from collarbone to waist. Grabbing a third heathen by the arm, he threw him ten strides.

Strain evident on her face, the Gifted did all she could to maintain her Ingonyama's transformation. "The champion has called a retreat," she shouted to the Omehi soldiers within earshot. "Get back to the ships!"

The girl – she was too young for Tsiory to think of her as much else – gritted her teeth, pouring energy into the enraged warrior, struggling as six more savages descended on him.

The first of the savages staggered back, his chest collapsed inward by the Ingonyama's fist. The second, third, and fourth leapt on him together, stabbing at him in concert. Tsiory could see the Gifted staggering with each blow her Ingonyama took. She held on, though, brave thing, as the target of her powers fought and killed.

It's enough, thought Tsiory, leave. It's enough.

The Ingonyama didn't. They almost never did. The colossus was surrounded, swarmed, mobbed, and the savages did so much damage to him that he had to end his connection to the Gifted or kill her too.

The severing was visible as two flashes of light emanating from the bodies of both the Ingonyama and the Gifted. It was difficult to watch what happened next. Unpowered, the Ingonyama's body shrank and his strength faded. The next blow cut into his flesh and, given time, would have killed him.

The savages gave it no time. They tore him to pieces and ran for the Gifted. She pulled a knife from her tunic and slit her own throat before they could get to her. That didn't dissuade them. They fell on her and stabbed her repeatedly, hooting as they did.

Tsiory, having seen enough, looked away from the butchery, urging the horse to run faster. He'd make it to the ships and the reserves of the Chosen army. The Ingonyama and Gifted had given him that with their lives. It was hard to think it mattered.

Too many savages had poured out from the tree line. They'd come in force and the Chosen could not hold. The upcoming battle would be his last.

# galaxy

*literary modes and genres*